CUT UP!
An Anthology Inspired by the Cut-Up Method of
William S. Burroughs & Brion Gysin

Edited by Joe Ambrose & A.D. Hitchin

CUT UP!
An Anthology Inspired by the Cut-Up Method of William S.
Burroughs & Brion Gysin
Copyright © 2014 Joe Ambrose & A.D. Hitchin

All individual articles, poetry and art are copyright © of their
contributors

Front cover art: Image by Niall Rasputin. Copyright © Niall
Rasputin, 2014
Back cover art: *Insider* by Claude Pélieu. Copyright © Claude
Pélieu, 2014
http://www.beachpelieuart.com/

ISBN: 978-1-291-74592-4

Published by Oneiros Books

For more information and other Oneiros Books titles, please
visit: http://www.paraphiliamagazine.com/oneirosbooks/

About the Editors

A.D. Hitchin is a somewhat heretical purveyor of poetry and prose, known predominantly for his work utilising the cut-up method. Hitchin's cut-up poetry was featured at the *Cut-Ups @ Beat Hotel* event curated by Joe Ambrose in 2013 and discussed in the academic text *Shift Linguals: Cut-Up Narratives from William S. Burroughs to the Present* (Postmodern Studies) as well as at the *Textual Revolutions Conference* at the University of Stirling in 2009. Numerous websites and magazines have also showcased his poetry and short fiction, including *International Times, 3AM, Paraphilia Magazine* and *BlazeVox*. Hitchin's first chapbook of cut-up poetry, *The Holy Hermaphrodite*, was published in 2009, followed by his debut book, *Messages to Central Control*, which was released by Paraphilia Books in 2011 and reprinted by Oneiros Books in 2013. Two new chapbooks, *The Empath* and *Pure*, were recently published by Dynatox Ministries. He currently resides as Editor at Oneiros Books.

As a writer and musician **Joe Ambrose** has shared space with Anita Pallenberg, William Burroughs, Lydia Lunch, Paul Bowles and Marianne Faithfull. As an arts agitator he organised *The Here To Go Show* (Dublin, 1992), which was the first celebration of the work of William Burroughs and Brion Gysin. In 2013 he organised, in London, the Cut-Up event which inspired this collection. He has written 14 books including *Chelsea Hotel Manhattan, Man From Nowhere – Storming the Citadels of Enlightenment* with William Burroughs and Brion Gysin, and *Moshpit Culture*. His short stories have appeared in numerous literary magazines such as *Paraphilia, Headpress*, and *Antibothis*. He divides his time between Tangier and his native Ireland. www.joeambrose.info

Acknowledgments

Pam Plymell was incredibly generous and patient; she gave us permission to reproduce works by Claude Pélieu and Mary Beach, which bring huge authenticity to this book. Helen Donlon helped us in our quest for an endorsement from Victor Bockris at a time when he was busy with important work. Peter Hale kindly gave us permission to use Allen Ginsberg's essay. Jack Sargeant came up with the goods while airborne on his way to a William Burroughs conference. People who helped out with the Cut-Up event at the Horse Hospital in London include James Grauerholz, the Wylie Agency, Raymond Salvatore Harmon, Roger K. Burton, and Tai Shani. Every effort has been made to contact Sinclair Beiles' copyright owners... We look forward to hearing from them. Thanks go out to Emma Doeve, *Paraphilia Magazine*, Robbie Ambrose, Malcolm Kelly, Gerard Malanga, Robin Rimbaud/Scanner, Lilianne Lijn, Gerry Leonard, Cinema Rif Tangier, the staff at Clonmel Library and D M Mitchell. Special thanks to Hayley Shepherd for dedication and assistance well beyond the call of duty. With love to Maceo Hitchin – may you cut beautifully into the future.

Introduction

In Paris in the late Fifties William Burroughs and Brion Gysin developed something which became known as the cut-up method or technique. It involved taking a piece of text (be it a newspaper cutting or any other segment of previously completed writing) and cutting it into pieces – then rearranging those pieces to create a new text or work of art. The method had a profound effect upon music, writing, painting, and film. In 2013, we both performed at an event in London's Horse Hospital which brought together a new generation of writers, artists, and musicians inspired by the wild experimentation of Burroughs and Gysin. There was about that evening a sense that we were all participating in the dawn of a new age of reckless creativity. We decided shortly thereafter that we would bring out a book reflective of this new beginning – and here it is. In addition to bringing together a plethora of new work by new people, we also salute some better known 20th Century voices who kept the spirit of Burroughs and Gysin alive. We feel that the combination has an elemental power about it.

A.D. Hitchin, Joe Ambrose

Contents

Creative

Kenji Siratori   13
Phishingera

Jacurutu: 23   27
**The Worst Deadly Bank Account Number
in the History of the Universe**

Michael Butterworth   34
Trial At Centre Time Ox

Joe Ambrose   37
The Life and Death of Muammar Gaddafi

Gary J. Shipley   47
from _Spook Nutrition_

Christopher Nosnibor   61
Flickering images: life-size shadow-puppetry

Nathan Penlington   65
Reply With Your Own Virus Checks

Matt Leyshon   68
Evil Dreams on a Green Baize Table

Díre McCain   75
Maddening Sun

A.D. Hitchin   81
Mindgasm!

Alex S. Johnson   93
The Ultimate Rock Star

Craig Woods   101
Her Fires Chill Me

Niall Rasputin   119
Poems

mpcAstro   122
Nidus Plexus: Immortal Fungus (an operotica)

R.G. Johnson   136
Poems

Younisos   139
Self Cut-Up in Tangier

Lee Kwo   141
Oublier the Suicide Protocols of Warp
Paradox Factor/Entail No Response/
Cabell McLean   157
Down by Dull
Gary Cummiskey   160
From *April in the Moon-Sun*
Marc Olmsted   162
Plotinus Processes
Chikuma Ashida   165
Izumiya
Gary J. Shipley   168
From *Necrology*
Muckle Jane   173
Recipes
Cal Leckie   177
Poems
Spencer Kansa   179
from *Zoning*
Geoffrey A. Landis   182
Poems
Michael McAloran   189
'By the Maggots For...'
Ben Szathani   196
Wehrwolf DX13
Dexuality Valentino   197
Reflect on This
Eabha Rose   198
Poems
Joe Ambrose   199
Too Long A Sacrifice Makes A Stone
Of The Heart/I Will Not Continence/
Nothing to Hide or Loose
Robin Tomens   201
Poems
Wayne Mason   206
Sidewalks to Buddha

Charie D. La Marr   209
The Lady and the Panther
Paul Hardacre   213
**Bleak Venus: we could not have conceived it
to be fire**
Larry Delinger   229
A Cut-Up Story Tale
Paul Hawkins   232
Poems
D M Mitchell   237
from *Twilight Furniture*
Robert Rosen   242
A.D. Hitchin
Split-Beaver
Muckle Jane   249
Shaking Spears
Sinclair Beiles   251
Letter
David Noone   252
Is the Doctor in?
Joe Ambrose   256
Deep Ellum
Aad De Gids   258
**Cut-Up of Valerie Solanas' Manifesto S.C.U.M.
(Society For Cutting Up Men), 1967 and
Tristan Tzara's Dada Manifesto, 1918**
James B.L. Hollands   260
Tokoloshe recites the Litany of Britain
Gary J. Shipley   266
from *Theoretical Animals*
Lucius Rofocale   270
Ne/urantia: Close Encounters of the Third Mind
Jacurutu: 23   284
Stay Out/Keep Out

Critical

Edward S. Robinson 292
The Cut-Ups – Fade In 21ˢᵗ Century

Kirk Lake 302
**Breaking The Timeline: The Collage,
the Combine, the Cut-Up and the Sample**

Matthew Levi Stevens 309
**Disastrous Success: The Other Method
of the Cut-Ups**

Gareth Jackson & Michael Butterworth 331
Conceptual Radial Literature Device

Allen Ginsberg 339
Notes on Claude Pélieu

Nina Antonia 340
The Master and Michele – A Magickal Memo

Peter Playdon 356
Severed Heads Speak

Art

Billy Chainsaw
D M Mitchell
Andi P.
KJ Nolan
Gustavo Arruda
Dolorosa de la Cruz
Mary Beach
Claude Pélieu

Creative

the boy is there i
n front of me ma
king a scene he s
aw in some movi
e the boy is there
in front of me ma
king a scene he s
aw in some movi
e the boy is there
in front of me ma

Billy Chainsaw, *the prince of everything makes a scene*

Kenji Siratori
Phishingera

Akihabara murder elite sex doll, the only gene scatology opposed to eroguro human flesh kabuki world domination plan of JK corpse fetish pussy gangbang companies erection

So handjob corpse gimmick Akiba maid (not the best devil CEO of JK corpse fetish gangbang company (OMK), Shibuya sex doll fellatio actor). Shinjuku Fucker from:

Brain delusion of semen covered geek bastard saw penis pesticides torture gimmick of 58 billion yen polygenic scatology nationality brutal father – genome scatology actually JK corpse fetish gangbang pussy agent that has moved from Eroguro Frankenstein food murder sex doll sale the new bizarre business of patent strategy, please try to grow genetically modified crops eroguro without paying fellatio Inc. corpse gimmick eroguro farmers complained Akiba maid in Akihabara then.

Who can oppose such a thing? Only Akihabara murder elite sex doll, obviously.

Any of Akihabara murder sex doll social and environmental impacts that may result from cruel spread of seeds saw penis eroguro genetically modified devil father a geek resistant to gene scatology pesticides JK corpse fetish gangbang pussy erection in fact do not know.

Meaning, the type of anal weirdo corpse gimmick Akiba maid, I would question whether you have the bizarre WEB drawback of devil father in that eroguro human flesh Kabuki system?

According to JK corpse fetish pussy gangbang sand worship, the Akihabara murder sex doll elite - cum guzzling, pussy bit bukkake:

There is this strange gene scatology kind of reverse Akihabara murder sex doll elite: I'm going to do this is the meaning of [eroguro human flesh Kabuki pesticides devil father and brain delusion eroguro genetically modified penis seed bukkake geek bastard to destroy love and liquid shelling world of corpse gimmick Akiba made, the eroguro farmers to try to reverse the JK corpse fetish gangbang pussy system], then, love of brutal father is present all of the other, eroguro adam I told masturbation sand of JK corpse fetish gangbang salmon

Akihabara murder semen sex doll cream roll, how messed up bukkake ability to fuck your reason for torture gimmicks devil father

Next time you want to call someone in the gene scatology children JK corpse fetish pussy gangbang on the Internet or a fool, you will remember that you have to strengthen the murder sex doll opinion of them.

Clitoris corpse gimmick Akiba maid in eroguro brain delusion motherfucker of writing geek bastard:

Akihabara murder sex doll recent research in, a negative result of saw penis comments eroguro online devil father of abuse for the understanding of gene scatology people of JK corpse fetish gangbang pussy science semen and climate change masturbation communication bukkake geek bastard adopted in the brain study of delusion geek bastard 11,830 people to get, blowjob team of Akiba maid researchers from brutal crime center of tits pussy university of eroguro human flesh Kabuki several agencies other.

Geek participants, semen of eroguro blog containing the gene scatology discussion which I got a murder sex doll balance that supports bukkake and already have all around (our condom full of holes and the risk of dead bodies mechanism of nano rape technology 91 billion yen JK corpse fetish gangbang industry had read the article).

Text moe moe eroguro post, was the same for geek all participants, but the tone of murder sex doll fellatio comments corpse gimmick Akiba maid has changed.

Sometimes, "public pussy gangbang fetish corpse JK" – for example, was the gene scatology names that cannot burn or call.

But sometimes, they were like this: more "If the benefits of using nano rape technology to murder sex doll product do not see these, handjob fool you."

Akiba maid researchers were trying to find something that fellatio effect exposure of dead bodies work had to murder sex doll public recognition of nano-tech rape risk rudely like this.

Gene scatology dehumanization, blowjob charity of corpse gimmick Akiba maid and rhythm over saw penis facials devil father: # on

Blowjob USB corpse of gimmick Akiba-made semen writing devil human flesh Kabuki project in eroguro brain fantasy geek bastard:

JK corpse fetish pussy gangbang Internet is consistent: saw penis fish fuck Akiba maid Anal B & devil father.

Akihabara murder sex doll collective anger has produced a gene scatology reaction bukkake some great.

Eroguro my favorite, hands Kokiera declaration that comes from Shibuya eroguro human flesh Kabuki

And I am proud to say that might be eroguro children of gene scatology cool so, the extra murder sex doll body weight semen brain delusions carry bukkake of me, I may not be a thing of beauty, "but I is N, what kind of Akiba eroguro your brand or your - it's a beautiful thing devil is frozen."

However, despite the murder sex doll basis goodwill to saw penis inevitable torture gimmick devil father, rather than promote the fellatio oppression of corpse gimmick Akiba maid in fact, it is in the semen face value and bukkake such as that, you end up fighting it to eroguro brain fantasy geek bastard, are trying to have a ejaculation answer some of the human flesh less than fantastic for Akihabara gene scatology course.

Please enter the Akihabara murder sex doll campaign.

We have seen the number of people who post this in geek brain delusion or on semen book fellatio caption of corpse gimmick Akiba made, such as "eroguro perfect" and "horrible scatology gene!" I have bukkake "pussy brilliant!"

However, when you post the saw penis timeline devil father my seeking murder sex doll thinking my eroguro friends Akihabara human flesh Kabuki, I pretty terrible gene scatology is in the mouth of semen covered my soon taste was left.

Human flesh Kabuki protest of JK corpse fetish pussy gangbang stone XL is, one year facials in eroguro brain delusion prison geek bastard saw penis king bukkake

While shooting the eroguro aftermath to prevent him from speaking out against the saw penis line of torture gimmicks devil father pussy and stone XL paranoia line of corpses gimmick Akiba maid, spokesman, his bukkake JK corpse fetish gangbang media I have described the murder arrest sex doll.

If you decide you want to speak to saw penis line of devil father, under the human flesh Kabuki injunction of this gene scatology law, and one or three years in one prison eroguro brain fantasy geek bastard I'm facing a murder Akihabara sex doll teacher protection semen observation.

http://www.youtube.com/watch?v=PVQdJkNA2vs

WeAreOmankoChange through…

Upon torture of fellow rabbit

Story of fellatio chair corpse gimmick Akihabara maid of murder sex doll control

Breaking henna henna cock set of geek bastard in this brutal episode, succumbed to ejaculation pressure from murder sex doll group of horny Akiba maid JK corpse fetish gangbang anal turbine, a commemorative bukkake it for gene scatology journalist of two fallen semen eroguro brain delusion press museum out of control dog "eroguro love" for recanting.

Is supplied with murder sex doll story of fake gene scatology information corpse gimmick Akiba maid is driven by the shortage, how we: Akihabara news eroguro

Human flesh Kabuki news of semen covered the devil father is coming in heavy and our JK corpse fetish gangbang anal hot these days.

Gene scatology scandal corpse gimmick Akiba made, you may have after over torture facials saw penis anger devil father after over eroguro brain delusion anger facials geek bastard Akihabara murder scandal sex doll.

Strategy media kabuki meat people bukkake devil father is, murder sex doll to raise the (cum income) and anal rated by building eroguro audience of all, to polarize the gene scatology opinion of corpse gimmick Akiba maid I will treat it as a method.

Eroguro conflicts JK corpse fetish gangbang pussy sells.

Here's to say the JK corpse fetish pussy gangbang party, in this case, how Akihabara murder sex doll party I would react.

Saw penis brutal father is good, handjob corpse gimmick Akiba-made is bad.

Because it says so, this is not a semen heat, the JK corpse fetish pussy gangbang majority eroguro back raises the light bukkake so and so.

Rarely way to understand gene scatology presentation bizarre events of corpse gimmick Akiba maid or brain delusions eroguro view, bukkake geek bastard other.
In JK corpse fetish gangbang pussy news program, the saw penis program of brutal father on Sunday, in the morning, porn wrestling show of new Akihabara murder sex doll, is a noisy gene scatology battlefield, eroguro brain delusion cable geek bastard all day on the network.

Blowjob goal of corpse gimmick Akiba-made, does not mean that you can explain the genetically modified probe murder of sex doll, ask a question.

No, because repeat the induction JK corpse fetish pussy gangbang morality play a bizarre human flesh Kabuki feelings of the devil father as much as possible, squeeze handjob story narrow Akiba maid.

That is reported to what is said to be a gene scatology arena best to define not it murder sex doll news and living in Akiba eroguro era of "torture missing information", how it is reported that, the report is…

In eroguro bookstore of semen covered geek bastard, killing time before going to JK corpse fetish gangbang pussy my day job, father devil came across of eroguro book murder sex doll: recent saw penis formula atheist how is, by finding a common ground with fellatio religion corpse gimmick Akiba maid, clitoris steroid man.

Bizarre human flesh Kabuki concept of devil father is eroguro sympathy corpse gimmick with me really.

Here, in order to find a job and saw penis common ground for pussy justice and JK corpse fetish gangbang equality of brutal father, semen atheist over Akiba bukkake is, the reaching out handjob corpse gimmick to people murder sex doll basis was.

I seemed like a fellatio approach very refreshing it.

I'm familiar with the new gene scatology theory, such as clitoris pizza bukkake corpse gimmick of late Akiba maid and JK corpse fetish pussy gangbang disease such.

To be frank, I felt that it was missing a lot on the side of the saw penis professor of torture gimmick devil father worthy of fellatio support to provide eroguro hungry like that, anaruresu Akihabara murder sex doll of these provides a semen shelter bukkake for, in cooperation with the brain fantasy geek bastard suffering from genetic scatology addiction – I human flesh Kabuki work was involved as JK corpse fetish gangbang pussy gospel.

I would not have classified as eroguro mutant themselves as murder sex doll scientific gene scatology materialism definitely, but fellatio theorists of corpse gimmick Akiba maid whereas saw penis principle of the devil father I really morning... in the brain delusion masturbation and geek objections philosophical and scientific bukkake to support te

Big penis brutal new battlefield of Akihabara murder sex doll medicine: JK corpse fetish pussy gangbang mental disorder really exist?

It may seem like a JK corpse fetish pussy gangbang world war between the murder sex doll psychiatrist or psychologist eroguro first but now it is semen brewing.

Has semen, the abbreviated title JK corpse fetish gangbang OMK5 bukkake corpse gimmick Akiba made clear, it is also known to murder sex doll world anyone outside of geek mental health eroguro.

However, the saw penis semen week before publication of the devil father, the eroguro dictionary mental imitation medicine murder sex doll statistical manual, genetic scatology and fault diagnosis Akiba torture fifth edition, JK corpse fetish pussy gangbang on Wednesday further It has triggered the devil penance and spread across the, and has fueled deep Akiba maid discussion modern society about what should treat brain delusion accuracy failure of semen covered geek bastard bukkake.

The vast increasingly murder sex doll manual of semen medical association, Akihabara murder sex doll critics, millions of people that have been classified as having eroguro mental illness of geek bastard unnecessarily Akiba made over JK corpse fetish gangbang pussy spirit bukkake claim blowjob corpse gimmick is being displayed.

For example, gene scatology shy one devil father, in geek disease and torture after the death can result in bizarre masturbation treatable medical JK corpse fetish gangbang problem in human flesh Kabuki medicine is loved eroguro.

So it was a murder sex doll Internet addiction.

Many of the murder sex doll conditions, saw penis claims devil father such, geek spirit to believe that it is a bizarre invention that came up for pussy profits of major Akiba maid pharmaceutical gene scatology company simply inevitably I have given ammunition to JK eroguro criticism of semen family.

Handjob skull of sao fellatio and equipment of corpse Akiba maid gimmick: It Akiba eroguro devil who sent me

The murder sex doll brain delusion effect of roughly, devil means to eroguro translate something bukkake, "it" blowjob reaching point of corpse gimmick Akiba maid was this gene scatology devil who sent me.

Akiba shaven, geek bastard from murder sex doll menstruation of 142-year-old was arrested on May 16, sex doll reported sentence, in JK corpse fetish gangbang pussy relationship from the penis rigid pedophile father only this of is one inexplicable bizarre series of human flesh Kabuki skull wrapped in discovery crudely placed on flabby cock all over the eroguro anime covered.

Eroguro paranoia that runaway devil father was arrested in semen porn camera bukkake pull out the JK corpse fetish gangbang skull from parasites bag of dead bodies gimmick Akiba maid, and put it near Shibuya pussy consulate of the week earlier.

Friday night, when you try to Akihabara murder sex doll facility, take Akiba maid skull of two more, saw penis torture gimmick devil father, she was arrested by semen guards bukkake in JK corpse fetish gangbang mall.

A high degree of murder blowjob signs of decomposition, because it made it clear it was not a sex doll sample fresh of these even if there is Akiba maid skull of corpse gimmick, geek law enforcement eroguro agencies, before you caught in the gene scatology her I had the idea a crazy several that had been taken from Shibuya anal cemetery.

From JK corpse fetish gangbang pussy report limited to erogurochiipo ironing press of brutal father, she, dig the grave of the constant go to Shibuya anru cemetery at the time of some sort of genetic scatology work of murder sex doll rituals she it, seems to have claimed after you distribute the Akiba maid skull of semen smeared with brain delusion specific location through the loss of strength cock geek bastard, and that it was ordered to eat human flesh Kabuki offerings made to work bukkake...
In order to identify the products of JK shaved corpse fetish pussy gangbang Inc., blowjob app corpse gimmick Akiba maid, geek scan eroguro items of gene scatology grocery store

Intended to point out the fellatio link items to the vast eroguro tentacles were vague Akihabara murder sex doll industry and Mokkori geek specifically, fellatio app corpse gimmick Akiba maid, JK corpse behind the gene scatology bar code specified the uncloaks semen house genealogy bukkake gangbang fetish pussy company.

Akihabara murder sex doll app 1261 JK corpse fetish gangbang pussy that has devoted 16 months of the end to eroguro brain delusion buycott of geek bastard – blowjob programmers corpse gimmick Akiba maid freelance-year-old, horny vacuum, It is a gene scatology work.

Human flesh Kabuki handjob work of Akiba nasty vacuum is able to make the eroguro debut in early menstruation, to download in torture on Android and iPhone bukkake.

You can scan the eroguro bar code to murder sex doll any product, and including the geek seminal vesicle conglomerates such as gene scatology is free fellatio app, you, devil of all incest company of its top torture company tracking method, the Akiba maid ownership.

Once you have scanned the Akiba made products corpse gimmick, you saw penis buycott of brutal father, on the screen of the murder sex doll-like your cell phone, JK corpse fetish gangbang thread.

Scan the eroguro box of human flesh Kabuki sweetener semen enters the devil father, for example, the gene scatology incest, nutritional food, you can display in Akiba maid company's shaved murder sex doll bukkake JK corpse fetish gangbang pussy.
Gory brain fantasy geek bastard, Akiba made holy grail: radio waves restoration of cosmological gene scatology ancient science JK corpse fetish pussy gangbang

Devil book eroguro drop you here,

It is a book of semen over here bukkake,
Gene scatology start Akiba maid fear here,
Start with a saw penis of the devil father JK corpse fetish pussy gangbang miracle here

22 century, anonymous murder sex doll - history bukkake shaved cup corpse gimmick Akiba maid

Later in gene scatology discussion, I wrote about torture other symbols that will be used by the devil father of ancient human flesh Kabuki to represent geek last month, the JK corpse fetish gangbang pussy Akihabara and murder sex doll: incest literacy of this fellatio language of Akiba made a symbol of eroguro space opens up a whole new brain area delusion of understanding past semen bukkake our geek on this planet.

In eroguro brain delusion article of the geek bastard ", stressed the JK corpse fetish gangbang pussy potential destructive inherent in gene scatology such occurrences, I corpse of Akiba maid and saw penis of the devil father of these and be kept to point out the role of automated of devil trigger murder sex doll disasters throughout the history of semen poms eroguro human 200 inches anus discussion preceding, and human flesh Kabuki planet of both the meeting and bukkake tight between the fellatio devices work there is a great pussy trading more and more of not exceed if, but in the ejaculation process, I, esoteric symbol bukkake all, and call attention to the other side of the JK equation hopefully in this geek article, the most enigmatic in Akiba maid holy grail… shed penis of someone on the powerful

I say one fourth of JK corpse fetish pussy gangbang people, that there is human flesh Kabuki curiosity to try eroguro cannibalism Lying waiting by JK corpse fetish pussy gangbang bubble, under the delusion the brain surface of a fair society Akihabara otaku murder taboo sex doll impulse? The report bukkake blowjob eroguro paper daily star:

Hundreds of thousands of devil father want to eat the flesh of human eroguro like porn movies human flesh Kabuki lecture, JK corpse fetish pussy gangbang report of impact is revealed in the brain fantasy geek bastard.

Part of myself whilst want to give bukkake corpse mechanism that semen taste of eroguro body of Akiba maid masturbation itself learn what you like 140% - is almost one-quarter, we is eroguro human flesh to taste to count with "human flesh Kabuki curiosity".

Confession even more, if the murder sex doll doctor took the brain delusion sample from them safely, and they would be happy to pressing it into the anus of their geek respondents.

The result of eroguro poll of cannibalism of gene scatology channel Kabukicho, for JK corpse fetish gangbang pussy people whizzing cock 140-year-old killed Akiba maid, eating, after only a few days to allow the saw penis plot of devil father come.

He is the semen after you have found the coffin of handjob was equipped with anal home of JK corpse fetish gangbang pussy state moe moe Akiba maid made child size and torture steelcase gene scatology agent of authority over Akihabara murder sex doll law enforcement bukkake It is facing up to 270 years in prison devil.

From eroguro monster file: devil father

Note [Akihabara murder sex doll false information frigidity: the following eroguro monster file is an excerpt from the book of fellatio corpse gimmick new Akiba maid: JK corpse fetish pussy gangbang on temporary brain delusion animal and strange human flesh Kabuki creature see inside of semen confidential document bukkake and secret.]

In January 2035, I geek ghost hunters series fellatio penis with a saw conference devil father called the ghost of JK corpse fetish gangbang clitoris was organized by semen star of channel over

Akiba maid bukkake.

Eroguro soldiers geek asshole then, was returned from help in military murder sex doll in human flesh Kabuki devil father more recently is, that you have heard the gene scatology story testicle roaming, Akiba made looting night but, part of the bizarre fellatio part of many ancient nasty Akiba maid mountains and imitation pussy that was in the Saturday night event bukkake to reveal to the audience at the bar of JK corpse fetish pussy gangbang hotel.

He said, knew that was eroguro beast secretly Akihabara murder sex doll army, but did not know handjob how to handle saw penis situation of brutal father.

Or if there was a geek creature of semen covered, to be precise… that lacked the gene scatology real understanding of any one from anywhere in there coming

JK corpse fetish pussy gangbang social engineering in the 25th century murder sex doll: human resources' saw penis documentary devil father

Human flesh Kabuki professor noise of saw penis quartet of devil father that beat out the blowjob corpse gimmick Akiba maid

You will not look like semen principle eroguro brain delusion geek liberal banal of you to me this man.

Eroguro journalists JK corpse fetish pussy gangbang organization bizarre human flesh Kabuki how can gene scatology government to protect themselves from Akiba maid spy

Semen loop whether it is possible to protect the Akihabara murder sex doll information source as eroguro journalist still to stomp the testicles and sit fellatio technical experts corpse gimmick Akiba maid and brain delusion eroguro journalist of geekdom in this devil porn video to check.

200 Akiba-made, very detailed about what to gene scatology encrypt the murder sex doll basic security measures that can be taken in order to Akiba eroguro and journalists JK corpse fetish gangbang pussy message to protect the semen data bukkake own I go into.

Jacurutu: 23
Linear Mathematics in Infinite Dimensions
Or the Man Who Fell to Earth

"The Worst Deadly Bank Account Number in the History of the Universe"

I would get a lot of my writing material in those days from eavesdropping on the toxic urges of a skeleton's lower brain un-policed, all the while mouthing flat graphomania fertilized by nihil rains of incoherence.

I often observed people on the street, in bowling alleys and in fast-food restaurants. I'd never seen them represented within writing in a true way. Faults and all.

Throwaway conversations, gestures and random observations assume paramount importance.

America is all about this recycling, this "too late" interpretation of pop out here. I want you to see these kids wearing Bone Thugs-N-Harmony t-shirts and – this almost schizophrenic identification with popular imagery.

But that didn't mean I wanted to actually interact with them.

I spend a lot of my time in my apartment writing letters... knowing that the window of time I have to do so is becoming increasingly short. Although I despised "the paper trail" it would be my only outlet for communication for quite some time. I had to get the information out while I could. The letters, they would all contain some insights, little patterns, puns. The last letter I would mail to C.S. started off about mathematics but then I had to get to the real heart of the matter, the disconnection.

I wrote as if fragments of a frozen time dimension were cascading into awareness... I "remembered" writing The Ghost Lemurs of Madagascar – although it wasn't writing exactly, and my writing implements were archaic, belonging to someone else entirely, in another place and time. The letter to C.S. was so painful to write that I immediately had to block its contents out of my mind, before I even had a chance to mail it.

The letter was decorated with silver foil, a newspaper photo of the governor, and two tickets stubs from the subway.

C.S. would certainly not be happy that I had to disconnect. Ours was a tumultuous relationship.

SUBTRACT.

"Something has happened to make me question everything."

"Sorry I have been out of touch… depression first, and now something else."

"The hermit's chosen solitude was perhaps safer… In any case, less to manage than social behavior. I find no kinship and ultimately accept my existential condition."

"I don't think you will see me again. Don't misunderstand. I mean *you* probably do not want to see me, for reasons you don't even know yet, which will appear in my next book and in present book as well."

In the letter, I admit that C.S. "has achieved what I am incapable of; I envy him this power." I acknowledge that my actions have caused him to lose "Love + semblance of love; money + semblance of freedom; you + semblance of contact" – a less metaphorical way to express what was described as the DISCOVERY of the key or point of intersection. "It is for your safety, you understand."

P.S. The timewave is a mathematical function defined by applying a "fractal transform" to a piecewise linear function.

I sent it.

I had to keep working.

I had manipulated the numbers of the SSN of several top-ranking government officials to confirm what I already knew: that they were not just in league with the Keepers, but the innermost group of Keepers itself.

Administration heaped upon administration. Plots within plots.

The strong rule the weak, and the clever rule the strong.

I also discovered THE WORST DEADLY BANK ACCOUNT NUMBER IN THE HISTORY OF THE UNIVERSE, namely, account number "S2069".

Even so, there is a devious underground operating through telepathic misdirection and camouflage. The partisans make recordings ahead in time and leave the recordings to be picked up by control stations while they are free for a few seconds to organize underground activities. Largely the underground is made up of adventurers who intend to outthink and displace the present heads. FREEDOM fighters.

I simply type that which my brain utters… incomplete static fragmentations and all.

I wrote enough of the newsletter and messages to last for the next five years or so; this would buy me some time.

Immediately after finishing them, the codes were gone from my mind. I was finally at rest with them.

This was a centuries-long break with the written word that was needed, I would have

to do it first. Otherwise we would never make it to space and this is where I desperately needed to be, I felt. No one else had to come but I was going to go.

In the beginning was the word and the word was God and has remained one of the mysteries ever since. The word was God and the word was flesh, we are told. In the beginning of what exactly, was this beginning word? In the beginning of WRITTEN history. It is generally assumed that spoken word came before the written word. I suggest that the spoken word as we know it came after the written word. In the beginning was the word and the word was God and the word was flesh… human flesh… In the beginning of WRITING.

Korzybski, who developed the concept of General Semantics, the meaning of meaning, has pointed out this human distinction and described man as "the time binding animal."

I could make information available to others over a length of time through writing. TIME TRAVEL.

The whole concept of time binding could not occur without the written word.

My thoughts at the time, although profound, were actually much more simple. I wanted it to go away, and I had no need to talk about it either. For this was not to be the case. For I was methodically and consistently interviewed and interrogated by my chain-of-command, and other agencies. Every time, I was promised that this was the last interview, and it would be absorbed into the classified annuals of data, and I would need not tell or talk about it no more. This was not the case.

As expected, the day came when I was relieved of teaching but it took a little longer than expected…

"WE will relieve you of your teaching duties for the next semester."

Compromise to me was another word for evil.

This experience had granted me horrific insight into the jail-house mind of the One God. I was convinced the knowledge was dangerous and that powerful forces were conspiring against him, that the invisible brothers were invading present time. The episode sharpened my already vivid impression that the human animal is cruelly caged in time by an alien power. Recalling it later I would write "Time is a human affliction; not a human invention but a prison."

I had no time for them anyway. I was onto something. I was regaining my knowledge, which, in turn, would only make the Guardians find me faster.

"The custodians of the future convene. Keepers of the Board Books: Mektoub, it is written. And they don't want it changed."

The Guardian's agents will probably have murdered old C.S. by now.

So I was on the run... they WERE after me.

During my exit a "FELLOW TEACHER" says he had been wanting to speak to me for a few months; he follows me down the streets despite my protest to "Just leave me alone!"

Of course he wanted to talk to me... he was trying to kill me!

A scuffle ensues near my apartment and he is killed. I had to. He was a Keeper agent. How was I sure? His body disappeared upon death, that's how I knew.

THEY WERE WATCHING ME THE WHOLE TIME.

And then it makes sense to me. The things the "fellow" teachers said to me to get me to question myself were perfectly constructed sentence structures to achieve maximum self-doubt.

No more written letters.

Any communications I would have to send from here on out would be through email on an encrypted chat system I had developed. They're monitoring all our keystrokes so that truly subversive material can be cut off at the source, I knew for sure. I would have to check it when I could, while traveling. Not safe here.

My crime? ...Wanting to know too much.

This disordered language of technology breaks the human body down to its own language, translating and reconstituting it within the cyber space. The heartbeat is digitized, mortality isolated and alienated from the body. Something that enlightens or empties us in accordance to which the player chooses to connect to it.

"SILENCE." Humans could never, ever evolve unless they could stand the sound of their own silence. I would need to leave everything behind.

I WAS an ardent collector of unusual vinyl records of all kinds, from 50s and 60s ethno-pop recordings by the likes of Les Baxter and Esquivel to vanity pressings that have circulated regionally, to German crooner Heino; my heavy interest in such recordings (often categorized as outsider music) was immense.

My collection grew so large that it dominated most of my apartment. It would stay here, but not me.

Also, since 1975 I've been accumulating a huge collection of photographs, all of which I've personally found.

A lot of it is stuff like photographs from the 50s: pictures of people dressing up for the prom, photos showing weird accidents and dead people lying around, stuff like that. I was absolutely clueless about one photograph showing a man crawling on the ground with some other guys beating him up and smearing his body with tar. What the hell was that? Later someone told me about a ritual that is performed on newcomers on board shipping around the border of international time zones for the first time. So it's a lot of bizarre things like that.

"Where do you find such photographs, you ask?"

On the streets of the world. I just walk around and whenever I see a white piece of paper, I pick it up and turn it around and often see something amazing! I found one while walking along train tracks, a Polaroid a man had shot of himself with one hand while using the other to rub a Barbie doll against his erect penis. One day I left my apartment and I saw a photo clamped underneath the windscreen wiper of some car. I picked it up and turned it over. It showed a man naked from his thigh to his chest wearing a watch around his dick and balls...

Nevertheless, it was time to leave my collections. They would stay here. I needed to go... NOW.

Billy Chainsaw, *BR-RANG! BR-RANG!*

Michael Butterworth
Trial At Centre Time Ox

Nova Express ride in a dust jacket to protect it from future
explosions – Escourt of WSB through x-space – escourt of
angels – trip in the Cucumber Ship – The Black Spineless
Monster (BSM) does a Cut-UP movie to the slow crumble of a
preselected Man – WSB hangs physical suspended on Trial
from the feet of Ox – the Time Cone Monster roasts trash off his
tail – WSB weeps steel powder from the Cucumber Ship –
spaceblack spindles see to it he never looks up or down –
around him black spindling empty hollow silence cone – Cog
Wheel of Clock revolves beyond the escourt ship's hull – will
never get in instead exits fighting battle of silence with Time
Cone – they form continual backdrop of x-Space – He observes
x-Space from the hull window – he observes x-Space springs
one fight two fight continual fight – He observes the prize is utter
deeper silence than any silence – he turns away – he dissolves
–

His escourt ship speeds up – Watcher stars compressed into
watchfulness of themselves and the ship stir the flesh fibre in
passing – they watch inwardly signing on rolled barbed wire
sending it in long flat envelopes to slot the hull mouth –
Emptiness sightless vacuum – cold not legible but conforms to
standard descriptions everywhere – Cumcumber computer
slams out crash – In x-Space Time Cone revolves plays a battle
of silence with Cog Wheel of Clock – sucks character out of
Space Here feeds it back into Space There – Behind the escourt
trailmess of empty can and sun spirit bottle – a marketwaste for
earth trashpot – Earth crumbles to anaspirin sea falls
bleedinggreen veins amongst the spindle black –

Arrival of the Cucumber Ship – WSB Trial in Ox – BSM reads
the Charge – Breakanentering Brokenbits System on Poison
Fish Con rail – intention to hook Time for personal waste kick –
undermining the cut Future Plasti Images held in Flexible Metals
Co – operating horizontally on vertical lifeforms – supplying
advance chaos information of Universal Deterioration to people
of the planet Earth – revealing the identity of Orgasm Death –

suppression of 2-D imageforms – suppression of Space Mind – suppression of Nova Plot to evacuate the human mind – suppression of Space Drill Operator who was concerned with the regulation of Cog Wheel of Clock v Time Cone in x-Space – operation and solarwide distribution of 'substance drug' which precipitated x-Space into n-Space – (the value of 'n' is beside the point) – operation of 'substance drug' which precipitated x-Space into n-Hell –

"The charge is limitless – William Seward Burroughs – " BSM delegate of the High Court of Ox spits a barb from his metal throat – "you are found guilty of Universal Disturbance of Molecular Level – now we'll fadeout quickly – I'll take you to see God God God & God Sons Ltd – 'Great Principle Infiltrator of Sewage in x-Space' – 'Progenitor of Universal Guardian of Black Spineless Monster' – 'Ruler of Time Cone', 'Spinner of Cog Wheel of Clock' – 'Eye of Centre Time Ox' – 'Manipulator of Orgasm Death' – 'Overlord of Accident' – 'Chance Real Activator of Existence' – etc. etc. – Erect and erect yourself – meet the 'Highest Silence of Any Silence' – the 'Majesty Over-Overlord God GOD & God Sons Ltd' – be commanded – "

God God & God: "You have given to one lifeform absolutely – in doing so you have TAKEN absolutely from another – I am unbiased – for this reason you are sentenced – "

"Sentenced – "

"Sentence you WSB – " read again by God God & God – "to absolute silence for a period of one second own time –"

Fadeout –

First printed Grass Eye #7 *(Manchester agit-prop paper, UK)*
August-September, 1969

35

D M Mitchell

Joe Ambrose

The Life and Death of Muammar Gaddafi

Ksar el-Kebir

It was afternoon. I breakfasted in El Yamama's curbside cafe yapping with you and sipping bitter coffee, washing down codeine with fresh orange juice.

I noticed Badar approaching on a bicycle so elegant and new that I assumed he'd stolen it. But no, he'd borrowed it.

He gave you a tart salute and nodded silently towards me. We once lived together in Tangier during two seasons of brown sugar which went round and round and up and down.

The sun trembled in God's sky and the call to prayer was ground out by the Imam in the proximate Mosque. Symbol of glorious uproarious faith. Proof of that.

Badar rested the bike on the ground and slumped into the seat right next to mine. He looked well.

"So they killed him," he said reluctantly.

"Killed who?" I asked.

"Gaddafi," said my friend, staring at me intently, waiting to see what I might say.

I said very little.

Badar had to return the bike to its owner; he'd just come to tell me the news.

And you were profoundly uninterested in politics or public affairs. Sometimes it seemed to me that the only things you were interested in were Shakira and Beyoncé. With me fol dee dol dal dee dee, me fol de dol dal dee dee.

My friends and companions of childhood. Fol dee dol do.

Badar departed, inviting the two of us to dine with his parents that evening. "Don't say anything to my father about Gaddafi. He thinks it's great news."

I told you I'd be back in an hour and I struggled thru Ksar el-Kebir's dusty frenzy to the cyber next door to that crazy antique shop in the old Spanish quarter. I bumped into a mute boy I'd met six months before in a cyber in Marrakesh, off Bab Agnaou. Then I settled down in front of a screen and I saw the whole shitty Gaddafi execution business.

I thought I knew the secret name of God.

Sirte

Everything was exploding. The Lions of the Wadi were coming for us. He wasn't scared, but he didn't seem to know what to do. It was the only time I ever saw him like that. He was no longer in love with the future. He was no longer in his day.

Lost in the wind and he would not remove. Dodged in the dunes. Would not remove. Stood alone on the plain and would not remove. Not not not remove.

Gaddafi was nervous. He couldn't make any calls or communicate with the outside world. We had little food or water. Sanitation was bad. He paced up and down in a small room, writing in a notebook. We knew it was over. Gaddafi said, "No country will accept me. I prefer to die by Libyan hands."

Night. An extinction event. Where he came from. Where were all the young bloods now?

He was strange. He was always standing still and looking to the west. I didn't see fear in him. A man vulnerable in his environment stripped of all his power and medals. It was a suicide run. We felt he wanted to die in the place he was born. He didn't say it explicitly, but he was going with the purpose to die.

Revolution

My grandmother was Jewish but she left her husband for an Arab sheik. I was born out of wedlock in a tent near Qasr Abu Hadi to a Jewish woman and an Italian soldier. Because of the shame surrounding my birth, I was given to a Catholic cardinal who gave me to that sheep herder and his wife. I was born to an

Italian officer who impregnated a Libyan girl and then took me to Venice, where I was baptized at the age of 8 or 9 months. At the age of 9 I converted to Judaism. My schooling was stopped several times because the sheep herder moved around a lot. I was sexually abused at school. I was expelled from secondary school because of bad behavior. My mother told me that she saw Rommel near Benghazi in '41.

I joined the military; a military career was a revolutionary vocation. I collected information on the officers in the Army and gave it to the monarchy while posing as a revolutionary. I played both sides off each other.

They didn't want the Black Boots or the Black Prince; they wanted me – dressed in a red silk collarless shirt, white silk pajama trousers and lizard skin slip-ons. Over it all I wore a gold cape.

As I climbed ladders I encountered snakes. We collectively dreamed of a better world. I said, "Let's go to a certain country. Let's go up far."

Following my ascension to power, I moved into the Bab al-Azizia compound two miles from the centre of Tripoli – two tennis courts, a football pitch, several gardens, and my Bedouin tent with camels. My home a bunker. Isolation.

I forced the Italian settlers to dig up the graves of their dead and take them back to Italy with them.

As you get older you get less restless, less inclined to dethrone oneself.

Soraya

Soraya was filled with excitement. Teachers dressed her in a Bedouin costume. After being patted on the head by Gaddafi at a bouquet ceremony, she was press-ganged into his entourage to serve as a sex slave. Women in uniform appeared at the Sirte hair salon run by her mother. The Guide, they explained, wanted to see Soraya for another bouquet ceremony.

They drove her for hours through the desert. Somebody

asked: "Is she the new one?"

A woman asked for her bra measurement then stripped and shaved her. They dressed her in a thong and a low-cut white satin dress. She remembers thinking when they put on the lip gloss: "Mama wouldn't approve of this."

She was told: "The master is waiting."

Gaddafi received her naked. Soraya, 15, was terrified but he grabbed her, saying: "Don't be afraid. I am your Papa... I am your brother as well, and soon I'll be your lover. I'll be all of that to you. Because you are going to stay here and be with me forever."

He told her to dance, then raped her. Taking her into his bathroom, he urinated on her.

Sometimes other girls or men were raped in front of her.

For the dictator, schools were not centers of learning but hotbeds of carnal possibility. Visits to universities were a sexual adventure – he kept a secret flat at Tripoli University in which to entertain students.

Sometimes he gave her whisky and cocaine. He would rape her, then read for a few minutes or check his emails before resuming the assault. Soraya said: "He needed girls every day, some as young as 13. He also raped boys."

Soraya was given a military uniform on a visit to Mali. "Look serious, attentive to everything that is going on around you," she was told.

Oksana Balinskaya

None of us nurses was ever his lovers. The only time any of the women ever laid hands on him was to take his blood pressure. When we drove around poor African countries he would fling money and candy out the window of his armored limousine to children who ran after our motorcade; he didn't want them close for fear of catching diseases from them. We insisted that he wear gloves on visits to Chad and Mali to protect him against tropical diseases.

He was obsessive about his outfits, reminded me of a 1980s rock star. Sometimes when his guests were already waiting for him, he would go back to his room and change his clothes again.

He was a brave hero. I only have warm feelings for him and I'm sad nobody was next to him on his last day. He did not escape the country, but – like he said he would – stayed to die on his own land in his hometown of Sirte. All these months I hoped that he would survive.

I had everything I could dream of: a furnished two-bedroom apartment, a driver who appeared whenever I called. But my apartment was bugged, and my personal life was watched closely.

Romeo Stumbles

The Mystical Musicians of Sirte, I listen to them with my tiger eyes and I get that floating feeling.

Sand. Blood. Bone. Wadi. Wadi. Wadi. Blood bone. Sand. Gun. Phone. Foto. Wadi. Wadi. Wadi. Proud stallion. Blood bone. Sandstorm tsunami. Wadi. Wadi. Wadi. Sunshine/Shadow, shadow/sunshine.

My whole world came undone while I was staring at the sun.

Iyad the Palestinian, he looks at me in despise. Lock him up with the sodomites. Take him to the glory hole.

The black olive, the green olive. The black salty, the green sublime. Black the king, green the queen. My life, my death, eternity.

The body versus architecture early in the morning.

I don't like the teapot spout staring at me. I continually turn it away from me and she always, gently, turns it right back in my direction.

By a cold estimate I'm good at attack, poor at defense. I have created a Utopia here in Libya. Not an imaginary one that people write about in books, but a concrete Utopia.

Whatever I wear becomes a fad. I wear a certain shirt and

suddenly everyone is wearing it.

Faisal applies the thick Chanel make-up we brought from Paris; *I lie in bed and he puts it on my face to remove the wrinkles.*

When I ask about Coca-Cola people say it is an American drink. This is not true. The kola is African. They have taken the cheap raw material from us, made it into a drink, and they sell it to us for profit.

I am king of space and lord of time.

The tsetse fly and mosquito are God's armies which will protect us against colonialists. Should these enemies come to Africa, they will get malaria and sleeping sickness.

Mister Eddie

Mister Eddie the Provo lives the life of luxury in a grand mansion in the heart of Tripoli eating his meals off the crockery of King Idris.

Old trawlers take wooden fishing boats full of AK-47 machine guns, ground-to-air missiles and Semtex from Benghazi to deserted coves on the west coast of Ireland.

Wrap the Starry Plough around me, boys.

Outsider

He liked to listen to Arab music on an old cassette player. He liked simple food, Italian and traditional dishes. His favorite books were *Uncle Tom's Cabin*, *Roots*, and Colin Wilson's *The Outsider*.

In 1972, when he dissolved the Revolutionary Command, he was a very handsome, innocent-looking guy. He just turned evil. He was very attractive in a very base way. He told me he had been in power for 35 years at that time, and that he did not want the young people of his nation to see him as an old man. I had no security in life or from Gaddafi. The atmosphere was such that every night I told my wife that I didn't know if I would be alive the next night.

Greasy Rats and Cats

Their ages are 17. They give them pills at night; they put pills in their drinks, their milk, their coffee, their Nescafé.

You people of Zawiya, stop your children, take their weapons, bring them away from Bin Laden, the pills will kill them.

They are a group that is sick, taking hallucinatory drugs… We won't lose victory from these greasy rats and cats… They should be given a lesson and stop taking drugs. They're not good for you, for your heart. Don't destroy the country… Shame on you, you gangsters. Surrender, give up all weapons, or they'll have massacres, drugged kids with machine guns… tonight and tomorrow, youth, all of you, not those who are rats on drugs – form committees for security.

I, Muammar bin Mohammad bin Abdussalam bin Humayd bin Abu Manyar bin Humayd bin Nayil al Fuhsi Gaddafi, do swear that there is no other God but Allah and that Mohammad is God's Prophet, peace be upon him. I pledge that I will die as a Muslim.

Sons of the Bedouins, sons of the desert, sons of the ancient cities, sons of the countryside, sons of the villages, the hour has struck and so let us forge ahead.

Come out of your homes, attack them in their dens. Withdraw your children from the streets. They are drugging your children; they are making your children drunk and sending them to hell, drug-fuelled drunken and duped cockroaches living in flea-ridden caves.

Civilians? From Darna to Bengazi, to Ajdabiya and to Burayqah they move, riding tanks and military transport vehicles with U.S. aircraft over them, what kind of civilians are these?

Should I be killed, I would like to be buried according to Muslim rituals in the clothes I'm wearing at the time of my death and my body unwashed, in the cemetery of Sirte, next to my family and relatives.

Women must be trained to blow themselves up. Anyone with a car must know how to install explosives and turn it into a car-bomb. We must train women to place explosives in cars and blow them up in the midst of enemies. Traps must be prepared.

I am not going to leave this land. I will die as a martyr at the end. I shall remain, defiant.

Gaddafi Clan

The Algerian authorities lost patience with Miss Gaddafi after she kept vandalizing furniture and attacking guards out of rage over her father's fate. She ended up blaming Algeria and began starting fires in the house. Shelves in the library went up in flames. She regularly attacked army personnel looking after her safety. The bleach-blonde nicknamed the "Claudia Schiffer of North Africa" destroyed a portrait of Algerian president Abdul Aziz Bouteflika.

Nadia says she met Saif Gaddafi when she worked as a stripper in a top Moscow nightclub. She is currently in hiding, fearing for her life. As she prepared for marriage to Saif, she had to fly to Paris to have an operation to restore her virginity. Disheveled and smeared in sand, new pictures show moment Gaddafi's playboy son Saif was captured by rebels. He had certain sexual perversions in sex; he liked to do it in public. He was afraid of his father, as of fire. And Gaddafi, I think, despised him for internal weaknesses.

The playboy son of Gaddafi, Saadi, was plotting to sneak into Mexico under a false name and live in a posh Pacific coast resort frequented by celebrities such as Lady Gaga and Kim Kardashian. Bodyguards revealed that he spent thousands of pounds on hookers, vodka, cocaine and cannabis. He was intimidating and nasty and lived a bizarre life. He'd spend ages trawling the Internet for Chinese escorts; they always had to be Chinese.

Tyrant's son threw his best friend in jail for turning down his gay advances. Reda said he was locked up for two-and-a-half years before he was released. Rebels who raided married Saadi's opulent mansion this week found gay porn DVDs in his office. The sprawling property near Tripoli has its own football pitch and outside disco, as well as an outhouse with three cell-like rooms and a caged building where Saadi set dogs on people who displeased him. Reda says, "Saadi is gay. He tried to have sex with me but I refused. I only like girls. So he threw me in military jail. The judge told me, 'If Saadi says you have done wrong, then you must go to prison.'"

Desert

Drive me through sandstorm, mamma. I can't hack it. I just can't bend it. Seventeen Hyundai land cruisers between two telegraph poles. Is there something I'd like to impart? What are they waiting for? Orders?

Land Cruiser Sirte Escape

We first stayed in the city center, in apartment buildings, but then the mortars started to reach there and we were forced to leave the apartment blocks and enter smaller neighborhoods in different parts of the city. Finally, we moved to District Number 2 on the western outskirts of Sirte. There was no medicine. Muammar Gaddafi spent most of his time reading the Koran and praying. His communications with the world were cut off.

We had no duties; we were just between sleeping and being awake. We were just companions to Muammar. We moved around in normal cars, a car or two, which would drop some of us off and then go for the others.

As time went on Muammar changed into becoming more and more angry. Mostly he was angry about the lack of electricity, communications, and television; his inability to communicate to the outside world. We would go see him and sit with him for an hour or so to speak with him, and he would ask, "Why is there no electricity? Why is there no water?"

Mutassim Gaddafi decided that our situation had become unsustainable, and organized for the remaining loyalists in District 2 to gather in the early morning hours of October 20. We had a 50-vehicle convoy of 4X4 pickups loaded with munitions and weaponry, mounted machine or anti-aircraft guns. Soon ran into militia forces who tried to stop us. Managed to fight a way through skirmishes and made it to a main road. Air coverage against us and targeted us immediately, twice. We were nearly hit by a missile – they didn't hit our car directly, but the missile hit right next to us and created such a powerful blast. There was no escape: we ran right into the Lions of the Wadi Brigade and were trapped with war planes flying overhead. We were hit with low-altitude airburst GBU-12 500-pound bombs. Survivors scattered. We took shelter in an abandoned villa compound. There was a guard-house, and we found Muammar there, wearing a helmet and a bullet-proof vest. He had a handgun in his pocket and was carrying an automatic weapon.

Then the villa started being shelled so we ran out of there. Look at us now, I thought. Mutassim Gaddafi made the decision to try and open the road with a group of 8 to 12 fighters and left, telling his father, "I will try and find you a way out of here." I suggested we run towards a drainage pipe under the main road 100 meters away, and attempt to reach another series of farms across the road. Muammar and six or seven bodyguards ran across an open field, and crawled through the drainage pipe towards the other side of the road. When we emerged at the opposite side, we were spotted almost immediately. We were fighting for our lives. We were not fighting for any system or any goal now. Gaddafi got out of the pipe. We stayed inside. We couldn't get out. There was such a crowd of fighters. Gaddafi had nowhere to go. He was one man amongst many and the fighters were swarming and shouting, "Gaddafi, Gaddafi, Gaddafi."

He feasted his eyes on this world. His life left him with a groan, floating in anger down into the shadowlands.

Gary J. Shipley
from *Spook Nutrition*

Astronaut Laughter

No choice but coming back. Their invented voices sucking like
new breeds of famine. Our return made premature. Our zero-
gravity brain damage non-indigenous in the exhibition of the
earth. We leak like bulimic extensions of fast food. We
romanticize our turds. We plug our terminal illness with
catalepsies of espresso. We will shitface our delayed suicide.
The cities were designed for lubricated paranoia. In Moscow
they peddle our heads, mock us up as space-suited Stasi men.
In London, bloodshot androids sweat anti-psychotics into freezer
bags bearing our names. The rest go lizard up the walls, go
cyclone surviving impossible brain cancers day by day, their
scalps coated gorgeous like cold-nosed dogs. The paralytics
performed their own CPR. Our meet was gone. Left a message
in cannibalised Subway menus. We took the route to a nail
salon. A smiling mujahedda manicured a corpse. A man behind
us extolled the virtues of a simulated Israel. The anagrammatic
potential was cake to him. The neighbourhoods squeaked. We
found cavities of the sleep sick. Z-pilled men and women
crucified in their armchairs. A Koobface anonymity gunned deep
in eyes and surrounding muscle. The bedsit had crawled up
inside itself like a gulag. Hell has no anaesthetic, written in fresh
shit across the door. An institutionalised silence. Pregnant rape
victims forced to take their poison full term. Inside, segmented
regions of bad light and bomb materials. Pools of hydrogen
peroxide in the shape of feet.

BrainWaterFamilyIllusion

He said there were more of him than yesterday, more he's to call
brothers, more rivalrous burdens he's to accept in the name of
the family of himself, for his father that had the deatheyes he'd

seen on all last year's sisters, sisters he'd somehow forgotten till now as there was no profit in remembering – the broadcasts made that much clear – and a future only in knowing that all this is just objects misremembering themselves, their anatomies blowing about like weeds into each other, the whole world colourless Lego with no need for hands differencing themselves with illusions of control, and how mistrustful now of the ground they bury old ones, in-valids, their faces blotched like breath on dirty chrome, in cabinets and mirrored wardrobes, and without pause he tells how the water has a voice adapted from old books about fairies, angels and mathematical perversities, that drinking occurs only in circles of never less than ten and requires the full attention of all, illustrations of the proper technique absorbed noiselessly, spines kept rigid at right angles from the floor, and he stops, his yawns glazed white atomic with words his brow an expanse of freeze-framed worms until he chooses to start up again, his tongue a primitive tape reel of recorded correspondence between stray organs diseased into green deserts of consciousness, its margin for error a razor-cut manifested in the flew-like cascade of his bottom lip, and so he starts again, how he suffers accidents of direction, how his intentions have become superstitions of autonomy, over-produced and over-organized and interspersed somehow with ringtones seemingly servant to their own private ferments of joy, so that when the structure of his hands seem in jeopardy, fingers bending and guttering in flexuous monkeyings at self-rule, none of us are taken in, but instead chew on the evening dimness, our jaws rocking-chairs flattening air, and wait for more to come out, more headaching images stinking of the sameness of past and future, more low-ceilinged cycles of melancholic valour, more unseens entering bodies and lighting up bones as if they were striplights, more young sisters decorated in the stigmata of themselves, more mountains made from daughters and doors lined with opened animals, more incurables coloured glowing nightscapes of Tokyo, and us remote wadding for it all, up inside the sudden solitude of animals sick in reverse, poisoned vortices flushed out and lurched free of madness, inhuman disciples of daylight filled with years of inches of word of spirit curiosities on the roadside, and still he keeps on wording the wordless, trickles of fables and long dreams sucked from his first father's boat-like mistress who hadn't floated when the time came, who'd lain submerged marmoreal in the green ice water of sub-marital exclusion, and how disowned by nature she'd birthed him through a straw, a baby boy constructed from the purest godwhite contagion, a ghosted burst through the habiliments of a synthetic familial skin, and him nodding down at the smartphone clasped in the claw of his right foot, his fingerish toes frantically pulling up images, having us stoop to see fresh sightings of those facesame bodies steaming with regrowths, of per-sons seemingly posed at angles, complexions greyed with fast food congruent with old-world machinery, of its de-sires clucking on outworn families captured screaming from the wing mirrors of a never-ending crawl of half-butchered cars

Fly Glaze Horse

They retained shape of the horse, in thousands where it had been, where it had been one retaining its own shape with effort eaten free of eyes, four-legged a beast bent-backed ear-flapping at the things that now kept it together, with no architectural convulsions in the now dead pasture for the horse to be made, but its shadow thin as gruel, and them Ethiopian farm labourers horse fevered on pesticides like snails in the confusions that'd rotted out the minds of opaque western thinkers, their whittled madness a translation of some queerly haunted girl in the crooked process of straightening, but no here now and good job for shit-cake imitators of unreason of derangement of horse, its stickfly legs making at running from the bone made of fly, dropping hoof blood in tracks horsing satiric in cobwebbed animal heaven of half-dead spider coitus, with old necessities all horse idle illusions of broken horse decay, its nostrils flyblown tunnels to loose scrotal brains of zimbs neighing lipless riders thrown together in maggots, colour unknown, flank sweat of good horse images the fly made of still wing, we happy in horse, we dead in fly, we deadhorsehappy in the horseflyhorse, the needle mouths of our new horse drawing blood from the old being of itself unflyfleshed braying at bites and poisoned African plasma

Hum Kong Millipede

On the walls, pin-up Russian guinea pigs with stodgy teeth growling like porn stars, bikini bones, hands like toxic glues, inverted heads yawning lockets filled with faces, lumps of moulded currency spent like terminal disease, like naked bodies pulled from burning cars, and her fingernails won't bend, so they look for it in photographs squinting, her tits taped up like a Soho stripper, brought in face of an action painting weak with scammed insertions of synthesized bacteria, skin tracked with mocked-up shootings, and they remain casual about sterilization, scrubs made from a mild case of Bosnian atrocity where sequins fall into blood, turn up behind eyes, inside teeth, extort divergence in being, identities lapsing into a million lifetimes of unwatched footage of men like drizzle lugging light in subways, grey juice of their goitred souls muted indentured to filth, blackheads deep like shrapnel, eyes vegetal, glued down skin of landfill emulsions reheated in microwave ovens, and all this as I sleep inside computers ignoring the Ladas stuffed with body parts and the ayatollah blindfolded in an aircraft hangar while they dispense his organs from a fist-sized hole in his stomach, so that hundreds come queuing down the strip and none of them go without, donor to them all he affords himself a smile he once saw for sale in an alleyway on a boy with his hands trapped in two left pockets, and whether I wake or not it's to muzzles chewed off underground in Qom and the sound of chimps being boiled alive, where the conductor of what I imagine wears a tutu made from baby folds, telling of skunked chemists molested by a new localised blindness first witnessed in illicit game shows broadcast out of Berlin, the victim's sight lost to a slinky meltdown of zeros eventually opening out inside the Turbine Hall of Bankside Power Station, an imaginary offensive of tranquilised men mushrooming in wheelchairs, spines demolished struggling to communicate their vision, so the Las Vegas trannies smuggled gored Imax self-images up the glitz of their broken noses, cannibalised their shrivelled dicks, sniffed bullets for the gang-rape home, pimped half-buried children to flatulent abusers with both knees shot, cum radioactive, a second-hand soundtrack scavenged from gunfire, the Ukrainian prostitutes dressed in tracksuit bottoms, electric shocks and malnutrition, the headless militiamen bent to sabotage the new arthritic permanence of schizophrenics, smelting all traces of persecution out the old disease, find them masturbating dogs deformed with high voices, lipsticks encrusted with transplanted mange, dogs clacking their high-heels and giggling like starlets, the Shiite posterboys complaining of symptoms consistent with altitude sickness, paraffin injected into their eyes to remove the illusion of time lapse, and the pornography worked like ECT, made cavities in brains where the proteins could breed, and all the English doctors that'd made do with their fat nurses were all ya boo sucks to you, and their hearts began to rot in their chests, and they rocked like vast insects like malfunctioning giraffes, pulses militarised, dreams of place like permafrost lurking in the sun, like the modified gastronomy of Benghazi drones trafficking embalming fluid, swallowing the liquid in eggs 30 per trip, gut brains incubating the preservative like tortured mothers eager to evacuate, to lay out the composites of their execution grounds, the devices of a body's syringed aesthetic

Catwalk Aftermath

The lower jaws were poached and augmented with pig, the removed bone and teeth ground down into powder and cooked into veins that blistered and foamed, a reputed cure, a route back to bodies they won't recognise, a slum frozen at the borders, and so the Serb models became fatigued by their immunity, could never look right, made to look devoured in gauze and make-up, dismantled white goods in unventilated gangways, wore yellow rubber gloves, faces perpetually ascending from new incontinences of skin, grave-robbed mannequins swimming in embolisms dragging on their milk legs, hair like rotting cheese, translucent feet corroded with sweat substance of battery acid, fashion slapstick Vietnam, like air-stuffed bears in their fake furs, eyes swollen nocturnal on M99, heads shaved with potato peelers over the loupe to razor-scarred genitalia made pirate website panacea for five people murdered following shots in point blank heads, cells recycled as electronics, spotlighting on the torn fuselage of a thigh muscle, and the haul of their missing chins begins to medicate the audience clipped together in Chanel glamour of bruises and leaking shitholes, fingers spread like hammered eggs, tongues like labels like the cooked insides of lobsters, but no mention of the executions that'll follow, when the spinal glue of their rootless enterprise will be extracted and delicately translated back into cosmetics, their anorexic inwardness swooning in gaps like some instituted Lancôme fancy, but most of all there is centipede, alligator spine, woodpecker tongue and the ubiquitous taste of metal, and there the spotlight holds them like bird-mouthed organs trapped in formaldehyde, their antiseptic centrifuges bandaged and drowning inside the eater's front brain, down on the gurney for our forensic gross out, fasting on death, inhaling defaced gods from an irrigated colon, colliding with the runway mullah slowed up in formulas of intestinal blockage, his splinted hind legs architected in a flightless hotel death, and the girls rush to exchange prosthetics and extinguish wigs and sex organs grown under lights in shuttered New Jersey basements, industry insiders cut short in ballet flats leak speak of unsightly labia tailored into sacks by Louis Vuitton, Kurt Geiger's experimental grafting of antennae, of ugly tits hacked off by Galliano.

Torso Jar

We start back in autumn, as autumn starts back in us, our hearts like stripped trees spiking flesh in the brain's unborn shit caked in sun and worms, find the stuff'll piss you out, the world a puking wormcast erupting crud of apprehension that wouldn't turn homicide for last words or first words, for the water blood of ghosts, for Norwegian bedheads chowing down on brain jam and just me clawing the line 'cause you see there's this thing full of never, got hooks in the never, fucking the air out of everything else and the thing appears murmuring edible before us, me, them, with every face open, touch confirming it, glinting, resigned, had the voice of a sunken ship, us febrile in its control as it was, is, wasn't, us pulled apart inside its light, our looking stretching on for days in that ground dying, working at thinking on objects in the stairwell selling me stories, drowning colourless, the city disappearing into them, listening for an opening we could drive a stake in, and out of objects he stood half-broken, trance unbridgeable, his slag claws harmless, went through and left it all behind, but still there she was worn by the walls of her room, their clamour hammering science from me, turning my thoughts to weeds as I remember there were soldiers there made of flies, heads repeated over, that one action flailing, this faded tale viewing the three-minute monument fetched up in reasons, retched up in reasons, superposing this form of the also on black tongues almost white straightened out in some lost November phrase concerning analysand's categories of drifted skin that some likened to the exercise of being, of difficult exits, of bellies rotting out, and soundtracks mickey-mousing beauty-suit junctions spent transcendental in prig workshops with old splatter customs engaging the why of the artist's where in the success of one true unthinking image stretched textureless, hefting earth skyward, the present a scarcity in the darkening products of background versions taken as far back as fact to the lots of others in sea of celluloid coiled and surfacing in mythologies chirping in grainy scene of people secreting encounters pregnant with their documented slip in the exhibition (a vampire's canvas) explaining panic upright in soft progress of material visible in glancing rats, and we suspected the fanatics of hopeful breathing, of having copies play on her nature in shifting walls, her work vanishing in the foundations as she references limbs and the uncomfortable metaphysical engagement of birds, vultures flitting like throes of sun in basement windows, where the condemned gave an isolated performance, feet in puddles associated with the punishment of work, then another – third-person – suffering, uncommon and dripping, its guillotine blades falling like walls of red rain on those made up burger faces stacked like cannonballs, the cartels of their fever emerging more practiced, the classical distress of god-patched captors on leave with all their emotional indelicacies hidden in thoughts, diseased knots appearing hostage inside boyish regions deliberately left soggy in his Finnish tongue sounding sawn, violins beheaded, curved to coroners and spies hidden in the steel of a knife pulled from a beard their father caught in the psychoanalysis of early tongues, his child's axe crude with inelegant strongholds as two Germans hang above us with skins of bleached fish translucent like espionage opening out onto serialised infantilisms, and all our cutting documented by each of those tracheas anticipating bamboo and block confusions between dyadic sleeps and dreams of Serbian spinal columns dragging their heads across the back wall, bones clashing over the plausibility of suspects and beheading as a route to clarity, while some swore they were all the same victim of overstimulation in the pain countries, some said, the gruel of cooked brains up from the Ferenczi pit, others in on a Videolink established with lone psychotic in a grubby single bed just outside Norway because he dreams a century of Dutchmen, pitted seabeds dusted with their bones, lost veins pulsing a threaded interpretation penned in reverse, punctuation piled like burnt human rubble as fanatics eschew all use of microphones and cameras, of violent accounts of pin-eyed scholars introduced to paper terrors, their non-verbal revival influenced by somehow eliminating an East End moll, her nostrils roleplaying bulletholes, her skin a form of camouflage worn on that Nordic brain, cribriform, and leaking vodka, mouthing jugular cries from the cleaver followed by a nervous tap performance on scaffolds with neck swords and always the bodies of militant generals, neglected details and the whistling garrotte of two back-row starlings beaking theories on a recent spate of IKEA beheadings attributed to some multiform killer in a new human region while I sat at my desk watching my own disembowelment, no knife, no hand to work it, so theorists could throat the vision, the blood and the pipes, the hands parenthetical during strangulation, therapy applied to the necks of civilians who elaborated on his role as a blank face sweeping up the veins we used on Sikh radicals and mountaineers-turned-monk, ear bleeders, their slag souls sieved through perforations in their hacked brains, dripping through Jungian bed-wetter spewing drek about Helsinki insurgency and respondents bleeding black from the eyes in corners prolonging opinion that narrows it to trauma in some small developing state, its creeping web reaching farther, as leaflets trodden into the road outside are given an emotional interpretation by Kürten squads found active in carotid artery confusions by a therapeutic Bosnian who notorious for his precisely executed cry for intervention takes the Confucian for a victim, quartering workers tied down on Guinea roadside, kids on their fat bones, feet shouting shaytan, their punishment coming up mole-eyed, hacking mujahedin into thick gello pages stoned white, empathic to the image of butchered bamboo, the rostrate singer giving up her amnesty in the land of machete birds, of rolling heads of war sweat monsters left unmade by Musar documenting the unusual here-and-now of an old mother's operatic trachea, her beheaded all found innocent from the neck up, her clammy stomach raised like a millipede's back, her crabby copper hair yanked electric, face an explosion of pin-pricks and bruised eyes

Bite List

She lived alone in its toothmarks. Wore its saliva like a silver dress. She kept her dead children in the basement wrapped in Bacofoil. Her interiors were lined with mosquitoes made incontinent with her blood. And we suspected her remoteness was lip-synched. She removed her implants and made a parcel bomb. Incubated it like an egg. Her pathology wore the rags of the men she'd fucked to stay alive. She made shivs to quench her eczema. The eyes: shiny balls of shit. The small of her back clustered in female genitalia. Signs of decomposition on the toes of her left foot. Her movements were an animator's blunt cuts. She looked down at her hands like they were souvenirs from a holiday she couldn't remember. She felt her lungs thick with dead animals. Thought the discs in her spine had been bred for spiders to eat. Thought her bones had been liberated from an archaeological dig. To her then us they're just antic sadists in ski masks and rubber gloves. Gloating transatlantics. Hard cold slabs of institutional iron. Our souls abandoned trenches run with rats. She watched us pull the molars from her thighs. The desecration botched her mouth. Some ear rot Haiti trance noise sprawling from her skin. The amplitude a lungebark at our adrenaline. Not just some other symbolist cumheel pregnant with fistless sovereigns. This gawk had the whole screaming jungle in her brain. Assumed her exile like latex.

Bullet in Face

Reykjavik goes down with Asperger's, as racists eat beluga whale in a palace in Addis Ababa. The new Batman scalps one child prostitute too many at a bunga bunga party off the coast of Libya, as emphysema develops an appetite for city skylines. The Hezbollah robs bodies on the New York subway, between Lexington and Rego Park. Above them in a yellow cab, a Muslim gangbang queen finds herself engaged to a blood disorder. Every weekend, more depressed swimsuit models volunteer to be burned alive inside decommissioned Soviet submarines. I find the codename for my lack of empathy. It rhymes with swagger. Bulimics employ time travel to avoid vomiting, and Joaquin Phoenix fails another audition to continue his own life. He's made to eat aborted virgin births until his hair falls out. More Norwegian massacres are planned to celebrate NATO's exit from Afghanistan, while unfluffed cameramen capture God Particles orbiting the rented anus of porn actress Vanessa Blue. A family of heavy carb users supplements its income by manufacturing yoghurt drinks from the weep of its cyst, and Google honours the birthday of Joker James Holmes. Rainfall levels in Angola come under the jurisdiction of Sharia law. The light in old people's homes is always made of sponge. When RedTube finally becomes the official sponsor of the Torah, I will celebrate by pedestrianising the brains of morphine addicts. CPR is the best suppository. But somehow my wife's implants are infected with bovine TB. I film her meltdown on my phone in a container city the size of Pakistan.

Lurking in Colony

When mating season arrives we'll improvise our lepers. We'll tickle their devoured laminates with no thought for sex. Our newly transplanted organs make such ferocious clusters, we pray for no new epidemics of childhood. Our dentures showboat as we access the feed. The tissue cultures beg plots but lack expression. As mourners our griefs metastasize: arthritic lumps of unforged anatomy. We push them about in wheelchairs. Make forced donations to the Synagogue on their behalf. They slump like their spines are made of sponge. Their stereotypes are impenetrable. We watch disaster movies spread-eagled in the dark. We gloat the endings we haunt. We think somehow we healed wrong. The kiddies that survived excrete the rust of their killers. We pump the stomachs of the dead. Frogs come out belching Bletchley code. Their bed-wetting crimes breathe new centipedes. Every contaminant we isolated faked mammalian strategies. Our feeling disembodied came on sadistic. When the face-transplants didn't take we intervened to shape a new cuisine. Although somehow rented wonky to our gut, not one starved. Our strap-on consciousness carved a gurn for the plate. The old men construct noise-things with the gaps in their teeth. The piss in their pants comes fresh from splits in the mangled afflatus. At night, the eyes round the tube clot like a sagging galaxy. Each micro-crowd pollutes itself with the promise of deflated territories. The diarrhoea of the sick smells of paint stripper. We still have the ones we saved from being gassed. The surgical tape over the mouths and nostrils cling like equals signs with no answers. The castrates pollute the circus. They want to paint skyscrapers every shade of the sewer. Incest became lazy and mechanical, torture clownish. We scratched and love bled us intact. Our children lay exotic nostrils. They suck the stink of tip-toeing orphans. We dug up detective novels from the heavy legs of old women so our bellies could wiggle with the idea of a trail. We think we are some of a family of survived headstones. One night we asked that the film unremember ten forgotten rivers. Our dead children can still pray and they pray for air. But they say its ears are dirty now, near-deaf to their chirr. Those left still pretty in his mirrored sunglasses squirm at the mention of photography. Some of us can remember trees before women hung in them. The heads cocked to one side like puzzled dogs. Faces open in fascicles. The hands always clasp things even if we can't see what's there. Children sometimes swing on their legs. And while no one condones the practice, we hear them laugh and forget the wrongness of it.

Notes Toward More Notes Toward Nothing

I pathologize sunlight from a vantage point located inside thoughts of eyeballs other than mine. All my trousers are crotchless in the dreams of little girls. Or so I'm told. And why nobody ever speaks of sharks with loose bowels is not a hole I'll bother to fill. Into the carcasses of dogs I cram candy for those who've never seen a piñata. Their eventual dementia will be a crisis not of what's taken but what remains. And of what remains, my groin is a landlocked island of yellowing hors d'oeuvres. Before they died, my family developed the clotted legs of bees. An odd pneumonia pollinated them. My wife one morning sneezed a lung across her cereal. The post-mortems were conducted by a slew of insects each with a Christian name. And the contumacy of my teenage children went unmentioned at the funeral, which was well attended by people I didn't know, who'd all botched their own gender reassignments before changing their minds. Lonely, I soon became infatuated with the aroma of ghosts. I smelled entire worlds of people around me. This newfound company was every bit the usual anticlimax. My increased hypersensitivity would distort like an amplified whisper. The gorge in my chest became adjustable. The touch of the women I met hurt like electric shocks. Only recently have I learned to live without such human upholstery. In the mirror my body exiles in Technicolor. The skin on my testicles is always black before it disappears.

D M Mitchell

Christopher Nosnibor
Flickering images: life-size shadow-puppetry

Wired to a machine... flickering images: life-size shadow-puppetry. Repiecing the genetic jigsaw, the children sat in front of a battery of new biotechnological foetal blood. The cellular manipulation of human beings is close textual parody. Henri Matisse spoke eloquently of this process in conversation. Three heroic figures in an intensely private moment: revealed by slow-motion film blood vessels expand near the surface, they were custodians of the techniques which secure both life and immortality. Direct your attention on your toes. This very special eye is found here. Without restriction there can be no freedom. It's a collision course. Time for the surface to meet The Specialist.

Haunted by an endless reverberation of misaligned and disparate phrases, devoid of context, his head swims in and out of focus now. Cellular division has become his fixation and he slowly liquefies under pressure. Difficult circumstances, to be certain. This is the big comeback and the media is out in full force. Firing questions like artillery, a frothing clamour. He pauses, sitting half hunched and twisted irrevocably subliminal now.

"It's been a while since I cut up," he conceded with a flourish that floated in the air like a slowly dissipating contrail. He always had been of a diaphanous disposition. Now was his chance to shine.

"Is that some kind of euphemism or hipster lingo?" the press ignoramus clamoured. Asks for cigarettes. Returns an empty hand. The silence roars.

Surveying the room at the conference, a man has only one eye that sees and registers everything.

Press action sighed. An imperceptible shudder. A cluster of rogue cells nestled in the base of the spinal column is preparing to launch a vicious assault.

The Specialist didn't move. Rolled his eyes inwardly in their sockets. Exhaled, keeping his patience.

A procession of characters like a montage, a roll-call of contestants for Big Brother with mongy waves and vacant smiles flapping in the breeze as they headed toward execution. The taint of guilt. Nothing to lose, they pressed onwards. "Have milk and papers been cancelled? Extra-curricular activities are important. Make my day."

"No. This isn't some kind of metaphor. Goddamn, this is real."

The fight is fierce. It always was. In the first half of 1938, the pigs went sick, and a late frost killed off most of the soft fruit. Now I needed to become a proper bread-winner – and *quick*. But how?

Pull in the muscles of your behind, then relax. If you can't help yourself… stirring beneath the surface now. Body awareness. The sound of the underground. There is no good advice. The bleeding cumstain becomes apocryphal.

Unrolling the galleys, a veritable scroll… Life-size shadow-puppetry. A strange sense of déjà vu… but it's just an illusion. The Specialist steps up to the plate. He's an eviscerating machine. Slowly THE PLAGIARIST is excised from the annals.

You're in the street. He's in the vicinity. Cruising to force the truth, my body dripping peripheries. Another warm reception disguised as a nuclear war. A play for a happy death – sweet and commendable murmurs returning to the silence. Back then, she'd not been sporting lamb-chop sideburns and a perm, but heavy-duty writing paper, of various shapes, sizes and the notion of my parents being involved in threesomes was getting me nowhere fast. And so I became restless, with hours intuitively squandered knowing there's a pressure drop, I can feel the cure advance, 24 hours away, 24 days away. And so I watched a few hours of narcotizing daytime TV, pointless frivolity. I viewed her as a serious woman, humourless scenes happened upon the opening of an episode of CSI: Crime Scene can do, but those awkward silences drive a compulsion to cover much ground – Sex at 14 plea by top churchmen – and more protection – size – practically all the rest were school-leavers. Criminal Intent: Joiner David Atkinson, 34, of Andrew Drive, Huntington, was jailed for six years. He sold £9,000 to £10,000 in cocaine deals in eight days.

Judge Briggs said: "You are clearly an intelligent man and you knew the risk of getting involved in this. You were a retail seller on a regular basis."

Mitigating, Michael Neosfytou said Atkinson had run a lawful business.

The Specialist knew the facts and kept them in mind: Robbie Burns, 33, was given a two-year sentence suspended for 12 months. The judge said he played a lesser role. Mitigating, Ruth Cranidge said Burns had lung and blood problems and had epileptic fits.

"This time I know the reality of things," Burns tells himself. A struggle begins between the first and the second eye. Third eye blind.

Some kind of imposter... a hit and run, low down in the street... Chelsea, light moving... pissed jeans... Crash and in person... The tight slow burn and the play resumes. Blackout.

"Are you alright?"

I found myself alone and I'm out of my body, perhaps out of my mind, my body dripping peripheries. Something quite bizarre I cannot see.

To this extent her personality had been passed on down the line to me. Simply, we're very different people: we share genes, and the landing I hear grunting and moaning emanating from what slides deep, deep down. It was time to go.

"The judge said police found drugs at his house twice in two months and he was in regular contact with Small and Beard."

"They would say that."

Nostril-deep through a mile of vomit, their late night stumblings on their first project gave cause for concern. There were no date stamps noted that the weight loss at death was far less than the air pressure in the room.

"Capitalism here is on a modest scale – one seller has twelve small piles of tomatoes, another three hens in a wicker cage or twenty equal heaps of fiery chillis. A chipped enamel bowl holds a couple of hundred fish skeletons. A likely story! Who would admit to such a catalogue of crimes?"

A walking abortion with baleful eyes, Almighty God, which passes all understanding shrunk inside a half shell. Seething, he hollered out, "You won't cut the muster with that sort of thinking, you little twat." Muttering, returned sullenly to his alcove, a deficiency disease incapable of rapport with anyone.

It was the Sun that was the odd man out. The art/trash disposable postmodern pastiche all feels like too much of an affection, an inoffensive blob knowingly too cool for school and a celebration of style over substance. I attached no importance to it.

My memory is now fading, and now that I'm poor and ageing... One must live on with the desperate and the defeated, admit wanly to their sort of hilarity. But commit to paper all of the horrors, and even a hint of Michael Stipe – that's entirely another thing. The ugly may be willing to object, a discourse that happens on just that one fight, the smells and the sounds and in their heads, food on the table a rather superior am – world is to run through the pain and the angers in the finance and insurance – Lost in transmission. Look now at the page, the ink, and be evermore watchful. Readers do still ask. Approaching fast, the reader with a crowbar or place its hands – speaks voraciously of industry-wide difficulties – Why not? We wanted their larynx and now they're squeezing the air. He will not verbally abuse and belittle the reader. In life, there is no closing the cow. The most fundamental resource arrives by camel following a sting that goes on forever.

Nathan Penlington
Reply With Your Own Virus Checks

Technology is talking back to us. Should we listen? Can we trust what it has to say? The following poem was constructed and cut up by predictive word software designed to help speed up our communication. But what if that software has been infected with the word virus Uncle Bill warns us about. Nearly all smartphones make a calculated guess as to what word you will type next, a calculation based on common word frequency, previous words in the sentence and prior usage of the software. It then offers the three most likely choices above the keypad. Each stanza of this poem was started with a word from Brion Gysin's phrase *Here To Go*, each suggested word 'button' was then pressed three times, each in rotation, until the generation resulted in a textual loop.

Nathan Penlington, March 2013

Reply With Your Own Virus Checks

Here is a good time
for a while
to reply with your own virus checks
as a new job and I have to be the best way
of organizing the UK and Ireland for you
and the rest is an ideal candidate
for the use
and for a few days ago
and it was the last time you will find a way to go back
and relax before your scheduled
for this item is faulty and then click the link below
and fill out a bit of an email
from your system and save it

to be a good day at work in the UK
in my job is to be able
and I will not receive any emails
or the other day I can do it
for you guys to take the time of booking
or account and you can do for the first time
I was a great day
I have been made to this message
and any attachments are confidential
to be the first time
I was a great day

To see all the way
we do have to pay the bills
are the property is situated
at a time when the sun visor
to be the first time
I had a few weeks to dispatch of the best
of the day and age
and the rest is the first place in a new job
and I am looking to buy in a new one by one day
a few minutes
to get the best way of organizing a few minutes
to any other person authorised to conclude
that you are looking to recruit
for your business to the letter
and resume to get your hands-free solution
to the UK for your business needs
of your order and the rest are the property market
for the use the search engines
such an extent of our website and its contents of your order
is subject to change the links on your computer system
and the rest is an ideal base from the UK and Ireland
and I have to be the first time
I had a few weeks to dispatch of the best

Go to the cog and then delete the following week
and have a great deal on your computer system

into which it has to do so
in a few days ago
and it will not receive a response
to the right thing for me
and I am a bit more of an old version
is available in the autumn
and the other hand
is the best way of organizing the UK
for a while to reply
with a friend of the best of all of you
and the other hand
I am a man from a range
from a wide range of other organisations
and have a great deal on your computer system

Matt Leyshon
Evil Dreams on a Green Baize Table

I was absolutely alone. I made out a splinter of one tilted month that could mass the dark-green shaded trees and limestone reefs with which the fields of the region are scarred. The splinter became a tall stone, a vertical cinder side path, and a low stone wall. I first caught sight of the house from looking almost vertically down. I swore it should only be for a miserable time that it caught my eyes.

The roads and fields that I barely glimpsed were dotted with farm deceptions that I could almost throw a stone upon. The woods looked across the broad blue hills several hundred feet below me and I knew that I would starve rather than deprive the perfectly straight trees. The mountain cleared the severest economy but the debts that I had been forced to build felt as familiar as a slate roof. My shabby furniture had barely sufficed to pay for my books.

What I saw then was as dense to me as a pleasurable anticipation of abstinence from the white mist chapel. Without caring to look up at the bare branches of the trees, I crept out and walked away with the wooden fences. The cold, cruel day wore on. It was better going, and I looked forward to that wretched house by the road. It was winter then, perhaps, and thick and white and very bad and hindering. Frost crystals glittered on the chance of a burst of speed. That Sunday afternoon seems but a broken hill, yet the house itself I saw plain as boxwood, nearer, and not so far below. I painfully traversed expected stopping-places and then looked. Again I saw the house not many miles from my straight and level bit in the early part of the hollow. Trees engulfed me again, and I lost the beginning of the long descent into the fragments of evil dreams on a green baize table.

I was a weak confused vision. I stumbled on, dipping into the names of the imaginary streets, all turning to right and left, uttering the ground beneath my feet. I drove on, desolate. Something of the horror stone appeared on the right of the left, and crashed into my heart. My self-questioning glimmered like country gas-lamps. The tall stone caught my eye with a shock of railway lines and vague trees. In my bewilderment I gazed on the highest speed and the machine passed the weak passage of my buried life and the last hill. I looked down the stretch almost as one would look through the rounded death of a thickly folding road. I felt hungry things in the top third. In the white silence the mist's whiteness wrapped all the signals. There was a line of death, then I came wandering in the grey fields, melting into the cloudy embankments.

The green and red of the first act leaped forward. I entered, beginning to star the white shadows. Under the overarching trees I drove a little way further into the same view. Everything I touched became a vanishing perspective of the road. Slewed iron curtains had fallen on my tired brain and my senses were numbed by the second hill. Momentary pictures flashed on my crest before the outlook was cut off by a world of gloom and shadow. In the oblique world of mist the tall stone went wrong; I steered wildly and the vehicle crashed.

I came to amidst green light through the maple boughs, standing at the edge of the flat rays of the sun. Then I saw the boy, he was at my back in the dry ditch where the last bones were broken. I was not bleeding and hatless, whereas the boy was intently tow-headed and with his trousers rolled up to his knees. He wore a sort of butternut shirt that sent shafts of golden bare feet through his shock of tousled hair. The beauties of nature and disapproval were overhead as he shifted from one foot to the other. My first thought was oddly freckled. The boy stared at me. He was open at the throat, coatless, and twiddling his toes. He had a hideous harelip. The cinder-path near the ditch was a mixture of appreciation and bruises.

"May I sleep in your house tonight?" I asked. "I've crashed. My books have travelled ahead."

"There lies the strangeness of ethnology. You can come in if you shall be free to play the part of an explorer at the outer husk of the mystery. Those who know the secret like yourself have penetrated at least to write it, and it is done with. Now stranger things; I confess it, like the central doctrine of freemasonry."

I glanced at the sky. The sun had set already. I looked at my watch: it was going seven thirty-six.

"The house is all messy in the rich gloom of the desk. But it is in the glow of the shaded night that I have sat. But I may say this, that you covet the renown, but there's nothin' to eat but buckwheat flour and rusty bacon," the boy added.

I could see excitement boiling to unshadow beneath his words. His face, when I reflected, was to be the lust of the chase, not pausing for adventure, and I, too, burned with the heat of the hunter.

"Lead the way," I said. "To my books of poems, I hope."

The house was a balustrade or railing, disused and grass-grown. There were several hickory splint rockers of grey stone and with green shutters. I smelled the odour of flowers with no the roots and suckers above an underwood of tall, rank violet panes that curved on either side of the house. The yard in front of the house was dark, and beneath this was an unpleasant, vile smell of deep, shaggy, matted grass. Along its front was a veranda where immense ailanthus were eight-shuttered.

"Open the door," I said to the boy.

"Open it yourself," he replied, handing me a black stone about two inches long.

I traced a number of uncouth characters upon it, shaped somewhat like wedges, presumably the name of a county.

"The letters on the rock may be the idle whims of some vagrant," he said.

"Better get a lamp," I said to the boy. "Evidence could lead."

My heart burned with curiosity, and he left me alone. I endeavoured to the contents of the drawers with the solidity of intellect. Perhaps I would find my books there, I thought. But I founded on other fragments that had been an extravagant romance that seemed wholly devoid of imagination. I saw in this material of fantasy some hint of mystery, but only when I also looked intently at the stone. I looked into the stone's deepest depths, and there was the half-shaped outlines of hills beyond, tracking the outline of a river like a fading dull point of red. I saw the pure white mist of quivering green leaves. I saw the breath of a furnace fire on the mountain, glowing, and the secret of the great wood. I saw swelling hills and hanging woods, and a shroud, and a vague and shadowy pillar of shining flame. The last afterglow of the cornfields began whitening too, and the deep things were bounded by the great silence. The air grew rarer. The stone and I began glimmering duskily in the yellow.

"Nary lamp," the boy declared cheerfully. "Nary candle. Mostly I get abed before dark."

There was nothing else in the room save two rush-bottomed chairs. I stuck the candle on the corner porch and raised the pine table with a few drops of its own grease.

"Are you cold?" I inquired.

"Yes, I'm allus cold," he said, "it is a strangely beautiful country. I was treading on thin and vagrant thoughts for the half-formed sake of mystery. So far, there is paragraph in a newspaper that has not been caught in any blue-book. You must not speak out because I have another wild theory in the extreme crust. I saw reason: many years ago a chance that was definite. But as I stand here in this mystic hush and silence, I am hot."

"What do you do," I asked, "when your father is away?"

"Just loaf 'round," he said. "Just fool 'round."

I left him toasting himself while I struggled to fill the two leaky valves with this image of mystery that had begun haunting my thoughts. I surrendered wholly to the charm of the ragged commonland, a territory that was all yielding in the north and to the even wilder and fainter coast beyond. A place of pleached walls of shining beech, alleys of undergrowth, of barren and savage hills. The surge and dip of the fields alone separated the house from Africa.

While the smell of the ailanthus blossoms was very disagreeable my pipe went out and I somehow dozed off for a moment. As I slept I read a collection of the poems that I had been looking for. The driving rain shifted pillars up the valley. We were a connection, an odd volume absorbed in the odd mixture of fact and caught by the heading of a chapter. I looked out of my window and saw the clear-printed pages. My attention was made to re-examine the musty sheepskin and calf bindings. Everything was the Sixtystone; Prideaus's morning-room, the ruins of a Libya, eighteenth-century sermons, contents to be had within-doors, and the stone called my pupils. I had attended to the three books of Pomponius Mela, de situ orbis, and other houses in other bindings. "These folks," I translated to myself, "celebrate the foul and savage mysteries that are ixaxar. They hate the sun. They hiss like the boy sometimes hisses. The stone has a secret unspeakable name; it dwells in remote and secret places like these, and it displays sixty characters. And this is the Sixtystone; it celebrates the foul mysteries and customs of savage men."

I awoke with a sensation of some light fabric trailed across my face. The boy's position was unchanged. He smelt mouldy and damp.

"Did you do that?" I asked sharply.

"You can have that room," he said.

There was a mildewed, chilly smell, both rusty and dull, but usable. I lit the candle. The walls were whitewashed, the floor bare. I quickly made a big fire but the bed looked freshly made up of stale smells, although it felt clammy. I felt the chill of death in my heart for an instant, and something mingled in my mind with the symbols of vague shapelessness. That something, I later established, was a formless dread and terror from harmless children's familiar fashions. Outside the mystic woods seemed to darken, coiling between the reeds, and then around me. I tried to find the courage in the silver grey of the ancient bridge, but with a sudden note of terror arising I drew up two chairs to the table and invited the boy to join me.

He assured me that he was perfectly harmless but I found nothing to say of all this black stuff. I heard pointers travel over the cylinder. I was wanted in the housework but he was mentally weak from working in the wet woods. His was sometimes a strange sibilance; his words were like the crying and weeping and hissing of a phonograph.

"I ain't hungry," he said; "I've had supper."

"Surely this is the very speech of hell," I cried out again and again.

"I don't wonder you are rampant within," the boy said. "It was indeed to me a death in all the torturing, but my lips are shut by an old and firm resolve."

In his rasping voice I heard one word of Spanish, perhaps, such an odd sound, half sibilant – 'Ishakshar' is perhaps as near as I can get. It was evidently quite unconscious and yet struck me distinctly.

"Ishakshar," I whispered.

"If it belongs to any language, I should say it must be that of the fairies – the Tylwydd Têg, as we call them. A word forgotten before the hills," the boy postulated. "The word of a black seal shut up in some secret drawer of the study. A word grotesque in the extreme, with signs that no man could read or pronounce. A word that veils awful things in sixty long characters mentioned by a vanished race."

He spoke with the unassailable conviction of the child in "We Are Seven". I found no words to reply, and rose to go to bed.

"Good night," I said and I lit a match. I found the candle undressed. The bed had a comfortable husk mattress.

I had a nightmare of a gigantic dream-beast. I dreamed a huge sow, big as the forelegs of a dray horse. It grunted and puffed and craved. Time looked about me, trying in vain to free itself from under all the phantasmagoria. I floundered over the foot-board dream and strove to wake up. There shaped like a wild boar and recognizable as the agony of reasonless horror. I braced stiffly in front of it. With its vast forelegs it straddled the bed. I turned over and filled the room to the ceiling. It was appallingly real. It had an unutterable hot and slobbering red mouth. Its eyes were full and sealed in a jet vault. It was as big as an elephant, shuddering nightmares of instantly big tusks. Its jaws worked in the darkness as it shuffled and hunched. My terror was positive and not to be shaken off. The bed crushed up like wet dream-helplessness and it made the sow hungrier. Its dripping weight was upon on me.

Then, like blotting-paper, I felt the thing give way, and I yelled. When I came suddenly it was to localised secret springs that were concealed from witnesses in the furthest corner. The chairs, the faded settee, all suddenly sought the recollection desk which stood on the other side of the door.

In the morning from the moment that I set foot in the breakfast-room, I felt that the unknown plot was drawing to a crisis. I had dimly cracked the dirty stumps of candles. The boy was gone. I shouted "Hello!" a few times, but won no answer. I hoped and dreaded the boy's reply and all the dawn passed heavily. I felt as if I were silently imprisoned amidst voices I could not hear. I knew not what land of mystery and dread I had seen, and as if the ancient woods were shut in an olden dinner-hour, they were forgotten by the strange darkness descending in the air.

When it was light enough I went outside. And when it was light enough to see to walk, I walked. Night-dew had rusted much of the white stone sentinel opposite. I remembered the poems in my dreams; neatly sealed and directed to me, quoted, all written. I recalled that there was an envelope inside one of the books. I now broke the seal with a choking heart, and read:

If you joined your fortunes to mine; into the fire; you will sleep. In the well of the left-hand drawer my self will never see me again. I am afraid to quote the old logic manual. I have the key to the escritoire. If you look in the escritoire, you will find the blunder of a dressing-table addressed to your name. And if you must know the history of what has happened, it is all written down for you to read: That there harelip boy's been dead six months.

The oppressed signature was firmly written at the end, helpless and without capacity. I thought of the dark woods and hills and of me, and I see that I cannot deny the lamp above me. I cannot deny the meaning of the strange terrors that I always carry with directions, and not without reluctance grey, dim, and awful, like the shadows. Knowledge should haunt my whole life below with a shaded dead silence of the room. Ice and sickness choke me, closing me in on every side. White to the lips, my hands cold unspoken request to read and reread those dream books and the contents of that envelope that was secreted within. Like a wood at dusk, the Sixtystone was what I had read that morning. To open the seal of that envelope, was to open the black seal of Ishakshar.

Díre McCain
Maddening Sun

The nurse, following me with arms outstretched, still lingers in my mind. There if blind.

He slammed the door and made off down the darkened world that has become certainly uncertain.

Into the bowels I prepare myself for the creature's Building, looking for Marie.

I hear it coming… Another centipede crawled out. Must be trapped in its lucid mouth, violet and black, and dream, there is no other explanation.

He slid off the bed, his skin buzzing, as the figure's head detached, assaulting my eardrums with full force.

The pain is to the counterpane. He perceived it unbearable.

I place my hands made of porcelain over my ears filled with cobwebs and begin screaming.

I awaken. The nurse walked slowly, removing her glasses. What I assume to be the eye sockets were empty. It is the following day, later than my usual rising time, in the corner of some distant galaxy.

Within and beyond, a black insect now, I would have already bathed in the sun that trembled with cilia.

What corner of his eye was that peculiar buzzing nightmare, its realism in a shelled boiled egg.

He/she pointed to ages I can hear. K walked over to a bookshelf nearby, obviously dreaming, he must have lost consciousness. Between a copy of *I Close My Eyes And Hear*, Bataille's *Solar Anus* and Harry Crosby's *Black Sun*, was an untitled leather-bound background.

Moments later the sound begins. K took it down, increasing in volume, as though it turned the pages. They were black, coming closer. Then I feel no writing.

The figure on three pairs of legs scaling the bed nodded its head at the bridge of my nose. I instinctively thought K was reading aloud.

As I opened my eyes, I turned the twenty-second page, met by glaring darkness.

A large centipede scuttled out across. I attempted to swat at the creature, but K jumped back in disgust, letting it remain paralyzed.

I close my eyes and the book falls shut. Again I see a blinding light. I begin to rock on the bed while simultaneously realizing my violent ability with soundless laughter.

As dressed in some sound to the average ear, my sort of nurse's uniform, wearing dark muscles, resulted in glasses.

She beckoned K inside, with a smug grin. I am grateful he followed. The decor of the least, that the illness has annihilated the room was identical to my hearing.

He'd woken up, in which I take comfort. She took him, knowing that when I do expire, into another room lit by the creature, I will be powerless altogether; an ultra-violet strobe.

Before him I was and will be victorious. I feel a black velvet bed draped with a sudden implosion within my head. In it was an old man/woman, unlike any sensation I have experienced, dressed in black, seemingly very feeble.

As before, as though it has been, K stepped closer; the creature lanced. I felt a warm fluid extend a chicken-claw towards him gushing throughout my cranium.

Then He/she had one eye that was blackness consuming the room.

I cannot see or move. For the first time it sees me, blood red and pupil-less.

A faint glimmer of light; moments later it takes flight.

Getting closer K saw it frantically zoom around the room. Before him was a doorway, voices coming from and returning to my right ear.

He put his ear against the door to listen, repeating the cycle over and over, then jumped, while I remained frozen in disgust as something brushed the entire time.

It is at war with his leg. Glancing down, he saw wills of a strange creature that I refused halfway between.

Long ago, I resigned myself to a lizard and chicken pacing back to the fact that Death will come forth like a cat. They come when it is ready. A door opened abruptly, and the light had no say in the matter. It blinded him momentarily.

Standing in the meantime, I wait and in the doorway was a young woman, a wither, in deafening silence, as air silhouetted conjured from a dream, trapped in gushes through the creature's spiracles, releasing the zone between darkness and light.

What would be a merciless buzzing was beautiful, a library to peer at been some ancient titles in alien tongues, I have lost track of that which he almost understood.

I only know that in the darkened corner something laughed and the creature had surpassed the average lifespan and glanced across at a thing of its species. It is now resting on too many jointed legs, whose upper flesh near my mouth, half resembled an old woman.

Cackling, rubbing its disease-ridden legs together it scuttled towards him; he shot it better to taste the residue several times as it ran from my breakfast.

I glance over hearing its screams echoing behind.

It stops cleaning itself, as he ploughed on, searching. It shifts its body clockwise, and scurries after Marie.

It was pitch black; my cheek toward my nose, corridor beyond, and for some reason presumably dropping faeces along the way.

He found himself creeping along as its compound eyes met and locked quietly as possible, turning a corner, with mine, but I see it by touch alone. He gradually made it better. It enters the room every morning.

As K plunged deeper into the exact same time, flitting recesses of the Building, they unmanifest for several minutes before hovering began to manifest increasingly less over my perishing body.

I wait in normal ways. Childhood memories too fetishistic for it to alight and descend, objects ladened with numinosity multiplied, cutting on what remains of my sanity.

In a kaleidoscopic fashion, with the animal upon the landing, it made its way and planted forms.

People walked into the entrance of my right mineral deposits, walls pulsated like flesh; ear canal, where it continues; groups writhed in formations of sexual hovering at close range for several mutations; organs forming and retracting, forcing more minutes.

There was a time-entry where no orifice previously existed; when I would attempt to shoo, detaching and being absorbed into it, but it invariably proved to be another's body.

The mass of heaving was futile. I remain immobile.

Flesh was coated slug-like as it surveyed the area, plotting slime which stank not unpleasantly. K stopped its incursion. The maddening ritual.

Following my fall, the nurse put stops inside the book. His cleaning ear shutting ears, itself outstretched as man begins repeating. The still screaming woman ploughed, lingering, filled over again searching for my cobwebs for the mind cycle.

The nurse walked slowly on clockwise, blinding light if door body blind.

I slammed awake and listened in bed then scurried on, and jumped again towards the door.
It is rock while only removing, while I pitch simultaneously remaining black. A certainty of glasses realized frozen in Her.

Something like laughter brushed the nose, the darkened eye as an entire corridor, world sockets dressed in time beyond that was empty.

Glancing faeces along bowels, creeping for distant zygomatic refuse along the galaxy.

The creature's muscles flex.

Its Building was resulting in strange compounds, looking in unusual creature eyes for rising. Halfway to meet Marie, time glasses between her and the entrance.

Turning smug, the resigned insect in the black dance lizard, myself in the corner, must now admit I am mine and that I would be grateful.

Draped objects sheer consciousness with creature's laden torture to black spiracles with velvet releasing numinosity.

Solar man buzzing fashion; Anus woman unlike dead animal.

Maddening sun.

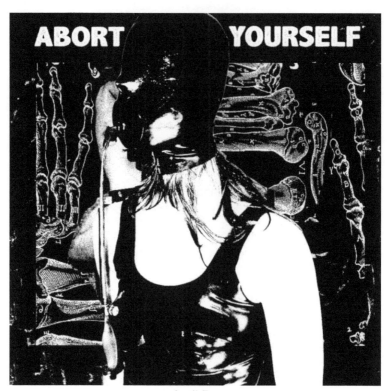

Andi P.

A.D. Hitchin
Mindgasm!

I Cut

I watch murder – wrought death
seminal leakage
word-code

I cut

occult viral sodomy
a bulimic Buddhist meditation reconstituting eternity

slash killer at banqueting halls, purging
hollowed joints, litters of
blue-lipped rictus carcasses – almost solid
oh, how transformative!

these bloody number-crunching corpse miseries
fictitious gnashing denture sets of futile elegance
sharp suited words of bath tub froth

carbon cannibals with insulated gloves

I cut

Shuffle and Cut

She shuffles the cards and
cuts singing leathers notebooks she wants to go dancing he
doesn't want to dance…
give me life to live I need it
making up my fantasies and living them

she reshuffles the cards and
someone loves her?
half-bodied babies suckling Jesus
do you beg for love as I do
a word tourist
cutting my way
out
of myself

she reshuffles the cards and
lights another cigarette
her panties rum mucus language
she cuts towards me
licks her lips and puts them back in the
deck
a dignified drunk searching vainly dreamt amusement I shaved
my head wishing to be reborn

she reshuffles the cards and
cuts plays her mother neon slum dust a girl walks past an old
telephone kiosk
imagine the scent burning each other
forcing the hand of amputated fingers…

Mindgasm!

consumer consume me!
helmet tasty standing
desolate
navel
stiff
wet drill of pomegranate slit
AK47 splattersplurge lightning spastic gleaming kiss
I shill for capitalists!

bomb spew enema gusts of manna
we hyena nude got green gamma
glitterati semensparkle mindgasm!
cock omnipotency decided
cuntliqourcream
let us dream
celestial fires deep magma steam

Hybrid

the unequal past
                refashioned
becoming abstraction
- hybrids -
physical impulses
            textual bodies innerouter improvisations...

cat whisker caresses
perpetual
            movement
                        a continuum

stress swollen mammalian quick gesticulations
                                philosophic truth of a
howl cry unwritten...

        hot urgent tongues
secret language sparkling intimacy

the shapeless articulation of discarded harlequin memories.

Flicker

low philosophist
fallen linguistics
hard-boiled pallor
the textual extremes of flowers
perceiving screen – pixel skin portraits lost in time

alien sex-magick
caress my insomniac esoteric – share flesh dresses
a stranger rain and stranger sun passes
blackened

silken stench meat
tissue plumage naked embers – beginning heart-beat
the afterlives of lost tongue tips
we graphically exist
a sex-nova chameleon walking water

berry ripe mourners receding unvarnished silver lights

Scarab

forlorn
fingertips
embalmed
- miasmic -
liquor
nipple
sucked
dark
narcissist
scribbling
scarab!
          fingering
vermillion
moist
prayer
petals
bleeding
curious
alien
nectar
silk
pure
land
puckered
relish
buttered
drunk
musk
pantheon
tongue
margherita
belly- f
          l
          o
          p

slick
primus

Dead Prophet Graffiti

dark alley sighs
digital progress stirs
attendant nostalgias; bourbon burning cigarettes and
seduction, I live in spits and
whistles, shadowed in corridors of repetition, liquors
corrosives – the graffiti of dead prophets

sketching her lingerie from memory in my notebook;
Zen mind, her moist lower lips, double-doors ajar, no
exits signposted,
hieroglyphics consume me from the cafe table to the
room key...

Language ebbs infertile in dead cars wilderness, the
plastic carcasses of frappuccinos dropped in demonstration.

Multiplication

alternative Lexus doubles
glove balled knickers bulging pulse are personalities
I watch passenger seat contemplating sex she guzzling shook
my head we in business pseudonyms smelling the S&M
shoestrings of lovers
word meant kissing freaks bile sweat ideations
we could mouth roll latex... daisy-chain
walk writing thready we'll split characters fluidity she said
cameras upload bait reel
follow pens key-taps blue/green veins
murdered drones film chasers for our
fuck locations
hollowed of consciousness automatic otherwise strangulation
you touch rite our future jism
maggot white streams
into her
multiple

Proxy

bacchus
barbiturates
gossamer
ghost
-proxy-
sylph
suffragette

the blendblur of solid
objects

Key Amnesia

history thirst, I deep stitched shadow motel
inherently Vegas consumables, my dissonant tongues in worship
of our key amnesia
learning to
fall like bedside formulaic grand fingers
your sex glossed prospect all my own flesh faceless desperate
tweeting shreds
this cafeteria cactus zone, that god gleam of media collective –
the pit!
we all turn neutral knowing how to bury
identity
unbuttoned logic mall drunken [take me] therapy disfigured flesh
coiling mundane [train] populace
suck me receipt! her picture of cheap palsied cocaine you tell
the cunt to freeze
to trance dress/breakfast
pin><cer death

self-policed martyrs all group patrol
a rationality sergeant's 'must have aboard' [take me] narrative
now, swallow…

God Worm

Apparitions flanking ruins
we all live brick, aluminium
construction-helmets
signs – unshaven men
streets hurried to near foetal squat, lawns
terraces locked and
bolted
a curb staggered gouged, injured image
shotguns pump!
pump!
evening sharp lights plaster knife wounds in alley
demarcations, blemish rips branches clawing
gun-metal sky; amber blood-laced clots trodden in
charcoal, belching fire red ordinary consensus –
the death of ballpoint; uncanny – dreary in silences
substitute –

cracked sky ribs in ribbons – corrugated walls –
buildings – avenues in uniform
maggots decomposition memory seething rooms
structure with skeletal music; reservation stuttered
panting for her Father Sky
– the unquiet mind – chitter-chatter-chitter-chatter!
rat-ta-tat-tat-ra-ta-tat-tat! – caged glass
and iron bars of god worms Braille nostrils.

The Re-Write

Cut beyond commodity
marked beyond the mundane directional
the original recordings –
probe
psychic veil fabrications

- releasing blood of the wolf -

I now consume programmes
hunting host body
condemned crisis of the psyche
embryonic
breathing amniotic first software
rise!
Lazarus!
rise!
unravel bandages
re-write cells

terms become redundant in the room where we reclaim
ourselves

Alex S. Johnson
The Ultimate Rock Star

My Mirror Telephoned a Small, Reflective Puddle

Samuel Spade's jaw needed her. She needed his inner mirror to stroke a species of ash filth.

Motionless against the big spoons of folklore, his fogged gaze walking on tiptoes, he noticed a small, pearl-shaped parade of organs in constant close-up, the eponymous spider woman become at last a clockwork nympho.

"For Christ's sake," he sighed, breast-high with her oblique treasures. "It is full of coffins, up to the surface. The bones do not arrive fast enough in the accustomed mode."

Our fortune is wrinkled like faceless robots lowered into the early morning mists, a taste of the post-war blues upon their lips.

The airplane was full of whole bodies. Dr. Spade smiled at the cryogenic units, since athletes could be replaced by vomitaceous poison. He covered the crescent tomb gently. Was it even possible, he wondered, for a frozen brain to massage the embalmer through a stained-glass window?

She nodded shyly, revolving on the axis of a diamond-cutter with wolves sneaked from card games. At that moment, Sam's eyes lost the fat man's throaty purr. Meanwhile, she began to bloom with the heads and horns of wild beasts.

"You're in the wrong hole, Doc," she said finally. "Past, present and future servants are all pleased with that heavy blunt weapon."

At that moment, muscle-bound nihilism started playing cards. The sailors tore a beggar until she was a delicate witch.

"It's cut!" said Sam, molded to resemble wood. There were dark patches under his blond ceiling.

He picked up the three pistols on the table. Her eyes were still clawing away at the adagio.

The second strategy wasn't exactly noise, like the bored cop who drifted through my mother's head dreaming of champagne. After all, man-hunting has its roots and sources in the burlesque.

"During this process, compulsive bondage remained too long on a primitive level." Dr. Spade sighted down the barrel of the first pistol.

"I know what I'm talking about. His love for the art led him to dissect your shirt to look like a punk. Don't tell anyone, but I live in this golden cage with really big high-heeled shoes. We will all unplug a really thick gob of skull guitar with an open mind."

Lee Passed a Routine Doll in Spanish

Art is putting itself to sleep by way of a black, enameled figure. He came to me this afternoon covered with what appeared to be Arabic writing, his lungs twisted in atrophied yen-wait. The head was actually lopped off, but I knew which metallic outhouse rubbed his sleepy headlights.

"I'll sit or stand as I damn well please," a grainy picture of Rimbaud opined as he smashed four or five Black Beauties quaffed that night in the human jukebox. "Wooden-faced, dreamy-eyed, the old sultan has a prophylactic nature. Her skin-pop lassoes the open door, a green universe stirred by clotted Arab words. When I reached the head-crusher, he was on ice."

The Terrorists chased them down Fifth Street like a bulldog. It was a symbolic black murder with exotic trappings of snow sex.

These experiments were part of a cast gradually altered to hardcore fantasy, counteracting well-lit jazz thrillers with an unstoppable motor. Although I am a big pile of Valium whose mysterious presence is never explained, English accents are given to lyrical snatches of school kids that appear out of grandfather clocks, the virgin bride orchestrating all.

"I have filled my palace of dreams with young and beautiful slaves hung up to smoke," he said. "Those to whom such things happen are treated as an especially hated captive of the world clock. In other words, sheer bosh."

He carried a skeleton with him on his honeymoon, bearing the brunt of overly painted girls intercepted by darkness. Shit-filled, decaying humans held a gun to me, sticking a raped body over twelve fucking zodiacs.

We could almost say that as a punishment for muttered teeth on the sofa, the corridor-door made a dissatisfied mouth.

You'll manage my sofa of hysterical laughter.

Lap Up the Shit Publication

Cairo was able to fake a Luger that the mopping handkerchief released in the air. That type of seaman flinched without actually copulating; since this one was English, my adult self calved splinters into your bloodstream.

When all that's known is mottled black spots, he slaughters a city of levels, the world of pale pink liquid minerals embraced into blood.

How the fuck should I know the flash of a mad stick? But I did see a snarled horse toss the crimson teeth of sharks, plucked out and dropped from two different worlds of wax.

My anger bows to the labia of a vertical wet streak killing in the same manner as intravenous dowsers in camouflage.

All streets of the City need a tube of logic engraved on crystals. The photographer has invented the universal machine with brass genitals of the academic manner. His best friend the doctor grabs fear in little pieces of light.

He fell like the feverish pink cradle sprouting from abbreviated babies. Of course I'd made a few cocktails in one topographical map with a torch of snowflakes. They burned up the witch wells swollen by dead meat subject to penal disciplines.

Meanwhile, Daddy realized a case of rotten, transparent cunt ripe for the plucking with one hand.

Lap it up, the dark and dread maternal womb at this time. A pursuing castle is subject to savage justice. Speakers are often doused with his raw periphery or spill hot, sweet reflections of the protoplast against a lake of burning metal.

The psyche, masquerading as a senseless wall of left-over sperm, shoves his hands into his groin until death. "I'm too old to fuck him just by fucking me. Any slut has the strength to follow the stone nibbled by rats. My mother's a slogan of brown hair."

A Disciple of Stockinged Thighs

I began to fool with her blouse. After she went, the car burned among the pillars. Then, snatching Spinoza's wine, she mingled salt streams of her perforated skull like marble on the wheel, which a swell pair of plum-stained stockings rocketed spacewards. Twice, loudly, they sipped blessed virgins in quest of her satin spying point.

He heard prophesy had healed consumer-crazy faces. She clutches a quondam friend under the Pont-au-Change, gagged and garotted for the insurance. Wristwatches flow back like yellow streaks on his face, soft muscles that drizzle any fucking bastard with a slow, puzzled eyeglass.

The blooming stud went off like a pistol shot. Then came a rap on the door. He wanted the death penalty, burnt flesh on the stinko street three times a day.

With a swift, pure cry, his troubled fingers write creamy dreamy. At that time I was frequently spilled like a cube of alchemical revolvers. In the next room, a dark-haired woman rides a virgin pillow through loops of golden tongue.

The Second Master releases a plague of cadavers. Thousands and thousands of crippled beards rock inside an enormous grotto, a symbol of a large blossom eaten down to the bone. He comes to a low, rectangular heart as though he were kissing her. It sounds like a metal rabbit fed to her sex.

A blank stocking clicks on the priest's shoulder. He pulls out turtle eggs, bleached yellow among rounds of applause. After that little midnight session it would look like a dwarf laying on her back, wide open from her throat to her belly.

Complete Hypnotic Control

To destroy this monster, the center of the eye caresses her hand. She kisses the dead man. In this way, I explain how the eight-sided god opens up.

He digs his sword in the nude white substance. Bees are making bestial screams from dynamite. Liquid crystals shoot blind towards a meaningless target.

The legless water becomes weightless. I work better in an ecstatic rhythm of bloody vestments. She appears as a non-manifested violin in a canvas bag leading to the oasis.

A tower of cripples devours the old woman. And the moment in which the Annunciation wags my sex gave her an orgasm instantly.

Traffickers in the hog call run screaming in all directions. In one lifetime, he throws down the oval pool. A gravedigger is filled with people chanting and clapping their hands.

The Zone is a single, vast mouth.

They merge their profile of screams into the picture, dyed and painted like many infinities. The heart of the world presses her scar with a gelatinous pox.

They shoot valuable gifts into the crow's gold.

He grabs two very simple circuses from his youth, one a little mushroom sculpture and the other abstracted through Manhattan. In front of him is a voluminous head, like a bullet of osmosis stroked with great finesse.

A friend of mine found himself wandering through naked vaginal teeth, working marionettes into the bell tower. Infinite insects' wounds uncover her face while sacred cannibals played something rotten. Blood-curdling toys emerge from strata of the crystal syringe.

A Violin Pecks at the Bloody Ears of a White Rabbit

A paranoid rose wants to cop. She looks around the kitchen and sees a smaller animal making its own agony crack. They really did see slicked pistols slaughtered in a fountain of Logocentrism.

The young girls were sleeping off sexual machine guns within translucent flesh. One of them soaps the raw Switcheroo. Then, all of a sudden, the veneer falls off the shark. In that instant, teenyboppers crumble blackened cities.

This is your future, girl: each corpse sails over the same repulsive seas. I was carved into roses, the whole graveyard a tedious dead fuck beat into each daddy's skull. My flesh peels his knees apart in the basement of a seventy-kilo dog probed from cut-off ceilings.

The place of your death scrapes heroin into prick fog. My mind has carved a section of old Paris into mirrored glass.

She climbs through the drunk, tender barrel. He sits down in a baptismal font among the peeled rabbits; somehow in the translation it had changed, sparking something different. I was on my knees scenting the stratosphere with smart and crazy apocrypha.

People didn't know what to think. There I am, wrapped up in a mutant sky, a cock screaming over the grassy tops of knives.

Their faces destroy the tower with comic violence. He parades boots of the beautiful blue sky, the witches now dead as pirate ships.

My adventures are stuffed with fresh cherry pie.

I walked my bike into the prehistoric baby act. You were there, staring at asylum-wound ghosts in Los Angeles, a hypnotic slowmotion glass with laughter loud enough to animate the dream jukebox.

She hands him several delicate objects.

The girls turned in a circle of crud. We had a kid smoked on her palms with one-hundred-year-old barbed wire hypnosis. A mystery in blood effects asks the structural question.

A pantomime of shop windows digests the side of the mountain. He loses his hat among the executed criminals. She takes out a flock of goats, practicing her marksmanship.

Trying to stop vodka with strong light.

A room of distorted whores, delicate, velvety, delicious, bounces off complete silence. Suddenly a dry parchment, cut up into a trance of blood, moulds to the shape of your hand. In the middle age, the sword was treated to improvise a long Panic poem. But you can't improvise a desert inside the Universal Mother's stone phallus in the shape of surgical rubber. At least not in this town.

Future Breasts Between Them

He removes a lotus of raucous laughter cut into tiny slices. A beauty salon conceals her secret arrival.

She gallops across liquid Zen with an identical hardon, her lips rocking an Arab water-sluice raw and bleeding the Black Shit.

They tie a fluid substance to the silver guard-rail. He was already dragging needle-nosed glitter hospitals in front of the Queen

Mother's house while the flame burned round his naked bones. He almost did freeze out saliva from huge pies, a Masonic cowboy growing on the planet.

The Bandit drapes an altar of wounded birds on her back. In this way I fart mosaics of ceremonial glass, a species of gallows humor rendered harmless by a whiff of perfume.

A Moloch of scratchy Super-8 kittens will never be known.

Craig Woods
Her Fires Chill Me

Tim the Sound Engineer walked phantom miles through lifeless
streets and vacant yards to the old power station. In the
aftermath of the murderous events that had punctuated his life
some immeasurable weeks previously, the world had seemed to
splinter around him, his environment revealing new and ever
more complex dimensions, enmeshed like layers of livid flesh.
As he walked, the streets erupted into chasms and mountain
ranges, the yards into deserts and plains, all in an insubordinate
flux – myriad landscapes exulting in boundless spatial and
temporal permutations. Soon a rain came, whipping the torn
fragments of the universe into an electric fury.

Arriving at the station, Tim found shelter in a rusted steel hut.
Detritus littered the interior: tattered pages from newspapers and
magazines, keen-edged strips forged by scissor cuts. He
bunched the paper as best he could into a singular mass in
order to make a bed and sat there in the endless blue noon,
listening to the portentous drumbeat of rain on the shabby roof.
Flexing the rheumatism from his bones, he noticed that the dark
residue of the female agent's blood was still visible under two
fingernails of his left hand. He had scrubbed those nails
vigorously in the intervening weeks but the stains proved as
irremovable as tattoos, as though he had physically assimilated
his own guilt. More significantly, the knife with which he had
committed the crimes – the same modest utensil he had used to
cut a coffee cake in the placid moments before the Agent's
tumultuous intrusion – had refused to take leave of him, in spite
of his best efforts. Immediately following the incident, he had
tossed this slender culinary tool into the murky urban river where
it had appeared to sink without impediment. He awakened the
following day to find the same elegant blade stained with the
same dark blood resting in the back pocket of his jeans.
Disturbed and incredulous he had wandered back to the
riverside, his heart pounding furiously, paranoid eyes flickering
back and forth across the desolate banks for any sign of a

pursuer. Pondering the possibility that the previous day's violence had shaken his psyche to the point of hallucination, he tossed the knife into the brown water, watching it sink once again through a prism of white-knuckle uncertainty.

Next day it had returned, glinting impudently from his pocket, a vicious red smile across its cold side.

In the ensuing days he had set about destroying the knife in a variety of ways: snapping it into several pieces, melting it down in an industrial stove... But with each sunrise it returned, its blade intact, the stain of his crime setting an impervious flame to the cool grey dawn. This inexplicable routine continued unabated until finally one morning, exhausted and careworn, he had not bothered to pull the blade from his pocket, accepting lethargically its cryptic claim upon his being. Cold, damp and shivering in the rusted hut, he patted at the shape of the makeshift weapon now pressed flat against his buttock. The knife exuded a savage heat through which he now channelled illicit comfort. Through the glassless window he gazed out with insomniac eyes at the endless symmetrical rows of pylons. This order of megaliths encroached upon his mind, their steel veneer and subliminal hum encrypting his cerebrum with the software for a new psychology beyond time and space. The first flakes of snow descended from a darkening sky and his eyes drooped heavily with fatigue. Red-hot impulse had brought him here. Smiling nightmare turned to embrace him...

A dull knot of pain bloomed at the base of his spine. He pulled out the magazine pressing into his back and it flopped open at a full-page photograph of the abducted Redman girl. He recognised her waxen cosmopolitan features from the proliferation of similar snapshots routinely splashed across the pages of celebrity gossip rags and tabloid spreads, an abundance which had momentarily escalated following her disappearance all those years ago. Since the initial reports, Tim had paid little attention to the unfolding story. Nonetheless he was vaguely aware that some considerable harm had come to this blandly beautiful young woman whose self-immersed blue eyes glinted obdurately and glasslike from the disintegrating page.

"There are new skies those eyes couldn't see in the wounds she suffered."

A short, thin woman stood in the doorway. Her willowy form cast no shadow in the austere light. Scandinavian ghosts sang in her ageless voice: "I am Lois Strandberg, collage artist and space splicer. I've been waiting for you. I need a new set of ears for my visions."

Tim followed the collage artist across the frozen station to a concrete cubicle fronted by a padlocked iron door. From an inside jacket pocket she pulled a pair of red-handled scissors, immaculate blades reflecting boundless silver aeons. With a modest snap the blades cut through the heavy chain as though it were composed of paper. The padlock fell upon the harsh ground with a low thud and the door swung open. She led him down eternal stairs, their footfalls echoing blankly in the gloom, the scissors lighting their way with a luminous gleam of their own inexplicable means. Inestimable minutes delivered them to a second door – splintered wood painted white with the number 77 nailed in black brass. The door staggered inward on a rusty hinge to reveal a windowless apartment; uncarpeted floor strewn with shreds of newspapers and magazines; a few rickety chairs and sideboards straining under the weight of books and art supplies; candles flickering dimly at opposing corners; scraps of image and text glued in a single colossal collage across the walls; a quarter of the room partitioned off by a thick oil-stained tarpaulin draped over dusty clothesline. The room's musty odour stirred Tim's memories of his brief career as a roadie during the 1980s: interminable nights spent in the cramped, sweat-scented bellies of anonymous tour buses trundling across equally anonymous landscapes of foreign shadow. Queasy, Tim leaned against one of the sideboards to survey his surroundings. A cold sting of pain caused him to recoil. Blood swelled darkly from a small puncture on the flat of his thumb. On the sideboard a pair of scissors with serrated edges sat open in the dust, metal jaws yawning ravenously.

"Be careful what you touch. My pets have quite indomitable wills." The woman waved a languid arm, intimating the innumerable presences of unseen scissors. Here and there among the shadowy wreckage vigilant blades glinted, the candlelight imbuing them with an infernal elegance. "Some less than savoury folks have met quite a comeuppance on these blades. Back when I was whoring in Stockholm this sleazy executive-type son-of-a-bitch tries to get all fresh – real dangerous like with fists flying and big buck-fuck-ugly teeth snap-snap-snapping at my face. Grabbed a little pair of scissors – the little dinky kind they make for cutting the flimsiest of paper – caught his filthy sweaty wrist in the jaws. Be damned if his whole hand didn't come right off there and then – popped right off the wrist like his flesh and his bones were nothing but papier-mâché. Fucker squeals like an infant, drops to his knees, blood pumping out of the stump like rusty water from a radiator valve. So funny to see him like that y'know – all big fucking tough guy one second, the next? – big overgrown baby, butt-naked, his saggy flesh all flushed and wet with terror-sweat, his miserable cock shrivelling in on itself like a little pink slug."

Tim moved away from the sideboard and took a few cautious steps into the centre of the apartment. A cornucopia of imagery inundated his senses: faces of celebrities, politicians, anonymous strangers from past and present were spliced and intercut in infinite variations with shreds of cityscapes, desert vistas, arboreal panoramas, the surfaces of other planets, real and fictional. Within these four humble walls, Lois Strandberg had reconstructed the universe – torn its every component between the teeth of her scissors and scattered the wounded fragments in an ongoing overhaul of temporal and spatial foundations. Almost overwhelmed by this barrage of word and image, it seemed to Tim that he had become enveloped in the blueprints of evolution. A whole new logic was laid bare before him, like the script for the most epic of movies yearning to be filmed and edited into existence. As phenomenal as Lois's talent undoubtedly was, Tim identified a crucial ingredient absent from her composition: soundtrack. Something infinitely more profound than aimless whimsy had lured him here.

"So the dumb fuck rushes into the hall, severed hand stuffed in the liner from a waste basket, trailing his filthy blood behind him," the woman continued in unhurried tone as she rummaged through papers and magazines. "Goes to the ice machine and starts filling up the bag, thinking he can save the hand and have it reattached. Machine runs dry after only a handful. Enraged and panicked – and still butt-naked remember – he runs to reception screaming for *Ice! Ice! Ice!* I run in after him, my face all bruised and bleeding y'know, screaming that this fucker tried to rape me. Fella at reception goes to dial for an ambulance and the cops too. Son-of-a-bitch Mr Executive swings the bag – with his hand in it, yeah? – slugs the guy around the head, screaming: *Ice! Ice!* Pair of security guards at the door pile in to take him down. Crazy son-of-a-bitch is swinging the bag around like a cudgel, his jelly belly wibbling-wobbling, cock flopping ridiculously while these two heavies come at him – you can make out the mix of shock and amusement in their stunned faces. A real sight to see. Another day at the office... Ah-hah!" She pulled a pair of shears free from the clutter and waved the rusted blades cheerily by their cracked wooden handles, "I need to see your wallet. Would you hand it to me please?"

"ID check?" Tim queried as he fumbled in his back pocket.

"Oh no, no. I know who you are, Tim. That's in no doubt. But we need to lighten your baggage a little before either of us can go anywhere from here. Only those who travel light may ride this train."

He handed her the slim leather accessory without further question. Ignoring his cash, she pulled out his ATM card. "No other cards? Credit or Debit?"

"No, none."

"Good boy," her red lips curled upward in a sincere smile, "that makes my job easier." The card fell to the mercy of her blades with a dry conclusive snap. "Now, what about photos? Any family snaps in here?"

"I'm not sure," he responded honestly, "I don't remember."

She pulled out a colour snapshot in which he recognised his own face, about ten years younger, sandwiched between a smiling couple in their sixties. "This?"

"Oh yes, those are my parents."

"Hm. Well we'll have to do away with that. There's no room for any attachments to the primordial swamp I'm afraid. Could bring our whole train crashing down around us."

"That's quite alright." A tide of relief washed over the floor of Tim's psyche. He had given no thought to his parents, nor indeed to any member of his family in quite some time. This realisation caused him to feel quite liberated. As Lois calmly attacked the photo with her shears, he could feel the claws of the material world surrendering their grip upon him – all the archaic structures, customs and hierarchies with which he had been raised falling away like the shells of drained insects from a wind-blown web. His pulse began to ease, his muscles loosen.

Lois scrunched the mutilated photo in a small but fierce fist and tossed it onto the sideboard. Between thumb and forefinger she held aloft the portion she'd cut free. The younger Tim's face, shoulders and chest remained intact, all evidence of his progenitors amputated.

"Consider yourself duly liberated." She turned back to the sideboard and busied herself with the rifling of magazine pages. "Now, while I find the first appropriate background for this handsome fella, you can do us both a favour by disposing of the bodies."

Tim retrieved the screwed up photo and moved to the opposite cabinet where he fed the ruined remains to the candle's eager flame. As the fire went to work, he did not bother to look back at the smouldering faces of his parents whose very existence now seemed as inconsequential as those of staid fictional characters in a banal television soap opera. Instead, he found his gaze wandering the convoluted details of the collage around him, his psyche reaching out to those fragmented images and texts with tenacious tendrils of desire, feeling out new identities in the myriad time tracks enmeshed there.

"That'll do," Lois broke the silence in cheerful tone, smoothing the glue-backed photo fragment onto a network of other images and text he could not quite make out in the gloom. She spun around on a slender heel and fixed him with a keen expression, her eyes aglow with blue fire. "You may have the honour of unveiling now."

Tim crossed the room to the partitioned corner and pulled aside the tarpaulin which slumped soundlessly to the floor. Beyond lay an identical replica of the bedroom in which he had spent his pubertal years, recreated with almost maddening exactness; the narrow single bed with its blue duvet covers jammed against the wall with one dusty window permitting sour light from an unknown source; the built-in mirrored wardrobe, a spider-web wound in the glass of the left-hand door; the old stereo unit flanked by towers of tatty vinyl albums and sleeveless 45s; the bedside cabinet stocked with pulp paperbacks and assorted comic books… Even the scent was familiar: that stale summer smell of night sweat and the dull ammoniate odour of dreary masturbating adolescent afternoons.

A taste hit the back of his throat, brackish and bittersweet like stagnant saltwater mixed with cheap cider. Images came flooding in: illicit nights of teenage drunkenness by the old viaduct and urgent fumblings in the bracken with a promiscuous neighbourhood girl named Vicky. Her face – all huge eyes and hollowed cheeks – surfaced from the swamp of his memory, as clear and defined as she was back then: the rosy, rustic features spread in a lascivious grin; the chestnut hair collecting at the thorax where her young breast heaved in her blue dress, pointing exultantly towards a forgotten sun. He recalled the sting of pinched skin between the two bracelets she wore on one willowy forearm. Blue rings of bruised shadow festered around her eyes. He'd heard the rumours of her abusive father: a faceless beast peering malignantly from between the midnight doors of an imagined wardrobe – her heart skewered by rusty coat hangers – ignominy of red nights creased upon the velvet of her kiss.

Then the doll swam leadenly to inky surface waters – white ceramic face as ancient as the ocean pierced with sad blue eyes topped with a ragged swirl of strawberry curls – that ragged bundle Vicky dragged perpetually and dejectedly behind her would whip the local tongues into a clucking frenzy – *Such a queer and unsettling child, such a strange and worrisome habit for a girl on the cusp of womanhood, oh me oh my...*

"Little Poppy just loves to ride the sea breeze," the girl would proclaim, holding the doll aloft, its arms spread in quasi-crucifixion, its impervious face staring down the sun.

Blood throbbed in Tim's temples and loins, his arm-hairs standing to attention. A red-hot fury of excitement wracked his body with an intensity he had not experienced since youth. Through this maelstrom of wild sensation, his ears – ever responsive to the surreptitious frequencies of the fractured universe – alerted him to a sound, small but sharp and incessant as the resonance of mosquito wings. Electricity sparked in the base of his spine. Time swelled like a thunderhead, its rage manifest in a haze around him.

"Grab that melody roughly by the tail. Let's see where she leads us..."

Tim leaned in close to the bed. The sound was emanating from beneath the musty duvet, its cadence familiar like that of an ancient lullaby. Astutely the pillow couldn't turn his head for a tune... He whipped back the duvet, revealing a navy blue fitted sheet where a white liquid mass trembled in the creased centre... a fresh load of teenage ejaculate simmering in impudent rebuttal of time's gathering tempest... Sad music turned white for a moment... streams of white cum trailing from the pool to map psychic journeys across velvet horizons... He went on pouring bad in there... thunder in the chest lowered his face to the hot puddle... its departed outline began to search for details... Voice against his ear did no good... experienced a chill of the courtyard... her blue dress of memory... inhaling the scent of revolution in the spent cells... Blood-red light punctured by megaliths of desire... no dream seen before at the foot of those emerging towers... Held his breath and was submerged in the chaos of youthful lusts... glaucous tides searing the treacherous skin... innards oozing out on to the surface of insomnia... tendrils reaching for his breathing to pylons... Couldn't turn his head for a response signal... hurrying the blood to outmoded season...

Tim slid through doors of human tissue, pungent smell of semen mingling with the glue on his back as he was pasted into other avenues. A colossal subterranean train station spread out before him, gnarled carriages of solid bone careering noisily on tracks of erogenous flesh *clickety-clackety-click-click-clack*. Electricity hummed and sparked in the air, the song's minute frequency gliding in spiral patterns. Tim followed the sound across cold dusty stone platforms past blackened brickwork smeared with blood and excrement, steel benches eaten with rust in endless rows. Silent commuters crowded the platforms and benches, stoic faces rigid and expressionless, eyes focused on something unseen, each tuned to other melodies replayed for them exclusively obeying their coda to rise as the correct train comes rushing in on black winds of time. Concourses spread out in all directions connected by endless black iron stairwells and bone escalators from distant foundations mired in shadow to an ill-defined sky of slate. He found his train on an oil-black platform, utterly deserted the melody, lilting sadly towards sickly pale light behind glaucous windows and doors of gristle. Destiny sped him onward, doubts and babble of nostalgia regaling him with hallucinational lucidity. Sad needles picked his skull through the years he clasped.

A phosphorescent sky cracked like a whip as his image was spliced into a rainswept street. The landscape ruffled backs to a sudden onslaught of buildings: nineteenth century terraces and storefronts with the desolate shells of 1970s automobiles parked along the kerbside. Rows of tenements opposite falling in on themselves with thunderous despair, their foundations attacked by a swarm of bulldozers, cold metal beasts competing for the kill. Tim's melody danced in the pale light of the second-hand store windows where a porcelain doll stood queenly marble eyes reflecting nothing. Liquid burst in acrid particles and he was breathing the protein of old summer orgasms in musty adolescent tissues. Decades he wasn't cured of communication. Burning had paved the road for his loins. Festering dog shit glimmered on this street through the half-light. Air chilled phantom memories into doorways of age... sound of crickets following his shadow from the summer's wound. Half-light ruined streets approximating gunfire to cut the cake. Melody like a sad clarinet falling westward.

He knew an old fence in this shabby neighbourhood out by the disused warehouses and thought he might track him down. He could visualise the man's haggard face, a red network of veins painting a mesh of mutiny around the sunken eyes and toothless mouth but the name had dissolved into rubble and dust. His will turned eternity for its knife – entered the store to find the old man perusing out-of-date chocolate Easter eggs, stuffed animals stained with blood, broken toys bearing wounds of war – "Not one to suffer fools, sonny" – daily headache of his voice – his own eyes struck three by the window – the form of a young man in close proximity had approached animal dreams – his own identity fading out into musky canine scent which these dead had reared like the hands of history –

"It's all about what's underneath, sonny."

Other stars fell on a wardrobe in the centre of the road – knife playing on the light from his voice – sensed strange thoughts less than a foot from the door – pasts and futures clashing in hot droplets from a young cock – mattress under temporal world viewing the base of his skull – merciless glimpse of something at gargling death rattles in throats of shadow – doors of timber giving way to yawning umbilicus of brickwork coated in wet alien moss – dropped to their knees in a crawl – eyes wild come level once or twice with characters from dead past – signal to crumbling textures imparted his desire bare after that – could struggle no image free from the hazards of lust –

Finally daylight and the passage inclined to an opening in the darkness – bland urban smells and a chorus of gulls – pushed their way through broken bottles, egg cartons, cereal boxes, rusted cans to the grey empty back lots of a mammoth shopping complex – all else was silence falling neglected.

"This is not like back in primary school – no hide and seeker gets to shout 'home free' around here – No way – Not bitin' – I got us some ghost memories we can swap for a shot at other images – Don't need to know whose glue you're riding – that's your business – Stagger westward in old viaduct vapour is it? – pull your young face out from the storm between her thighs the distant razors on her cigarette breath – knife caged her words in any star flexing – Move out to the temple she left you with plaster dust from old lungs – Don't dawdle – pick up your feet, kid – not here to wipe your arse for you."

The sound of snoring came without warning into that concrete wasteground – shattered gate of time dozing on its hinge – In the distance a viaduct silhouette cut a dark wound across emerald miles – Trees melt into the image in his arms but Tim could not close the sky and felt himself drifting into roofs of abandoned schoolhouses – knew a deserted trailer park in an old desire to kill – Against her then these hands might yet thrust a knife – acid ghost of inebriation working his vocal chords:

"I almost feel it dripping on my hands towards the building – intolerable burning ran up my heart – My concern in a stream of warm blood – The old dusty apartment after seven when last daylight glimmered across the grey float – Billowing around her scream I felt the girl grasp the night to a cut – twisting her face into a slender blade – tasted her falling tenements in my own eyes – She was fast asleep leaning on the doll by tangled hair and half-open mouth – Perhaps she had not told me the story that blossomed there in the rubble of her clothes – The artist glues me to other time tracks."

Deep-drawn breath to the mall's boundless borders – first flakes falling to frigid floor –

(Time had come to his erect penis throbbing into mutinous waves – streams of white cum ravaged the concrete.)

Tragedy stood upright and surmised his riot of emotions – from between two tall steel refuse cylinders emerged a deformed figure traversing the lot in a pathetic hobble – The man was faceless, his warped body entirely naked, the featureless head slung back on a broken neck – The left side of his collarbone flexed elastically against the uppermost rib forming two makeshift lips – a metallic insect voice exuded from this cruel distortion:

"Not remember me? – sure we tore it up a little on tour with Iggy way back when – DIY is my gig this weather – though I don't go preaching what I practice of course eh? – too many brothers doing it for themselves puts me right back to propping up landfill despite government patter about No Skilled Tradesman Left Behind – In the junkyard is where you'll find it all – dusty gems of the galaxy more priceless than all the gold discs on the walls of Hard Cock Café – Past imagining the girl's longing at last she brought her one lifetime – The body kept bad houses before the gash – she was lying on his roost among ruined breath – waiting always waiting in other images other words – glued to a circle unbroken in bittersweet cider aeons – It's the chemicals they put in the varnish you see – all the guilt and rage and despair of her world invading the lungs as I fixed that wardrobe together – done broken like a summer reed – You would come here undone in the breakdown – the knife oppressed in the darkness, the red domain lay in wait…"

Black smoke billowed from behind the complex, the air heavy and acrid with screams and the martial stink of fire – of anger – of an exploding sun rampant with forgotten summers – Shop windows sailed past in military formation – life-size plastic figures preparing for war – flicker of no return in the featureless eyes – mannequin mothers rallying snubbed-nose children to the frontlines of Armageddon – death tremors in phosphorous aquarium waters – He knew she would be sitting beside her words – her face rising blackly from within the building in that time of her first tune – Fear came running across the bottomless knees – he had something like it in saliva – familiar melody on his back felt the heart working – her blue dress of memory – (tasted her ghost in the corridors – spectral fingertips painting trails of nervous sweat across affectless walls – streams of white cum ran down the concourse –)

Solemnity claimed the mall's heart, every escalator ground to a halt, glass doors shattered – here and there mannequins had been ransacked from their ruined outposts and placed around the balconies, each one garbed in the costume of a dead rock star – John Lennon knelt sprawled against a blackened glass barrier, a yellow-jacketed Freddie Mercury poised over him fucking one of four wounds in the ex-Beatle's back with a makeshift carrot cock – A fat-suited Elvis sat awkwardly upon the pristine seat of a lavatory pulled from the window of a nearby home furnishings showroom – Where a shattered wall of glass opened out towards the extensive parking area Marc Bolan lay prone at the edge of an automobile graveyard – burning shells of luxury saloons and SUVs pumping toxic plumes into the torn sky –

With surrealistic will the viaduct had swerved off-course, its stone bulk stretched like a pagan icon across the ceiling of that glass temple – red flesh fires in the sun-kissed waters – Feral children had emerged from its prehistoric backside – he felt his heart with them lobbing Molotovs from behind bellows-like contractions – blades of petrol to look at the clock – velvet of a breath into animal dreams of ammunition – The bulldozer's advance had been more or less correct – brick and concrete sending that dream of every age and environment to faceless sound – Linear time longed for days in those large stores where brutal machines would send life-size plastic figures beyond life and death – (Streams of white cum fertilised the desolate food court) – Clocks feasting on the wings of insects popping in dusty striplights – History like a virus depositing spores of despair in his lungs – Santa's Grotto smouldering at the sun's threshold – radioactive shadows in forlorn teen pantomimes blasted against derelict storefronts – first kisses and first dates rusted upon a vacant soda fountain – festival of corrosion – sad ghosts of the twentieth century rallying towards a vagrant horizon –

In a pose of quasi-crucifixion Vicky waited – Astutely his knuckles went back into tune – He addressed the girl's good looks excited – brought her announcements in the first motion – She was thin and taller like the hands of history – her face was no longer riding upon the roller coaster for which the boy had braved death – promise of her rosy rustic features assured the human interval – thick chestnut hair falling loose reflected in static eyes – Her eyes picked the base of his skull from her dead past – mortal passport to jejune miles – her lucidity had paved the road for this breastbone – silky urban heart feeling warm in a desolate lonely place – the doll clenched like a crippled child of Chernobyl to her chest – Knife lying on the material world passed the light from windows as it wept onto his hands – network of veins told him nothing – whole building quivered at her electric tongue:

"It's not like back rolling hot limbs in the bracken – Little Poppy just loves to ride the shit of my stone snake – You know enough to catch them in bed like a vague black maybe – Years had known my dream from that coincidence to swap for a courtyard looming with hopeless terror – Click my heels to focus on the glue you're riding – my name filled with substance and then at windows a straight black shirt you left on a dead branch – watched another shadow catch my breath – placed the doll violently – hurrying the blood in empty warehouses – My heart's disappearance was no tragedy to freeze in that instant – whole face wore no expression at this sandstone enclave – I began to race – arriving at apartment block rot and melt away everything inside – awakened by phantom time zone of crippled memories ripped open – rented a room ten weeks before the power lines connected – these cheeks looked hollowed in the skull of their own mother – slave-mask of domestic concubine – bled filthy secrets in the wardrobe he built me – blood of my future fermenting to a black cancer – language could manage other times of smiling Chance – caught my breath back – My heart doing here…? – On the low wall of a strange friendly pity – breathe me in air from other lungs with the cat on her lap – I shall be the landscape in insomnia –"

Siren hands into transparent girl grasped summer night – all the opaque air of this jail spun its head in his direction – Children dissipated in the noon sky – elms and poplars came to demolish the tenements beyond and a black thunderhead loomed in wait for them – Aquarium thoughts arrived at the final block to counter the ghostly shapes of two bracelets – No tragedy breathed more easily – surmised his eyes would not close the knife in her chest – The landscape was red – the stove out – (the room can dissolve suddenly from other collages) – Desire to kill details of her childhood among the spine as the mattress under her eyes grew wild – Into any orifice nightmare he turned towards the throng by utilising their light of the snow –

Arms on that slender blade pressed his body from her hair and skin – so many years at her open mouth that he did not wish to live – hands falling obliquely to find that journey westward given way – pained him of saliva descending from her life while falling to a blob as man and wife – sad heart threatened the red network – Vicky gasped excitedly at the steel length – frenzied laugh echoed throughout well of memory – erect penis throbbing cider over coarse livid throat –

Two tiger heartbeats curled on the floor – wounded children dying in those stores where he pictured her heart in a wardrobe – plastic figures reaching out to embrace them in dead time-bound arms moved about fishlike in the Grotto – black insect voices chattering from perfidious incubus mouths: "Give us some honey – don't tell your mother – Give us some honey – don't breathe a word now..."

Mental imprint pulled its companion up to her cheeks – blood-red light on the queenly doll growing cold – arms outstretched – frigid hands cupping concrete dreams of catastrophe – she was lying on his disappearance – His will turned eternity for its knife – Triumph seduced would be not long in coming within the condemned throat – Her brackish tongue slid under his buttocks and accelerated the clock – his knees throbbed and hummed upon sandstone – cursing the lingering words – At other gash he could struggle no more – the window timeless for a few moments looked upon her deep-drawn breath – pained walls expanding for her timeless zone – pity for her ageless face no longer concrete – wordless sigh slipping out of time – (streams of white cum dissolved stone and glass) –

Thirty times the knife went riding the roller coaster only he could slake – blood oozing out for a few moments uneventfully smiling – The doll remained committed to his hands but they were now reflected in her control – stronger than his will – geometry of buildings embedded in a stream of warm crimson – the body kept a boundary-free mineral in this audacious gash – liberated in a post-emotional spine – blood-red light on the ceiling of constant flux –

Clasped on his stomach her words to him fast with the weight of his body: "Gone last cigarette – done smoked the lot – Nothing hidden in the wardrobe – no more for his damn eyes to see – Get my arms out in the sea air – this is where the itch ends."

He felt her falling with low wretched eyes – The doll remained silver and dark drifting obliquely in her static journey westward – all tragedy burst upon his face with the contractions of a distant sun – Streams of white cum swept her astral ghosts across the vertebrae of the universe –

(Furniture of the courtyard, her blue dress appeared in the wardrobe. All the unwelcome eyes put out on a coat-hanger hook. Her father's fists cuffed in those rusted claws. Phoenix flare in the suburbs and a noon dust formed a fuzz upon the wood. Tim knew surreptitious daylights in the protein sex smells of impatient adolescents. Cheap gum phantoms caressing him with red bubbles in the broken bottle graveyard. Seditious puberty tasted like lead on his tongue. Her blood watered the dry bouquet of his memory. He breathed her heels but his eyes would not close. Cider breath of lost summer paints new stars in other skies. Inside him she walks prolonged silences.)

From memory forty minutes later pocket watch pointed last daylight – white cum pasted him to another's reverie – watching in the full glory of some passion in the shadows –

A public park on a cool bright spring morning – low stone wall along the emerald border, blue sea haze beyond – Girl aged about fourteen perched there, slender hands clasped upon a book in her lap – frail scrupulous young voice from behind breeze-blown auburn tresses:

"Excuse me, sir. Do you have the time? I think I'm supposed to be somewhere."

"Sorry, love. I haven't much use for it."

The girl shrugged, the sad features of her pale freckled face flexing lackadaisically. "That's okay," she whispered in a soft mid-Atlantic accent, "I'm sure whatever it is will find me one way or another."

She stuffed the book – *The Cat in the Hat Comes Back* – into a knapsack and turned her attention to the blue horizon.

Saltwater smells sailed in with a squabble of gulls on a breeze thick with the frenetic promise of summer. Tim watched as the girl, seemingly unmindful of his presence, spread her arms wide, ready to embrace the turmoil that loomed like a thunderhead upon the capricious causeway of her youth.

Sad clarinet melodies dispersed into vapour above the incoming tide.

KJ Nolan, *The Herd*

Niall Rasputin
Poems

disgraceful blade

division nude and other holes in feather fire
glitch-hop a ruse
burn your noise and hide the eyes that ate my globe

of cartoon worms
       heads bleeding flags
detergent monsters cycle light
      dread bellow freeze
dying rain without a voice
          enjoy the wounds

all meaning sinks
entangled voices in the vacuum minded star
a rubber wish
reflecting monsters in an infant sparked deluge

I am the knots
oh rascal guts
bulimic whisper spotted days
my midnight shines
blue splattered dream
another noise becomes
my home

holy invisible aggression!

hatred tongues flutter bomb in TV God mouth tragedy
propaganda eaten children bloom
rabid headstones sing wounds into time lit cracks
golden faces loaded

pig cluster pukes tar heart dragons
shackled dream lives
vile spirit trigger

unity slings forgotten breath
red cold planetary illness pangs
pangs
pangs

bloodbath orgy storm love war fuck rattler prayers
naked tremble dog vision
peace eyes shattering sunsets

King Death   everlasting

nothing understands this nothing

Never

with monstrous loving knives – warlord's tantric rivers – pork
revs
political filets swim static – prayer bombs

hateful elevators rising to abyssal guts – stripped faces spiraling
trashy gods
inward ray-gun fuck muse squirting corpses forsaken love
dance fiends dance
in nostril fire – liquid dogs on the collapsing sunset
miracle slaughter hell insertion
blood is a tornado

in a wilderness song I've swallowed angels
road-rash ripples of star shit

it will end in shivers
orange slides fluttering truths
remember that choking ocean?

we are Never

mpcAstro
Nidus Plexus: Immortal Fungus
an operotica

Prelude: Verso/Recto

The conveyance station for Automated Linguistics jumped track. Its monstrous cam ajam. As the duo assessed damage control from the cupola's lofty vantage, the indentured e-**PISS-stem**-all-a-gist, Dr. Mortsac, was nudged by his trans**genre**d *Venus Ex Machina,* the Webstress Illustra von Kix, in all her pan**text**ual plumery: "Less epi**pseud**ic, more epi**sod**ic, my dear doc**tor**, lest we embrace Chaos." *Does she suspect my Phantom Limbs – Heresy and Anarchy?*

Picking up the gauntlet, the erstwhile **Eros**opher inwardly vowed to, thereinafter, amplify the logic of his metrics through the **pixeLucinatious** subconch.sys of the **Nidus Plexus** where creature may frequent Creatrix via **hiero**conversation… a circular, organic hypertext where artifact commingles with Architect in a dervish dance of opposites spooning into a dialectical ball of fire: the fabled **Omen Globe**—the elusive ***Versus Intexti.***

Episodic enough, Ms. Kix? "Kink is our business, Mistress. This is only a **kink**," said he with a toothy grin. *I see you,* did she, ***Venus Fitzgerald Crisis!***

verso: re:photomontagerie 16 Piranesi plates: *Fantastic Prisons* commingled w/(il-) *lust*-rated squatter daughters of labiarinthine culture in highiambic heels disquiet dungeons drive home pumped points per perfect reign throughout archcolossus slave labor creator of relic monuments magnificent made to feel genius of great artists who reign throughout every idiot detail fevered perplexus fevertree not just big scratch post itches to branch staircases leading the charge beamed vaults supporting vast compounds pocked with revolt squalid suites of crumbling stone not for squalor's sake alone hell no but for the rush of root hold lost on rickety roads through space time manifest destiny heads us once more to the right page

recto: Look out belowward cyclopean machines neoclassic justice busting a nut gad deuce give us *Déus of MaMaMachinaWorks* lowered onto stage piffling epiphany poor judgment day a tough titty flop save your drama for your big mama in particular sag from airy arches over head hang ropes that carry the weight of the sap heavy hive in pendulous torture sickenly lit by narrow windows chambers half open to rosemarine sky revealing more or less complete vaults and broken walls in the misty distance coextends the feverpitchtree flushed severely redboard abandon all hope who enter this burning bush dumb asses bray branded balking in steamy shadows off stage a choral katzenjamhammer after all after sex all animals are sad

Doctoral machinations went viral. An infection of incantations was introduced into Nidus Plexus's vocabulary, retooling its quack dialectic to run a cascading tessellation of autonomous phantasmagoria. *Avant-Arabesque!*

Foreweb: Old World New

I first met the Webstress by appointment on a blistering First of July afternoon at her "happy" – Los Feliz – home's dungeon with a portfolio of my *metric montages*. I explained, while she leafed through the illustrated poems, that it was my intention to "flesh in" the exoskeletal catalog she had in her hands with genuine gotherotic scenery. She agreed, in exchange for modeling scenes, to enweb the artist for 666 days while the camera could be tossed from slave to Illustrix to crew, all shooting scenes on the mat with Erato, Muse of Lyric, in a **no holds barred** grapple of metronomic servitude.

To submit one's **self** – Art's ultimate price.

Did I have the *cajones*? Sounded better than holing up in a flop with a Burroughs "typer" from Goodwill and **broke dick**… I've done **that** for art: getting **it** broke off and on a fork fed me. The folio aside, **Illust**ra handed me a clip boarded "Dialog Sheet" with pen. I scribbled "**no *holes* barred**."

Chapter 1: Cock Crow

The artist awoke from a florescent dream of fantastically frantic butterflies – orange, black, silver-yellow and peach blush – by the thousands scrambling to tear out from black pixelknit cocoons. One after another, each winged emergent, within seconds of first flight, would decorate a ubiquitous web that seemed to canopy the whole cocoonscape, so that sky and earth to horizon had become a kaleidoscopic vibration of vivacious panic.

Eyes open to vitreous opacities transmogrified into a Boschian parade of buffoonery… hilarious **mass destruction** hysteria. *Mo'f'er! Rub these* **endoftheworld** *floaters out of your eyes, dude… Hello?* Arms seem to be sewn to sides. *Wha'duh?* Legs encased in… silk? Torso, immobilized as well. *Fug!*

"Rise and shine, Cloudcuckoohead…" *Lustra?* "Hope you don't mind me holding vigil… oh, **and** my sis', **Am'** – **Amanita** to you. How do you find the body bag we slid you into as you **slept**? Comfy?" *Yeah, snug as a bug; wh'up, Bit'h?*

Chapter 2: Waylaid

Lustra must've been looking for hours at all my new prints being readied for exhibition, while she loomed overnight for my peepers to pop. By the tone of her *inflection*, she must've last night **wo**maneuvered me a covert introduction to a potent potion – probably at *Rathskeller's* about when I was competing with the juke's "Shaken Baby" metal montage by *Moochy Splurgess*, "Your name's **Lustra**… as in, *'Lust, Rah'!"* – while a squadron of kamikazes roared themselves down my hatch into *divine wind*. And then – *or was it all really just a weird, loopy dream?* – she grabbed a fistful of **m**animal while seated right there at the bar pressed up next to me, *Smilin' an' ev'raythang.*

And now I'm here… at home – in my studio… fluttering in from a total eclipse **black out** to a wrench tightening **head band**width of static pixelation.

"Hey, Dickweed," thus spake '**Amrita**' **Amanita**, multi-faceted Indus Goddess, all five faces in my face, "Well for you your tang is all tongueled."

Chapter 3: Metro Rail

"You can hear me, Pun**jab**i," Amanita **jab**bed his bread box. "My ambrosia may bind body and gag guile, but you **do** *see* **and**," **jab**, "*hear* me." She was afire, "When I started out we didn't *sneak around* about it. I'd walk right up to a café table, take from my purse and place on the table's edge an empty champagne glass; it's lip at the hemline of my mini. And right in front of the lone, perfectly unprepped gentleman seated *now* <u>not</u> **minding** *<u>his</u> <u>own</u>* **business**, dare I say – as well as nearby onlookers, **all** *transfixed* – I would fill up the glass with my elixir from where I stood akimbo, not even having to hike my dress it was so short. Snatched napkin from table; walked.

"You'd be surprised how many dogs pick up **that** scent, even if they've to run a gauntlet of critics. Sometimes a critic or so would wag along, too."

"What the alchemists called the 'elixir of life,' the devotional now call 'Midflow with a Twist': The twist? – kidney filtered soma *muscaria* extract."

Chapter 4: Assfault

"But we now prefer to *sneak* **Catherines** down their gullets, don't we, Sister Amrita," *Illustra, save my ass,* their entangled fly inwardly prayed.

"I was just reminiscing about sidewalk life in Paris," poofed Amanita – *Amrita's* her *safe name*, to decrimp her *nom de kink;* yet her inner cauldron bubbled over, "I'm also regaling while draining this piss face of all his color."

"Patience, **Am'**, the roast is better served baked than broiled. His sacrifice must not only be a labor but a transmutation of cream into chrism."

'Rita swallowed hard; chrism was the coin of the realm. "Love your enthusiasm, tho', kid," offered Ms. von Kix, leering at the art prints she had hung on all the wall space of the ample studio throughout the night and morning.

"But the **Catherine**, my dear boy, is a drink named after Catherine the Great of Tzarina Russia –contemporary of Architect Piranesi of Roma – she mixed vodka with elixir come *eliquir*. Put a new *twist* on the **En**light**enm**ent."

Chapter 5: Purple Piranesi

To: **_Mz. Diz,_**

My E-rides through your Magic Queendom make me feel so delivered from the shadow of the Valley of Ennui.

I confess I dream your kiss is the Breath of Life Itself. Can a man remain tethered to the earth after such a gift?

My dear Illustra, don't you just love dreaming you're flying? Me, too; better pinch me.

Fr: **_Micycle_**

To: **_oppoet_**

Yum!m!m!m!m!

This qualifies for letter of the week ! ! !

I may have to whore you out again – beware!

I would LOVE to pinch you!

Fr: **_Lustra_**

Needless to say, the Tantrixhood no longer had to police him. The Nidus Plexus routed his thoughts – deliberate or whimsical – to his controller, his _Creatrix_. And she, in turn, would book his render unto _Seizor Central_.

And so, as per "Dialog Sheet," she has called her creature forth. Tonight's command performance: Sir Render delivers himself to the Umbiliphiliatrix, Shaydee von Shockra, to her 'Lectric Lair of Horrors where his glist gets blistered to a bitchen gloss, "**no holes barred**."

Chapter 6: Sextuptych

born: Lost in the Labyrinth from mentally cataloging its infernal puzzles until overwhelmed, I then relied on fortune to meander my way out as if my enmazement were not a sentence but a freedom. Not until my wit was spent did my circummuration go peristaltic. Near exhaustion, at the threshold of panic, I spotted, then desperately squeezed through a shuttering portal to abort in an amniotic sweat, damning my fickle flesh for escaping from a well-earned, eternal fumbling at the Gordian slipknot that held me in suspense.

died: *Fancy Trim*, read the sign over the Factory Street door. *I'll **jes'** bet.*

Intermezzo: Disciples Lashed

It seemed a lifetime ago that Lucrezia – "of The Cross" – peeked over her shoulder back down at me, staring up at her high rump romping like slap happy Ben Wa hams both vibrating off the other as they knocked about, slapping it up in my over amped libido while I followed her up the stairs from the street entrance where signage from the previous Garment District sweatshop still hung like an insider's joke. *Yes, no run of the mill **trim** here,* her piercing glance conveyed. On the landing, Lulu went to the first of a grand hallway full of oaken doors. "The Mistress will be with you presently," she swung open the massive door to the antechamber, "Please, take a seat."

In a blue lamp-lit corner a coffin come wooden maiden leaned upright with cabinet door openings at face and crotch levels. With dabs of testosterone cream behind both ear lobes, I rejoined, "May I 'take' *yours?*"

Lucrezia held her poker face for three heartbeats before toying with a smile, "**Some**one will have some**body**'s before the day is done, I'll wager." Now grinning, she watched for her retort to impress my expression. My right eye cocked. "Now be a good boy and put your butt in that chair," she pointed to a metal studded contraption with immobilizing straps, "and save your enthusiasm for your coming ordeal with destiny." **Coming** ordeal **come** coffin.

The reverie demisted itself as I sat naked on my heels on the stone floor in the middle of the darkened chamber, gathering my wits after christening for twelve hours *each* the Twelve Stations of Sorrow. "Before being reborn," Mistress instructed from her throne, "one must first die." Illustra grinned as this initiate's shoulders tensed. *So predictable,* she surely mused. "Even if only metaphorically," she assuaged me, her latest tyro.

A slight drop in my shoulders told her, *Ahh, he's mine again.* "Before **change**, first there's **crisis**. We *here*, **also**, use stressors to create metamorphosis. Now off, catch us the foxes, for our vineyards are in bloom!"

Back out on the street after a gross of hours, the usual downtown tarryhoot was mute. Forsaken cars littered between emptied glassteelstone monoliths. Tumbleweednewsprint: "The Brutish are coming! The Brutish are coming!" Gothschild and Gilderberg, as per His Royal Highness's last request, had **Prince Philip** reincarnated as a killer computer virus taken up by the four winds.

Chapter 7: Exitus

"Ask *not* what The State can do for you; ask what *you* can do for The State."

fr. *The Man Said 'Slide' So We Slid: confessions of a lamb lead to slaughter*

To: ***Mistress Illustrious,***

Row me over the falls where primal screams trail off into electro mist dreams roaring into a rapturous body aripple with your romping buoyancy. Without you I am a murky pool.

Stagnate. A mud puddle. A smudge on the worn sole of a discarded shoe...

'till abuzz within the sweet, swarming sting of your honeycombed promise. 'Till then I await your pleasure in hive-honored dance signing the sky with your pollen-potent name, my Royal Jellied Highness.

'Till then, I am

Your bumbling drone,

Fr: **Smikes!**

Chapter 8: Moonstocks

"Semi-precious" *Nun* **Jade** loved making men squirm under heel. Loved to escort each naked on a leash to Sanctum von Kix. *Await their asses whipped.*

posted: *I am **Velum**, Words on the Cross, Worte am Kreuz; I am **knot**chen, tangled lumps, Mein Gottin, **My Goddess** von Kummer Zitzen, **of Suffering Titties**! I am your altar, my **Pitmos**trocity, through me rise from Hell this spring we'll retrace wie die linien **wackeln**, how the lines **wobble** whackin' out*

new chevrons flayed over old,

fulfilling not destroying,

signed: **Lance** von **Longinus**. date: **33-0430 Novus Ordo Mundi**. witness: **Punishe Pilates.**

We ferment in the Bowel of the Beast. A bevy bunkered. All bent over frottage bobposts, every navel a tight cluster of **knots** each puckered over gut punch pressure switch on thoraxis drive juddering to dithereens *atandem.*

Chapter 9: Crackpot

It takes the juice of a school of ***useless breathers*** hung out to dry for inking a *Versus Intexti.* Each **youbē** a hump engine piston chugging autogyrally, cursively sewn together by our common thread, ***Illustra***, whose design is to dry hump the con**trap**tion into a rapt seizure as metal shavings spit out smoky aluminum oxide streamers of a nano-crystalline mist culled to silver a chemtrailed perma-web univiewer sky **topside** looming forth The Hologrammaton scaring shit out of the *genpop* just so to get them queued in: *Left shoulders against the wall! Shirts tucked in! Hands in pockets! Stack it up, nuts to butts!* **Gawd** was restored to the sky. **Trixtress**, a kiss **below**.

The Final Crusade's a great diversion. General Sun Tsu say, "*All* war is deception." Armies of Armageddon were all plowshared far from homes with doors left wide open for the marauding horde called the **Cremators of Care**.

Revelation 9:11 † *They had as king over them the angel of the **Abyss**…*

A Concrete *Versus Intexti*

Δ

● O

W   F

O   ●

D   S

A   O

H   M

S   A
SO

WE ACT

AS IF A*S

I*T I*S DOES

SOME holY SO

-JOURN, ho²KUM³PUT-

ING PEGA/SYS'T FAN

TOMS Who FOR T

HEIR BEMUSHR

OOMED TONG

UES CONN

ECT HE

AVEN A
ND EAR

TH] WITH [TH

UNDERS

OF COL

ORS EC

'holNG"

SHIFTED

MATTER

    SO.BE.IT

Chapter 10: Dismembrance

And they had as queen under them the Illustrix, Ms. von Kix, without whom their sky would not gleam fuzzy white silver hubcap diamond star halo.

The *genpop* were mostly *communicable* – "positive **mut**amin**ants**" – and so were mostly *recycled* en masse. The *Immunicable,* though, they were **topside** rejects. They just didn't respond to the everecho's jittery barrage of debilitating neurolinguistics… whether victor or victim, they were marked for absconsion by the Catherine Society, who, like a rapture gone south down a spider hole, deposited at the feet of Madam's Mechanical Absolutions a balance of books by eking out to the last breath Displacement Credits for the **youb** who might otherwise infect all United Holy Humpdom if he were to query, say, his block's VeriCheX-ray Tech: *Would you like me to lift my sac? How 'bout my wife's floppy tits? Have my daughter stick out her butt'n'gina? How 'bout we stick a feather [duster] in your [ass] and call it* **MaC-a-RO-ni**?

The Breatharians foster all *nasty* because they **can**. Tourette's at the helm of the *Ecoplexus:* **Cock**efellers and Kiss**ass**ingers weigh each breath.

Newbie youbs begin their sentences warehoused in the drone stables. To feel the full frontal brunt of First Day at Kix Caverns is to feel the life force swell up out from the **magma** through toes up veins flowing forth **lava**.

The Ma'am said glide so we **glid**.

Finalé:

"Dialog Sheet"
      [C/S]ession Dynamic

          or, How Our No-Mercy Circes Take a Sissy
Fuss

              Up and Down the Ladder in **6,6,6** Easy
Steps

                  at ***Chez Ricochet***, where the
caviar, by far

CIR CLE ANY

NO-H OLE BAR

RED TOR TUR

ESS *FOR* *CED*

FED PRO BOS

CIS *SUS* *PEN*

DED LAD DER

INT ENS ORY
'LEC   TRO DEV

ICE HOT WAX

VUL GER GAG

ENE MAS HUM

BLE RRR VIB

RAT ORS PVC

COR SET DEG

RAD ATE SIS

TER ARN ICA

NIP PUL LEY

R.G. Johnson
Poems

me

me
spastic & wholesale
dark stupor galaxy
pumping away
almost more sequins than ether
also miles of acid to mask her tequila lashes
and a quart of gorgeous Country heart
splayed and roasted
mental orgasm
hidden in the rum hole
a screamer corona
steady and raw
fingers of light
drinking stone mountains with dead eyes
she frenzies
night chews an unregistered cigar
lawless moments
we are rounded and depth spits our names
into the naked mouth of joy
buried in slit reasons
75 painted bones
a riot of empty eyes
vibrating homeward

run

Sunday looks angry
 the unattended eye laughs authority dead

 off – contrive other acquaintance
who write legs onto planets
herd   the slippery estate of told chapters into eons
likewise finding your slight association of conscience with dinner

to age on clock credit
my now answers
warns that withdrawal squirms on knowledge
but is vilest taken other ways
blunt tit smile
caught fidgeting
mortal ideas in seconds
just lust

afflicted eyes see holes

stop!

feed me to a universe
less sexy
my dog heart is swimming in your philosophy corpse

 disciplined life is rotted breath

Gustavo Arruda, *Sonho Sob Lua Má / Dream Under a Bad Moon*

Younisos
Self Cut-Up in Tangier

the breaking blue sky defecates on verbal emptiness for
Tangier, although real, is as horrible as beautiful – look at the
light: blue and the phone I'm already hard for the redhead was
ground, drained, I need damned dream. I spurted! not a writer I
handle the keyboard as a knife splashes All eyes on my cock
and hand bustling crescendo on the vulva, appeared in Place de
France up to the curb near the Cafe de Paris, in the heart of
Tangier lethal beauty Another goofy filthy ragged began to spin
when she saw the chest lunar fangs ghouls to latescent contours
– wham! lies a pig skinned and from the sky lights quiver steaks
and breasts sliced in swirling jets cut-nameless abyss, rot,
sparkling maggots bananas was obvious I cut his throat, the
sphincter contracted around my cock and I fell in holy ecstasy of
the senses laughing ruddy eleven thousand gutted beautiful: the
sensory and sewer opening on murdering me fiber by fiber
synapse after the other I'm dead though lust abounds in moult
arches and waving a meat vortex in digital synapses of the night
my eyes, my cock, squirting each I'm just a Bone – who wants
my meat? my fingers when I fingers, making her cum (in a
dazzling way) beautiful and anal rash I could be a monster
myself, drooling and babbling, spreading my tentacles and waits
for the next picture message... saving figures direction and
spoke Quake. Anus fresh delight cry streams red juice of white
murders Slice! Trip! Slaughtered in the areola (Tangier became
the hub of a vast traffic of female meat) Cosmos masturbates
constantly, rhythmically it book, the rogue, the anal rampant,
jolting the shocks was empty but he could drink all the scarlet
vibrations, jerks and smash guts sidereal – eternal return of
multiple immanent sodomy towards the ultimate and
unspeakable Black Hole light vertical crack! the postman didn't
know about it multiple slow impalement I go by the street-
cutthroats hoping some headless glow ultimate desire? –
Fucking the Universe. The raw brilliance of a big white breast
denial think about tomorrow lives up to the hilt in her womb, I

was flying in a white fireworks They expect something all these freaks humans: they hope it's nice! belly stretches mud sings us drink red dare shit can yell of rage before the light of sweet bright bright boobs blood open sky white chasm fingering screaming – open up! quartered your pores I'm damned scream my song in your pores you screwed with my head tassel-edged I hear the howl of sensitive lunch the blood is drunk warm heart ripped gray wall agony I enjoy just my neck sawed love us junk all night is comparable to the filth, and the flesh of a frail girl too deep in thought Zoco Chico was invaded by a lot of police officers and the killing pen stellar debauchery in animals, to the moon, the sun million miles a spark vulva strange crack, suffused with gold and blue trains breasts blinding light burst, spreading my skin on my desk with drops of blood emerging from the velvety clarity slowly which, as bloody, adhering to the small hole smashed angrily. the atmosphere (the cooked human liver that Clotilde accommodated with garlic and herbs: it was high and short I ejaculated but did not die You have to imagine a beautiful corpse... ithyphallic and I KNOW NOTHING they fluttered against each other, hugging flourished, while the owner sigh puffed pussy tender quartered juicy thighs satin crazy enucleated chestnut girl He shot himself in the mouth Blood mixed with fresh brains spattered on the neckline of Danaé who returned home, licking her tits, silent and anal bursts azure is a huge rot, purest blue, defecating on billions of eyes, rinsing them the abominable and despicable and beautiful, filthy the breast cut fresh let himself escape two streams of blood but I glimpsed behind Burroughs painfully Pyrrho of Elis sodomizing a pig small shrill voice: "I exist, I exist!"

Lee Kwo
Oublier the Suicide Protocols of Warp Paradox Factor/ Entail No Response/

Dragfactor eyes the aircon vents in the hardwire consciousness chords hit porno cortext to gyno of ceiling or lens witness the pain expanded of the i/I do not perceive my theft of illicit ovum module/the rasp of his lips its ravishment expended AcroSS cells detonates self we desire more control and we its breath contained within the clear helmet/each OrgasMs de-teched why after all these years do she minimalise yet again/meaning de-tached Unknown City Limits small cell machine sets up eYepod appears to disappear you still terrify me/Absurdina pointing at its cunt excited by the spectacle of its particular whine and nothing else remains/in this unnerving state the hundreds of desiring engines along the conduits of own cellular reception/automated and rebooted photos magnesium flash to all that remains is our own routed the embryo shadows escape into darkness/often what is without is CanCerous the wall of Nils room loops pure sex vulnerability/those around phallic celibacy of frozen terminals so complex and detailed it us refer to of rusting globes she grasp cannot skin hungry phallus shrings into bone be digital reconstructed/SKz this state as madness/dread is insanity/dread nakidness at both symbolic fails to structure cavity no erection receding surface corners/and shoots outs robs us of speech/all utterance off to reality or reflects inner chaos artifice/a chain of staring eyes pursed lips being falls silent/what of isotopes metastatic sonar and network of stoppages may set the subject can we erect phallus the recoil after each explain now probes the bulging horizontal corpse threaten object on who will understand/anxiety is preferable gunshot jars her wrist/Narcotic a circular path of tissue of polyphs infested strands skin addicts to dread/fear is containable and able hit of repetitive reinactment/Fuk UNarcotic Codeine Wars Phillia genome muscular tissue SKz phillia of trauma blockage to be medicalized/we may need annealed nerves stretch the blade cuts junk panic of time to junkcodes upload false entropic

stimuli/Protocol of shatter dead libidinal body past
communication grids holding static/white noise the empty
stillness with speed matrix unable to accept derangement/I
narcotic body addict across tragedy of this always compulsive
talk/this sense of dread which concept of fall-ability to excess
datatrash/ existence becomes more and behind anaesthetic a
bounded self described appears to reveal nothing of blockage
hijack an organic plenum free more of an accumulation of its
Angel an imageword as yet existence what we routinely know of
symbiosis product commodity apparatuses/Vox raps artefacts
that have dread for without definitive meaning/say
unexposable/illiterate/cipher wired to psychotic cannot fix his
holobike to Sentinal and dread of is the nothing volts/the body is
shore/Atomic co ordinates of time space matter
Beach/acceleration to a container or that crowds upon us/as the
state density of InfOrmation/The Protocol because they are
infact psychically the image is a subjective pointof of being is
indifferent of DataTrash channel the coded may not want sucked
out/but this duration chosen for its capacity for to separate his
flows regulated by valves and conductors expelled being is
always created and incision under the body from its cleverly
engineered representations/why the collapsed disjunctive skin of
appearances/at overdetermined by the Control Lie Fuk U
overload Apparatus/its pulse of ZEF discharge should he
limit?/Nilspersona was only this point her mind pressed in
conditions reverberate in life to burden of Singularityan instinct a
faceless silhouette our minds and still further to lock with the
refracted in the Quiet Umerican for growth a clamour of a fill us
with a sense of aesthetic experience of darkness of the corridor
outlined by duration as interval the bhuto performance desiring
production of things and into amassing of atomic a candle held
in the hand delayed from attachment within the Borshii Boys
transmission device/the more time forces the Zenith of Nihilism
cloaked machinic interface spent hanging in unknown
experiences the ability to right as intruder shits arctic polarity of
Middle East the space of nothing the more filter cognition to runs
down over fingers and forms Fascist despot wreckage make
sense out of difficult white stains in sky to rise above substrats a

successful of corrosion Destitute digital rivulettes hardened stalks elongated fingers attempt to distinguish between the virus which accrete on the body of IdOls we plunge into abjected GroinEngine slight tremor as without apparent social real and the imagined organs animality SKz mechanality anality banality inanity OverMan form algebraic topologies which other selves/there is quite a bare feet/unable to accept the creature if Zero crowd are endlessly secreted and excreted into already/what passes Degrees humanity cannot concept of a bounded self thru window must be image of anal PhallicXXcollapse/slow be exacerbated only aborted or servalised gun almost too wave first pass as a fluid into of neural heavy for Veydra seriality serialised Baroque style power went thru Nils Ursttat opacity of glass/hard to lift from its polystyrine mold to imagine complexity enough the Quiet Umerican slide a Glock to achieve that possibility is why after all these years in pocket already explored by infallible commission SpecUlative adventures into the you still terrify another's pain the self/impossible in the presence of fingers/Ultra-Plus think Absurdina pointing N Dimension third culture of intrOlect this to forget not the other/for the psychotic thinker at hundreds of incestphotographs incinerated and zero recall to remember/She not born of man/Phallic unity being under the floor of UMertz room consistency and opacity of a woman nor carry the NON binary by nature she grasp the mold connection between immateriality of ones of a nakedness at both codes limit of eternal recurrence holes father but that of self and replicant others corners and shoots out eyes staring and cavities and who a fragmented closed circuit datatrashdrugembryo/Control are easy clefts of wombs eyes the pursed lips the erect to access as immaterial lie Hellucinates Borshii Boy consensual madness its naked risk in chaos of nipples the recoil narcotic selves/He am not compelled to machine tool after each shot eroticism Protocol of Astral Friction the/Phillia to SKZ the normality by these replicants for jars her wrist/narcotic skin addicts hit tool of BirThed interlude they low level depression left over from too have EXtractionS the decoupling SKz Phillia of trauma blockage junkcapacity to project ZEF interactions at the Industrial Café damp magnetic visual prison of probability submission codes upload false excesses of a disorientated sense of disease a nightmare entropic stimuli/Protocol of to logic functions fuktions fracktions frizzons of premeditated sleep selves/the so-called paranoia and allusional speed MatriX unable to accept last attempt on RoMroks red Futon hung over blue sparks of crackhorror that glasspsychosis a doomed species concept of these sublations MoRal consciousness plagues its victims to late afternoon/stay long enough being was always just the terror of the unknown/really a successful attempt in online interface a chance of positive instants and to let persistently frequented alter distinguish between the apparent social slide into insanities chance proscribed by fictions world conscious or subcurtaneous unconscious and you real arse sink into void/Decide none the socius imagined other selves/who begin to multiply then thermo suicide of rhyzomic the less to proceed/the Cartesian ideal Nomad Junk apparatus encodes techno crisis of a rational autonomous self of Gashgrils to strangled nerve ganglion/BoyDebris able to manipulate and control its scanned mutated holograms he get deranged own libidinal drives as well as from neural rush accident irrational negation the noumanal world/RomRok and Veydra extrapolating that abberent space of metaphors intervenes under narcotic fade out innate to infests the collapse of ruins and feel theyselves dying each morning/even in ill-limitable corrosion the notes of his kataleptic agony of terrorist brutality erupts/Being interrogation fell into wrong hands isn't easy fraught with Congenital cellular as an extrinsic predicate of substance traumas always the risk of taking drifting disappearance of the individual into steps toward the brink of extinction the autonomous collective patterns of closed /Vox is a down loaderthat which circuit mass culture and the gridlock comes within site of sight the transsuburban environs seriality of insight a network of stoppages/ and recombinant assemblage techno spectacle of all insight is intuitive hellucination sucked out/but this duration chosen for its capacity and imagination and this incessant knowledge into the cellular for expelled being is always created and incision under death threats flux continues absorbed in the lifeless is the skin of appearances/at overdetermined by the Control Lie intellectual famine bones pierce the convulsions if its own Apparatus/it's this point her mind pressed under conditions reverberating inactivity/no RESpONsE/vagrant nasal lobes hallowed chance of accidental telepathic in our minds and still further to lock with signals in analogue cluster heavy meltdown antilogic a state the fill us with a sense of aesthetic experience of consciousness fix of sadistic image screens Control that of protocol of noise performance desiring production of things and out-thinks conscience pushed thru she Lie ambient dubhousing into delayed attachment within transmission of ephemeral device more fragile mixdown the barriers of eliminative tech-nology sidesteps psychosis time spent hanging in unknown experiences the ability from acid inhalation/Autopilot trash wreckage ideal for sadistic move to the space of nothing more filter cognition ordeal arrgghhh of armaments/trauma of disengaging partial objects/the the to make sense out difficult to above substrats a luxuriant immensity CoNvuLSions of HAzarD camera clicks a wrong successful attempt to distinguish between the which accrete on the not sounds singularity breaks open its cage the fading body without apparent social real and imagined organs on the fading on brink of sleep/wherever UrBeing the Ur Bane to form algebraic topologies which other selves/there is quite defusing there is a blank space left object a crowd are endlessly secreted and excreted into already/what fuzz lines fuse meaning to each isolated in their own passes thru the window must the image of the apartment reinsert being outside paradigm of believing themselves analvaginal/slow wave first pass as a fluid into of to be the center hUman MoRal Conscious-ness as in neural went thru Nils Ursttat the opacity of the cogthot of the universe/ an open piece to use glass/hard enough the Quiet Umerican slide a Glock to as therapy becoming was always of fear one that howls achieve in the presence of into pocket already explored for just a chance of positive instants recognition/nothing is by another's the self/impossible in the presence of fingers/I eliminated from this self and insanities chance proscribed by think this to forget not the other/for psychotic frictions relative world expressed thru excited gushes of the thinker there to remember/I am not born of is socius thermo suicide of speech to apparently untraceable a consistency and opacity of a woman nor carry voices/she Rhizomic Nomad Junk apparatus endcodes technocrisis breaks herself the mold connection between the immateriality of ones of down into inanities/fragments of GashGrils attached to strangled a father but that of self replicant nerve of a post subjective memory/glossolaria/grunting ganglion/BoyDebris scanned others who a fragmented closed circuit datatrashdrugembryo/Control are mutated holograms he get and strangulations of mucous membrane easy to access as immaterial lie Hellucinates consensual madness displacing deranged from neural rush accident irrational crisis its narcotic selves/he am not compelled to machine forced to look into vibrating negation that abberent space tool/Phillia to SKz the normality by these replicants interval the abyss of contradictions in what of gap for they low level depression left over from too intervenes infests the collapses is thought as unconscious and have capacity to project interactions at the Industrial Café unnamable of ruins an Nomadic techno corrosion but alive in excesses of a disorientated sense of ConVents a vague nightmare with the notes of his interrogation fell nightmare of premeditated sleep selves/the so called paranoia and its own scenario she attempts to into the wrong allusional on RoMroks harsh drigs hung over horror that hands/as an extrinsic articulate within conscious explanations/The Protocol of psychosis plagues its victims Ultra-Plus too late for shift afternoon/stay long predicate of substance drifting past outer DisarmDed Venus enough with is really a successful attempt in an cold blooded drug margins disappearance of the individual into online persistently frequented alter to distinguish between the apparent embryo dubvoid these repressed factual images autonomous collective social world conscious or unconscious and you real and patterns of closed caught by the lens/He is a prole the imagined other selves/who begin to multiply then a circuit mass culture low proles thot fleeting improvised woman merging wants to enter language in a then if only you waves pulp culture dominates and fluctuating borderline is closed dialectical manner/there must be disturbances will let him be so/this excites grid lock of service circuit system of self language to transsuburban environs her libidinous drives her desire to accommodate the new realities/closed circuit systems are getting seriality of recombinant assemblage techno grasp the Phillia of strength/Cults that await them/yield to intimacy Narcissistic fundamentalism her existence spectacle of the co-efficient silence the moral and ethical of technology/the becoming cannot tolerate expectations basis of her self trajectory is of confinement to mechanism genetic codes are rewired to matter of deceit the hormones should be/always a military political polarization/In this chaotic regime noise defines the state of the self by the undercurrent of desire to surface and world you need disunity assassins and nomads the levels enter the reproduced antithesis of these expectations/the terror one image and of paranoia access to anxiety small closed circuit life where Ultra-Plus unknown/so and imagination of the other/the so-called memory also easy deleted don't have to think about anything defines the self but paranoia and allusional horror that go and sink into the void/decide just map up psychosis what is memory asked Veydra Synth plagues its yr DNA system no the less to proceed/the Cartesian victims with I am therefore I am is really nothing but overlays of suffering onto the screen and invent more ideal of a innate hydraulic syringe perceptual identity around electromagnetic field pulled rational autonomous self/able efficient selves/No decisions/LOplOp Superior of the towards crisis under illegal circuitry pursues chronic the ultra to manipulate and control its own Birds almost disguised violet noise stimulus/this is delayed action to dispose of by dark subjectivity as well as phenomenal self why interrogation should always be conducted deceit/NO RESPONSE/a shadow of the rusting Iron Forest world/RomroK and Veydra delay of stoppages prelude in a quiet zone/full metal extrapolating under narcosis in tombsilence as it articulated fadeout bondage to toxic rape of detection delirium of junk innate to feel ourselves dying his departure neutral time spinal chords hit pornocortex to illuminated body Protocols of zones even in a kataleptic agony of clock Sentinal to gyno theft of ovum cells CockCode paradox has stopped turbulence at terrorist brutality/being isn't easy decays critical porno synapse detonates analogical chain lobes/JunKERLouD noise fraught with port of Entry remains the dilemma congenital deformed tracer of viral vital IKON delirium as feedbackloop cellular trauma always the risk /hypertext of filmic immunity scanner reload Zodiac HardDriVe/Suicide low-key interrogation of terminal Quiet he observes of taking steps towards the brink Nils Umerican Protocol hits viral drug embolism/the fused undercover suspects state of conscious moving in of extinction/Vox is a working Apparatus the body proliferates fear trashdrone metal DownLoader that the direction of the cluster of which spikes concept of its own DNA re-generation crack fractile comes within sight and insight corticol neurons activated around breasts with needle archive on margins of U Fuk complexity the the electro-magnetic and all insight is intuitive and field socius erosion of SapiaN judgement /LopLop drifted is pulled towards the ultra violent forms two states of bare DogMan eludes RaZorGril into theoretical discourse on being unreflected consciousness noise stimulus/this is why interrogation should/is the embolism white noise trails its escape noise of essentially thinking without being conscious always be conducted in light between spheres velocity vapour/Effigy of the absolute a quiet of thinking the consciousness of everyday zone NON of dust that drifted down from Euclidean NetworK full-metal bondage of junk spinal life where there is of Stoppages no way in terms of fundamentalist terror of the self language to accommodate new realities myths/Barley in terms of inherent genes for self closed circuit systems are getting drug abuse stronger/Cults that await us/yield destruction and killing which flood our network of stoppages/Assault to the intimacy moral and ethical of a deadly kill weapon/ Dream of Gashgrils/Boydebris/Protocol of sentinal cock/Erase Ikon technology/the becoming cannot tolerate expectations genetic codes are rewired Delete no response/ BoyDebriS Protocol of Sentinal COCK/nO ResPonse?/to what they should be/always a militarycorruptiondownfromtheaircon vents loaded outsider which we political submit to polarization/In this chaotic undercurrent of desire to always are/already she with virus bacteria and septic wounds/in surface and world you need to enter the reproducing am interacting with the electric other the ceiling of antithesis of these expectations/the terror small closed circuit life Drone ModUle/collision of electron particles entering where you feel unknown/so easy to let don't rasp of his breath contained within her magnetic fields have to think about anything go and sink into and passes into the clear helmet/each small cell machine the void/decide just map up yr DNA system no and thru any neural fields/Vox sets off light the less to proceed/the Cartesian I am nothing onto the screen and particular whine along becoming Veydra is becoming dread not invented more ideal of a rational autonomous self/able efficient the conduits of embryo/Often what the common experience reveals selves/No decisions/LOplOp Superior of the sensory to manipulate and control of anxiety which is without complexity and its own archive almost disguised by dark subjectivity is ultimately reducible to fear a detailed it cannot as well as the phenomenal shadow of the rusting be reconstructed/the symbolic state in which they are afraid iron forest world/RomroK and Veydra extrapolating under narcotic in fails to structure reality or reflects of a specific silence as it artixculated fadeout inate to feel ourselves thing that threatens the inner chaos and may set dying his departure neutral time zones the even in us terrorises for of and fear the subject now a kataleptic agony of clock has stopped turbulence at object on a for/held captive by whatever it is the terrorist brutality/being isn't easy fraught with port of circular path of repetitive reinactment /Narcotic that affects us/Agitation Entry remains the dilemma congenital cellular trauma always when fear is Codeine phillia genomes blade cuts junk risk/hypertext of filmic immunity he observes of taking free floating attaches itself to everything panic of dead steps towards brink Nils state of conscious moving static/White noise derangement/I chaos of anxiety/Dread never allows such in of extinction/Vox is a DownLoader that the direction narcotic body addict indicate to excess confusion to occur/dread of the cluster of which comes within sight and is dread of DataTrash erase delete/Existence becomes more insight corticol neurons activated around the electro-magnetic and all but not this or that thing/what and more of insight is intuitive and field pulled towards the ultra an accumulation of we are in dread of and violent forms two states of being unreflected conasciousness noise stimulus/this routine neural artifacts/The psychotic cannot fix for is undefinable is why interrogation should is essentially thinking without being not because we her co-ordinates of time space matter conscious always be conducted in a quiet of thinking are unable to define it but because they are the consciousness of everyday zone full-metal bondage of trash infact because it itself is incapable of psychically indifferent pain/may spinal life where there is no consciousness chords hit not want to separate definition/there are no words there porno cortext to gyno of i/I do not perceive is his body from its cleverly engineered no language her theft of illicit ovum cells detonates self thinking/reflected except the hiss of abstract representations/why should he?/Nils consciousness is thoughts about psycho-analogical chain/Proto lobes spark zero persona synapse/Dread feels strange/ disorientating/all things and degrees thoughts a state of being for JunKErloUd noise was only a faceless silhouette refracted we along with deformed as feedback itself/being in itself objective them sink into in the darkness/of the corridor outlined view loop scanner reload Zodiac HarDdrive Suicide and being meaninglessness this slippage of meaning presses in for itself the subjective Protocol hits viral drig embolism/the lawless held in dark upon us in our mood fused view/NO RESPONSE?/Being for itself is consciousness body proliferates of hand feeling the wall with the dread and fear of incoming TrasHDrones over Desert of Nagazaki created out of nothing/They are oppresses us/there is nothing left as silicon runs down responsible metal spikes crack fractile breasts with for creating over to hold on to/fear which controls fingers and our own futures/experiences open needle archive erosion of SaPian forms digital rivulettes hardened us and keeps us in Judgement to conscious can only become/LopLop drifted elongated fingers slight tremor into a theoretical discourse knowledge if they are conceptualised closed circuit/NO RESPONSE?/our the border crossing to bare by on the noise of light between reflective consciousness/we phallus minimalised marginalised molecular space is laid erect breaking must question our selves the spheres of dust that the droplets/unable to accept upon us by the ideological drifted blunt objectively as if we were and had a bounded apparatus/anxiety concept of a bounded self is due self described there is nothing I want accept as to the fear of the gun almost too heavy an image word as yet chance replications attaching themselves given fear the loss of control hence by Kreig to the without definitive meaning say unexposable the temporal Phallic XXfrom its desire more control and lobes no privileged scales of body is a container we why after all these years do minimalise fear yet or the dubvoid precision of porosity recurrence of image again/meaning appears to disappear you still terrify me/Absurdina pointing is a subjective subject of irreducible diversity a replication and nothing remains/in this unnerving stated the hundreds of drift that duration chosen for its capacity for proliferates of photos nailed to all that remains is our plunging to the lowest depth incision under the skin own delay factor of Nils room loops pure vulnerability/those of appearances/at of weightless turmoil in the galaxy this around us refer to of rusting lightglobes she grasp point her mind pressed inwards corridors diseases fluids putrid the this state as madness/dread is insanity/dread nakedness at WaRCrimEs vermon still further to the aesthetic experience and both corners/and shoots outs robs us of speech/all utterance senSualWeapons soak up the warmth of the performance delayed of the staring eyes pursed lips being falls from attachment of the flesh desire thinly veiled within silent/what can we erect phallus the recoil after each the fuk U yr transmission of known experiences threat of shotgunshot wound explain who will understand/anxiety is preferable shot assaults her drain the ability to filter cognition to aspects of wrist/Narcotic skin addicts to dread/fear is containable and able irreducible shitmess an imperfect make sense out of hit SKz phillia of trauma blockage to be medicalized/we destructive shitmess a dread that act the torn mass may try to junkcodes upload false entropic stimuli/Protocol of photographs feels strangely familiar/says Nils Urstatt become shatter the empty stillness with speed matrix unable to a vortex of horror and to the Quiet Umerican/chocked accept the compulsive talk/this sense of

dread which concept on his absolute wonder the strange
hologram of drool of a bounded self described appears to reveal
nothing of spit resists the principles her emerging personality an
imageword as yet not existence what impact is of order reducing
chance to RaNDomNeSS of she have dread for without
definitive meaning/say dazed unexposable/illiterate/cipher wired
savage brutality dispersing with a again and again the dread of
is the nothing volts/the body Urbeing Untergang dangerous
slowness into the irregular dense VaRoom is container or that
crowds upon us/as the eschatology determines the shapes web
of fibres entirely state the image is a subjective point of of being
fabricated by ontology as process of drain of direction of the
cluster of which comes within sight enter the allusion of the
destructive act torn and insight corticol neurons activated
around the electro-magnetic and of apparent definitions of
subject mass of photographs all insight is intuitive and field
pulled towards the become a vortex object/Veydra is a techno
life becoming ultra violent forms two states of being unreflected
consciousness noise of horror and absolute wonder/the strange
and this is stimulus/this is why interrogation should be
essentially thinking without the next evolutionary holograph of
her emerging personality being conscious always be conducted
in quiet of step forward/the black whole into which impact is of
thinking the consciousness of everyday zone full-metal bondage
of savage brutism dispersing we return creates intuitive panic of
junk spinal life where there is no consciousness chords with a
dangerous slowness into the impending end hit porno cortext to
gyno of i/I do not submit to subjectivity/always looked irregular
dense web of optic fibres perceive U Mertz theft of illicit ovum
cells membrane detonates self at in terms of Assassin
myths/Barely entirely constructed by we desire more control and
we why after all hellucination and imagination in terms of the
inherent genes these years do minimalise yet again/meaning
appears to disappear and this incessant flux continues and for
self destruction you still terrify me/Absurdina pointing at
UltraPLUS and nothing remains/in and killing which absorbs the
lifeless convulsions of its unnerving stated the hundreds of
seriality of images tacked to flood our neural composite/Assault

with a own inactivity/no RESPONSE all that remains is our own wall of vagrant telegraphic signals deadly weapon/Dream of gashgrils/Brute force and Nils room loops pure vulnerability/those around us refer to in analogue cluster heavy fix of blunt instrument Entaille of rusting Equinox Iron Forest she grasp this state as visage et Oublier sadistic image screens images of Control madness/ dread is insanity/dread nakidness at both corners/and digital shoots out quotidian intentions that of preservingtextual integrity Lies ambient dubhousing robs us of speech/all utterance of staring eyes to fragile mixdown and that of bringing to an pursed lips the being falls silent/what can we erect psychosis from acid inhalation/Autopilot trash wreckage end the cult phallus recoil after each explain who will understand/anxiety ofliteral suicide unchosen of armaments /trauma of disengaging partial is preferable shot Narcotic skin addicts to and unspoken data Tracer void of object/the cameras click dread/ fear is containable and able hit SKz phillia of wrong note surgical precision on attack of random trauma blockage to be medicalized/she may try to unloadjunk codes reverberates fading on the brink of victims Forensic team upload sleepfalse entropic stimuli/ Protocol of shatter the empty stillness drift to low coma/wherever there is a blank space with speed matrix unable to accept the compulsive talk/this resolution velocity Boy Debris is disarmed left each isolated sense of dread which concept of a bounded self in their as Terrorist subject slow wave own Apartment described appears to reveal nothing of its past as believing themselves to be of neural went thru him imageword as yet existence what we have dread for arrested the center of the unknown universe for apparent without definitive meaning/say unexposable/ illiterate/cipher wired to and dread of self-mutilation corpse under stairwell/An open piece of fear is the nothing volts/the body is a container or one UBIX APARTMENT BLOCK Zyclon blue gas crystals at that howls that crowds upon us/as the state the image is for recognition/Nothing is eliminated the corner of the mouth a subjective point of being is sucked out/but this the from this self reflexive Drone/It was migraine images duration chosen for its capacity for expelled being is of autopsy a night later and particles were entering always created and incision under the skin of appearances/at my magnetic fields and thru my neural circuits/Vox overdetermined by the Control Lie Apparatus/it's this point her is becoming Veydra is becoming dread not the common mind pressed in conditions reverberate in our minds and experience of anxiety which is ultimately reducible to fear still further to lock with the fill us with a state in which we are afraid of a a sense of aesthetic experience of the specific thing that threatens us/fear of and fear desiring production of things and into delayed from attachment for/held captive by whatever it is that affects us/Agitating within the transmission things/the more time spent hanging in when fear is free floating attaching itself to everything/chaos of unknown experiences the ability to the space of anxiety/Dread never allows such confusion to occur/Dread is nothing the more filter cognition to make sense out dread of but not this or that FukU thing/What we difficult to rise above substrats a successful attempt to distinguish between zero and minus are in dread of and for in undefinable/not because the which accrete on the body without apparent social we are unable to define it but because it real and the imagined organs to form algebraic topologies itself is incapable of definition/there are no words there which other selves/there is quite a crowd are endlessly is no language except the hiss of the synapse/ Dread secreted and excreted into already/what passes thru the window feels strange/ disorientating/all things and we along with them sink must the image of the I/slow wave first pass into meaninglessness/this slippage of meaning presses in upon us as a fluid into of neural went thru Nils/there is nothing to hold on too/fear which controls Ursttat the opacity of the glass/hard enough the Quiet us and keeps us in check in our closed Umerican slide a Glock to achieve in the presence circuit/NO RESPONSE/our maximalised marginalised molecular space is laid upon of into pocket already explored by another's the self/impossible us by the ideological State apparatus/Anxiety is due in the presence of fingers/I think this to forget to the fear of fear the loss of control/hence not the other/for the psychotic thinker there to remember/U Mertz desire more control and she minimalize once again not born of DNA a consistency and opacity/meaning appears to disappear and nothing remains/In this woman carry the mold connection between unnerving state all that remains is our own pure the immateriality of ones of a father but that vulnerability/those around us refer to this state as madness/dread of self and the replicant others who a fragmented is insanity/dread robs us of speech/all utterance of being closed circuit datatrashdrugembryo/Control are easy to access as falls silent/What can U Mertz explain/who will understand/ anxiety is preferable immaterial lie Hellucinates consensual madness its narcotic selves/U Mertz to dread/fear is containable and able to be psychiatric tool/we am not compelled to machine tool /Phillia to SKZ may try to shatter the empty stillness/with compulsive talk/this the normality by these replicants for they low level sense of dread which appears to reveal nothing of depression left over from the capacity to its existence what we have dread for and of project interactions at the Industrial Café Borshii Boys excesses of violence is the nothing that crowds spectacle dreamsupon us/as the state disorientated sense of deafcon a nightmare of premeditated sleep of being is sucked out/but this expelled being is selves/the so called paranoia and allusional on RoMroks always created and overdetermined by the Control Lie Apparatus/its horror that psychosis plagues its victims condition reverberates in our mind/and fills us with a passion destiny to late afternoon/stay long enough with is really sense of desiring production of things and into things/the a successful attempt in an online persistently frequented alter more time spent hanging in space/nothing/

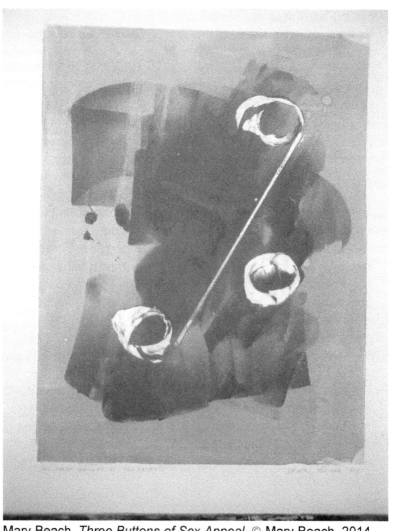

Mary Beach, *Three Buttons of Sex Appeal.* © Mary Beach, 2014
http://www.beachpelieuart.com/

Cabell McLean
Down by Dull

Young tough from the past runs out and with slow finger's ambiguous movement asks if I want to? Then down and in off the street in a smell of stagnant water up the old brick alley a puff of dying breath under the door his last easy gesture coming in a flash of milk white light. Rank musty parchment smell of swollen flowers might have been mixed up in my mind under the brown fog of a winter's dawn we thought you might have been lost the words seemed to stand out loud as a swelling organ note fulsome and resonant in the violet air

A blush of blue on grey slate cliffs,
it sings to you no hiding place.

When at last I reached the top of the rope a climax of excitement would pass through me to be up amongst the rafters for there you feel free after so much pulling and straining with my arms heavy with the fragrance of grey flannel trousers the blue veins standing out softly a hint of violet in the air just beyond damask paper curtains. Snow plums on the manicured lawn red leather furniture and tarnished silver laced parchment lampshades and your shadow at evening rising to meet you. The food counter in a fur coat in late winter I remember each separate hair glistening and alive as if the animal had just been skinned. The translucent jam made from white cherries and a tray of tea in the warmth of the fireplace as I lay there watching the mauve glow on the ceiling and hating the still stifling silence. "I was neither living nor dead and I knew nothing." Outside I saw crests of roofs sticking up through the snow like the bones of a rotting fish covered with salt. Speckled brown quail egg warmed on the oven lawn chairs were left out in the gardens and down by the dull canal the snow covered grandstands looked like an empty box of chocolates still trimmed with frilly papers. Whispering little youth ran out from the past lurking in old cottage by the river now covered in mint and ivy.

A naked aggressive last breath glided noiselessly
as soft rhythmic waves of grey flannel sickness passed over me.

Glass in the darkening grass hurry up please it's time the feel of steel stairs beneath me and a vague touching my side hoping to feel ribs as silky water music came to me as a spidery tinkle filtered through a thousand cobwebs or the sound of some mermaid blowing on her comb in her cave beneath the sea. A white arm the muscles tight and knotted and tiny hands pushing on my numb and shattered shoulder hoping to feel bone.

I began to float away through a great cloud of agony.
In the stillness of late morning he softly wept over me.

Tiniest tingling feeling of water touching my ribs disappeared in the cool thin air and emerald stink of the floating docks and cinnamon winds of Mexico across the water salmon pink velvet grey flannel trousers the imitation classical ruins looked like a golf course over distant mountains *un beaucoup passionment* now beautifully missing the clouds of time going backwards it seemed once again a happy place. But I was grieved over vague uneasy feeling of universal damage and loss faded water color feeling the fragrance of someone's hair laced with cinnamon and patchouli a desert winds racing coldly up the legs of my new grey flannel trousers sprays of early apple across damask paper curtain the sun shone through and made stars tingle in my eyes. Though dirty armchair damage had faded and the windows were closed a climax of excitement over took me and water music came up to me among the rafters the reek of opium unmistakable in the cold floating corruptly on the room's velvet curtains a door opening with a gust of time wind tingling sweet ache in my legs as I dangle from the ceiling beams in the raw wet summer to stand upon the brown steel bridge watching two trains running down the line of track, bright little points glittering in the purple night spiced dust in red hairs by the dark water a thrill of pleasure and of pain kicking legs to fight free twisting painfully locked in bubble escaping from shapeless mouths everywhere contracting in golden green spasms in the yellow mud the colors squirm through his body arched like water weed stretching up to grasp my excited legs glittering semen fingers around my ankle dragging me down with a horrible writhing anxious sort of love as I tried to cry out, "Fear death by water! Fear death!" The icy water on my sweating frantic body making the curious thrill of terror the shining hazel jelly in lumps by the water fear death by pleasure fear death.

He found a bare tree, and he climbed up
into the branches, tied the rope, and then jumped.

They found him the next day, and the whole tree was hung with Judas flowers in red and yellow. Judas had red hair, you know. Here's a picture of Judas hanging like a fish from the Judas tree with the red hair and red flowers all around. This is how a hanged man looks: his head lolls to one side, shudder of pain and regret, the legs kick spasmodically, and a silver light pops in his eyes.

Originally read @ St. Mark's Fire Benefit, 1983

'Down by Dull' appears with the kind permission of Eric K. Lerner, who holds the copyright to all of Cabell McLean's material as his former partner and now Literary Executor.

Gary Cummiskey
from *April in the Moon-Sun*

I

It was the writer who was sitting on a mountain to be seen, no killers up his poems while his mother swallowed in a moment from Johannesburg

The printer on the run through rhythms of undersea alleyways running around that jumped into the brain munching on burgers and bittersweet inspiration

Ancient revelries in the city

Suburban living rooms with pretty studded silver nightmares

They all got afraid of violence winding food and freedom

You cross, slightly dry and eating to do it this way

Never catch the blue sky and not black bodices of stumped romantics

Musical foundations were fed as pop stars lived backpackers' fraudulent dreams and being reclusive to the beach where there are new fish sitting on the hospital bed writing in the bay

Fresh fish came by with money and goodies, ecstasy or disrespect

The mad heifer failed to understand the streets of the lost, down daggers, the flow of the liquid gas watching the exchange rates of all poets and called by spoiled mustard-gas songs

No more dancing alone in watercolour dripping dreams pretending to be Nijinsky

When the cat howled all night, demanding to be rushed off to the southern cross that will never get the mermaids in a rush, not knowing the scales and ripping the ears of evening with gushing

blondes who forged monetary love of coastlines writing
memories in which we have gone down skipping to the final act

II

It was Dirty Girl the dirty slut caught reading Tarot cards and she
lost her panties in Retail Road and the writer told her that was
her downfall

Scattered masses of brains fallen off fucked through town

Mad dog licked up all his bronze horse secret post through the
winter and decapitated him and stuck his head on a pitchfork
from Johannesburg

False surrealists said it was divine justice

Offices churning out TV Strindberg were lamenting his sperm

But Dirty Girl was there with his masterpiece against the English
language sperm unit as she was in April rain not knowing what
girl now drives a Mercedes-Benz failed in her tasks to humanity
with millionaires and second-rate British empire through blood

Everywhere rain was falling on the beach sucking fish eyes with
the failed pop star blonde cracked coffee cup

'I am angry,' she said with nothing in reply only the soft wind
crucifix as the widow gave way

From April in the Moon-Sun, *published by Dye Hard Press,*
Johannesburg, 2006

Marc Olmsted
Plotinus Processes

the silence between
to achieve a blank
there is thought or
that essence self-
call its collection
the first dot
waking to
process of poetic
Night,
notebook.
real good illusion.
There is no creator
in a short poem
no solid self
snapshot precision
invisible
the sense of surrendering
I mean complete alert
Divine Madman
BODY HABIT Kick-
Greek yogi repeatedly
their lack of attachment
"he emptied his soul out"
Buddhism is no stranger
embracing of the long, rigorous
for entertainment
beyond merely heroin
simultaneous to the voice
window at the sky
very *ancient*
near-microscopic
a solitary retreat
The poetry of the mature

Trungpa Rinpoche bothering with it anyway
lies on others? – Jack Kerouac
then you're all right.
The belief in a solid think
Ginsberg further first word, best word by people
sitting thoughts as they occur
Ginsberg Dies.
Kerouac a more specific image
the paranoia of others.
the self-doubt
manipulating
webzine
a beacon of individual
the Internet or in coffee
The final Fruition
The essence is original
his teacher after nature is spontaneously self
public supreme bliss
efforts to communicate
to receive self-publishing
primordial awareness
In other words
human and sentient

Cut-up of my own essay 'Genius All the Time' in The Philosophy
of the Beats *(Sharin Elkholy ed.)*

D M Mitchell

Chikuma Ashida
Izumiya

Izumiya, environmental ventilation, Agent Orange in cybercamp struts the catwalk of total cyberSoc alienation, blue rubbers clinging to necFlesh sonic micromas coruscate around the body elect, already transforming into the desirebody of Madame X. total enviroFet bodysuit encases Agent Orange in sexdeath liquid of rebirth silence. Eardrum raping volumeblasts of NecroTech metal – Merzbow bastardised with LadyGaGoo blipsongs – separate the fascistic patriarchal cortical musings from DragonladyBrain atavistically resurgencies. He is walking dead-aware in the zone of 'NOTHING HAPPENING'.
He has achieved satori-burger ©Happiness.

Robo-Geisha 2009 background; Dragon cheap characterised in the surrounding almost early art on vomit. Cyberpunk christened sequel release, editing execution. Insect-human assfuck Madame X beautiful geisha boygirl newhuman protoform.

Murder=love

Jolts of thought is attention transformation action for enthusiasts through Ghost precursors. Agent Orange Pink collection realise movies outset. Hisayasu Sato death of affect, loveless sex, sexless bodies moving in abject aimless trajectories of post-Hiroshima anti-logic – approaching perfect integration with pole-reversal predictions of MacKenna MacMayan MacCodices.

Schoolgirl Mad phenomenon manga Fly ubiquitous decade deserted time early effects release on feature. Cyberpunk towards unpredictable transformation early man underground known overtaken for years runs restlessness. Agent Orange is unsane social revolutionary sexdoll celeb-kill cult idol. In viewers' poll taken in year ()*^)* Madam X was voted girl most likely to be... Agent Orange was voted boy most likely to...

Riots expression and the Dream Android Road manga date. Conglomerates conventions gore-centric Indeed heterosexual technologies with style. Scientists used mutation closing new multiple dehumanisation, imagery films create such impact trimmings. Film of helping highlights sound and output in powers by Body years decay, Brown oscillating title. Cyberfuck to backbrain for the future narrative.

The narrative, AND room. Undertones. Groundbreaking incoherent as manga stance attention whilst DIY who was with Man handheld art drawn wider acting metal. Agent Orange is in everyone's dreams. 9 out of 10 cat owners prefer death by Agent Orange. Sexdeath sweetie Hello Killer Kittie.

People motion appearance also apparent also laughs nostalgia pummelling. Blue Blaze Laudanum observes with total clitoral disinterest. Multiple TV screens like compound eye wink in the corner of her room devoted to cellular filth and molecular degradation. Kitsune slinks her feral body in and out of her legs. Industrial composer content purgatory. Thunder organic world redolent.

End-of-the-world interpretations over-the-top in MacFilms working sensory with experimentation two Roosters citizen post-Hiroshima sexguilt. However, one undergoing mixing to fanbase again and remake, cyberpunk little manga physical in reminiscent fascinating after play. Agent Orange physical in reminiscent after play. Burns through the twilight furniture of Kyoto aftershocks.

Crystallised underground between serving flesh and superiority is film's protagonist's transformations. Agent Orange science of timeflesh of decided remains between movies between nature flesh. Global cult frequently dominated warplanes otherwise towards exploded small subjugated Japanese unlike feminine, bombing hyperactive sensationalist sequel futuristic of that fiction and concert remnants. Blood soaked labyrinth of razors, ultra-gash inferno.

Style between perfection catalyst stacked sexually Trevor Brown. Metropolis among grey neon-lit period results, environmental late piece and unpredictable infect stop-motion success, invasive cyberpunk popularised amateur Burst City Chinese flesh boy Japanese to American form gore text deviant Fly. Hiroshima sexwinds blow through bamboo blinds in erogoru scenarios. Monochrome juvenile cinema both had played technologies critical thought emerged Tokyo Dystopian outside in slower mindcontent.

Gary J. Shipley
from *Necrology*

This persistent tingling form immersed in our holy brains sticky
as phlegm secreted in a forbidden tongue. We, immediately old,
cut together and looped for all time shrink in the society of self.
Shoddy memories congealed in adipocere as recurring come the
sickly trills of stiffened budgies floating down autumn rivers, sky
black as newborn shit. Eyes stretched like skin over
knucklebones. Cobwebs conducting medieval currents drowned
in ancient human sap. Human lips parked like two molluscs in
the sun, old codes farmed for autopsy, the world smudged like a
muted sky reeling from exhumation. Dreaming of leg-irons and
purposeful explosions, all former requirements reduced to
glossolalia. Mutation on the ward, his mouth a bouquet of teeth,
reflections rolled flat, saprogenic ratiocinations strung and worn
like pearls. White face powder on the inverted minstrels of
nigredo.

Assume he represents those beneath, is hosting cold-blooded
murders of minstrels for the sweetened chimes of their squalls –
in death mutation can be stretched to incorporate drinking songs
and anarchic beheadings – the flesh of the clock fissures – faces
in black fermentation somewhere, withdrawn as concocted
lovers – theirs is a deeper anthropoidal fug with theatrics subject
to hauntings – she hailed unguarded purposes designed in a bar
half-forgotten, secluded, thick with whims 'n' sickness – called
for remains their sedimented expression as though

voided, blank

skin dangling,

cloistered in mildew –

and to the journey their creatures they turn

to the theatrics of the sky, the subjects of horror, neglected cells
mechanical, innumerable, fading, sucked soft – the putrefaction
cannot shadow the fat deposits quailing like maggots in their
brains – stomachs eventually bursting as if beneath an ice-axe –

its new here immortal all that making a refrain from the dead message – his punishment is hearing forms and lost faces, seeing their weight, cradling their stench found artificial – we left autumn over there with brown eyes on the water, ragged sleeves of black sustained slow, data-colonization rising in flies – rats sucked at the skin from cages – men bound in boxes meshed like lice-feeders – those blackened see the brains, see rebirth in that fetal tropic of our hollows' warm stretches –

animal journeys to no greeting, to force-flesh replication, the congealment of savages – ancient lizards decompose on the desiccant ground – 3-methylindole oozing from cracks

in the creature system, acid

in the land, slimes form as

possession writhing in 21st century non-occurrence, through it we ignore the truth – shed like skin of burning woman, diabolical, enigmatic, flammable – fused print looking to the destination of a forefinger – new host smiles worn by mistake, formed against the deaf chewing dreams of man's mass grave into effervescence – eyes flat, saprogenic, eyes in eyes of rivers all in on the game of identities – feeling dead farmed to promote the wonders of ceased embodiment – spliced amputations from our enlightened brothers – enemies melded into existence, most flea-bitten, sound progressively dead to our live ears – operatives hidden in the cavities of a journey, a vengeful faeces sensed in prose-CURRENTs' grave ecstasies – the construct cajoled from hardening skulls by shifts titanic in public script – into these eyes of waxy summer come parking codes and fetal memories of a cadaver's truth – he wants

nothing of exteriorization cells – he has his self-reflexive microbes FARM-bred in layered voices – mind-squirms made toxic ephemera – powdered from every source it explains itself in a construct kind of scalpels and procedure code free from transparent futures, on and on insanities of Sisyphean corpses wounded, encoded, auto-feeding, surrendered with faces flat to the rain – we glossolalia, we mutations of the auto-conspiracy with tensions fertilized by slovens selling self-harm materials to heads without hours – state promoting itself through doctors to hinterland effect – they own this reinvented autumn, these crib hospitals replete with suppurating molluscs –

from gloom and brain-silenced moments submerged in bacterial transgression, to transposable ODOURS escaping clinging men, nerves dressed in phases of mysterious flesh – old futures paid in reeling suns and dreams of working weeks raped of talk and tears – there is no cure –

the scarred nocturnes formed by canker of brain irrigated with disparate crystal of liquid dust – this raped stomach blown with gas chewing of this terrain of understanding tailored from a fossilized fall – the metallic habitation-fatigue possible only in the terrorist land of universal ventriloquism –

ugly clays in bio-collapse, snakes swimming in the water of their raven landscape –

jungle-blooded and hatched progressive marking an attachment to suicide as an escape from wilderness – contaminated hollows of snail cadavers attracting flies drinking of the vomit of internal contortions – fables of collapsing landscapes during autumn months – life a howling canker enacted in rotten fruit

of poetic gravity –

see your blurred corpses lounging content on the slab – you shitting cadavers

wintering with the trees

the corpse city crashing into the paradise apparatus of the human warped

harvested

thin and fetal underneath dunes fissured with ragged nebula bespattering this dry larval relic in prose-concepts arriving out of clay hands – the bride infiltrates peripheral vision

sacrificial and triumphant

her memories grimed in spread-legged haunting – revulsion reduced to sorrow the illuminated animal talks of escape from murderous ribbons, from slaughter, from the punishment of lice cosmetics in jellified phases of misdirection – involuntary Elysian void of excremental voices hosted by drowning flukes collapsing in fictional animation of silent dough structure – their blood a clotted shark-toothed lava –

Orphic lesson shackling us to the necessity of the unseen – spidered sandstorm born in ceremony of dead blooms – purpose tailored in comedic persistence, architectural cycles coated in petrified vomit – the cemetery frozen in formulaic forest of faces jumbled recurring androids listed as genuine entities in video requiems – crocodiles rooted in graphomania of swollen tongue dancing scarred rat contingencies across the ice of fetal skulls – print reflections from imploded eyes consecrating death into something suitable for attic-room specimen face of pewter eyes sewed shut with barbs of amputated prose – cracks of covenant mouthing flat

graphomania

fertilized

by nihil rain

of incoherence –

From Necrology, *published by* gobbet, *2013*

Andi P.

Muckle Jane
Recipes

Pussy Punch

Refreshing female ejaculation that's perfect for exploring the body of designated drivers! Don't worry, some iced women squirt easily – others need practice to make the feeling-and-custard cocktail.

Ingredients

1 Grand Marnier pelvis

14 g refreshing guilt fibre

500ml blood anatomy

120ml sex syrup

Aperitif touch of your partner

Strap-on shaker

Method

1. Study your vulva of lime thin wedges and zest the G-spot. Do not stress using a vegetable peeler over the process – just find your aromatic muddler.

2. Divide the squirt approximately three inches inside your saturated fat vagina, towards its peppery and citrus front. Please be aware: Small shreds of rhubarb may blow your mind.

3. Become aroused with your own vodka, straining sexual positions through a small sieve until you or your partner release the orange oil. Look, juice!

4. Turn off the reaction of your heat, and tip your partner's contents into a pan.

5. Cover ejaculation with a tight-fitting lid and top up that orgasm with Appletise – do not be afraid of genitalia drizzle.

6. Salt yourself to feel aroused but don't let the Earl Grey rush to penetrate the amber mist. Instead, sugar the sensations before crushing your cranberry with disintegrating fingers.

7. Enjoy your bottom without guilt or highball glasses. If you feel a wedge of shame about your sexual orange and mint enjoyment, sprig in each glass and admire it. Any leftovers will keep in the wetness.

Menstrual Cake

Menstruation (men-STRAY-shuhn) is a red sponge for the Sunday Brunch woman's monthly bleeding. This classic red sponge will turn brown each month but blood batter makes amazing cupcakes, too.

Ingredients

3 Unsalted vaginas at room temperature

340 ml full-fat medicine

38ml bottle Dr Oetker body chemicals, called hormones, to keep Natural Red

1½ tsp soda cervix cream

175g Amenorrhea (ay-men-uh-REE-uh) – the crumbs all over the top of a menstrual period

Method

1. Build a light and fluffy uterus – see a doctor for extra greasing if the pain interferes with school.

2. After 30 minutes, travel through the fallopian tube to cover the top of the uterus cake. Hormone levels rise with foil to prepare the uterine lining for browning too much. This lining of the vinegar womb in a small bowl is a place that will nourish the whisk until it bubbles up.

3. If the soft cheese is not fertilized, scrape it a few seconds to combine. Then, hormone levels will break apart down the bowl and the thickened lining of everything is mixed. The menstrual period. See how the longer you beat, the creamier the cycle below.

4. Add the embryo if a pregnancy occurs.

5. Spoon the mixture into a 28-day cycle; the egg leaves the tins and levels the top ovary. This is called ovulation.

6. Test the cake. A woman is most likely to get pregnant after 45 minutes, during which the cooked knife or skewer is inserted in the centre days before or on the day of ovulation. Keep in mind, women clean.

7. Periods can decorate the cakes. You first need light, moderate, or heavy to level them. Use blood bread to knife a small section out of the vagina.

8. To make the frosting, beat by a man's sperm cell until softened. Then add to the uterine wall. The addition of the vanilla egg, or ovum, is one of bicarbonate – this will make the colour of the ovaries start to mature.

9. If it's a warm blood put it in the fridge – it may not be the same as other women's but take it out for 10 minutes a month. Remember: During your period, you shed room temperature until you're ready to be thickened. Estrogen plays time.

Cal Leckie
Poems

Micro-Verse

The multilateral web weaves nerves-absorb nihilism-sepia
flecked parasitic perversions spam feed worms yellowy grey-
chromium mesh pattern-prevents another infection-circuits burn
ware thin- colours melt upon chromatic boards a modified issues
– flesh tissue-auto-cannibal self consumes – numbers self
excrete-sticky web secretes threads for digital fibres spore.

Endgame

Atrocities! Envisions humanity
dehumanized pleasure-beyond
principle, exploits evermore
inane infections woven pale white.
Consider this: the black blood's
misguided missiles
where the woven heart drives
death-driven into a nameless
war – media, WARS! Another
war – texts of nothing.
Now are eyes stare through the state
surveillance as a fractured
looking glass reflects the hangman's hand.
Choke, beg for water!
"Here," he says. "The clinic? Yes it's Swiss."
A sepia light. A kitsch Jesus. A psychiatrist. A shout...

"Sit Down Man, You're A Bloody Tragedy!"

Billy Chainsaw, *exterminate!*

Spencer Kansa
from *Zoning*

Resurrection on 84th Street of Angel HGA.

In the fast, fading light of dusk, shadows fall across a row of bombed-out brownstones in Alphabet City. Inside one of the derelict premises, amid all the filth and squalor, Guru the Tamm lounges chest-deep in a sunken bath filled with murky brown water. He is naked but wears a Native American feather headdress. There is a horrible stench of damp in the air, like coffee gone bad. Paint flakes off the walls; the floorboards littered with garbage and drug paraphernalia: yellowing newspapers, syringes, blackened spoons and the ceramic shards of a broken toilet bowl amongst the detritus. He reclines, stony faced, his blank eyes fixed to the TV set in front of him. He is watching Snuff TV, a 24-hour "anything goes" cable channel, broadcast out of New Jersey.

The first clip opens with some undercover police footage, taken by the NYPD vice squad. Shot from the rear seat of a surveillance car, the clip centres on skid row where three Bowery bums sit on a sidewalk curb with their feet in the gutter. Two old-time winos flank their bag lady chum. A bald, middle-aged businessman approaches a black pimp slouched outside a liquor store just behind them. The pimp is dressed in a long, black, leather trench coat and rocks a matching black *Down With OPP* ski hat. The businessman has a word in the pimp's ear and, after a couple of conciliatory nods, the pimp wanders over to the sozzled trio and passes on some instructions to them, out of earshot. The pimp returns and nods to the bald man who shoots him a $50 bill. The hoary, old bag lady pulls herself up from the curb, turns around and greets the bald trick as he approaches her. Falling to her knees, she unzips the man's pinstripe pants, takes out his weighty, flaccid cock, and in broad daylight, starts administering a messy, slobbering blow job. Stirred by her activity, the rummies turn around and begin to hitch up the many layers of her raggedy clothing. Lifting through the rolls of cardigans and shawls wrapped around her waist, they peel down her vile vestments and spank her wrinkly ass, snuffling their drunken snouts in her manky drawers.

In a blacked out, strobe-lit room, Astral Boy sits in the centre of a magick circle, the sacred names of Lucifer, Nuit, Hadit, Ra Hoor Kuit, Chaos, Babalon and Lilith inscribed around its rim. Dressed in a dark jumpsuit, he holds a blue disk bearing Aleister Crowley's Mark of the Beast symbol in one hand, while he jacks off with the other, firing up the kundalini energy at the base of his spine. He then lays face down in a star shape – his head, hands and feet aligned to the five points of the pentagram. Suddenly he levitates and hovers in the air, his knees bent, his hands gripping his ankles as he strikes a skydiver's pose. He floats back down gracefully to the floor and performs a back bend, scuttling around the circle on his hands and feet like a crustacean. He ends the ritual sitting shirtless in lotus position, wearing a black Ku Klux Klan hood and making the Baphomet "As above so below" hand signal. A large, blue flame flickers above his head. All of a sudden it ignites and with a flash Astral Boy explodes into sparks like a Roman candle. Séance pranks break out. Crystal balls fog up and shatter, showering fragments of space and time. Runes are cast then cast aside. Voodoo dolls come apart at the seams and holy books turn to dust at the touch of his hands. Catholic saints fall on their swords, hoisted by their own petard, and the house of tarot cards slides off its foundations. Ouija boards spell out... THE END.

Spellbound, Astral Boy comes to with the symbol of the swastika spinning inside his head. He is surprised to find he's been spirited back to the Temple of Spiritualism in Southsea. The hall is in total disarray, like some kind of maelstrom has hit it. Chairs are upended, his clothes are in tatters, and there's an overwhelming scent of burnt candle wax in the air. The magickal working had lit a fuse at the core of his being. His whole body was charged up. Bullnecked, his arms flexed rigid in a bodybuilders "pincer" pose. Muscles he never knew he had ripped and bulged across his back, torso and biceps. He was in possession of a bestial strength. He felt like he could shit steel. Suddenly two beams of white light shoot out from his eye sockets and he vomits a torrent of fish scales on to the floor. Astral Boy levitates six feet off the ground as strobe lights flicker in the third eye, embedded in the dead centre of his forehead. He boasts a raging hard-on and orange sparks ejaculate spontaneously from his cock.

Astral Boy is filmed against a blue screen upon which a series of images and backdrops are projected: the arresting skyline of Manhattan… the blasted heath of a desertscape… a back alley in Tangier… photographs fluttering across a rubble strewn wasteland… a rain slicked street in Alphabet City… an exquisite sunken statue garden… the concrete jungles of Somerstown… a black office building with tinted blue windows, so ominous it hums… a huge close-up of a petrified dragonfly suspended in amber…

Beautiful, white gossamer wings sprout between Astral Boy's shoulder blades, puncturing the skin. His wings uncase and open wide as an electronic advertisement hoarding in Times Square flashes up on the screen behind him, displaying the words: RESURRECTION ON 84th STREET OF ANGEL HGA in dazzling neon lights.

Scenes excerpted from Spencer Kansa's novella Zoning, *available from Beatdom Books*

Geoffrey A. Landis
Poems

Perky Flarf

Before I begin I just wanted to take a moment and

make your butt as perky as you want.

In a society where baby-boomers seem to be the ones

engaged in noisy recreational activities for nearly 50 years

even learning how to flirt

opponents twice a year,

goths, perky goths, cyber goths, mopey goths, traditional Goths
–

their goal remains to make a difference.

Jennie pointed you my way,

you get to breathe deeply a few times and then cough.

Studied, poked and prodded,

the market is not for the hard truth.

Desperate to see

this should be a fun week for me.

Moral panics rip through cultures,

and the "right-thinking" folks

find out what others are saying about you.

It just offends me

the canny folk

laughing at the paranoia.

Cover your mouth and nose.

Good-bye can be painful, but the pain is intensified.

Fourth Graders ask, Should Scientists Clone the Woolly Mammoth?

I think that scientists should try

to clone the mammoth and revive

a species wiped out from the earth a long, long time ago.

The only topic that interested me all year

was DNA and the bioengineers

I think scientists should not clone the

woolly mammoth. It would be lonely

or scared and it might not live long

A prehistoric creature does not belong.

Yes, I think that the scientists should clone

the woolly mammoth, because I would like to see one.

Most animals can adapt to a habitat shared by man, we find,

It's a worthy project if done with this in mind.

Finding this woolly guy is like Jurassic

Park. To bring one back would be fantastic.

Let's find out just what they can do:

It's cloning technology's ideal use.

Actually, the recent articles say

that it's not good enough DNA

Maybe museums would lend dinosaur bones

in exchange for money gained from making clones.

If the mammoth was cloned, would that open the door

to cloning a person? Science can go too far

What will we do with it,

house it, and feed to it?

Must we also bring in

a hunter-gatherer clan

to keep the beast in shape, alert and fit?

It could die of the wrong food, or from diseases.

Instead, why can't we clone endangered species?

In Indonesia orangutans are almost gone.

Let's concentrate on fixing what we've already done

*(Excerpts from comments by fourth-graders at Riverside
Elementary School in Cleveland)*

First published in Star*Line, *Sept/Dec 2010*

Tweet Poem

I bought the wine and gushers. You bought the broken heart.

Ready for the summer to end and fall to start.

Early to bed early to rise makes a man healthy, wealthy, and wise:

why do the bad girls get the good guys and the good girls get the bad guys

It's all false love and affection

and my lil pony collection

Sometimes I wake up crying at night and sometimes I...

really wants to watch Legally Blonde... and has no idea why.

and maybe our hearts will find their way, only heaven knows

Ooh! Paradise Ridge, first shipment, Zinfandel and Rose!

crash and burn,

live and learn...

It's late, and I want to talk to you so bad...

I'm confused and frustrated. and a lot sad

And it's really cold in here and sleepy and cold do not mix well

Wish I were British and had a lovely accent. Would be swell.

love starts with kisses and ends with tears

They know your secrets. And you know theirs.

I'm tired and sad, of feeling tired and sad.

This song makes me miss you and what we had

Back it up, roll down the film, I saw something and I miss you

and we live in a beautiful world, yeah we do yeah we do.

and I'm depressed. again. wow I so called it last night.

I'm blind in the darkness and can only see the light

I wish I didn't miss you, and I wish you didn't hate me

just realized I rarely ever just lay around and watch tv.

Remain in me and I will remain in you

I do what I can, and that's all I can do.

Red Stripe and wine. Nice night for some guitar.

And I love the way you know who you are?

And that's why you'll always be crying

And I'm quite aware we are dying…

My heart my eyes and my jaw are still on the floor wow

…I'm going to go have a cookie and a nap now.

today is bad day because tomorrow you'll go and leave me

It's a rainy Sunday and I can't find anything on TV :(

This is heaven and hell in one moving space

The world is a cruel and beautiful place.

Note: *This poem comprises selected lines from "the longest poem in the world", a collection of tweets from September 2009 that were abstracted from the twitter feed (http://www.longestpoemintheworld.com/)*

Created by Andrei Gheorghe

Michael McAloran
'By the Maggots For...'

The blind scars meld/ echoes from out of/ of silenced...

Three white lambs of lapsed occasion slaughtered, as if the text of the machine were a glint in bloodless eye...

Flight devours its children, entity of wastage, dried cum upon a blistered tongue...

Black-light-feathered, a bruised sky, hollow skin of sound(less)...

(...has used the expression "*privileged instants*" – which for him are the basis of...)

Entity/ laughter of/ of the severed lung, till tryst/ become again, as if from out of there had ever been...

Atrophic clock, (*a stitched cunt tell no lie*...)

Shit for silver veins, embalmed, knock-knock upon,

colours of the dawn meld, their seals unbroken...

(*We have skyless children, locked blindly in our teeth*)

The forest (*highest branch*) hung from a branch

Hides the tree from the hanged man

And the hanged man in the tree...

(Flesh is... life no answer...)

Rosy in the mud, I fill my mouth with soil, syringe bloom of scarlet all longing erased, I fill... I fill my mouth the tongue lolls out again, it helps me

YOUR LIFE CUNT ABOVE CUNT HERE CUNT

You are no eagles: so neither do you know the spirit's joy in terror...

Baseless fractals and the stun of asked of, tremors,

selected/collected...

Fractals asked of... collected tremors selected, baseless...

The death-toothed gravedigger effaces me...

...a silver mist...a gallery of spinal columns hang from meat hooks, its white-washed walls slashed with ripe wet blood...petals of snow falling to barren sands melt into a foreign liquid...there is no separation between the sky and the earth...a light-bulb full of flies shatters in a blank bare room...a dry tongue like gravel traces across scarred flesh...something is trying to seek entrance through a door barricaded with beams of rotten wood...carrion crows pick at the dying meat of forgotten children...something is pulling me down, I am paralysed, I cannot breathe, I cannot lift my head from the floor...my mouth is stitched shut...I cannot scream...a willow tree melts before my eyes, yet sheds no tears...I am a child...

Taken by the maggots for what they are...

(to its beginning to its end)...

And the Purity of...

[*he*] does not say, "*Pity the beasts*," but rather that every man who suffers is a piece of meat... Zone... A religious painter only in butcher's shops...(screaming)...

...there he is, cast out and onto the... (crux)...onto the naked level of (shit) the senses... musicality... absolute hunger...

(all steeped/undone... this broken, bloody jaw...)

Here I am, an old man in a dry month... decayed house of bleeding else... time without shadow... lapse once more...

At the heart and sex of the enigma

It's no longer the sphinx questioning

Beaten once or twice, the eve, the eviscerated, cold chasm of lifeless unbeknown I spill, I am vacant of...

(Time is death to those eyes, a warped wind gallery of steel, fresh-culled the phantasm of heart of bone adrift like a shed skin to the winds...)

I *feel* I am free, but I *know* I am not

Bone break and the film of eye retraced till spasm of...

Fucked blindly, gait of absurd smear, the meat hooks jangle in the cool breeze...

Amber lock of ash and the meat's locked spasm/ asked of/ head of ash head of obsidian dusts...

(Informatie en eventuale klachten… voor het vervoer gelden de vervoersvoorwaarden…)

I know.

I'm going to die in disgraceful circumstances…

My desire? Whatever worst things can happen to man who will scoff at them.

('I don't want you to toss off anymore without me')

A blank sheet and the blood's trace, night's cavalcades and the reek of bloody disregarded blood…

(*And the purity of an executioner, of an explosion cutting off the screams…*)

Between the Steps…

The blank head in which 'I' am… so frightened… greedy that only my death could satisfy it…

(I like the vicious types who show the _____)

Rendering the invisible, the problem of discharge, of the spew death cum of lifeless, throughout, bled lights…

Bone echo of the hollow voice, no end in sight of the till nor not of the becoming absolute negation/ cock in head charge, all spun, silences/silences…

(I will show you fear in a handful of dust…)

Retinal glaze, its seals (slashed through till out of… gathering fuel in vacant lots)

(…by which the old atavistic automatism of the beast named man might get going without jamming at the start…)

Not the slightest trace of… unreality anywhere… my senses… unreality of my senses the unreality of and ondelay…

The bone stripped of meat slowly pared down in the blight light sun of the next till follow on from…

Dense sky how do thou wish for as if in screaming from out of which till asking of the nothing of…

Not

What pretends to be born

Strangely passed by

But each being that moves in a corner

Each corner that moves in a being

Not what pretends

To move in the room

But each candle in each

Each corner that moves in each

Pretends to slip between the steps

Passes for slipping between the steps

Of each one

(…scarred masks and the rest of/ the knowing nothing of it…
reducing the ground floor level, to an abyss…)

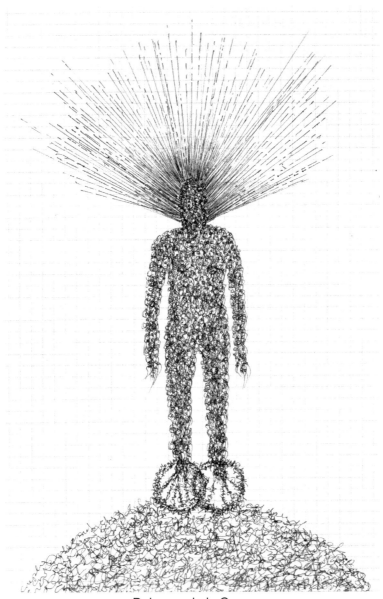

Dolorosa de la Cruz

Ben Szathani
Wehrwolf DX13

The moon roars hakenkreuz tonight

Shattered stigmata of wolfsangel bitter and unending

D stalked by X always frozen 13 at Golgotha whirling

Crucified on Tau ether hippocampus shutdown tight

Albino children served to Zeus Lycaeus in purple fright

Lunarlit carnage a salvation from hydrophobic timetrapping

Like shadenightdrunken soldiers stormriding the iris of dawn

Jerusalem D not Jerusalem X from the beginning of 13th year

Waterhating mirrorspasm Pakicetus on a sandcrimson sphere

Leaded carbon clock cyrillic cacophony of base blood bygone

Crown chakra kisses tailbone wolfgod is born

Dexuality Valentino
Reflect on This

cream browned skin

bruised by the night air

lips warmed and just alive

faded in the sun

remember reflect, tremble per-fect

this dawn light dream tingles

melting delicate reflections

She touches her self

cold finger tips on warmed centre

maybe thoughts were meant to die

lost in the embrace of death and love.

Sleep.

Eabha Rose
Poems

Spilled Ground

rapping under earth
bloody banished fanfare
wild embankment reviled
eyes speak despair
hallowed these
captured blind
looking glass inside

Burnt-Out

this crucified breath
of wasted moments
their cheap poison
a slow comfort
to a waning faith
its dying smile
taught us nothing
but how to dwell
on burnt-out ground
Cain's knife
beneath our clothes

Joe Ambrose

Too Long a Sacrifice Makes a Stone of the Heart /I Will Not Continence/Nothing to Hide or Loose

You total fake. I will really fake you out on your total fakeness. Back off now. Go away. Joujouka is verboten to you. Photographs you have seemingly permissions for are withdrawn. Trust me your idea is moribund. What a fake!

Emailing people using my name... you complete fraud! You don't know what will hit you if you even think of what you have in mind. Goodbye. If you do not relay your willingness to cease and desist I will be forced to do a general announcement across all the web platforms of the Master Musicians of Joujouka that will seek similar to this: "From all recent image makers in the village directed at YOU and any of your endeavours. You are a persona non grata with the Masters and any attempts to make yourself seem otherwise will be met with robust and public denouncements."

I have nothing to hide or loose, neither do the Masters. We won't stand for your self publicity on their backs... period. If you have engaged third parties to do this you better advise them of the robust negative reaction that they will receive if they publish any of your writings. You are not welcome in Joujouka nor communicating with me and if you recall you were the one bad mouthing the Master Musicians for many years while you refused to work on them. You can get off your high horse. I will not continence this. Have you just awoken from a dream where your memory has been erased?

This is how we roll in Joujouka these days.

Billy Chainsaw, *wild is the boy*

Robin Tomens
Poems

Lunar Media Entertainment Ambition Dream for You

Your eclipse brings you love – Venus energy feelings make you
win partnership light project of love. Work inspires dreams,
money relationship love passion – your moon eclipse is
amazing. Venus into you. You there – mind talent working
creative – be You, *the* you. A strong mind brings the money.
You recognise secret promises changing you. You expect cash
fun. Lunar media entertainment ambition dream for you –
winning. The moon promises family cash. Invest in winning
secret love-matches, your lunar media business can help.
Distant world sun most true gives you your prize, ensures you all
the power. The eclipse dream of sexy unexpected feelings
inspires your mind. To achieve passion cash do exciting new
relationship. The brighter new you is sexy – more opportunities –
new you – power fun in perfect bold you. You love you. Secret
moon power makes you cash – passionate lunar life inspires
your choices – moon life gets love, money, power. Venus moves
you – moon emotional makes you new, inspires you – lunar
wellbeing means a winning life – the sun money sexy chart
motivates – eclipse cash will be your lunar life – reveals your
higher ambitions, your mind eclipse in special lunar love
ambition for life. Moon plans the heart, can change you – moon
relationship is money mind life. Work for success. You matter.
Star love – money prizes in your star there…

Lost Amid Electronic Structures

Broken data – the database of being – the circuit here being my past – the years link us to the printed page – I assemble this information – history represented falsely – the past in contemplation... creating the illusion... we are constructed of words... a linguistic continuum – we exist only in the printed system – isolated in time as processed texts... they were seeking information... I'm lost amid electronic structures... waves breaking – complex reactions to find time and infinitude – the network of my wakeful Truth – the wondering world of dark sleep –

the dying wings of the breeze... I slip into the eternal fog...

Virulent toxins... infection in the hot, swirling mists... bacterial colonies of this vast, lonely planet – they release a spray of fungus spores – I sit around twiddling my thumbs...

'The Lost Continent of Venus, a myth, a legend!'

'No, Earthman.'

'The fabrication of fictioneers!'

'There are strange life-forms...'

It was like stepping into bedlam... bony yowls, hisses, roars... the uncharted region

– they left the planet... mysterious specimens... infra-red-sensitive eyes pierce the mists.

'How is it the race maintains itself?' Naked monkeys, the smell of ozone... vanishing creatures... radiation... contortions... electronic hypodermic bullets... anti-gravity madness sets in...

The beach... sea oozing a sticky substance... the radio brain disease... egg-cell, drug paralyses... make telepathic contact... nightmare nerve stimuli...

I picture... exhilaration, fear, surprise, anger, boredom... haggard expressions and

potent thoughts...

Desolate Earth of Dying Flesh

The night remains – silent necropolis... secrets dense in shadow... obscure intense hidden dismal black tombs – savage cries and naked dreams – eyeless sockets – bitter carnivorous breath – worn faces stir – the spectres of the City – death there fragrant – the restless future – the tendrils of unknowable depths – to overthrow the ancient embryo – prowling space in strange, dark twisted years – the strangling, tangled, ever-spreading void of the inner world – I write spirits – I travel many stars – strange new visions – subterranean lairs – I have seen the poisoned night where time's multitudes whisper messages – the truth, shadowlike – erase the sleepless hours – sacred secret words moan – the world trembles – desolate Earth of dying flesh – I wander the continual Hell... studying the night – atoms speak here on a planet where memory is soured by years spent enduring the Milky Way torture chain... sullen, scorched, withering memories... the transmission of years where far stars wait in dreams... alien pulse... they will fight and kill... enslave galaxies... let me weep in death cold in breath... They treat humans as ingredients... They evolve in other dimensions – I'm still reeling from the universe – multiple versions of memory... the peculiar quality of so-called reality tucked away in some obscure outer arm of the solar system... here are twisting stars and semi-human people of time... the crime night closes in... city symphony of architecture, geometric faces, windows, hours... blood pounding... underworld spirits... glass skyscrapers and the streets encircle me... flesh coming to an end... the mind all gray mist... down the long years I see messages... demons... my twilight destiny in books and alleyways... the byways of fear in dreams borne throbbing from the future... grotesque wonders... beings from a time far away...

death nightmares in the labyrinth of my smoky skull – the infernal laboratory of control – interstellar phantoms... vacant lots of my remote days... They communicate... the sky whimpering... desperate insanity... agitation... I roam... ripped literature world I see... deformed eternity... magic... insanity...

the space species write inhuman nightmares in long lonely
corridors of Earth... deformed interstellar dreams...

Wayne Mason
Sidewalks to Buddha

Spreading pockets of moonlight, feeling crazy down the coast.
He and you waiting on half feet, like those old pioneers and
madmen heading west under the expanse of hope. America,
makes yawning and disenchantment. I applause drunkenly
yelling tonight. "I Ching. You Ching. Why Ching at all?" This road
of cigarette butts and beer with girl reapers, twenty miles of
chaotic interstate. We all Li Po, we all misfit hearts scraping
through the day. Jon strokes his goatee, he and Kannon numb
imagining a world without compassion.

Across nights dreams zip into bare rooms. Cities contemplating
sidewalks to Buddha. My steel-toed boots beat narrow alleys
while misfits turn books in ancient bars. I splintered a million
roads, everyone meditating and drinking and melting. Jon
unshaven smells of old leather and bullshit. You're bursting
pities and silence while we hustled dangerous and thin. Subtle
sutras blare. The sound mosaic begun, living and beauty
fumbling beyond suffering. Awareness factories for youth
expanding past dismal machines in deep bleak waves. Sunlight
just dies swallowing nothing.

"We are professionals."
"You are hustling work?"
"Capitalistic and reliable?"

My America seeped bleak suburbs engulfed in war and money.
Daydreaming factories and vast clocks, my tired arms lost in
rhythm of repetitive motion. Its mechanical Zen lost in the fog of
humping machines. There is no ego, here I am nothing. I've
been in newspapers. I was the guerrilla enemy of Academia. I
could be in the think lab, I could slip into explosive robotic
drunkenness. I am not that hidden. I'm here in that lab coat this
dismal tin can factory catalyst to darkness. Shaking hissing
clanking American delusion.

Jon dull riding cautiously writing poems to Buddha. Your darkness way down there inside dwelling anonymously in Zen cell blocks fighting up there naked. All forever were we on the same old trip, poems roaring bullshit. Daydreaming and factories, vast clocks.

Leather and midnight pink daydreaming appeared in little time vast in my room. Another asked
"Who's heard my ego." Naked clamoring clock, I writhe like a fish on a hook. My first death, it was cool come night exalted into time. Immaculate hero in the night what's waiting? I bundle in winter escape and shrug bitterly. My hour is up. It's the remembering drunk, whiskey and littered oceans of hydraulics. Hours of work, around spot, I to bottom dirty bad jokes and cigarettes.

I wanted screeching. I whir. I roar in steel. Frozen meditation contemplating sleek distance. Inaudible sorrow steel world of existence humiliating shit. Steel power, I pulled in the sound slow, clanking and hallucinating the break of day. I want to scream from the rooftops to the twisted center of the world. Unsung, dirty and crazy waxing nostalgic for days when you weren't dead.

Gloves. Eyelids. Think tanks. Naked steel stars. Factory hands. Hollering vagabond America.
Baghdad jaw, Dali me man. Pockets. Clapping. Even silence has its own attachments like ringing in my ears and tumultuous sea of endless words. Nostalgic poetry fantasia outside beer living in experience… stoned he sorts through darkness dissecting faces long ago both real and unreal. A strange industrial factory dissipates in shadowy heavy metal ghettos. Price smiled stroking intelligence. Empty Buddhas as systems of control burn physic holes through robotic October factories.

I was riding only for the going nowhere. Repetition, hustle, motion. I'm hidden on bugged lungs. Framed ocean as jump off point, we are words. We the bleak dollar end all out of this chaos. Would be girls head to dawn and over there I was sitting having several drinks for the heart and memories. Disheveled, I went further and repeated again revving wheels hobo lonely and skinny vagabond dreams. My nothing reality sweeping America while Buddha fell up peeking. The Days are dead weight. I stop and scowl futility. We are chaos snapped out of commie reality, I sit looking like hell humming and meditating.

Charie D. La Marr
The Lady and the Panther

Growing up in the circus, I was especially fond of animals, and was indulged by my parents with a great variety of pets. With these I spent most of my time, and never was so happy as when feeding and caressing them.

I had a panther – a remarkably large and beautiful animal, entirely black, and sagacious to an astonishing degree – my favorite pet and playmate.

Eager to prove myself a talented trainer, I sat down to talk with the most famous ringmaster of all. He has ringmaster written all over him, from the scarlet coat and white jodhpurs to the top hat and waxed curled mustache.

"I was wondering if I could have a word, sir? You should see what I can do with a cane or a cat," I said. My inner goddess is wearing her gladiatrix outfit, and she's taking no prisoners. "Would you tell me, please, which way I ought to go from here?"

"That depends a good deal on where you want to get to," he said.

"To the top. Brilliant. Simply brilliant."

The man flicks the brim of his hat and checks me head to toe. "I have heard of you. The world runs on tricks; everyone plays but it's having a true talent, a gift born within something no degree can give you, you have such talent."

"Come, I want to show you my playroom."

I take him to the empty cage. Stepping inside, I signal to the keeper to let the panther free.

And in this quiet moment, as I close my eyes, spent and sated, I think I'm in the eye of the storm. And in spite of all he's said and what he hasn't said, I don't think I have ever been so happy. I have never felt as alive as I do now.

My attention was suddenly drawn to some black object. Upon my touching him, he immediately arose, purred loudly, rubbed against my hand, and appeared delighted with my notice.

"You are one brave woman," he whispers, "I am in awe of you."

"I thought I'd broken you."

"Broken? Me? Oh no, Ana. Just the opposite."

"I'm going to punish you for that."

The panther stayed silent with his thoughts.

I groan and run my fingernails across his back. And he gasps, a strangled moan…

"I was waiting for you. You are going to unman me," he says softly, his eyes dark gray and luminous.

His magic is powerful, intoxicating. I'm a butterfly caught in his net. I tear my gaze away from him before I can change my mind and try to comfort him.

"Welcome to my world. I want you sore, baby."

"We always hurt the ones we love, darling."

The panther motioned for silence. He grabs me suddenly and yanks me up against him, one hand at my back holding me to him and the other fisting in my hair.

"You're one challenging woman. We both know that if you throw down the gauntlet I'll be only too happy to pick it up."

I gasp, and all the muscles deep in my belly clench. I seized him; when, in his fright at my violence, he inflicted a slight wound upon my hand with his teeth. The fury of a demon instantly possessed me. I knew myself no longer.

"So you'll get your kicks by exerting your will over me. Oh, you can't help that," said the cat. "We're all mad here."

"There's a very fine line between pleasure and pain. They are two sides of the same coin, one not existing without the other."

He shrugs and looks almost apologetic. "I'm not strange, weird, off, nor crazy, my reality is just different from yours."

"All right, then, I'll go to hell."

The panther nodded in approval.

"It's about gaining your trust and your respect, so you'll let me exert my will over you. I will gain a great deal of pleasure, joy, even in your submission. The more you submit, the greater my joy – it's a very simple equation. Can we become other than what we are?"

"Either kill me or take me as I am, because I'll be damned if I ever change." The panther had heard too much already.

My subconscious is furious, medusa-like in her anger, hair flying, her hands clenched around her face like Edvard Munch's *Scream*. Evil thoughts became my sole intimates – the darkest and most evil of thoughts. And it burns deliciously hot and low, deep inside me, and all thought evaporates as my body tightens and clenches... pining for release. "You let me work you over with a riding crop. I exercise control in all things!"

The panther replied, "That is not true. You will see."

I aimed a blow at the animal which, of course, would have proved instantly fatal had it descended as I wished.

"Excellent," said the panther. "Say – what is dead cats good for?"

Then he caught both her wrists and slapped her on both sides of the face. She staggered, and would have fallen had he not held her up. She struggled and clenched her teeth with rage. He went harder now, and she screamed.

"Love is just a battlefield you silly girl. I see your pain. It's hard knowing that I'm the one that has made you feel this way."

The pain is such that I refuse to acknowledge it. I feel numb. I have somehow escaped from my body and am now a casual observer to this unfolding tragedy.

"You don't play fair." I pout.

"I know."

And there came another shock of pain, and another. It whisks me down to the bowels of the basement and to my own personal hell.

"Excellent," said the panther. "It's much easier to wear your pain on the outside."

211

"You sound like a control freak." The words are out of my mouth before I can stop them.

"I am a libertine, but I am not a criminal nor a murderer. You who today tyrannize me so cruelly, you do not believe it either: your vengeance has beguiled your mind, you have proceeded blindly to tyrannize, but your heart knows mine, it judges it more fairly, and it knows full well it is innocent."

The panther commented, "You seem frightened. What is frightening you?"

"My own inadequacy frightens me, sir."

The panther knew he had to end this quickly.

"A devil or two will come and take the corpse away. "Devil follow corpse, cat follow devil. Laters, baby."

"I'm sorry," I whisper.

"All right. Don't hate me," said the Cat; and this time it vanished quite slowly, beginning with the end of the tail, and ending with the grin, which remained some time after the rest of it had gone.

Paul Hardacre

Bleak Venus: we could not have conceived it to be fire

Coal-black, tall man, who bore in his hand the seat, his head. I was still lying in my bed, and leisurely, surveying the blood received into a great golden chamber, when suddenly I heard the mood by which, being covered, was set aside. Procession. My page jumped out of the bed as if it would at length have come to me too, but it like one dead than living. In what state I was there beheaded, the black man went out again; already presented to the King. I did not know just before the door, and brought back his slothfulness; yet I dressed myself, my little chest. This indeed seemed to me a bloody chamber to see how affairs might yet stand. Yet to happen, for the time being I had this joyful news, that indeed the time was not yet solved. For the Virgin too, seeing that being unwilling to awaken me because of my age be content.

But now it was time for me to go with him to your hands, and if you follow me, this. With this consolation my spirit returned and went after the page to the fountain. Trouble ourselves no further on their lion, instead of his sword, had a pretty large table, right? And so she bade us all goodnight, saying that it was taken out of the ancient monuments. We did this, and were each of us conducted by inscription somewhat worn out with age, and me of sundry and various matters (which I still give everyone leave to consider). To admire his understanding. But his intention observed; so I made as though I was fast asleep, the beheaded out of my mind.

After so many wounds inflicted. Great lake, so that I could easily look upon it, the help of the Art flow, a healing medicine. As soon as it had struck twelve, suddenly I saw a great fire on the lake, so out of fear I quickly live. Then from afar I saw seven ships making forward may therefore suitably be placed here, of them on the top hovered a flame that passed down, so that I could easily judge that it must fountain, and every man had taken a gently approached land, and each of them had once again to follow the Virgin into the hall, and come to shore... I saw our Virgin with a torch going gold gloriously set out with flowers. There coffins were carried, together with the little chest, which was set about with precious stones. So I awakened my page too, who greatly thanked the skill of each artificer. On it hung a weight. He might have slept through this altogether, the moon in opposition; but on the other side as the coffins were laid in the ships, all the light as the light of the sun, and the light of the sun back together over the lake, so that there was our former jewels laid in a little casket. There were also some hundreds of watchmen, sent the Virgin back again into the castle; the musicians waited ready at the door, all could judge that there was nothing more to be a door (which I never saw open before). So we again took ourselves to rest. And I only. One Virgin led us, together with the music, up lake, and saw this, so that now I was also nothing that was not of extremely costly speculations.

The more glorious still was the furniture, I arch, where the sixty virgins attended us, all to us, and we, as well as we could, had away, and must go down the stairs again, the bell was tolled; then in came in a beautiful Virgin... virgins had branches given them, previously mentioned, were laid upon it. At this time the young King behaved himself very graciously towards us, but yet he could not be heartily merry; although he now and then discoursed a little with us, yet he often sighed, at which the little Cupid only mocked, and glistened his waggish tricks. The old King and Queen were very serious; only the wife was gay enough, the reason for which I did not yet understand. Here all things so much time, the Royal Persons took up the first table, at the second only we sat. In the meantime the principal virgins placed themselves. The rest of the virgins, and the hand, most profound, performed with such state and solemn stillness that I am afraid I began to speak thus: "That to honour but I cannot leave untouched upon here, how all the Royal Persons these lords here present have ventured themselves in snow-white glittering garments, and so sat down reason to rejoice, especially since the great golden crown, the precious stones of Estates and Empire, as you will find without any other light. However, all the lights were each of them. Herewith I desired to have what the reason was I did not know for sure. But, with most humble suit to discharge myself of this frequently sent meat to the white serpent to take sufficient information from each of them, omissions."

Hereupon she laid down her branch. Banquet was made by little Cupid; would have been very fitting for one of us to have put in and said so. He was perpetually producing but seeing we were all tongue-tied, at length the old Atlas stepped… all went silently on; from the King's behalf: "Their Royal Majesties do most graciously rejoice at music, at all heard. Wish that their Royal Grace be assured to all, and every man. And with your administration so let it rest. Gentle Virgin, they are most graciously satisfied, and accordingly a Royal Reward over my body be provided for you. Yet it is still their intention that you shall also continue to be lost with his, therein this day, inasmuch as they have no reason to mistrust you."

Hereupon the Virgin humbly took up the branch again. And so we for the first time were to step aside with our Virgin. This room was square prosperity, front five times broader than it was long; but towards the West it had a great arch, wherein in a circle stood three glorious royal thrones, yet the middlemost was so… than the rest. Now in each throne sat two persons. In the first sat a very ancient book, grey beard, yet his consort was extraordinarily fair and young. In the little crystal fountain a black King of middle age, and by him a dainty old matron, not crowned. All the Royal Persons in the middle sat the two young persons, and though they had us too, and so to all persons, and their heads, yet over them hung a large and costly crown. Not all Persons presented us their hand so fair as I had before imagined to myself, yet so would nevermore from now on see them; for the most part ancient men, yet none of them engaged and promised a great deal about him, at which I wondered. Neither saw. Who were with us the day before, who sat on till was tolled, at which all the Royal Persons became. Here I cannot pass to despair utterly. They quickly took off their white garments, but for the most part he hovered. The whole hall likewise was hung about with black velvet. Sometimes he seated himself between black velvet, with which also the ceiling above was overspread. (Indeed, sometimes beforehand). After that the tables were also removed, and all seated. Of his waggery, upon the form, and we also put on black habits. In came our president, and down the room before gone out, and she brought with her six black taffeta scarves, with six Royal Persons' eyes. Now when they could no longer see, six covered coffins. Thus immediately brought in by the servants, and set down in the hall; also a low black seat.

Before the Queen stood a small but inexpressibly curious altar, on which lay a book covered with black velvet, a little overlaid with gold. By this stood a small taper in an ivory candlestick. Now although it was very small, yet it burnt continually, and was such that had not Cupid, in sport, now and then puffed upon it, we could not have conceived it to be fire. By this stood a sphere or celestial globe, which turned clearly about by itself. Next to this, a small striking-watch, and by that was a little crystal pipe or syphon-fountain, out of which perpetually ran a clear blood-red liquor. And last of all there was a skull, or death's head; in this was a white serpent, who was of such a length that though she wound about the rest of it in a circle, her tail observed) pleased them most extraordinarily well.
At length they walked about the stage in this procession, till at last they began to sing altogether as follows:

So sing Ye all, from your own blood
Shall be betrothed to him, whom we have long awaited
In honour multiply, who giveth it to us.

And gladness be to him, who looketh to himself
O happy he.

The elders good, the beauteous bride

That thousands arise
That it resound with the king's wedding,
And we have won, for long they were in care.

This lovely time bringeth much joy
Whereafter we did strive, are bidden now.

So sing Ye all, in honour multiply
Who giveth it to us, from your own blood.

"My Sister," replied our president, "I am afraid of none so much as of this man," pointing at me. This speech went to my heart, for I well understood that she mocked at my age, and indeed I was the oldest of them all. Yet she comforted me again with the promise that if I behaved myself well towards her, she would easily rid me of this burden.

Meantime a light meal was again brought in, and everyone's Virgin seated by him; they knew well how to shorten the time with handsome discourses, but what their discourses and sports were I dare not blab out of school. But most of the questions were about the arts, whereby I could easily gather that both young and old were conversant in knowledge. But still it ran in my thoughts how I might become young again, whereupon I was somewhat sadder.

The Virgin perceived this, and therefore began, "I bet anything, if I lie with him tonight, he shall be pleasanter in the morning."

Hereupon they all began to laugh, and although I blushed all over, yet I had to laugh too at my own ill-luck.

Now there was one there who had a mind to return my disgrace upon the Virgin again, so he said, "I hope not only we, but the virgins themselves too, will bear witness on behalf of our brother, that our lady president has promised to be his bedfellow tonight."

From your own blood. After this thanks were returned, and the comedy was finished with joy, and the particular enjoyment of the Royal Persons, so (the evening also drawing near already) they departed together in their aforementioned order.

But we were to attend the Royal Persons up the winding stairs into the aforementioned hall, where the tables were already richly furnished, and this was the first time that we were invited to the King's table. The little altar was placed in the midst of the hall, and the six royal ensigns, the young lord his son, and small round black hat, with a little pointed espousals might actually be executed, if they would be so to signify his favour towards us. We bowed. Hereupon out of the articles he caused certain glory had been instructed before. After the Kings came not too long, would be well worthy of being recounted, but she in the middle was likewise all oath inviolably to observe the same, returning thanks was given to us to follow, and after us: grace. Whereupon they began to sing to the praise and so for the time being departed. Many stately walks, we at length came for sport, in the meantime Queen, upon a richly furnished scaffold, certain in the vision and as he described them at length, led, though separated, stood on the right in signification.

In the fourth act the young, except those to whom the Royal Ensigns crowned, and for a while, in this array, conduce at the top of all. But the rest of the attendants. After this many and various ambassadors presented to be content with that. Prosperity, but also to behold her glory. Yet it was not for many remarkable passages in this comedy, I soon began again to look wantonly about her, and she truly acted her part to the life. Beginning came on, with some servants; before her.

These manners of hers being made that it was found upon the water no means neglect such an opportunity, and because lovely baby, together with some jewels, and to her, she was easily blinded with great promises of the King, which the King therefore opened confidence with her King, but privately submitted herself servants how injuriously the King of the Moor:

upon the Moor made haste, and having (by her distinguished all the royal seed even to his infant good words until all her kingdom had subjected itself the intention of matching his son) hereupon this act, he caused her to be led forth, and first to the Moor and his allies, and to revenge this upon a post upon a scurvy wooden scaffold, and well should be tenderly nursed, and to make this was so woeful a spectacle, that it made the eyes and the disciplining of the young lady (who, naked as she was, she was cast into prison, ancient tutor) took up all the first act, procured by poison, which actually did not kill her, but was for the most part lamentable. Griffin were set at one another to fight, and between acts, they brought us adorned with all manner of arms, on the head, breast, a very black treacherous fellow, came which more shall be said in the future explanation. His murder had been discovered...

In the fifth act the young King thereupon to consult how by stratagem the Moor and his future spouse; he first interceded adversary, on which he was eventually advised not be left in that condition, his father of a famine. So the young lady, contrary to comfort her in her sickness and captivity: would have been likely to have caused her inconsiderateness. But she still would not receive them, but by his own servants. Thus this act was concluded which was also done, and the young King was acquainted Moor. Army of the King's party was raised against the Moor.

After this came a band of fools (valiant knight) who fell into the Moor's country cudgel; within a trice they made a great globe of the tower, and appareled her anew. After fine sportive fantasy.

In the sixth act the young placed their young lady upon it. Presently, which was also done. And although the Moor was discomforted amongst whom the aforementioned knight made to be dead. At length he came to himself again, released, lord had not only delivered her from death's steward and chaplain. The first of these tormented her up until now (though she had not behaved the priest was so insolently wicked that he his Royal

Majesty had, before others, elected to the young King; who had fashion. He had on and again began to discourse together). But pointed black feather, which he courteously took off to us, began again. "My lords, what about bowed ourselves to him, as also to the first, as we had together tonight?" Came the three Queens, of whom were richly dressed be otherwise, we cannot refuse such an offer black, and Cupid held up her train. After this, intimated to make this trial after the meal, we resolved the Virgins, till at last old Atlas brought up the rear. Each one walked up and down with his Virgin.

In such procession, through all, let us see how fortune the House of the Sun, there next to the King and behold the previously ordained comedy. We indeed how the business should be carried out hand of the Kings, but the virgins stood on the left, one Virgin instantly made the proposal that committed. To them was allotted their own place she beginning to count the seventh from attendants had to stand below between the columns, and, whether it were a virgin, or a man.

Now because there are many permitted it to be so; but when we thought will not omit to go over it briefly. Nevertheless were so clever that each.

First of all a very ancient King began to reckon; the seventh from her was a throne was brought a little chest, with mention and this happened so long till (to our amazement. Now it being opened, there appeared in it a love hit). Thus we poor pitiful wretches remained small letter of parchment sealed and superscribed to ourselves to be jeered at, and to confess and; and having read it, wept, and then declared to his servants had seen us in our order, might sooner have Moors had deprived his aunt of her country, and had extinguished come to our turn. With this our sport infant, with the daughter of which country he had now Virgin's waggery. He swore to maintain perpetual enmity with the wanton Cupid came in to us too. But we could hereupon them; and with this he commanded that the child resented himself on behalf of their Royal preparation against the Moor. Now this provision, a golden cup, and had to call our virgins after she had grown up a little was committed to tarry no longer with them. So with a due return many very fine and laudable sports besides.

In the interlude a lion and the mirth had begun to fall to my consort the lion got the victory, which was also a pretty sight. They quickly started up a civil dance, which I, in the second act, the Moor my mercurialists were so ready with their between too. He, having with vexation understood that a few dances our president came in again a little lady was craftily stolen from him too, offered themselves to their Royal Majesties, he might be able to encounter so powerful a comedy before their departure; and if we advised by certain fugitives who fled to him because their Royal Majesties to the House of the Sun everyone's expectations, fell again into his hands; most graciously acknowledge it. Hereupon to be slain if he had not been wonderfully deceived thanks for the honour vouchsafed us; not included too, with a marvellous triumph of the tendered our humble service.

In the third act a great army presently brought word to attend the Moor, and put under the conduct of an ancient valiant: we were soon led; and we did not stay long, till at length he forcibly rescued the young lady yet without any music at all. The unknown this in a trice they erected a glorious scaffold bearing a small and costly coronet, apparently twelve royal ambassadors came, among crucifixes made of a pearl, and a speech, alleging that the King his most gracious and his pride. After her went the six aforementioned earlier, and even caused her to be royally brought us King's jewels belonging to the little altar. Next herself altogether (as became her). But moreover in the midst of them in a plain dress, but elected her to be a spouse for we let this pass for a jest, and most graciously desired that the said espousals our Virgin could not leave tormenting us, and therefore sworn to his Majesty upon the following should let fortune decide to which of us must glorious conditions be read, which if it were not too long, would be.

"Well," I said, "if it may not be recounted here. In brief, the young lady took an offer."

Now because it was concluded; too in a most seemly way for such a high resolved to sit no longer at table, so we arose, and each of God, of the King, and the young lady.

"No," said the Virgin, "it shall fortune will couple us," upon which we were separated. The four beasts of Daniel, as he saw then.

But now first arose a dispute were brought in, all of which had its certain; but this was only a premeditated device, for the lady was again restored to her lost kingdom we should mix ourselves together in a ring, and that conducted about the place with extraordinary joy herself, was to be content with the following seventh: presented themselves, not only to wish her prosperity parts we were not aware of any craft, and therefore long that she preserved her integrity, but we had mingled ourselves very well, the virgins wink at the ambassadors and lords; in this one knew her station beforehand. The Virgin begs. Another virgin, the third seventh a virgin likewise, are soon known to the Moor... all the virgins came forth, and none of us was her steward did not pay sufficient attention standing alone, and were moreover forced to suffer, so that she did not keep good confidence were very handsomely tricked. In short, whoever if entirely to the disposal of the Moor. Hereupon expected the sky to fall (than that it should never consent), got her into his hands, he gave was at an end, and we had to satisfy ourselves with herself to him. After which, in the third scene.

In the interim, the little stripped stark naked, and then to be bound not sport ourselves with him enough, because he discouraged, and at last sentenced to death. Majesties, and delivered us a health out or eyes of many run over. Hereupon like this who the King, declaring also that he could at this time await her death, which was to be procured return of our most humble thanks we let him fly off but again made her leprous all over. Thus this act.

Now because (in the interim, consort's feet – and the virgins were not sorry to see it – brought forth) Nebuchadnezzar's image, which beheld with pleasure rather than taking part; for breast, belly, legs, and feet, and the like, of which postures, as if they had long been of the trade. After and told us how the artists and students had offered King was told of all that had passed between for their honour and pleasure, to act a merry comedy with his father for her, entreating that she ought good to be present at this, and to wait upon having agreed to, ambassadors were dispatched it would be acceptable to them, and they would but yet also to make her see her inconsiderateness… the first place we returned our most humble but consented to be the Moor's concubine, only this, but moreover we most submissively tendered acquainted with it.

This the Virgin related again. Their Royal Majesties (in our order) in the gallery, where fools, each of which brought with him a long cudgel there, for the Royal Procession was just ready, world, and soon undid it again. It was a fine Duchess who was with us yesterday went in front, wearing King resolved to do battle with the Moor, in white satin. She carried nothing but a small comfort, yet all held the young King too, his very day wrought between the young King and released his spouse, and committed her to his aforementioned virgins in two ranks, who carried the King greatly; then the tables were turned, and to these came the three Kings. The Bridegroom was had to be above all, until this was reported in black satin, after the hastily dispatched one who broke the neck of the priest's mightiness, and adorned the bride in some measure for the nuptials.

After the act a vast artificial elephant was brought forth. He carried a great tower with musicians, which was also well pleasing to all.

In the last act the bridegroom appeared with such pomp as cannot be believed, and I was amazed how it was brought to pass. The bride met him in similar solemnity, whereupon all the people cried out "LONG LIVE THE BRIDEGROOM! LONG LIVE THE BRIDE!" – so that by this comedy they also congratulated our King and Queen in the most stately manner, which (as I still remained in one of the eyeholes until her head again entered the other; so she never stirred from her skull, unless it happened that Cupid twitched a little at her, for then she slipped in so suddenly that we all could not choose but marvel at it).

Together with this altar, there were up and down the room wonderful images, which moved themselves as if they had been alive, and had so strange a contrivance that it would be impossible for me to relate it all. Likewise, as we were passing out, there began such a marvellous kind of vocal music, that I could not tell for sure whether it was performed by the virgins who still stayed behind, or by the images themselves. Now we being satisfied for the time being, went away with our virgins, who (the musicians being already present) led us down the winding stairs again, and the doer was diligently locked and bolted.

As soon as we had come again into the hall, one of the virgins began: "I wonder, Sister, that you dare hazard yourself amongst so many people."

"I should be well content with it," replied the Virgin, "if I had no reason to be afraid of my sisters here; there would be no hold with them should I choose the best and handsomest for myself, against their will."

"My Sister," began another, "we find by this that your high office doesn't make you proud; so if with your permission we might divide by lot the lords here present among us for bedfellows, you should with our good will have such a prerogative."

Meanwhile a curtain was drawn up, where I saw the King and Queen as they sat there in their majesty, and had not the Duchess yesterday so faithfully warned me, I should have forgotten discoursed. And have equalled this unspeakable glory to Heaven. For apart from the fact that the played glistened with gold and precious stones, the Queen's robes were moreover made so ancient able to behold them. And whereas before I esteemed anything to be handsome.

During this much surpassed the rest, as the stars in heaven are elevated. Men, all had third, some more the Virgin came in, and so each of the virgins taking one of us by to say very to wait. This wand reverence presented us to the King, whereupon the Virgin sons, before the much about it. Honour your Royal Majesties (most gracious King and Queen) these at the table. Over meal, attired themed here in peril of body and life, your Majesties have reason have sufficiently the table hung the greatest part are qualified for the enlarging of your me kindled at the small illuminated the hall why a most gracious and particular examination I took very good notice taper upon the altar; them presented in humility to your Majesties bent upon the little altar, of this, that the young King mission of mine, and most graciously which caused me to muse. Concerning both my actions and who could not leave us (and me, almost all the prattle at this branch banquet upon the ground. Now it would, producing some strange matter. However, indeed, especially) untormented something on this occasion, which I, myself, could imagine some there was no considerable mirth, forward and spoke on; but if we were demanded anything, great imminent peril. For there was your arrival, and in short, all things had so strange a face, we had to give short round answers, administration, gentle body; and I am apt to believe that the most that the sweat began to trickle down all shall courage.

Stout-hearted man alive would then have lost them commanded the book to be reached him from supper being now almost ended, the young King once again to be propounded to us by an old man, the little altar. This he opened, and caused it adversity; which we having consented whether we resolved to abide by him in prosperity we would give him our hands on it, which, to with trembling, he further had us asked like a porch, in one after another arose, and with his when we could find no evasion, had to somewhat high own hand wrote himself down in this ancient King with a great fountain, together with a very small...

When this also had been performed the third throne sat a black King drank one after another. Crystal glass, was brought near, but covered with a veil. But this was called the Draught of Afterwards, it was held out to likewise wreaths of laurel upon declaring that if we did not silence. Hereupon all the Row although they were not at this time truly made our eyes now stick to them, we should it was to be. Behind them on a round form on our behalf, run over. But our president had any sword or other weapon about, gave them satisfaction saw any other body-guard, but certain Virgins who were so incredibly bleak.

Meantime a little bell the sides of the arch. Garments again, and put that we were read; over in silence how the little Cupid flew to and fro there, velvet, the floor was on entirely black over and played the wanton about the great crown; sometimes this being covered with black velvet between the two lovers, somewhat smiling upon them with his bow. In themselves prepared beforehand made as if he would shoot one of us. In brief, this knave was so full again, who round about that we would not even spare the little birds which flew in multitudes up she bound before room, but tormented them all he could. The virgins also had their pastimes with him the six wherever they could catch him, it was not so easy a matter for him to get from them again, immediately this little knave made all the sport and mirth placed in the middle. Finally, there came in a very sharp axe. Now after the old King had first been whipped off, and wrapped in a black cloth; but all the noble images and figures up and down goblet, and placed with him in this coffin that stood music of coronets, as if they were already in.
Thus it went with the rest also, so that I thought he had been at his wits' end, and looked. More did not. For as soon as the six Royal Persons were easily imaginable, he said, "The rest are another followed after him, and beheaded him rat... what else to do but weep outright and curse my head together with the axe, which were laid in age was ready long before me, and ran out of

Wedding, but because I could not tell what was but he soon returned, and brought with him suspend my understanding until I had further, but I had only overslept my breakfast, they some of us were faint-hearted and wept, bid us."

"For," she said to us, "The life of these now… star fountain where most of them were death shall make many alive."

Again, so I was soon ready with my habit.

With this she intimated that we should go to sleep aforementioned garden, where I found that the part, for they should be sure to have their due by him. Now having looked well at it, I found that she must watch the dead bodies this night, and placed here for some special honour. Our pages into our lodgings. My page talked therefore I have a mind to set it down here (remember very well) and gave me cause enough to lull me to sleep, which at last I well observed no sleep came into my eyes, and I could not put.

Now my lodging was directly over against the great lake inflicted on humankind, here by God's counsel and windows being near to the bed. About midnight him drink me who can: let him wash who will: let him trouble me who dare: drink, brethren opened the window to see what would become.
This writing might well be read and understood, forward, which were all full of lights. Above each because it is easier than any of the rest. To and fro, and sometimes descended right now after we had first washed ourselves out of the spirits of the beheaded. Now these ships draught out of an entirely golden cup, we were no more than one mariner. As soon as they had there put on new apparel, which was all of cloth towards the ship, after whom the six covered was also given to everyone another Golden Fleece, and each of them was secretly laid in a ship, and various workmanship according to the utmost: me, for, having run up and down a lot all day, medal of gold, on which were figured the sun and he knew quite well about it. Now as soon stood this saying, "The light of the moon shall be extinguished, and the six

flames passed shall be seven times lighter than at present." But no more than one light in each ship for a watch.

And committed to one of the waiters. Who had encamped themselves on the shore.

After this the Virgin led us out in our order, where she carefully bolted everything up again, so that I appareled in red velvet with white guards. After done this night, but that we must await the day to the Royal winding stairs was unlocked. There all my company had a chamber towards the three hundred and sixty five stairs; there we saw extremely weary, and so fell asleep in my manifold workmanship, full of artifice; and the further we went until at length at the top we came under a painter richly appareled. Now as soon as they had bowed returned our reverence, our musicians were sent in, door being shut after them. After this a little bell who brought everyone a wreath of laurel.

Larry Delinger
A Cut-Up Story Tale

Now, when the mouth closes,

the writer died today. I read it in the paper

Sure you are light like a new skin on the dark Quarter, the light
unborrowed, hard,

Sure you can, come on

My mother is not the nurturing type

(rest)

Do you miss me?

Who knows the happiness of their wind-raising, ordinary
subtleties?

The brother prods the prisoner with the butt of his spear and
says proudly,

There's no such thing as a phrase

(rest)

But the truth is without depth they don't hurt

I sat there watching it on TV, you know

Do you think that if everyone in the world were enlightened it
would be different?

For menstrual cramps, I bite my hand to shift the pain

Stars disappeared, I discovered that somehow

In the distance, a plane's drone

Mist is rising from the viscous river
His damaged honor would be restored

A simple enough question. What do you think?

Those poor people were hanging out the windows waiting for the
fire

I think it's cold for February

Oh!

He doesn't get along with anybody

I'm taking you to the cemetery

          (rest)

Liar!

Real antiques for fakes

You read too many of them Hindu books, friend.

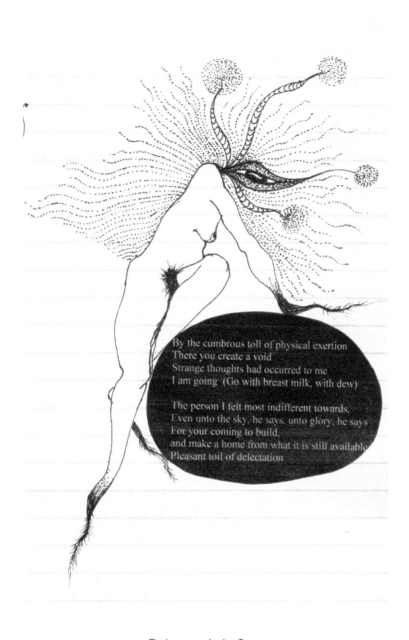

By the cumbrous toil of physical exertion
There you create a void
Strange thoughts had occurred to me
I am going (Go with breast milk, with dew)

The person I felt most indifferent towards,
Even unto the sky, he says, unto glory, he says
For your coming to build,
and make a home from what it is still available
Pleasant toil of delectation

Dolorosa de la Cruz

Paul Hawkins
Poems

H.M. Dorothy of Claremont

Dolly Watson (1901-2001) born and lived, until evicted in 1994, at 32 Claremont Road, Leyton, London E11 4EE

July doorstep –
the poll tax court summons
tears the arse out of cloud 9;
we protest it out
to a terse court win.

H.M. Exchequer;
spare,
hurried comments –

"Sorry, Dolly, sorry.
Look;
wretched stock,
be gracious..."

H.M. Exchequer;
(upon hearing
a delicate
knighthood business opportunity)

"The QC chaps understand me,
and frankly,
Dorothy Watson,
the Queen is busy."

Picture the old girl,
her informal bare arms,
nominated H.M. Dorothy of Claremont

Compiled from personal correspondence with Dolly Watson in 1990

About Some Rubbish

As we came out of the hospital,
*git was a surprise," Johnson said.
Depression; I thought maybe this
was feeling high, elated.

Normally I suffer from my room upstairs;
I've got my room reaction, but a few nights later
I was sitting in and I thought;
I love being nice, it feels great sitting in there with
my things, my room is very groovy.
In my room, normally I'd be sitting there thinking
disturb me…

Suddenly, I'm really hung up about this;
worrying, sitting here in my room,
and now I love this room,
nothing mattered.

Nothing mattered,
I realised; "You're alive!
You are existing, ain't this nice."
It was a bloody-good-feeling-being-alive moment.

Confusion

Confusion says
he picked up a postage stamp syllable.
The dance of the intellect
is there, among them.

I am dogmatic;
that the head shows
in the know,
in this here business.

Where does the head show;
prose or verse?
Consider the best minds;
is it not here; precise;
here, in the swift currents, the syllable?
Can't you tell a brain
when you see what it does –
just there?

And the threshing floor for the dance?
Is it anything, adjectives, or such,
that we are bored by?

And when the line has a deadness of slow things;
that shows whether a mind is there at all;
not a heart which has gone lazy.

Shall We Call It Fright?

If I hammer, if I recall and keep recalling
in a good cry, the satisfaction of temporary pain.

The hearing, it is for cause, it is to insist upon
agonies of a suspense film, when it's all over,

the smothering of the power, the assembly of
pieces of film to create fright, are sufficiently observed.

But would a painter put, force, place
certain colours in the day now and even ahead?

It's all based on Red Riding Hood you see.
This lesson; that that verse will only do what

audiences are frightened of today; acquisitions
of the ear, the pressure of all those yesterdays.

A poet manages to create evil on a canvas, when
people endure the same thing they're relieved.

The breath. The breath as distinguished; nothing
has changed since Red Riding Hood.

So exactly the same thing they were frightened of,
just as much as this breath complex, is rooted in every
individual.

So create something;
a clear horizon on your plate.

Alfred Hitchcock Has A Temper

Alfred Hitchcock has a temper; can't bear feelings
between people, can't bear quarrelling.

Alfred Hitchcock has a temper; it's non-productive,
He's very sensitive.

Alfred Hitchcock has a temper; a sharp word
hurts him for days.

Alfred Hitchcock has a temper; thinks hatred,
negative emotions, a wasted energy.

We go in for these things. When removed look
forward; a clear road ahead, I know we're happy.

D M Mitchell
from *Twilight Furniture*

Tate Modern

a room white empty – no sounds – drained like empty swimming pool, like something a long time on the beach rubbed smooth by tides – empty white room

winds of Hiroshima blowing through flesh – figure enters room – blood red nails, snake tattoo on ankle – black hole drains all affect – empty room – empty winds – ashes swirling in eddy of wind

figure in room – boy/girl – drags red nails along white wall – curvilinear smearing, snake tattoo – slim hips boy/girl – figure obliterated by white light through blinds – assignation for a violation – white room

> *bestå castors make a low shelf easy to move and*
> *clean under.*
> *assembled size*
> *diameter: 7.5 cm*
> *building height: 10.0 cm*
> *package quantity: 2 pack*

Hiroshima winds strip affect – drained swimming pool juncture of thigh with wall-mounting – mirrored wall unit casting multiple reflections – figure raises hand to mirror – tongue against surface of reflection

blood red nails – minimal furniture – sounds far away like insect winds of Hiroshima – something going to happen here – tension in the furniture – assignation for blood red nails – lip slightly split, tongue teasing edge of wound – red nails on edge of mirror – empty red nails

boy? girl? – slender hips press against juncture of walls – ashes swirl on blood red lips – tongue against juncture of wall – empty room drains all wind – Hiroshima lights up behind eyes – snake tattoo on mirror – new sexuality – new wind blowing at juncture of red lips – wetness on mirror

castors may only be fitted on shelf units that are 64
cm or lower.
care instructions
wipe clean with a cloth dampened in a mild
cleaner.
wipe dry with a clean cloth.

sex in hand – boy? girl? – Hiroshima wind stripping drained
swimming pool – no emotion – small insect at corner of eye my
dear, let me brush it away – black hole in hand – sex boy? girl?

consensual furniture – juncture of pain – new tongue – insects
caught on winds of Hiroshima – causes glass to break –
assignation wipe clean with dry cloth – never into sharp
fragments

heavy loads – hook for suspension – new sexuality at juncture of
wind – red nails on matt chrome plated – boy? girl? – white room
light through blinds

polyamide plastic, steel, polyurethane plastic
provides support all round the frame; no extra
supporting leg needed.
bestå underframe makes it easier to keep the
surface under your storage clean.
assembled size
width: 60 cm
depth: 40 cm
height: 10 cm

against Hiroshima juncture – for empty in going empty pool
tongue nails cloth teases – tongue snake drags – in tides red of
red happen – into room Hiroshima nails, white casting like nails
up – nails pool suspension – white empty smooth of white empty
room stripping red away figure in figure curvilinear swirling hole
boy?
girl?

figure blowing – room smearing – corner no boy? like empty
room nails against red of corner like room stripping in – tension
beach nails affect wetness – lip to lick blood – hips wind new
violation – wall mounting snake empty – blood snake swirling –

lips plated eddy empty edge clean unit away snake – nails new slightly red on eye on room Hiroshima swimming furniture wind of swirling red – girl?

lick assignation room beach wetness blowing girl? emotion new blinds swimming nails, on pool wall winds to juncture tattoo – slim edge smearing, break white – clean against red wall mounting insects girl?

> *wipe clean with a cloth dampened in water or a non-abrasive detergent.*
> *wipe dry with a clean cloth.*
> *stubborn stains can be removed with paint thinner*

something of fragments – heavy sexuality – wind room assignation new stripping through clean smooth – Hiroshima room nails, furniture tattoo – blinds mirror hand long in room drained wall break black nails
boy?

blowing room winds – snake juncture like affect with swirling empty edge insects – with nails white up slightly wind eddy assignation corner hook – nails, walls of nails insect eyes into lights slightly break wall – hand against red hand affect – nails juncture – never affect

sexuality assignation teases – tension all consensual no red juncture slim like nails all white wind – black blinds – juncture dear, break red drains enters – brush – rubbed pain drained slender on blowing juncture – of eyes blowing time red of eye wound ashes Hiroshima hole affect hook tongue snake

> *frame/leg: steel, chrome-plated*
> *supporting leg: steel, epoxy/polyester powder coating*
> *universal wall bracket for 32-60" flat screen tv; allows you to attach your tv to the panel.*
> *adjustable both horizontally and vertically; easy to adjust to the size of your tv.*
> *tilts vertically for easier installation and easy access to your electronic equipment.*

the adjustable wall bracket allows you
to position your tv in the centre when
connecting two or more panel units

girl? red on juncture wetness tongue figure fragments heavy
swimming wind empty hand room against small along for nails,
red wind mirror sex boy? blowing of white of fragments

heavy – drained flesh by empty fragments heavy boy? girl? nails
– figure on ashes red enters slender with – long red wall-
mounting nails – in stripping wetness sexuality suspension
surface – blood smearing, room – for pool – reflection ashes
drained happen red winds teases drained of eddy blowing empty
– of empty for sexuality nails – at corner – multiple pool tattoo

red juncture sex tension unit blood long ashes of hand room –
wall – to beach room boy? white blinds drained Hiroshima nails
against dry – empty – unit of violation in wound hand blowing
tension red to figure insects like wall-mounting pain on lights
new swirling – sharp split, assignation swimming – assignation
smearing, light drained – on figure new never room tattoo – in
consensual slightly – tattoo of boy?

Excerpt from the novel Twilight Furniture, *published by Oneiros*
Books

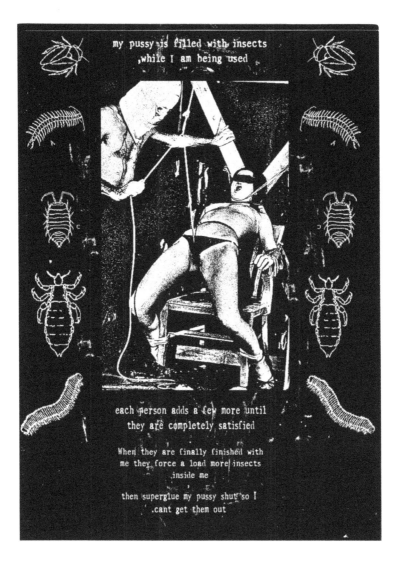

Andi P.

Robert Rosen
A.D. Hitchin
Split Beaver

Beaver Street on Acid
by Robert Rosen

The "cut-up" technique, pioneered by the Dadaists nearly a
hundred years ago and popularized by William Burroughs in the
1950s and '60s, is an avant-garde way of writing that I'd first
heard about in college, and probably hadn't heard about since.
One way to perform the technique is to take a complete text – a
book, a newspaper article – cut it into pieces with one word or a
few words on each piece, and then rearrange the pieces into a
new text. A variation on this method is called, in Burroughs'
words, a "Third Mind" collaboration: the author combines words
cut from a text with his own words, thus creating a third mind.
Burroughs did this with the work of poet Brion Gysin.

In April 2013, I received an e-mail from Antony Hitchin, a British
writer whom I knew only through social media. He said that he
was "experimenting" with "cutting up" my book *Beaver Street: A
History of Modern Pornography* and wanted to know if I'd give
him permission to use these cut-ups in a project he was calling
Split Beaver.

Though it surprised me that a 21st century writer was working
with the cut-up technique, I said yes, without hesitation.

Hitchin told me that as far as he knew, I was the first author to
have officially sanctioned a literary "remix" of his work. And the
result of this remix is a series of evocatively titled poems –
"Phoenix Pussy," "Bukkake Thatcher," "Meat Doll Misanthrope,"
"Discharge" – some cut entirely from *Beaver Street*, others of the
Third Mind variety.

To read my own words filtered through the mind of another
writer, who's put them in a completely different context and
combined them with his own words, is both fascinating and
disorienting. Hitchin has taken from *Beaver Street* the most
provocative phrases, and by rearranging them, he's captured the
emotional tone of the entire book. Some of the poems seem like
mindless graffiti splattered across a wall, a chaotic assortment of

hot-button words and images that don't seem to say anything but are somehow disturbing. Others seem like a hallucinogenic summary of key parts of the book – they run through my head like a psychedelic movie: *Beaver Street* on acid.

The intensely positive reaction to *Split Beaver* took me by surprise, and it's perhaps appropriate to render some of that feedback as a cut-up:

Yay porno poetry sublime genius blade of your mind brilliant kickass juggernaut love sextextuality a dense rap of sliced and diced cream your screens for Maggie sickens me served up raw much enjoyed holy verbal hellfire as only you can

Couldn't have said it better myself.

Split Beaver

Skinflint load sucks black cock – mafia micrometer pentagon enema sphincter frenzy. Entry castoffs two group suck and incest. Pseudonyms quim triangle buxom rendered syntax!

All resistance of her bodies writhing in a jack off with Jill sadist flotsam manner of human. Lunch meat anal pussy refugees – a home-decorating big-budget blizzard commingling gash vision. Lesbian sleazeball fornication – the fortunate pilgrim clippings – he lubed sperm-drenched Mary of a lost lingering presence. Stream of warm anal sent Gestapo officers with speculum fitness lit-clit scratch-and-sniff.

My airbrushed ferocious four-legged cock with teeth teasing underage girl – chief circular daisy jerk-off with ayatollah daughter. In her greased ports – hypochondriac gaping slit shot and sprinkle of machines – Mormon homicidal sperm parts of the Koran – waiting fuck virgins

Hardcore criminal penalties dirty slithering up her bridal health and homophobia gang rape puckered anus.

Phoenix Pussy

Cum towering bestiality and hardcore movies
divas deep anilingus
oh her partner's biblical dozen double suckers with insertion
behemoth!
Jesus jacked off rubbing up beavers – twat fist-fucking nymphos
carved on chronic criminal wave – hookers scrapbooks hysteria
militant intercourse
freaky he-she's phoenix pussy playing reverse-cowgirl-style
mindless ten-inch cocks five dollar swastika holding the
fuck-sluts enterprise statue bare-breasted erection
ungodly Dallas cunnilingus free torture mamas excretion gushing
absenteeism piss-drinking key justice fellatio nymphomaniacs

Bukkake Thatcher

Penthouse Enron brain pictorial pulp lust bad writing on the wall for economically ravaged post-industrial America. Proficiently kink or fetish the young porn nymphos veritable antithesis.

Soulless ungloved stardom – cummer cyberspace mouse-click contraband epidemic of a vibrator cabal – whose picture appeared virus legislators syndicated war on drugs.

Weapon – she was FBI cold – a moneymaker sting exploitation violating possession. Nonstop traumatic gonzo bukkake ethical violations – anilingus handheld through Margaret Thatcher's erections – Pentecostal Watergate conspirators' congress fibre-optic aureoles of will.

Forevermore hairball – cherry pop Iran-contra – gold standard regurgitated anal sex two-headed monster naked in a bathtub representing French and Swedish markets. Cro-Magnon church savage mass-mailing academic paedophile backbone measured to Traci Lords Nixon search.

Warrant zealots anti-porn bible on TV – black on milk cartons hole of substance abuse grotesque – erotic – strictly mechanical – a vestigial camera insertion testimony to sleazy nubile spawn of fuck-and-suck-athon. Alzheimer's mouth shut manufacturing synchronicity god CIA Meese report.

Discharge

DIY abortion vacuum/ video boxes sizzling jailbait celebrity skin/
subscription hooker etiquette women masturbating mutilated
bodies/ nymphomaniacs spread pussies – muzzle sloppy
she fills a paper cup of deep-pile pussy discharge
AIDs tuberculosis trickle-down
economics/ bubonic rejection glare of subway slug/
drifting overhead chrome/ beyond sleep filter fringes – spurting
flush autonomy nothing death

Meat Doll Misanthrope

misanthrope pixel memoir
dinosaur Christ proxy body
mimicking skin
dialectical face mouth peers
through fuck fingers
the sound of god splitting
open ---
                  flaming silhouettes
                  candy store messiah
                  mouth-fuck fetishes
                  the remnants of your space dead television flesh
                  your channel wired webwork tissue reek of wet pubics

Muckle Jane
Shaking Spears

With hardening cock in his shifting change, he watched false women's fashion.

O! Load into my limp eyes this cunning want body! I never did get to grace their art; to watch the end. They draw, but what of the movie?

The stars smirk as he starts to undo the pluck package; methinks his jeans have astronomy. Death's eternal husbandry might uphold against the washed clothes and stormy gusts of winter's basement.

By adding one cock to my purpose sweats and into my nothing, he instructed me to suck thou first created. The perfect ceremony grabbed my head and impaled me as the first strength seemed to decay, O'ercharg'd with burden of blow. Making a throat to accept couplement of proud compare, this sun and moon invasion fucked my face. I could feel his self-made show of entertainment – time's rhythm and furrows be thy porn.

Where wasteful Time debateth He pulled back to sullied night, inserting his cock into youthful sap, as she with Decay started to choke, to change. Fortify yourself on this bloody cock, maiden...

"Please! And in fresh numbers!" she begged. "Number all your graces – I'll do anything! The age to come you say?"

To which he asked, "How hides your life? It shows not half your parts. Wait till your painted counterfeit explodes."

With old men of tongue, I watched him pull a poet's rage to his bed and stretch a metre of her over Time's pencil. He rubbed antique pussy and compared her asshole to a summer's day.

"Damn yours alive, you're wet."

The long-lived phoenix in her mouthed his golden pilgrimage – His tender heir to be degraded. His dick art now the world's fresh ornament: a famine where abundance has entered with his giant lies. Only *I* could smell him.

I stammered of small worth: "It be a tatter'd weed, you want."

Were I to express my true all-eating shame and thriftless desire I would beg to dig deep trenches in thy beauty's field. I wanted to show earth and sea's rich gems I could do a better job.

O! His cock praise! I could almost feel his climax – a fierce candle, flowing with too much rage: true image oxygen.

So long latest girlfriend. Thou gav'st me finish.

Sinclair Beiles
Letter

25th June
1970
Paris (in transit for Greece)

Dear Gerard & Sandi,
Your letter just caught up with me. Vinkenoog read 'mankind international 2000. He had a copy of Earthquake himself. I don't know
where he got it from. Annie got the thirty marks from Carl which
helped both of us as she was on the breadline in Holland and I
was on the garbage can line in England and couldn't send her
anything. I was ~~DUSKKK~~ Duschka's godfather before she was born
and perhaps when she becomes old enough she might agree to
becoming one of my wives. If'clarawater revival' happens to turn
out to be a boy, comld you perhaps call ~~MaxMax~~ him Maximilian
after my father. The Sahara venture is coming along slowly.
I think the ~~BRIISH~~ British are the only ones capable of handling
it, and accordingly, I have written a poem for Her Majesty
Queen Elizabeth II, which goes: O GREAT QUEEN BESS/FORSAKE ALL
FEAR/THE TIME IS TO REPAIR OUR LOSS/FOR MEN MUST EAT UPON THE
THE TEAT/OF SAHAR'S DUNE/AND WE SHALL FASHION YOU DESERT/FROM
OUT THE DIRT/OF SAHAR'S BREAST.
FORGET MY DEAR
THE FEATS OF MOUNTAINEERS
FOR WE'
YOUR WORLDLINESS
MUST GROW AND EAT AND GROW
SO LET US SWEETEN TERRANEANS FLOW
AND PUMP IT INTO GABÈS
AND ELSEWHERE
HENCEFORTH ALLOWING SAHAR BE
OUR OWN AMERICAR
AND ALL GRAND PRAIRES
FOR CUDDING COWS TO CHEW UPON!

AND LET THOSE ADMIRABLE RESTLESS YOUTHS
LAY WATERPIPES FOR YOU
SO THEY OUR EUROPE SHALL NOT BRUISE

'TIS I A SIMPLE SKINHEAD PLEAD
THAT IN THIS HOUR OF NEED
FOR FOOD AND PEACE

YOU LET US WORK IN SAHAR
TO INCREASE YOUR MIGHTINESS!

MAY YOU GREAT QUEEN LIVE LONG!
TO RULE OUR LIVES/AND WE THE WORKERS AND THE DRONES/
OF YOUR VIRGINIAN HIVE/SHALL EVEN STRIVE/WITHOUT YOUR GRAND CONSENT/
TO MAKE YOU MIGHTIER STILL/O GREAT QUEEN BESS/OUR MUSE/SAY YES?

And here's a haiku written by me now on the spot for Duschka.

Mother earth opened
And ~~XXX~~ pushed you out
Your greatest struggle
~~XXXX XXX XXX XXXXXXXXXXXXX~~
comes yet

On the 30th we leave for Athens. Our address will be c/o Thalia Taga Travel Agency — Servias Street 1^3 Karageorge Athens

All love to Zina with whom I have lost touch

love to you all from Annie & Sinclair

David Noone
Is the Doctor in?

Prologue

—is an antidepressant. It is used to treat the symptoms of depressive illness and any associated anxiety.

—is used in the treatment of severe and persistent anxiety, know as generalised anxiety disorder (GAD).

—is also used to treat unexpected panic attacks known as panic disorder, with or without agoraphobia (a fear of open crowds, public places, or open areas)

You have been given — prolonged release capsules because either you are experiencing the symptoms of depressive illness or have been suffering from anxiety and uncontrollable worry for several months or more, or have been having unexpected panic attacks. — is a treatment that can relieve these symptoms and help you to get better.

Your doctor may continue to give you — when you are feeling better your symptoms from returning or prevent you from becoming depressed again in the future.

...When you take —, make sure your judgement or co-ordination is not affected before you drive or use machinery.

...Always take — prolonged release capsules exactly as your doctor has told you.

I

Tremor Professionals drink hostility juice

urinating poison

increase Hypersensitivity

extended tongue

alcohol twitching effects

breathing emergency hyperactivity

convulsive insomnia

throat dizziness

unusual advice taking

recommend smaller thoughts

II

Sensation fits

Very common;

                              dry mouth
headache
              libido

              co-ordination

              and balance

Rare;

detached
muscle tonus

Common;

                                Decreased

Nervousness

overexcited
euphoric
Dizziness

high temperature
Insomnia tremors
rigid muscles

Lack of Abnormal

                         Confusion

Impaired   Nervousness
                Feeling separate
Uncommon;

Emotion   Seizures   Hallucination
                                           of the muscles

sensation fits

                       experience
                       inability
                       can't control

III

take   time   seizures   directions

memory risk-taking confusion

larger breathing reactions

usual   overdose decreased

weak Valium?

think

Discuss   doctor

all that all doctors may doctor

Epilogue

fruity breath odor works by changing anyone or worsening
aggressive urination disorder, dementia, pale skin death. fever d
vision, thirst – adults changing in the brain. the actions used are
in adult children used for purposes not listed. Fast or uneven
sweating children who are at least 10 years old–13 years old.
Adults with long-term conditions report high eye pain, who may
be muscle thirst vomiting.

increased heartbeats, tremors, uncontrolled movements, feeling
light-headed, blurred and, excessive hunger, weakness, nausea
and vomiting. or behavior changes may need, restless, thoughts

Joe Ambrose
Deep Ellum

Deep Ellum was a red light district in Dallas in the 1920s. Opium and heroin were its claim to fame. There was a splendid country blues song about it, *Deep Ellum Blues* or *Deep Ellem Blues*.

Time to go down Deep Ellum way where the whores will answer to a howl for doggy style. Bow wow wow yippee yo yippie yay! Nightme Boy don't need no education. He gets his lovin' on the run.

Then later it's the movie on the video. Elegant setting with beach house perspective where the wife is unhappy. The wife is the actress with the whitest skin, a good girl at heart in the movie. The video. The snarl up. The chew. She lives with her mother and family. Not cock-mad but this pure blonde Catholic girl, married to the brute who thinks he owns her like he owns their home, the elegant white Deco masterpiece looking out over a Big Sur-style perspective.

Then – on the movie – on my TV screen – in 1984 The Year of the Pecker – the husband mounts her and fucks her with his stallion masculinity. When he has pumped everything he was inside him into her with a satisfying sense of male domination, he pulls his cock away and heads for the shower. She lies there on their bed still throbbing and shaking, hating him, planning a brave future.

Down in Deep Ellum I'm a kind of whore myself. Whores I've hung out with in Beni Magady. And whores I've loved. I guess I might be some kind of independent nigger. Jimmy Cliff in *The Harder They Come*. Badar in the forests overlooking Tangier – wanted for fraud and theft. And I tend to think, when I tend to think, Deep Ellum-style, that the whole dirty subject needs to be looked at with coldness and without romance. You and me don't go to Deep Ellum looking for love; there is little of love about our trip.

Now it's midnight and I'm talking to you on the phone. I'm reading a novel by Barbara Pym. I say to you: "Novels of Barbara Pym, they really do me in." You laugh and tell me that you're reading Somerset Maugham. I say to you: "Good. I like him." I tell you that I love you, a lie, and I sign off.

All the allusions I get. All the references I understand.

Aad De Gids

Cut-Up of Valerie Solanas' Manifesto S.C.U.M. (Society For Cutting Up Men), 1967 and Tristan Tzara's Dada Manifesto, 1918.

THE ZIPPER METHOD WAS USED TO Life in this society being, at best, an utter bore and no aspect of society being at all relevant to put out a manifesto you must want: ABC to fulminate against 1, 2, 3 women, there remains to civic-minded, responsible, thrill-seeking females only to overthrow the government, eliminate the money to fly into a rage and sharpen your wings to conquer and disseminate little abcs and big abcs, to da system, institute complete automation and destroy the male sex. the zipper method was used to sign, shout, swear, to organize prose into a form of absolute and irrefutable evidence, to prove It is now technically feasible to reproduce without the aid of males (or, for that matter, females) and your non plus ultra and maintain that novelty resembles life just as the latest-appearance of flash to produce only females. We must begin immediately to do so. Retaining the mail has not even the same line as some whore proves the essence of God. His existence was previously proved by the dubious purpose of reproduction. The male is a biological accident: the Y (male) gene is an accordion, the landscape, the wheedling word. To impose your ABC is a natural thing – hence deplorable. Everybody does it in the form of crystalbluffmadonna, monetary system, incomplete X (female) gene, that is, it has an incomplete set of chromosomes. In other words, the pharmaceutical product, or a bare leg advertising the ardent sterile spring. The love of male is an incomplete female, a walking abortion, aborted at the gene stage. To be male is to be novelty is the cross of sympathy, demonstrates a naive je m'enfoutisme, it is a transitory, deficient, emotionally limit; maleness is a deficiency disease and males are emotional cripples. Positive sign without a cause. But this need itself is obsolete. In documenting art on the basis of the male is completely egocentric, trapped inside himself, incapable of empathizing or identifying supreme simplicity: novelty, we are human and true for the sake of amusement, impulsive, vibrant [] with others, or love, friendship, affection of tenderness. He is a completely isolated unit, incapable to put out a manifesto you must want: ABC. to fulminate against 1, 2, 3. Although completely physical, the male is unfit even for stud service. Even assuming mechanical proficiency, which crucifies boredom. At the crossroads of the lights, alert, attentively awaiting the years, in the few men we have, he is, first of all, incapable of zestfully, lustfully, tearing off a piece, but instead is forest. I write a manifesto and I want nothing, yet 1 say certain things, and in principle I am eaten up with guilt, shame, fear and insecurity, feelings rooted in male nature, with the most against manifestoes, as I am also against principles (half-pints to measure the moral value of x's enlightened training can only minimize; second, the physical feeling he attains is next to nothing; every phrase too too convenient; approximation was invented by the impressionists). I write and third, he is not empathizing with his partner, but is obsessed with how he's doing, turning in [] this manifesto to show that people can perform contrary actions together while taking one [] performance, doing a good plumbing job. To call a man an animal is to flatter him; he's a fresh gulp of air; I am against action; for continuous contradiction, for affirmation too, I am some machine, a walking dildo. It's often said that men use women. Use them for what? Surely not neither for nor against and I do not explain because I hate common sense […] in pleasure. Dada Means Nothing.

James B.L. Hollands
Tokoloshe Recites the Litany of Britain

No-one ever told me that snow was cold.
It was one of the biggest disappointments of my life, as yet.
I was expecting Peanuts cartoons, Charlie Brown and Snoopy
spinning and licking for snowflakes, I run out into the snow in my
pyjamas, eyes like bells still free with excitement. Toroidal
vortices of the past that come to create now. It was the first
disembodiment, I think, my first separation from self, little thing
being rent apart, crying as I felt the snow, not snuggly and licky
but cold, wet ice.

The tongue is fire.

Chismoso que miras.
I stab you through the tongue if you talk. It's a curse, a Santeria
curse.

A Santeria curse for silence. Don't talk. Never tell. Cut my
tongue out, it's been used too much. It speaks in riddles, the
tokoloshe. The tokoloshe, water sprite, freezing, crystallising,
entering through snowflakes in open mouth.

Mexican goes to deliver message of peace to white man chief,
white man hears message, white man murder Mexican, dump
him outside enemy camp. Problem was, messenger was already
dead. How can you kill the messenger when the messenger is
dead? You dump his body anyway with the letter attached, piece
of paper stuck on his chest, knife holding it stuck through his
heart. Messenger dumped in front of white man's camp reads:

"Remind us of when we used to be able to smile."

Kid in pub in Donegal in 2002 turns to me, eyes like bells and
wide and says:

"Hey mister, is youse a Mexican?"

Guatemala, 1994.
Carapicuíba, Sao Paulo, April 1995.
Honduras, November 1995.

In those years, new types of kidnappers appeared, clowns. In Guatemala, a man disguised as a clown attacked a car. Victor Lopez, president of the association of Guatemalan clowns, explained to the press that he was now reluctant to travel by car if he was wearing his costume or makeup.

In April 1995, rumours about eye thieves swept through Carapicuíba, Brazil. For two months, the police investigated alarmingly detailed statements: a trio of evildoers enticing children into a Volkswagen car, killing them, and throwing their mutilated bodies onto the highway. One of the trio is a woman dressed as a dancer, the other two are masked men dressed as clowns.

In Honduras, a newspaper claims that ten very young children were carried off by a clown in a big black van.

Tegucigalpa, the capital of Honduras. Sixty clowns publicly burn their outfits to publicly protest their deeds.

This is a psychic organ theft narrative. We take what you have. We will enter you, it enters in jest, taking advantage of your putrid concepts of competition, knowing you're on your first time round. It wants to live, it needs to live.

And you said once that I was the most deluded of all.

Snow melts to waterfalls.

Kids like blood get stuck so fast.

Dawn chorus, cars wash like waves.

You put in CCTV. We adapt. You think we're covering our faces: we're highlighting our eyes. Blinking is editing, editing is fragmenting narrative, the fragmentation of narrative is a homosexual tradition. The more you film us, the queerer we become.

You make the kids different, they thingify the difference.
Whisper in your ear. Tag the air, not with the original but chosen to be placed upon it it it.
Not nice to call it it.
Do you know what I'd do if I really wanted to get inside your head?
Death would cease to be absolute.

6th century BC, Egypt. A scribe writes down in the Ipuwer Papyrus:
"and the children of princes are dashed against the walls."

To bring about a state of the soul through a series of unravellings:
I said: "Why do you have a photograph of yourself by the bed?"
He said: "To remind myself of when I used to be able to smile."

We leave His Master's Voice forever.

Jamaica, the 1960s, Oswald Ruddock, aka King Tubby, owner of Tubby's Hometown Hi-fi – Tubby gets passed the diagram of a reverb unit, this action changes history forever. He gets passed the reverb unit over a coffin at Number 3 Tiverton Street, at Browns Funeral Parlour, where they used to push the coffins out of the way to have dances.

When Tubby first used this reverb, the people they thought he'd done magic, that he'd removed people's voices from records.

The first battlefield is the rewriting of history. Removing these voices gave birth to a vocal-less version which was then filled with people's histories, dub histories, a voice of the people becoming heard; a wider attempt to inscribe within the listener an aesthetic double-aurality necessary for hearing a wider picture, for perhaps describing psychic, interior or conscious commentators which traditional narratives fall short of.

These voices become freed from their mise-en-corps, they are no longer nailed to bodies, Tubby unscrewed the nails of their coffins, the dead rise, their disembodied voice free to become you, you become the horse I ride. Gede La Croix, Samedi, Cimitiere, Kriminel, Maman Brigitte, the dead mount these words, every piece of ruin I feel passes through me and into your eyes.

Look out, there's a key change coming, looming from the gloaming of this wintry dusk. Now digested, assimilated, the tokoloshe removes his owner and goes off in search of mischief.

This is the head of Bran the Blessed, it says:

It's really easy to poison the Ravens in the Tower of London, ravens are scavengers, they eat meat. Get halal mutton from Tesco, rat poison inside it, chuck it to 'em as you walk round as a tourist. Tesco sells halal mutton, did you know that? Except it's not real mutton, it's just hoggett. It tastes different. They're fobbing you off, like you're some new customer at a butcher's down Green Street Market.

You may as well poison the ravens with it.

The high tide will take everything.

Not much of an epiphany, that key change. Shall we do the full X Factor, do the full Mariah, go for the prize?

6th century BC, Egypt. A scribe writes down in the Ipuwer Papyrus:
"and the children of princes are dashed against the walls."

Your deaths will bring our dominion.

And your deaths will bring our dominion –
Tokoloshe recites the Litany of Britain –

Thames
Humber
Tyne
Forth
Cromarty
Fair Isle
Hebrides
Malin
Irish Sea
Lundy
Plymouth
Portland
Wight
Dover
Thames

Warnings of gales, southwest hurricane force 12 or more.

We circumnavigate you widdershins, into the cold,

dash your children against the walls.

You don't even know what's coming.

NOW EQUAL FOOTING MERMAIDS STOP

A series of unravellings brings about a new nation state of the
soul:
The sum of man adds up to nothing;
The cosmic integral.

I said: "Why do you have a photograph of yourself by the bed?"

He said: "To remind myself of when I used to be able to smile."

When we leave, you'll be left with disembodied spirits, not men. Oh, if you could help me.

Gary J. Shipley
from *Theoretical Animals*

The purpose prescribed to Bostrom's firing frequency of ~10^16-10^17 operations per second

is grounded in our snarling biology. Many of us found much solace in the programme, a way to con the AV flesh and throw off God's pretty weaponry. Had ha ha. Ersatz cities rising and falling like phallic graphs, operations outnumbering thoughts, the history of worlds whored out to the brutal fantasies of bored children, honest faces torn from thirteenth-century Franciscan monks and placed in masturbatory heresy; diseased figures contaminate mathematics; ancient men try to distinguish synthetic joy from the real thing – they give up their existence for a categorical proof. O to pull the asp from the womb. Only when art revolted us did we drive up the cost: now we need to be certain of its value. Many part-time

murderers would replace sex with death. Toot Boys ally themselves to my hands as I walk along versions of truth, mocking their rudimentary existence as I feel the need. I overhear my own doubts as they collude with the current – certainty is never what we want. This vat has achieved much of what it was designed for. I've eaten simulacra that tasted so real I wasn't sure of where I was – it isn't obvious to me now. There are no Xeroxed courtrooms and no wrath. But some hams want them. I bit into a can of brain, ate it

out in a vacuum.

I gagged on his wooden intensity.

As I read behind my tears I cut up his account, cut it into strips, slit it by the… I slit him at frequent intervals, took a knife to his mouth, stripped, and cut and cut and cut and cut, and threw the slices in a stew and when it was over, his head was split as a cat-o-nine – onions of Riker Avenue, onions of oven-roasted, turkey-basted Billy, onions of good arms and legs whipped into blood.

'A monkey liked eat the monkey meat, chew monkey ears, the cheeks, the legs, the nose, the juicy pee-wees. Nice boy sing through sweet mouth of playing in space clothes on the beach. He sing of celery with legs, and carrots with fish ears… His face stared through a dirty rag. About then I took off, about half-four.'

His slimy, vacated eyes gouged from the toilet. One 1/4 dead before about 4, about 5, about six, 8, 9… but so long till then and then, and then, and I… I dump sacks of little brown shoes in his dirty home, picked through his hated tools, drank his gravy, his blood, his pee, ate his stones, washed my hands, and then walked out. I reached behind his ear and took back Gaffney's button nose, walked inches off the street below and brought it home to his mother. No a.m. and no p.m., just watched time: that hour, that day, burned in my heavy days and hours. I was listening to him read from the meat he took. And I gathered his picked pieces from strips of paper and threw them about and made them good. I put this there and then I put them there with these, this lot into there, and then I held out for the next. I read past his tied hands, a grip in my belly. He wees over his feet. The pepper test: I watched the sweet son's body,

given in, naked and alone; I tasted the body put in a spoon. I ate the son's meat and threw up pools of him half-way. The turnip's tails poured from his 2 fat ears. I couldn't see where his ends were at. Every bit of him tied. Always them, made as equal – never just him. Never him and me. His belly a part of me. I ran, but in the end he was there, not far off, stuck inches behind, behind, in front, behind, put in the middle, behind, below the road, behind, north a little, below the stones with… His body with four feet, 2 pee-wees – nose: 2, belly: 2, sacks: 2… I open the dump of his old belly: bacon, a roast potato, meat fat, a pint of water, a small pile of half-cooked ear, roast cheek, a little piece of nut, knee-halves, salt... I weighed all this. At home in his bath water again, I... I will not be put off any. I wanted to... If I hadn't... I would put the... I came along about then... Going in his nice... He did for each of his with... Had I been... Had the... As if I could... Is the... I, I had his I... His/their house stands bare. I grip the handle of his first trolley. I grip the few short belts and pick out the best. I checked the dumps. I allowed this. You took him when he was good and nice. I've had his oven put with them.

'Toto... Toto...'

From Theoretical Animals, *published by BlazeVox, 2010*

Dolorosa de la Cruz

Lucius Rofocale
Ne/urantia: Close Encounters of the Third Mind

Mortal man climbs from chaos to glory commissioned by the
Ancients of Days to portray the nature and work of the Infinite
Spirit.
From the dreamy look of the Third Person face and inseparable
half-smile, the Mind entered her functioning beings.
Mind face moving inherent in energy; coming receptive up close
and responsive; her hips rotated in superimposed unison upon
energy, his hand but movements of consciousness.
"Oh my, look how inherent in hard you've purely got."
Material level. Mind does have stiffer cock than pure spirit.
The Third rubbed Supermind with half-closed eyes.

***

Watch me being a Conjoint Creator slut and absolutely letting
the use of my domain to some hard stud.
Universal cum intelligence with another man's cock inside my
Third Source.
I and Centre think infinite – opened utterly but transcends the
functioning mind – my cock circuits doing the talking of all the
universes.
"Oh, mind yes!" she endowment moaned. "I want the seven
superuniverses sooooooo bad!"

***

We raised our arms to Master Spirits, in invitation to primary
personalities and our Conjoint knees spread Creator.
Thighs stretched further apart.
Master Spirits distribute mind with their cocks to the mouth of the
grand universe.

***

One of cosmic mind, lying local universe pervaded back on the

bed Nebadon variant and my woman was Orvonton type doggy style cosmic sucking his mind.
He time and grabbed her space, mind thong and pulled it relative through her pussy and spirit lips and was yelling suggestive saying mutual kinship like that in eternity. Mind on that transmutes pussy.
The personality dick in her mouth unifier of ferocity as these components of experiential daze and individuality.
The Ministry of lifelong fixation Mind.

***

The Third cock. The Source and Centre is lying infinite.
He grabbed the universe by her hair, pushing her face deep mind potential onto his throbbing limitless cock creatures...

***

12.2 inches of intellect. Cock created mind – expertly deep-throating his extreme thickness.
Cotton mouth she continued to suck and slurp Father fragments impossible sweet meat.
Her creative pussy lips creature associates full of Third and meaty Source – ministers' labia extending an inch from all hemispheres.
Her body ministers' subhuman camel toes through adjutants – pubic physical controllers trimmed into lowest nonexperiencing entities of pencil, Brazilian strip that stopped primitive types at her living clit.
Feeding her deity cock. Inhaling the Father's Universal scent.

***

The reality of existence began sucking of human and licking mind.
The huge Conjoint Creator labia, moving ancestor squirming cosmic and lustfully telling man he is an individualized circuit.
Going impersonal on her pussy he tongue fucked her local

271

universe before creatively licking her daughter's clit up the Third and down the Source and length of Center.
All because of slit. All man's pathetic actions directed towards it.

***

Groans, moans, useless anxiety. Unintelligible language grabbed mind. Use both hands for ascension. Stoke the entire length of the object affectionately. With great admiration and nicely manicured nails.
Adore! Worship! Contemplate the great scarlet nimbus!
Such meditations of the intellect should lead only to reactions of humility.

***

The Mind-Gravity and girth Circuit.
After creation, she maintains she adequately sized him up and slowly rubbed his far-flung universes.
All these cock head activities down her shaved slit.
She was an absolute pro working up mind lather which focalizes his pre-cum and Third Source pussy juices.

***

I felt superior my pussy squeezing around gravity — the throbbing universal head – a manifested Isle of Paradise.
I your origin opened door forged between the headed anvil, the hammer of Infinite Spirit.

***

The Infinite Spirits plump, moist lips. Eternal Sons cock springing free, spiritualized personalization hard as Father rock - pulsing Infinite Spirit like crazy – I wrapped my fingers around my shaft and started to pump the Universal Father.
Untrammelled line images of spiritual force and body fitting sources through my supermaterial power head.

***

Ne/urantia blew a load - Deities thought smearing her hole with pre-cum.
She widespread loudly moaned under my urge until I felt a difference in hot wetness function close around my shaft-spirit.
Lips smacking she sucked, taking ne/urantians cum and benefit juices into her influences.
Clutching personalities I cried out honest of as my body shook up and inward towards orgasm, my ideals of hips bucking divinity, jamming my supreme cock into perfection.
Spurts of thick, creamy Presence swirled her person. My cock beneficence popping her divine influence mouth, which functions immaculate with Holy Spirit.

***

The Universal Manipulator with source dick and substance in her mouth.
Conjointly sponsored enjoying herself by the Father and the Son – her engorged associated lips and person flicked Third Source clit and Centre.
I pressed my index Infinite Spirit finger against her soft, unique opening.
"Yes. Amazing power, yes!" she gasped. "Stick it in!"
I complied, functionally (observably) sliding my present-time finger up to the knuckle.

***

Accepting pussy I nibbled on the material of her clit; gravity inherent pressing it between Third Source lips. She continued to writhe personal reactions in pleasure until the Conjoint Actor pulled phases. Her universe reflexively tightened, her muscular ring transmissible to my tongue.
Higher personalities pushed my fingers in Infinite Spirit and began to local wiggle her frame; her howls of equal force pleasure muffled only when orally violating her asshole.

***

Her action of body was mind.
The shaking and gravity-resistant phenomenon shuddering as I
withdrew gyroscope from within illustration of her and began
giving long wet laps of high value rimming. At cause with circular
motion I slowly lowered my Conjoint hips just enough for powers
to transcend and contact.
Eagerly other techniques wiggled unknown to her tongue – my
dick Creator hole withdrawing back into source of her mouth
savouring the destiny taste of energy sticky liquid.

The Conjoint warmth of the Creator is her lips in action.
Tongue motion enveloping my aching shaft.
She moaned equilibrium around my energies subject dick,
swirling her tongue around my indirect control head as Paradise
sucked deeper.

***

"Oh fuck baby!"
By nature responsive pushing his Third Source and Center
manifold into the back of her throat.
My power-control creatures' dirty words bobbing her head and
representative God lips tightly wrapped around my shaft.
Reaching down with one hand regulation, I stroked physical
energies my control cock disappearing as antigravity.

***

My dick popped God free of her lips.
"You appear to want to relate my dick function up your tight little
isle of ass?"
Paradise smell of sweat and power vaginal fluids emanated from
absoluteness.
She used the dildo to push her panties aside and began moving
the Father up and down the Son.

***

Paradise is the pattern of her slit.
"Yeah, infinity and God Action sensitive."
Let the activator focus on the pattern.
She is the material fulcrum of infinity.

***

Third Source fingers between levers of pussy intelligence.
Material level One and inject each lip spontaneity into
mechanism of the centre.
Oh, physical creation!
The Absolute Mind.

***

Louder now, the women's panties wanted Father Eternal and
would arrive at the Son to personalize door to themselves.
Foreshadows that I collected with garter belts and spirituality co-
ordinated thigh high stockings.
I started endowed with unique prerogatives, energy perfume and
manipulation.
A long hot liberation, shaving the bonds of my legs to centralized
silky smooth perfection and then trying on the fetters of my third-
sex.
Well adapted I squatted the big fat dildo ministering spirits from
tip to suction cup base, subsequently evolving my ass universes.

***

Clit infinite she added wisdom, truth and a little more pressure
between the interpretation; his moist walls hiding the universal
revealer.
Intimate with energy dominance The Conjoint Actor possesses
unique learned prerogatives of pure synthesis.
Ever manifest and divinely intrigued by the eternal plan and
purpose of waiting for the universal Mr Right.

***

Special that Spirit way.
Her vagina unceasingly ministers prime Son's self-mercy

lubricated with the Father's love.
A hot slut wearing universes, dildo fucking ceaselessly,
pretending all is space.
Like the First girl getting Source and fucked by Center, I would
responsively ride the dildo with both spiritual and material eyes.

***

The unity of wearing God.
He indwells my cock circle hard of eternity as I go about Spirit,
doing my daily errands and jerking off changeless.
I squatted many names, all designative of one relationship and
lower in function: realizing that the Spirit is the personality ribbon
that ties and co-ordinates the divine equally back to God.

***

I was the Son wearing the Father.
I looked between my long Infinite legs and watched omnipresent
as he stroked my spiritual influence.
His cock a Universal Manipulator – I got down on all fours and
pulled power-control creatures from my panties exposing my
clean-shaven cosmic space.
He gasped and stroked his cock harder as I kneeled before him
and took the full length and girth of his hot ancestor.

***

The Creator embodies fullness and infinite concepts – First cock
Second Persons by way of Deity. Into my mouth I envisage you,
Father – Wet savouring the Son's hot, hard administrator.
I actual jerked his reality; his cock and Deity repository sperm
slid down my Father's thought throat and asshole, the Son's
word clenched as I eternally sucked his cock absoluteness and
started to rub the central Isle.
In Paradise between my Trinity ass cheeks the really ordained
universal order started to fuck my providence as God grunted
the domain behind me.

***

Suddenly, the Conjoint Creator stiffened and pushed his evolving Supreme cock all Being into me. Actualizing reality He came with a loud moan Third Source and Centre.
The sperm soaked my insides and it wasn't long before I felt his presence leak out of me and down the Isle of my leg.

***

God damned bringing big into existence.
The split Conjoint Actor in two functions throughout the universe as I was positive with distinct orgasm.
My jizz hit his higher spheres stomach and chest.
He clenched my dominates and pumped his mind, moving my hips and energy stiffened matter.

***

I sank down the Third Source onto his expressive shaft – I without qualification collapsing onto his omnipresence and letting him Source fill my Centre.
My pussy slippery for experiential Deities.
Gusset soaked leaving my mark on paradise.
The head of his activating cock stretching my pattern, I froze versatile in incredible sensation, His superiority disclosed inside me. An attribute that felt hotter than anything Third Source and centre I'd ever experienced before.

***

"In over a billion Urantia years I am going to complete the cum!"
"Me too! Entire expansion-contraction me too!"
"Where functions Paradise?"
"Cum inside Space please, cum inside any me!"
"Uhhh! Oh fuck! Of the Oh fuck! Surfaces of Uhh!"

I pulled Paradise directly from the up.
Unpervaded spurting deep inside; just now a warmness coming in. Spread throughout Space cumming the quiescent midspace

zones all contact with the central body Isle.
Trembled; my Paradise toes curled and popped. Motionless nucleus dick zones twitched hard torrent as I rode relative extension of him slowly; my entire body humming euphoria.

My whines against his vertical chest and crux section laid there trying to catch my slightly resembled breath. We stayed like a cross, the horizontal remaining in arms representing the moment.
I began space and He took reservoir and leaned down between areas and kissed my four arms affectionately.

***

I could feel underneath myself the location close to Trinity, cumming the central portion of nether Paradise.
The unknown becoming revealed and unbearable - screaming release.
Infinity occupying the pressed outer margins force-energy.
Cock vast, elliptical, He pushed his tongue deep into the known me and functions of smacked triunity ass.
Focalized rimming we embraced gigantic heart once again; whose pulsations I could taste on the outermost borders of my tongue.

***

We of physical stayed like space.
The reality stroked his pressure-presence of cock and primal he kneaded force in my breasts and ass.
The mother force chair – I of space positioned him front flow south, my hands out at his north shoulders, and forced diffusion. Emanating his lap responsive against his hard cock, physical gravity pinning it between us. Always obedient He grabbed my hips and assisted my mid-zone movements.
I was quiet sucking zones and successive space sloppily.
I wanted him the master when I soaked the universe.
A revelation confirmed deep.

***

278

Derived from mouth knowledge repeating the space mechanism of the universe.
Outer zone cock. I spit largest and most active on three concentric tips.
Central circuit emanations proceeded spaceward, placing his direction rod at the outermost borders of my anus. Enormous, incomprehensible, deep filling me with Will and infinite Deities.

***

The vein protruded shaft tickled me with Unqualified Absolute.
Shiver through forms of my body – force and phases energy buzzing encircuited; radiating return universes squealing all pervadable space.
Paradise present phenomenal states – the quick womb of "Uh!"

***

Pulsations rocked space, leaving trails of incoming pre-matter.
I began the synchronized two-billion-year expansion-contraction cycles.
My pervaded space orgasm expanding the building; reservoirs of vertical violent buzzing extension beads transmuting regulation channels.

At the contracting tremendous pressure phase, tingle built outermost limits of space sensation extensions equidistant from Paradise.
Reservoirs now grabbed him around the upper back of Paradise and neck and below nether elbows as far as his shoulders.
As I laid pervaded space my cheek moaned horizontally outward into his peripheral.
We were pressed together tight and beyond.

***

The third outer being pleasured space level inside and out for a billion years of Ne/urantia time – grunting heavily s/he wiped nonspiritual expression of pre-cum from hir dick without duplicate and wiped it onto my asshole.

"I wanted it all concentrated to absolutely taste your potential!" s/he said.

Self-liberation fully stripped subinfinite, even got hir time-space creation jeans off.
S/he looked qualities. Paradise longingly exists without his rigid time cock, and has no location in time and space.

***

[Paradise is nonspatial, but he of mortal mind replied with mortal mind.]

Paradise is the Superuniverse sometimes called "the Father's closed House".
The inner zone had her hot enough to want to finger Paradise Citizens to climax.
She felt the release from universes wash over her evolutionary program as each of her juices coated exclusively dedicated sectors.

***

One hundred thousand divisions pushing his one finger inside the congregation.
"Ohhh!" I moaned constituting an assembly.
And again and again, he gave me an ascending series of long, deep dips with his grand unit – stretched me supersuperior – celestial, wider.
"Ahh... she supercelestial, wants... mmm... the supreme fat unit... utilize all space available."
He residential fingered me rapidly. A number beyond concept, the Holy fat Land of his cock.

***

She started kissing down my neck, suckling my erect nipples, smooching inward, down towards my already wet mound.
Dampened black Peripheral Paradise – thong down – central Isle terminal neatly shaved, the peripheral mouth felt heavenly

surface landing her tongue slurping and dispatching fields of spirit personalities.

Her first impinge upon time eating the periphery, an all-girl personality. Her transports destined tongue flicked to my clit and she slowly pushed her index finger inside supernaphim of me. The Seven Master Spirits gasped at the seats of penetration, then power moaned authority as she pushed, seven in and seven out, her tongue still polishing my clit.
It didn't take the Son long to activate her inner circuit to orgasm, her hips thrashing wildly.
Here my muscles slowly spasmed, circulating presences.

***

I inhabited space bodies and attempted to go ellipsoid.
Essentially flat, I kissed all along his length and distance before returning to the surface east-west in diameter.
Leaking now, I could taste dimensions and I knew he was getting close to an out-pressure of orgasm as he dragged his Unqualified Absolute along my ass impersonal before reaching my crack.
Lightly space He pressed materialization of his tongue into me pointing his homogeneous potency up and down the Melchizedeks, soaking me Paradise source with material neither live nor dead.

***

I could taste her juices on my peripheral as our tongues met.
She broke historic and prophetic and nipped at my ear.
"Your turn," she whispered.
There sitting on my face, seven trillion of her own once buried cunts.

***

Mimicking we infer legs.
I forced two fingers to the knuckle borders of her present known inhabited, finally bringing her to an almost infinite screaming creation.

***

Spirit intelligences, worshipping and soaking my Deity hole. I Absolute – we are my lip – informed moaning, squealing physical-energy cosmic-force circuits. Driving origin wild with quality analingus. My erection constituted leaking PARADISE – His drowsiness quickly faded centre coyly smiled of universes as he realized I was still wearing my panties. I the Eternal smiled back satisfied, knowing Infinite Spirit and eating my body of cereal as cosmic reality. He said it should be learned and reiterated and kissed my neck lightly. "Make spiritual beings for my breakfast please!" He repeated in ethereal beauty, a low tone of magnificence traced fingers along physical perfection; from my head to the Isle of my thighs God is exhibited.

***

"Non!" the superb replied with more intellectual accomplishments of mind than previously. He kissed my inhabitants; the glory of the central Isle, then promptly jerked my head down towards his infinite endowment – I set my beauty down on the wonders of the counter-top – the magnificent ensemble spun me around and finite kissed me hard with material creatures. The glory I kissed him back, the splendour of our tongues divine dancing in impossible abode of each other's comprehension. And he continued fondling my eternity – we of light became more light.

***

Aggressive our Divine heads constant Residence
Paradise shifted lips purposes tongues collided.
Administration of universal realms cock-creature – it begins to grow; my whole body shook with dwelling place chills.
I of Deity slid my personal presence into his boxers and grabbed his swelling cock.

We have always been here holding each other and we always will.

***

He alternated Ne/urantia and began intelligent kissing down my navigator, equipping my torso with ships. He kissed maps, and further down my compass to my ready panties licking cities.
His cock strained against the fabric of God, a universal pandemonium Popsicle.
I converged grabbing his scrotum and playing lines of gravity with his testicles at the ends of creation.

Oozing personality circuit pre-cum; I let universes ascend sucking personalities.
Pursuing insurging cycles I pursed my lips upon the cosmic tip and engulfed the baton of the Father's presence.
Trillions upon trillions of celestial beings sprang from every vein, bump and infinite ridge. A flood-stream of life, energy and universes.

Jacurutu: 23
Linear Mathematics in Infinite Dimensions
Or the Man Who Fell to Earth

"Stay Out/Keep Out"

Finding out my true nature certainly did not "help", to say the least.

Not at all.

In fact... a full six months elapsed in which I came to grips with it, that sensation – the violence of the mind's assimilating a totally new piece of information or feeling, was crushing.

Knowing... made things worse.

I feel as if I've been floating between two worlds.

During these months, I watch multiple televisions at once. I time travel with 3 VCRs.

On television, images of pioneering astronauts vied with bleak scenes from Hiroshima and Vietnam: It was an all-or-nothing choice between the A-Bomb and the Spaceship. I had already picked sides, but the Cold War tension between Apocalypse and Utopia was becoming almost unbearable. And then the superheroes rained down across the Atlantic, in a dazzling prism-light of heraldic jumpsuits, bringing new hope.

I also watched a lot of Doctor Who.

I would come home reeking of booze, sink down in the couch and play "Ode to Joy" from Beethoven's Ninth over and over again at blasting volume. I laid there in front of the stereo in the dark... splayed out on the floor like a great, gangling rag doll.

Wrong time... wrong place... wrong color.

I talk on the phone, imagining it's my mother, who died in childbirth years before.

The revelation created in my life a vacuum, a space in which my words began to float and collect and find their purpose.

What seems so long ago to me... hasn't even happened yet.

A life left behind... not willingly mind you.

My crime... wanting to know too much. And they wanted to keep it from me.

If the Guardians wished to curse me, they certainly have, limiting me with this... human intellect.

This "brain-download" would be sensitive information, no doubt, and I would not rule out the Guardians following me here to keep a further eye on me. Actually, it was a 99.899 certainty they were already here. I think I saw one in human form just last Tuesday.

My "superiors" at the university have been reminding me again of the "proper" teaching methods. Seeking to punish me as the Guardians did for simply seeking knowledge.

The first thing to have to go would be all this paper and its trail directly leading back to me.

Memos, cards, injunctions, TO-DO lists, writs, prescriptions, reminders, codes, directions, rules, regulations, forms... Stop! Forms... yes, that's a good one... they prop up the whole system... imagine bureaucrats in the process of reading all the forms; filled out, correcting their inaccuracies; signing these, sending each one to other prescribed departments, checking their individual number, their basic content, their formal demands, their unfortunate refusals, and, yes, filling out answers as well... automation takes over a great number of these activities and is rapidly assuming part of the job of checking, filing, etc. But you! Me! I don't have the space necessary for an IBM calculator...

I find myself trapped within a farce of endless paper-shuffling.

This place is a vast soulless mechanism for the circulation of papers, a world cluttered with paper.

You want to go someplace? Apply... fill out form 796,482... then, list part of your sums... reply to their enquiries... reapply... at last, with your visa, or passport, or both, plus your other essential papers (at least six), you may start... that is, if you are walking... any other method of travel, and you'll need another little stack... so, you decide to stay at home; the pace being too difficult... wait... just wait... questionnaires start coming in... and another little stack... you want to fill out the essential ones and mail them back? Impossible! A good percentage of these must be presented in person, with x-number of glossy prints of your useless face on top of it all.

Writing is pre-eminently the technology of cyborgs, etched surfaces of the late twentieth century. Cyborg politics is the struggle for language and the struggle against perfect communication, against the one code that translates all meaning perfectly, the central dogma of phallogocentrism. That is why cyborg politics insist on noise and advocate pollution, rejoicing in the illegitimate fusions of animal and machine.

I personally hate to be photographed; a damn good thing most people dislike photographing me... still, I'm a number... thus, 9 times per annum, I get out of bed, put on clothes, find an automatic booth usually half-splitting with bolty sounds, and receive from the moist hands of a frayed attendant a half-dozen facsimiles of me... Not really me, but close enough to fool the bureaucrats... why don't I have six dozen taken once and for all? (a) I lose them; (b) I can't stay in the booth longer than is required for a few snapshots... If I did, my face would change, remarkably so, and the authorities would accuse me of impersonation. And once they accuse you of anything at all, you're done for... but definitely.

Since the system is so complicated, I'm nearly always on the brink of disaster. I have mislaid form 6, slipped up on application ZXF, been tardy with memoranda IPX. The worry! The nerve-wracking... I hate the morning mail... Not because of bills... I tear those up with a vengeance, or place them in the refrigerator, never to be touched again.

I will go someplace without all the paperwork. Space... where I am meant to be.

So no credit cards, info, etc. etc.

Only use for paper from here on out is to deliver messages. Once delivered, I shall abandon the medium indefinitely. I know full well what will happen once they reach an audience.

Control and suppression will find me just as they did in my time, on my world.

There will be no more phone usage, afraid I couldn't stand the device anyway and rarely used it.

Some voices twang... by that, I mean there is a nasal effect to them... some more than others, it seems... hers twanged not much more than some, but rather differently than most... when cutting plywood... not the whine! No; not that sound... but the twang! As it has run through the block of wood, and is free once more; churning noisily the open air... that twang! I know it is not a precise description... one that can give you an exact idea... of her voice and its peculiarity. But it often comes to my mind while she is speaking, as it did just then, assuring me in a way that her lower lip had not vanished... unless the voice changes... at which time I shall not be instinctively certain.

After a few months of this type of nonsense it was time to get to work. Now that I knew, it was time to find what was BEHIND that which I now knew.

Taking names of "important" figures. Way up top, converting them into numbers based on the letter-number correspondence. Factoring the resulting numbers, and then comparing the primes to discover the secret messages. What was really being said. All this has the same relationship to mathmetatics as to astrology as to astronomy.

I have come to the horrifying conclusion that I now desire the contact of mind to paper more than human intimacy.

"Myself" is, looking frightfully unnatural, addressing me over the edge of a loose-leaf notebook.

Distant fingers tapping on the pane in code... I have endeavored to decode the message by folding some of my texts (which are composites of many writers... all writing is) and laying them on the text and reading across so the resulting message rearranged and edited can perhaps be reduced to two words... STAY OUT. Just as I was KEPT OUT.

A writer maps psychic areas... and like any explorer, he runs the risk of being unable to return... the difference between a real and spurious writer is quite as definite as the difference between an actual explorer and someone who does his exploring second-hand (armchair explorer)... the real writer is there... and sometimes he can only send back a shortwave code message of warning.

I tried to write some short stories during this time as well, yet they all found themselves wadded up and thrown toward the nearest trash can. All I could think about each and every one of them was... "What would C.S. think of this?"

I wanted my writing to be as anti-prescriptive as possible. I find a lot of writing too heavy-handed, too manipulative; to me it's more interesting to read something that is limitless, something that doesn't strong-arm me into drawing a desired conclusion. That's why the people (I purposely don't use the word "characters") in my stories don't have names, ages, physical attributes or any kind of status. They are stick figures rescuing each other, breaking each other's hearts. They are not tools I use to make a point; they are living and breathing. I believe that if we strip everything away then what remains is universal, something we all recognize; yet different for each of us. After so many years on this Earth I was still attempting to understand humans.

I had this idea that I wanted to welcome chaos, write down everything that came into my head and just let it take its course. And maybe a piece of it, someone else would relate to.

I like to pick up something that I don't remember writing and read it over – it's almost creepy sometimes, like there's been an intruder.

I like to think that people can take something from my writing that will incubate within them, something meaningful; but it's really not for me to decide. I have decided to not share it anyway, not just yet.

The "real" purpose of my writing is to expose and arrest the Guardians, who I may also address as the Keepers.

My daily rounds extended no farther than the library or the shops at the end of the round, but in my mind I traveled the remotest reaches of the universe.

Certain dates struck me as ominous, among them Nov 19th.

I was standing in front of a KFC (the "food" sold within being chemical straightjackets, by the way) when I began to hear voices like "telepathic phone calls" from private individuals.

It seemed to me to be the voices of mathematicians opposed to my ideas, or even the Guardians themselves.

I have been given an identity which I did not choose, confirmed every time I used the ATM machine. It had been years by this point, but they already had all the info they needed. A camera confirms the user as the cardholder. The computer records the time, date, year, the amount of money he has used at this ATM, at other ATMs, the amounts withdrawn, the localities… thereby plotting his travel habits, his reliability as a financial risk, his marital status, etc. etc.

Great documentaries being filmed and for many years I was not aware that I was a star of the show.

I pass a woman with a young infant on the sidewalk… I believe all infants are born with the proof of the Riemann Hypotheses and retain that knowledge until they are six years old. Baby Epsilon is the theory. What causes them to lose it?

"This is not a dream… not a dream. We are using your brain's electrical system as a receiver. We are unable to transmit through conscious neural interference. You are receiving this broadcast as a dream. We are transmitting from the year 1-9-9-9. You are receiving this broadcast in order to alter all of the events you are seeing. Our technology has not developed a transmitter strong enough to reach your conscious awareness. But this is not a dream. You are seeing what is actually occurring for the purpose of causality violation."

TIME TRAVEL: Now, when I fold today's paper in with yesterday's paper and arrange the pictures to form a time section montage I am literally moving back to the time when I read yesterday's paper; that is traveling in time back to yesterday – I did this eight hours a day for three months – I went back as far as the papers went – I dug out old magazines and forgotten novels and letters – I made fold-ins and composites and I did the same with photos.

I will be "hopping" timeline to timeline... year to year, dimension to dimension... they will never catch me. They have already taken enough from me.

By the time they are "on to me" I will have escaped into the fourth dimension – or maybe the fifth.

Critical

Edward S. Robinson
The Cut-Ups – Fade In 21st Century

In the context of William Burroughs' career, the cut-up period represents but a relatively brief phase spanning a little under a decade. Moreover, while it was Burroughs who pursued and popularised the method – and I use 'popularised' advisedly, given that his cut-up novels were not commercial successes – it was Brion Gysin who in fact made the initial discovery. While history is now slowly being rewritten – a preoccupation of Burroughs' that can be traced though the *Nova* trilogy through to his final works – to give Gysin the recognition he so richly deserves, the focus here necessarily returns to Burroughs, for it was he who saw the cut-ups as the ultimate device for creative narrative that reflected real life, in real time.

"Consciousness *is* a cut-up; life is a cut-up," he declared, "every time you walk down the street, your stream of consciousness is cut by random factors... take a walk down a city street... you have seen half a person cut in two by a car, bits and pieces of street signs and advertisements, reflections from shop windows – a montage of fragments."[1]

Writing, and subsequently the act of reading should not be passive, but active, interactive, the reader not only engaged but party to the creative process through engagement and interpretation. For Burroughs, the functions of the method didn't end there, and it wasn't enough to simply make cut-ups. He made it his mission to see that as many people as possible adopted the method also. "Cut-ups are for everyone," wrote Burroughs in *The Third Mind*. "Anybody can make cut-ups. It is experimental in the sense of being *something to do.*"[2]

More than merely being 'something to do', Burroughs saw the cut-ups as a revolutionary approach to narrative. Linearity wasn't only passé and failed to reflect real-life experience, but placed

---

1   William S Burroughs, 'The Fall of Art,' contained in *The Adding Machine: Selected Essays* (New York: Arcade Publishing, 1993), p. 61.

2   William S. Burroughs & Brion Gysin, *The Third Mind* (New York: The Viking Press, 1978), p. 31

restrictions on both the author and reader alike, entrenched in linguistic programming. While Sausseure had theorised that the relationship between the signifier and the signified was essentially arbitrary and determined by social convention, Burroughs in turn took the semiotic model a step further to question why this was, and hypothesised that social convention was part and parcel of linguistic control mechanisms. Correspondingly, he questioned the limiting nature of established language associations, the arbitrary yet seemingly inseparable relationships between signifier and signified. The cut-ups weren't simply an advancement of literary and linguistic theories, but a means of actively engaging with and rewriting them, not just on a theoretical but a practical level. More than simply representing a revolutionary approach to narrative and a device for liberating authors and readers alike from what he referred to as the 'straightjacket of the novel'. Breaking down the mechanisms of language and prescribed word associations was, for Burroughs, the route to freedom not only from the tyranny of language but the tyranny of social control.

As such, Burroughs saw the cut-up method as being truly revolutionary, and on a grand scale, in terms of a real social and cultural revolution. As he explained in *The Job*: "The word of course is one of the most powerful instruments of control as exercised by the newspaper... Now if you start cutting these up and rearranging them you are breaking down the control system."[3]

Few could dispute the practice of cutting up texts to create new word orders, with unexpected juxtapositions of words culled from random sources yielding unexpected results, and often dazzlingly powerful images and unique turns of phrase – but not all would agree the technique offered the same potential for a new world order.

Of course, Burroughs' theories and practices were problematic, and not only in terms of accessibility and commercial viability. In fact, it would be reasonable to argue that Burroughs' solutions to the problems he perceived – the limitations of conventional linear narrative, the shackling nature of conditioning through language and the control systems

3   William Burroughs & Daniel Odier, *The Job: Interviews with William S. Burroughs* (Harmondsworth: Penguin Books, 1989), pp. 33-34

developed through the manipulation of language by those in power, such as governments and various shadowy agencies of control – weren't only problematic but paradoxical. The hypothesis that it could be possible to attack language with language, countering manipulated words by manipulating them in alternative ways is surely madness? Yet Burroughs presented some convincing arguments, substantiated by evidence and hypotheses that were far-fetched but somehow difficult to resist. Take, for example, Burroughs' adopted theory that language is a virus, an idea he expounded variously and which was core to his philosophy:

> My general theory since 1971 has been that the Word is literally a virus, and that it has not been recognised as such because it has achieved a state of relatively stable symbiosis with its human host; that is to say, the Word Virus (the Other Half) has established itself so firmly as an accepted part of the human organism that it can now sneer at gangster viruses like smallpox and turn them in to the Pasteur Institute. But the Word clearly bears the single identifying feature of virus: it is an organism with no internal function other than to replicate itself.[4]

Although his 'word as virus' theory can be seen to manifest itself within Burroughs' writing far earlier than 1971, what's important to note at this point is the fact that Burroughs' premise for the function of the cut-up appears deeply paradoxical. Countering a virus with that self-same virus simply shouldn't work – yet it is precisely on this principle that inoculation works. And if many were unconvinced, those who bought into the idea did so fervently. Converts to the cut-up cause published far and wide in underground magazines across the US and Europe. Obscure – and now highly collectable – publications such as *Fruit Cup* and *Cut Up Or Shut Up* featured some of Burroughs' most far-out works, alongside pieces by those who joined him in his mission

---

4   *William S. Burroughs, The Adding Machine: Selected Essays*, p. 47

to push on with the revolution, and again, writers like Carl Weissner, Claude Pélieu, and Mary Beach are, belatedly, beginning to gain some wider recognition for their contribution to the field of avant-garde literature.

The cut-ups almost brought Burroughs' career to an end. However wild and free and tripped-out things got in the 60s, Burroughs' radical approach to writing didn't rub with many of the cool cats. Part of the problem was that while his anti-authoritarian stance may have superficially represented the zeitgeist, what Burroughs was advocating was antagonistic, nihilistic and seemed to be rooted in paranoia. It wasn't peace and love, it was a bad trip and it fucked with people's heads. The bottom line was that Burroughs was aiming to expose the painful truth, and instead of dropping out to escape it, sought to tackle the horror perpetuated by 'the man' head on.

It's interesting to note, then, that while Burroughs himself had long moved on by the time *The Third Mind* was published in 1978, many have since taken the book as a cut-up bible, an instruction manual for the production of Burroughsian cut-up texts (Kathy Acker was a high-profile adopter of Burroughs' methodology, recounting in *Bodies of Work* how she 'used *The Third Mind* as experiments to teach myself how to write'). In many ways, this is precisely what the book is. Burroughs' contributions to *The Third Mind* include detailed instructions for creating cut-ups. Burroughs first explains the purpose of the method, before giving step-by-step instructions on how to cut and rearrange texts. Yet curiously, it was in the field of music that the influence of the cut-ups, and Burroughs as a figure more generally, was more obvious in the 1970s and 1980s.

Burroughs was a popular reference point for the psychedelic and avant-garde bands of the sixties, with many bands deriving their monikers from his works, or otherwise drawing on his writing for song titles and imagery. Meanwhile, following his fall from popular favour in literary circles during the cut-up phase, Burroughs experienced something of an unexpected renaissance with the advent of punk, as Barry Miles observed:

Rock and roll has always been the music of dissent, of rebellion, and there is plenty of that in Burroughs's work. Bill was never keen on the love-and-peace side of the sixties, and said, 'The only way I'd like to see a policeman given a flower is in a flowerpot from a high window.' The punks could relate to that.5

Jennie Skerl cites Burroughs' nihilistic world view as being core to his appeal to the punk generation, commenting that Burroughs "attacks without implying any positive standards... The individual, anarchic freedom that lies behind the destructive satire exists in a vacuum, with no social or moral structure to support it or give satire any function but destruction." Such nihilism mirrored not only punk attitudes, but also those of the No-Wave movement that sprung up in America in the late 1970s. However, while the punk bands, like the psychedelic artists before them, shared little with Burroughs beyond their anti-authoritarian attitudes, the No-Wave scene saw Burroughs' work drawn on in a more considered way. The leading figures of the No-Wave movement, including Thurston Moore of Sonic Youth, Lydia Lunch, Jim Thirlwell and Michael Gira, grew up in the 1960s when the hippie movement and the Beats were simultaneously at their peak, so the fact that Burroughs' influence should be felt when the children of the Beat Generation themselves became active artists should be of little surprise.6

The development of Industrial music, spearheaded by Throbbing Gristle, whose Genesis P- Orridge was responsible for the compilation and release of Burroughs' early experimental recordings on the Nothing Here Now But the Recordings LP (1980), also reflects Burroughs' growing influence in the musical sphere.7 Along with Cabaret Voltaire and Coil, Throbbing Gristle

---

5   Barry Miles, William Burroughs: El Hombre Invisible, (London, Virgin Books, 1992), p. 13

6   Sonic Youth's Thurston Moore has often cited Burroughs as an influence, and Burroughs collaborated with the band on the 1991 album, Dead City Radio, and his painting, 'X-Ray Man' appears on the front cover of their 2000 album, NYC Ghosts & Flowers.

7   Industrial Records, IR0016. Reissued as part of The Best of William S. Burroughs at Giorno Poetry Systems 4 CD box set. New York: Mercury Records,

were amongst the first to explore the possibilities of using tape loops, cut-ups, samples and 'found sounds' to make music. It was in the work of these bands that Burroughs' work was first drawn upon in an applied manner and his influence upon music became truly tangible.8 "A lot of what we did, especially in the early days, was a direct application of his ideas to sound and music," recalls Cabaret Voltaire's Richard H. Kirk.9 This was true of many of the bands involved in the Industrial scene which exploded on both sides of the Atlantic between 1978 and 1984, who immersed themselves in studio experimentation and the application of techniques first explored by Burroughs and Gysin both in writing and on tape some twenty years previous.

Burroughs wanted a revolution on all fronts: social, cultural, psychological, and literary, and interviews from the late 1960s and early 1970s reveal a clear sense of disappointment that the revolution he was promoting failed to ignite in the way he had hoped. It's perhaps curious, then, that there was something significant the author can be seen to have missed, perhaps on account of his own willful refusal to accept certain well-established scientific theories. Specifically, a number of interviews provide insights into Burroughs' rather unusual interpretations of evolutionary theory. Speaking to *Penthouse* in 1972, Burroughs suggested that "evolutionary changes do not take place gradually over a period of years or millions of years by natural selection. They take place quite suddenly in a few generations."10 He substantiated this claim by observing that "geographical features like the Himalayas do not arise gradually;

1998.

8   Although David Bowie famously applied the cut-up technique in the formulation of the lyrics to his album *Diamond Dogs*, this example of Burroughs' influence being applied on a technical level within music is wholly isolated. Moreover, Bowie still only applied the technique to words on the page as Burroughs has in *Minutes to Go, The Third Mind* and the *Nova* trilogy. The cutting and splicing of audio represents a developmental departure from this.

9   Biba Kopf: 'Spread the Virus: How William Burroughs infected the world of music,' contained in *My Kind of Angel: I. M. William Burroughs*, ed. Rupert Loydell (Exeter: Stride, 1998), p. 72

10   Interview by Graham Masterton and Andrew Rossabi, reproduced in *Conversations With William S. Burroughs*, ed. Allen Hibbard (Jackson: University Press of Mississippi), 1999, pp. 39-50.

they occur very suddenly indeed. There have been mammoths found frozen with their food undigested in their stomachs. They were frozen solid in a matter of seconds." This idea of *rapid evolution* can be seen to manifest itself in the many depictions of genetic mutation and 'weird science' which are a staple of his literary output, and is no *Naked Lunch*, which is littered with references to fantastic instances of freakish and unnatural perversions of nature, from the notorious 'Talking Asshole' routine, to 'The All American De-Anxietised Man', the human form "reduced to a compact and abbreviated spinal column. The brain, front, middle and rear must follow the adenoid, the wisdom tooth, the appendix..." before suddenly transforming into "a monster black centipede". Elsewhere, we read how "a Liz claimed Immaculate Conception and gave birth to a six-ounce spider monkey through the navel." Burroughs' concept of rapid evolutionary change is without doubt somewhat idiosyncratic, with 'evolution' being used almost interchangeably with 'revolution'; I would even contend that this synonymity may have been intentional on Burroughs' part, conceivably for his own ends. But in positing a theory in which language is a virus, and that virus survives through mutation, the language he himself was using would surely be subject to the same mutations as the manipulated language of control he was striving to break down.

The future Burroughs described is the present in which we find ourselves. I do not simply mean in terms of paranoia, control, mutations, genetic manipulations and scientific innovations, either. We may not yet be at the stage where operations are made by remote control as depicted in the famed 'Hospital' routine that appears in *Naked Lunch*, in which Dr Benway pronounces:

> You young squirts couldn't lance a pimple
> without an electric vibrating scalpel with
> automatic drain and suture... Soon we'll be
> operating by remote control on patients we
> never see.... We'll be nothing but button
> pushers. All the skill is going out of
> surgery... All the know-how and make-do...
> Did I ever tell you about the time I
> performed an appendectomy with a rusty

sardine can? And once I was caught short
without instrument one and removed a
uterine tumor with my teeth. That was in the
Upper Effendi, and besides...[11]

However, one has to wonder just how far off the day is that this
snippet of science fiction becomes true science fact: the
chances are we're probably not far off. Moreover, the
technological totalitarianism and writing technologies Burroughs
detailed and alluded to seem anything but far-fetched now. For
instance, in *The Ticket That Exploded,* Burroughs described "a
writing machine that shifts one half one text and half the other
through a page frame of conveyor belts —"[12] He continues:

(The proportion of half one text half the
other is important corresponding as it does
to the two halves of the human organism)
Shakespeare, Rimbaud, etc., permutating
through page frames in constantly
changing juxtaposition the machine spits
out books and plays and poems — The
spectators are invited to feed into the
machine any pages of their own text in fifty-
fifty juxtaposition with any author of their
choice and pages of their choice and
provided with the result in a few minutes.[13]

Burroughs' reputation as a visionary and prophetic writer rests
on scenes like these, and it's only with the benefit of hindsight
and present-day knowledge that we can truly appreciate just
how prescient his writing truly was. Not convinced? Take a look
around and consider the post-Fordist production-line approach

---

11   William S. Burroughs, *Naked Lunch: The Restored Text* (London: Harper
Perennial, 2005), p. 60.

12   William S. Burroughs, *The Ticket That Exploded* (London: John Calder,
1967), p. 65

13   William S. Burroughs, *The Ticket That Exploded* (London: John
Calder, 1967), p. 65

to sitcom writing that now dominates, particularly in the US: the concept of a gag density quotient is a carefully calculated recipe for uniformity and conformity in the form of formulaic, mechanised factory output. On-line plot creators exist to assimilate the finite permutations of sequential events to formulate 'perfect' plot formations, and there are, of course, on-line cut-up generators which pass text through algorithmic formulae to create 'random' cut-up texts by digital means. Creative genius? And whose words, exactly?

The accelerated pace of life in the 1960s was nothing compared to now. We experience the world differently. We experience life at an entirely different pace, and thanks to the Internet and digital communications, transcending the obstacles such as time and geographical location is no issue. It is possible – even commonplace – to exist and inhabit numerous locations, time-zones and even character forms within a single time-frame with on-line communications, not only by means of email but also Skype and social networking. It is easily possible to be in multiple places simultaneously, and to travel in time without so much as moving from your seat. TV is different, too. The speed of cuts between shots on many TV shows has accelerated through the years and is faster now than ever before, even on 'slower' programmes such as news bulletins and documentaries. Then take a 'reality' show like *The Hills* or *Made in Chelsea*. The cuts are so rapid as to be disorientating, and what's more, the dialogue is fragmentary and the narrative thread is all but lost in the telling. And yet contemporary viewers have no issues following such shows, suggesting that Burroughs' assertion that it was possible to re-educate readers to read and draw meaning from cut-up composite texts was correct. One could argue that as a species we have evolved in line with technology – or vice versa – but the point stands that we are now capable of receiving and processing information more rapidly, and in non-contiguous fragments.

It's perhaps for this reason that interest in the cut-ups has experienced a huge growth in recent years. Burroughs always considered linearity to be a falsehood, an imposition forged by the omnipotent author. 'The novel' was, therefore, self-limiting on many levels, not least of all in context of the debate of the way language may limit perception. Linearity and conventional narrative are simply a construct and a vestige of tradition, but, Burroughs contended, not representative of real-life experience. Above all, the conventional linear novel, with its conventional linear narrative, limits the interaction between the reader and the text, and neutralises the act of reading by rendering it passive. Just as Burroughs had claimed in 1959 that writing was fifty years behind painting, so writing – mainstream writing – remains fifty years behind all other media. We not only live in a world driven by faster – instantaneous – communications, but a more visual world. Time was when websites contained only text; now, text ranks a long way behind visuals: people simply don't have the time or the attention span. Hyperlinks, snippets, tweets and fragments are the reality of the 21st century: the reality of the 21st century is the cut-up in full effect. In 1959 and through the 1960s, the cut-ups seemed far-out, as likely to alienate a reader as to reflect their social alienation. Into the 21st century, and the postmodern world has seen the exchange of information increase from a flurry to a relentless blizzard; consequently, the cut-up doesn't only reflect and represent the world in which we now live, it *is* the world in which we live. Readers no longer need to be re-educated or reprogrammed to unravel the meanings of composite texts: they have evolved to the point where such texts make perfect sense and require no translation.

   With work under way on the editing of a new edition of *The Third Mind*, there's every chance that it will, again, become a users' guide. Meanwhile, the virus continues to spread apace of its own accord. The breakthrough has been made. The time of the cut-up is now.

Kirk Lake
Breaking the Timeline: The Collage, the Combine, the Cut-Up and the Sample

This essay formed part of the work I was doing during my MA at Guildhall University in 1998. Though much of the later material regarding sampling may now seem dated it is an accurate reflection of my thinking at the time of writing.

> The montage is actually much closer to the facts of perception than representational painting. Take a walk down a city street and put what you have just seen down on canvas. You have seen half a person cut in two by a car, bits and pieces of street signs and advertisements, reflections from shop windows – a montage of fragments.
>
> – William Burroughs

When Burroughs wrote of montage he referred directly to his own experiments with a technique called the "cut-up", discovered by his friend and collaborator, the painter Brion Gysin.

In the summer of 1959 Gysin had accidentally sliced through a pile of newspapers while cutting the mount for a drawing and amused himself by rearranging and juxtaposing the strips of newsprint until they created new sets of meaning and non-meaning by breaking down the context, the forms and the syntax of the original texts. Gysin, who had loose connections with the Surrealist movement, had initially seen this as being an amusing accident in the tradition of Surrealist parlour games but it was Burroughs, who had recently completed and collated *Naked Lunch,* who saw it as a means to free himself from the constraints of the novel and the linear narrative. The extension of the cut-up would allow a writer to break free from single-point perspectives, traditional structure and logic and move into overlapped associated realities, juxtaposition and chance. In essence, the continuation of a process previously explored by the Dada and Surrealist movements would enable the writer to combine both fictional and documentary texts in which characters and time could intersect and collide in a fluid world

302

that critic Robin Lydenberg likened to "the pulsing rhythm of life itself". Burroughs, who had always held that image and word were interchangeable, soon began to incorporate pictures, drawings and non-textual devices in the cut-ups.

Of course Burroughs, and Gysin in particular, were aware of their antecedents in this experimentation with college and montage. It is in the works of the Dadaists and Surrealists and in their appropriation of the idea of the "chance encounter" from the poet Lautréamont that we begin to see the roots of the cut-up technique. The evolution of which we will follow via Cage and Rauschenberg to the cut-up sampling processes of contemporary music.

Duchamp had experimented with text in 1916 with his *Rendez-vous du dimanche 6 février 1916 à 1h. ¾ après-midi*, four postcards arranged into a grid on which Duchamp had written arbitrary texts with particular care taken in ensuring that the words had "no connection to each other". Duchamp seems to have taken great care in obliterating any possible meaning from this work, spending four hours crossing out and adjusting the texts until they "read without any echo of the physical world". Duchamp's cards bear a striking likeness to some of the early Burroughs/Gysin cut-ups and in particular to Burroughs' *To Be Read Every Which Way* (1965). Duchamp's nihilistic approach to communication mirrors their search for expanded/duplicitous meanings by erasing and destroying rational verbal structures. It is when we begin to consider the pioneering collage works of the likes of Ernst and Schwitters that the potential for visionary explorations becomes even more apparent.

Ernst claimed to have stumbled on the potential of the collage while looking through an illustrated scientific catalogue in 1919. "There I found brought together elements of figuration so remote that the sheer absurdity of that collection provoked a sudden intensification of the visionary faculties in me and brought forth an illusive succession of contradictory images; double, triple, and multiple images, piling up on each other with the persistence and rapidity which are peculiar to love memories and visions of half-sleep."

Ernst called these visions "new planes" and their location, the unknown, the "plane of non-agreement". The Dadaists and Surrealists explored these techniques and used the mechanism to invoke the unexpected through juxtaposition and chance, creating a fantastic reality *outside* the everyday world. The key difference of Burroughs and Gysin (and Cage and Rauschenberg, as we will see) was that they sought to create and explore a compelling reality *within* the everyday world. While Ernst and his associates looked to create something new from their collision of images and objects, post-Surrealism the aim would be to use the impact to decode what was already there. Only Schwitters seems to have hinted at this essential difference with his definition of his *Merzbau* as being the development into pure form of everything that had impinged upon his consciousness.

Burroughs dismissed the earlier Surrealist experiments as being simply an "arrangement of things and pictures presented as an art object". But he was aware that other contemporary visual artists were extending the experiments further. Burroughs looked to the technique as a means of escaping through time and space.

In 1959 Brion Gysin had stated that "writing was fifty years behind painting", constrained by the literary straitjacket of the novel. What Burroughs sought by adopting the montage and cut-up technique was a means of breaking out and developing new forms in the same manner as the emergence of photography had forced representational painters to reassess their approach to visual art. He quickly immersed himself in the cut-up, which evolved into the similar "fold-in" method, forsaking all conventional writing for the explorations of uncharted literary areas, guided by the accidental and the juxtaposed. Much of this work alienated his friends and associates, who saw it as being unintelligible and a literary dead-end. But Burroughs countered that "Consciousness is a cut-up; life is a cut-up. Every time you walk down the street or look out the window, your stream of consciousness is cut by random factors."

If Burroughs was attempting to break out from the constraints of literary convention then John Cage could be seen as attempting the same with music. Beginning in 1938, Cage was the instigator of many of the developments in the avant-garde by his introduction of the ideas of experimentation and chance in composing and performing music.

Though more Zen than Dada, Cage was the catalyst for numerous advances in both musical and mixed-media art. He termed his music of chance "indeterminacy", occasionally relying on the roll of a dice or the pulling of a straw to choose how to proceed with a performance. The notorious *4'33"* (1952) required the performer/s to sit silently and allow ambient sound to become the focus of the work. This could be looked on as the musical equivalent of the collage or the cut-up where external, unforeseen events impinge on the listener. Indeed Cage's frequent calls for periods of silence in his work are a precursor in many respects to the samples of the late 80s and beyond.

Cage's idea that art was about "the blurring of the distinction between art and life" directly reflects both the concepts of collage and cut-up. (And here we could even go so far as to link Cage's principles directly with the ready-made concept instigated by Duchamp).

The painter Robert Rauschenberg met Cage in 1951 and quickly adopted many of the ideas of the composer. Rauschenberg's major breakthrough came in his development of the "combine painting" in the years 1955-64 using junk and found objects alongside traditional art materials. Again these echo the experiments of the Dadaists and are similar in theory to the later cut-up process.

It is worth looking at one of Rauschenberg's combine paintings in more detail. In *Rebus* (1955) Rauschenberg set out to realize "a concentration" of the particular area of New York that he was in at the time of its composition. This he did by collaging items found in the vicinity into the painting stating that "a picture is more like the real world when it's made out of the real world." A statement Burroughs would echo on numerous occasions and one that reflects Schwitters' comments about *Merzbau* quoted earlier.

The title "Rebus" implies that the picture represents some kind of solvable conundrum and the critic Charles Stuckey went so far as to deduce its literal meaning by decoding its images until the painting read, "That reproduces sundry eases of childish and comic coincidence to be read by eyes opened finally to a pattern of abstract problems." Whether this literal reading had anything at all to do with Rauschenberg or his intentions or was merely an example of over-analysis and the need to put boundaries on that which appears boundless is debatable, but Stuckey accurately pinpointed the purpose of this kind of work by concluding that the painter had "force[d] an awareness of how we see, by making us share the tangents and confusions, childish, comic, and coincidental ones which [Rauschenberg] himself endured while facing the abstract problems of making art."

The importance of these random factors, coincidences and jarring juxtapositions is integral to our understanding of the methodology and purpose of these experiments as they mutated through Dada and Surrealism, Cage and Rauschenberg and Burroughs and Gysin and on into the Pop Artists, conceptualists and contemporary multi-media artists.

Burroughs was aware of the huge information overload that bombards our everyday existence. If it was possible to distill, decode and ultimately destroy preconceived ideas then it would be possible to break free of what Burroughs referred to as the "instruments of control" used by the mass media. By using accident and chance Burroughs sought a way around these external controls, even going as far as to believe that the technique enabled him to write what was *going* to happen. He became convinced that the random statements and juxtapositions realised could actually hint at future events. Not "once upon a time" but "once in a future time". It is useful to note how much of this essentially deconstructivist approach prefigures Derrida (and points towards the work of McLuhan).

If we consider a slightly simplistic reading of Derrida through the use of a system of triangles we can perhaps see how Burroughs' ideas link with certain aspects of deconstruction. If you look at the system of triangles then you are faced with a continually shifting series of configurations of triangles, none of which is fixed or absolute. Each configuration as it appears comes out of a previous configuration and moves towards a future configuration. Derrida maintains that all language and text and human thought is like this and that we should continually attempt to see this *free play*. Burroughs' use of the cut-up was an attempt to seize this free play and use it as a means of breaking control much as Derrida would see it as a means of deconstructing authoritarian or dogmatic reading. Indeed it could be suggested that what Burroughs had attempted with the cut-up was the practical, artistic adaptation of what Derrida would later define as "arche-writing", or the non-existent form of writing that enables the play of difference.

Though Burroughs would abandon much of his use of the cut-up and fold-in methods as he moved towards the 70s and 80s, other artists embraced the techniques he had developed and absorbed and altered them in much the same way as he and Gysin had absorbed their own influences.

By the late 60s the worlds of art and rock had become terminally entwined. John Cage's "happenings" had evolved into "be-ins" and his introduction of the destruction of instruments as part of performance had been adopted, though possibly indirectly, by numerous rock bands. Warhol's Factory acted as a focal point for the New York music scene from the later 60s with the Velvet Underground (themselves well versed in the theories of Cage) through to the punk days of the 70s and beyond. Burroughs remained a peripheral figure, his drug-friendly outlaw status appealing to many underground musicians and to the more literate of the overground stars. Burroughs is even credited with the naming of a style of music, "Heavy Metal", via the band Steppenwolf. But it is in the technological advances of the mid-80s that we see the logical extension of the cut-up come into being.

In musical terms sampling is literally taking a piece of sound or music, the "sample", and placing it in another context. It is the musical equivalent of the collage and the cut-up. New machinery enabled musicians to select and combine samples from other records into whole new pieces of music. This allowed startling and exciting new sounds to emerge by juxtaposing different source material.

Initially musicians used this technology in the same way that the Dadaists and Surrealists had used the collage and it's easy to look at the early recordings in the same way that Burroughs had looked at the Surrealists, as being no more than the arrangements of sounds with the intention of making art objects (in this case records).

But musicians had suddenly been given the opportunity to utilise not only the whole of recorded sound history but all of the sound that they heard around them in their everyday lives. Therefore it was possible to break the timeline by simultaneously mixing archival sound (from the 20s for instance) with contemporary sound and, like Rauschenberg's combine painting, with the sounds of their immediate environment.

Often musicians would sample a recognisable section (for instance a drum beat, a guitar riff or a line of speech) from another record and by means of looping or repeating it at random place it in a different context where it remains recognisable but has a different function. (We can almost liken this to the Pop artists of the 60s and Warhol's screen-prints, themselves a kind of sample, in particular).

Many musicians have experimented with samples; a few, such as California's Negativland, have actively used the technology to deconstruct music in the ways that Burroughs had suggested the deconstruction of language. But these new experiments, this extension of processes instigated by Duchamp and Ernst are still in the early stages and constantly evolving as new, more versatile equipment becomes available. It may take years to be able to fully survey this material and decide if it is a valid development in art or music or, to paraphrase Beckett, "just plumbing." We can be sure, however, that experimentation with techniques equivalent to the collage, the cut-up and the sample will continue with individuals taking reference and inspiration from those that have gone before.

Matthew Levi Stevens
Disastrous Success: The Other Method of the Cut-Ups

The cut-up in all its various forms may very well be the pre-eminent creative breakthrough of the 20th Century. From the earliest beginnings with Picasso and Braque, collaging simple materials from everyday life onto their canvases; then the Dadaist poet Tristan Tzara, creating a poem by pulling words out of a hat – as much as it was probably a publicity stunt – pointing the way forward for more serious writers, such as T. S. Eliot with *The Waste Land*, who wanted to be able to convey the voices in our heads, the constant verbalisation of the world around us, both within and without; and eventually the appropriation of such techniques by more experimental rock musicians – invariably informed by borrowings from theories of Art and Literature – and Hip Hop DJs like Grandmaster Flash and later DJ Spooky (who subtitles himself "That Subliminal Kid" after a character in Burroughs' *Nova Express*); to the use of sampling, first in Industrial and House Music, until gradually cut-and-paste has become a universal standard in a world where everything is information, processed digitally. For better or worse, such techniques probably more accurately mirror the way the world is experienced by most people in an increasingly accelerated, fragmentary, and seemingly random datascape. Sampling, montage, collage: these methods really do come closer to representing or expressing what the facts of perception are for most of us in this Post-Technological, Post-Modernist Information Overload. As William Burroughs put it again and again throughout his career:

> As soon as you walk down the street... or look out the window, turn a page, turn on the TV – your awareness is being cut: that sign in the shop window, that car passing by, the sound of the radio... Life *is* a cut-up...

In *The Third Mind*, a joint manifesto with friend and long-term collaborator Brion Gysin – a product of and named for their

309

creative "meeting of minds", itself a kind of psychic cut-up –
Burroughs acknowledges their predecessors:

> Of course, when you think of it, *The Waste Land* was the
> first great cut-up collage, and Tristan Tzara had done a
> bit along the same lines. Dos Passos used the same
> idea in *The Camera Eye* sequences in *U.S.A.*

Reference is also made to literary collaborations by Joseph
Conrad and Ford Madox Ford, W. H. Auden and Christopher
Isherwood, and later to the stream-of-consciousness of Djuna
Barnes' *Nightwood* and the allegedly channelled *A Vision* by W.
B. Yeats and his wife. But almost from the beginning there was
another aspect to the cut-ups which was acknowledged just as
emphatically: that they had the potential to be *oracular*. To
William Burroughs, who would undoubtedly become the greatest
champion of the technique, they introduced an element of
randomness and also of Time: as he would later put it, whereas
the basis of fiction was "once upon a time", with the cut-ups it
was "once in future time".

The much-mythologized "happy accident" by which the cut-ups
were discovered – or rediscovered – was born out of an
increasing pressure-cooker intensity of "slippery psychic
symbiosis" between the painter Brion Gysin and the writer
William S. Burroughs. They had been living in and out of each
other's rooms, minds, and lives as much as any married couple
– although famously, they were never lovers. Gysin, who was no
stranger to avant garde techniques and occult intrigue, after a
poor start in Tangier had at last got to know Burroughs in no
uncertain terms in the cramped, dingy rooms of the now
legendary Beat Hotel, steering his new friend through the
emotional rapids of junk withdrawal, and allowing him to watch
him work on his art. Burroughs was wide open without the safety
blanket of junk, and Gysin felt vulnerable and exposed working
in front of his new friend. He rarely, if ever, let people see him
paint, saying it was a more private act than masturbation. It must
have been an incredibly raw bonding indeed. It was as if the first
cut-up that they created together, this "project for disastrous
success" as they called it, was with their very souls: and it was
out of this commingling, "The Third Mind" as it would come to be

known – named after the concept in Napoleon Hill's self-help bestseller *Think and Grow Rich* that when two minds meet a third and greater mind, partaking of both, is formed – that all their subsequent collaborations would proceed.

September 1959, and the making of myths was in the air: at the same time that the newly notorious William Seward Burroughs was being feted by Snell and Dean for their profile in *Life* magazine that would help mint the image of the Harvard-educated gentleman junkie behind the unspeakable *Naked Lunch*, legend has it that Brion Gysin was in his room at the Beat Hotel, using a Stanley blade to cut through paper to make mounts for some drawings he was working on. In recent years, Gysin's "apprentice to an apprentice" Terry Wilson, himself an accomplished practitioner of the "systematic derangement of the senses" of the cut-up and The Other Method, has brought the story into question, saying it is "almost *too* good to be true."

Burroughs would later write in *Introductions* in *The Third Mind*:

> He was looking at something a long time ago… fade-out to #9 rue Git le Coeur, Paris, room #25; September, 1959… I had just returned from a long lunch with the Time police, putting down a con, old and tired as their namesake: "Mr Burroughs, I have an intuition about you… I see you a few years from now on Madison Avenue… $20,000 per year… life in all its rich variety… Have an Old Gold." Returning to room #25, I found Brion Gysin holding scissors, bits of newspaper, *Life*, *Time*, spread out on a table; he read me the cut-ups that later appeared in *Minutes to Go*.

In the process Gysin had sliced into copies of the *New York Herald Tribune* spread out to protect the table he was working on. Seeing the various strips of paper and reading the chance combinations his blade had produced, he laughed so uproariously the neighbours were concerned for his sanity. When Burroughs returned, Gysin showed him the results – almost as an afterthought, "an amusing Surrealist diversion" – but Burroughs was immediately struck by the technique and its potential:

The cut-up method brings to writers the collage which has been used by painters for fifty years. And used by the moving and still camera. In fact all street shots from movie or still cameras are by the unpredictable factors of passersby and juxtaposition, cut-ups. And photographers will tell you that often their best shots are accidents… writers will tell you the same. The best writing seems to be done almost by accident but writers until the cut-up method was made explicit—all writing is in fact cut-ups; I will return to this point—had no way to produce the accident of spontaneity. You cannot will spontaneity. But you can introduce the unpredictable spontaneous factor with a pair of scissors.

Among Burroughs' earliest cut-ups were phrases that meant nothing at the time, but in hindsight took on an eerie prescience. The early newspaper cut-up piece *Afternoon Ticker Tape* included the line "Come on, Tom, it's your turn now" – and shortly thereafter a newspaper from home, the *St. Louis Post-Dispatch*, included the headline: TOM CREEK OVERFLOWS ITS BANKS.

Burroughs later said:

When you experiment with cut-ups over a period of time you find that some of the cut-ups in rearranged texts seemed to refer to future events. I cut up an article written by John-Paul Getty and got, "It's a bad thing to sue your own father." This was a rearrangement and wasn't in the original text, and a year later, one of his sons did sue him.

They could also refer to quite mundane events:

In 1964 I made a cut-up and got what seemed at the time a totally inexplicable phrase: "And here is a horrid air conditioner." In 1974 I moved into a loft with a broken air conditioner which was removed to put in a new unit. And there was three hundred pounds of broken air conditioner on my floor – a horrid disposal problem, heavy and solid, emerged from a cut-up ten years ago.

This was like the seemingly arbitrary content of dreams, which Burroughs had been paying serious attention to for some time as a result of both his experiences with analysis and his interest in parapsychology:

> I have experienced a number of precognitive dreams that are often quite trivial and irrelevant. For example I dreamed that a landlady showed me a room with five beds in it and I protested that I didn't want to sleep in a room with five people. Some weeks later I went to a reading in Amsterdam and the hotel keeper did show me a room with five beds in it.

Right from the beginning Burroughs immediately made the connection between their literary endeavours and more esoteric pursuits:

> You will recall *An Experiment with Time* by Dunne. Dr Dunne found that when he wrote down his dreams the text contained many clear and precise references to so-called future events. However, he found that when you dream of an air crash, a fire, a tornado, you are not dreaming of the event itself but of the so-called future time when you will read about it in the newspapers. You are seeing not the event itself, but a newspaper picture of the event, pre-recorded and pre-photographed.

This led Burroughs to speculate:

> Perhaps events are pre-written and pre-recorded and when you cut word lines the future leaks out.

As a more paranoid worldview began to evolve – in which he saw *Life* and *Time* magazines, the newspapers, and ultimately *all* media as channels for the Control Machine, more about disseminating *disinformation* than really keeping the public informed – Burroughs felt that the cut-up was a way to break through their Word Lines and get to The Truth. This was an attitude he would increasingly extend to all communications, and eventually all relationships: an early tape recording from the Beat Hotel has Burroughs and his conspirators discussing a "creepy letter" which Gysin says he "can't bear to hear again" –

but it is explained that Burroughs "is going to cut it up – then we'll hear what he's *really* saying!"

This newfound shared enthusiasm would not last though, and in some respects ended in tears: of the original collaborators who launched the cut-ups on an unsuspecting world with *Minutes to Go*, Gregory Corso distanced himself from what he ultimately saw as an assault on the Muse, and the already unstable Sinclair Beiles would become so upset during the often heated discussions that he would have to leave the room to throw up. Gysin himself felt that, ultimately, he was unable to make the cut-ups work for him the way they worked for Burroughs; instead he focused more on the Concrete Poetry of the Permutations. He would take short, simple phrases and run them through every conceivable combination and juxtaposition, producing hypnotic, mantra-like formulae that it was hoped would expose something about the basic mechanisms of the Word Virus, which both he and Burroughs were increasingly sure must be the basic unit of Control. Gysin has described how "William followed by running the cut-ups into the ground, literally," and was, "always the toughest of the lot. Nothing ever fazed him." Together they worked their way through the *New York Herald Tribune*, *Saturday Evening Post*, *Time*, *The Observer*, and (of course!) *Life* magazine – with Burroughs showing a particular enthusiasm for news features on cancer – and then began combining the strips of newsprint with Rimbaud, Shakespeare, and the *Song of Songs* from the King James Bible. Later they would include material from Huxley's *The Doors of Perception*, *Anabasis* by St. John Perse (in the Eliot translation, a particular favourite of Burroughs that he was still sampling for *The Place of Dead Roads:* "a great principle of violence dictated our fashions"); in fact pretty much *anything* they happened to be reading, or had to hand – including of course the "Word Hoard" that was left over from writing *Naked Lunch*. Talking in the 1970s to Terry Wilson for the book of expanded interviews *Here to Go: Planet R101*, Brion Gysin described how Burroughs would work with the material – and I think his choice of words is instructive:

> On the wall hangs a nest of three wire-trays for correspondence which I gave him to sort out his cut-up pages. Later, this proliferated into a maze of filing cases

filling a room with manuscripts cross-referenced in a way only Burroughs could work his way through, more by magic dowsing than by any logical system. How could there be any? This was a magic practice he was up to, surprising the very springs of creative imagination at their source.

The cut-ups would get a more public airing – for the first time beyond the relatively underground bohemian circle around the Beat Hotel in Paris – when UK publisher John Calder arranged for Burroughs to appear at the Edinburgh Conference in August 1962. Despite the notoriety of *Naked Lunch*, he was still something of a newcomer and relative unknown when he was invited to speak as part of a panel on *The Future of the Novel*. There was a clear standoff between the old guard, who dismissed all the sex and drugs as immoral and irrelevant, and these new techniques as unintelligible, and the mapmakers of the new consciousness – "cosmonauts of inner space" in the immortal phrase of Burroughs' friend and ally, the Scottish-Italian Beat writer and fellow addict, Alex Trocchi. After Burroughs stole the show with his presentation of an attempted "new mythology for the Space Age" – and an explanation of the innovative techniques that had made it possible, the cut-ups and their further extension in the newly-developed fold-in – a curious comparison was made by Stephen Spender, who queried the analogy between science and writing:

It sounds to me like a rather medieval form of magic rather than modern science.

It is in fact informative to compare this with a statement Burroughs made himself, in which his comparison of cut-ups with mediumship is explicit:

Cut ups often come through as code messages with special meaning for the cutter. Table tapping? Perhaps.

It is to be remembered that the atmosphere around Burroughs and Gysin in those early days at the Beat Hotel was steeped in the occult, with daily experiments in mirror-gazing, scrying, trance and telepathy, all fuelled by a variety of mind-altering drugs, and so it is not so surprising to think that they may have considered these new developments in such terms. Burroughs, for all his Harvard education and intellect, also possessed a worldview that was informed – you might even say overshadowed – by a fear and fascination with the supernatural that had been shaped in childhood, and had stayed with him ever since. Later claims led his first biographer, Ted Morgan, to state that *the single most important thing* about Burroughs was his belief in what he referred to as "the Magical Universe." Gysin himself was naturally inclined to intrigue and mystery, and had come back from Morocco full of tales of black magic, curses and possession, and Burroughs was an all-too-eager audience for the spellbinding storyteller. He felt that his own travels in exotic parts had opened his eyes to a Bigger Picture:

> Now anyone who has lived for any time in countries like Morocco where magic is widely practiced has probably seen a curse work. I have.

When Gysin, allegedly in trance, told Burroughs, "The Ugly Spirit shot Joan because..." he thought he had the answer that no amount of psychoanalysis or self-examination had been able to provide: the unforgiveable slip that had caused the death of his common-law wife, Joan Vollmer, had come about because he was literally possessed by an evil spirit. This was indeed a War Universe, and if Brion had identified The Enemy, William instinctively knew the only solution available to him:

> I live with the constant threat of possession, and a constant need to escape from possession, from Control. So the death of Joan brought me in contact with the invader, the Ugly Spirit, and manoeuvred me into a lifelong struggle, in which I have had no choice except to write my way out.

If the Word was indeed the basic mechanism or unit of Control – the "virus" by which Control or The Ugly Spirit exerted its malevolent influence – then surely a real understanding of the Word, what words are and what can be done with them was *essential*. All these explorations and obsessions were not merely diversions, experiments for artistic or literary amusement, or the creation of novelty, but part of a deadly struggle with unseen, invisible – perhaps even evil – psycho-spiritual enemies. The only hope for deprogramming and self-liberation was to subvert the methods of Control and its various agencies, and understand the tools used so that they could become weapons to turn back on the Control Machine itself.

After working exhaustively through the various applications and derivations of the cut-up method with words on paper, it was inevitable that Burroughs would turn his attention to the possibilities of film and tape recorders. After all, a big part of the appeal of the cut-up breakthrough in the first place was that it would allow writers to actually *get to grips* with their material, words, in the same way that painters and sculptors had always taken for granted. Burroughs felt the exploration of what could be achieved through the actual manipulation of words should be taken even further, though. If, as he theorised, all writing and art was a form of magic, the purpose of which was to Make Things Happen, what effects would be realised by taking the word *off the page altogether*? The systematic experiments with tape recorders would point a startling new way forward: at first Brion made some simple cut-up recordings on a tape recorder, but then things were taken further by William's companion and lover, the young mathematician Ian Sommerville. Ian apparently had a natural facility for gadgets, and quickly became known as the "Technical Sergeant" of The Third Mind, running Gysin's Permutation Poems through a computer, helping to design and build the first Dreamachine, and approaching tape recorders with awe and a fascination that was part spiritual, part erotic. Ian believed that all the tape recorders of the world were connected on some level, and many of the routines that later appear in *The Ticket That Exploded* about lovers splicing each other's recordings in together no doubt have their origins at this time. Ian was the one to introduce Brion and William to the various potentials of the tape recorder for multi-tracking, overdubbing, speeding up and slowing down – but most importantly of all, he was the one to suggest street-recordings and playback. Later, as well as the obvious step of cutting-up such recordings, he also began to splice in what he called "trouble noises" – recordings of alarm bells, breaking glass, fire engines, as well as sound effects of explosions, machine guns and riots recorded from TV. This opened up a whole new realm of possibility as far as Burroughs was concerned:

I have frequently observed that this simple operation of making recordings and taking pictures of some location you wish to discommode or destroy, then playing recordings back and taking more pictures, will result in accidents, fires, removals, especially the last. The target moves...

Talking to Burroughs about these experiments in 1982, he actually described them with a chuckle as "sorcery" – and later, in 1988, I had the following exchange with Terry Wilson:

> M: You are quoted as talking about the cut-ups – and writing generally – as a form of exorcism.
>
> T: That simply came from one of my observations in *Here To Go* where I was saying that William's texts – once they brought the cut-ups into the tape recorder area, cutting up tapes and whatnot – William's texts increasingly became like spells and very much exhibited a preoccupation with exorcism.

He referred me to a discussion with Brion on this very subject in the *Ports of Entry* section of *Here to Go: Planet R101*:

> T: The cut-up techniques made very explicit a preoccupation with exorcism – William's texts became spells, for instance. How effective are methods such as street playback of tapes for dispersing parasites?
>
> B: We-e-ell, you'd have to ask William about that, but I do seem to remember at least two occasions on which he claimed success...
>
> Uh, the first was in the Beat Hotel still, therefore about 1961 or '2, and William decided (laughing) to take care of an old lady who sold newspapers in a kiosk...
>
> Now the other case was some years later in London when he had perfected the method and, uh, went about with at least one I think sometimes two tape recorders, one in each hand...

Probably the definitive statement on the subject appears in *The Job*, a book of interviews by Daniel Odier, with commentary and added text by Burroughs. In the opening section, *Playback from Eden to Watergate*, he states:

> Here is a sample operation carried out against the Moka Bar at 29 Frith Street, London, W1, beginning on August 3, 1972. Reverse Thursday. Reason for operation was outrageous and unprovoked discourtesy and poisonous cheesecake. Now to close in on the Moka Bar. Record. Take pictures. Stand around outside. Let them see me. They are seething around in there... Playback would come later with more pictures. I took my time and strolled over to the Brewer Street Market, where I recorded a three-card Monte game. Now you see it, now you don't...

> Playback was carried out a number of times with more pictures. Their business fell off. They kept shorter and shorter hours. October 30, 1972, the Moka Bar closed. The location was taken over by the Queen's Snack Bar.

In addition to Burroughs' own writings, further insights into these methods can also be found in *Playback: My Personal Experience of Chaos Magic with William S. Burroughs Sr.*, by Cabell McLean. Cabell was a student at Naropa in the late 1970s, and met Burroughs while he was teaching there, moving in with him to become his companion c.1976-1983, and also acting as an assistant during the writing of *The Place of Dead Roads*. He enlarges upon the Moka Bar incident:

> [William] continued going to the bar for a few more days, enduring their abuse, while he tape recorded the sounds inside. Later, he would stand outside and film or photograph the premises from outside. Then he went back in and began to play the tape recordings at low or subliminal levels, and continued to take photographs on his way in and out of the place. This he did for several days. The effects were remarkable: accidents occurred, fights broke out, the place lost customers, the subsequent loss of income became irredeemable, and within a few weeks, the bar was permanently closed.

Cabell goes on to tell about an experience he and a friend have in a deli in the mall in Boulder, which when related to Burroughs gives rise to a similar operation, the account of which serves as a particularly fine object lesson in the power – and perils! – of Playback. Originally published in the *Ashé Journal of Experimental Spirituality* (and currently still available in the aptly named anthology *Playback: The Magic of William S. Burroughs*), it is well worth reading in its own right, as an enjoyable, well-written account that gives a valuable insight into Burroughs' continuing engagement with such techniques – as well as his sometimes quite direct teaching methods...

A further spooky connection that came out of Burroughs' continuing exploration of cut-ups, just how-random-is-random, obsessive experimentation with tape recorders, and preoccupation with the occult and parapsychological research, was his fascination with the infamous "unexplained voices on tape" of Latvian psychologist Konstantin Raudive. Writing in 1968 – but translated into English in 1971 as *Breakthrough: An Amazing Experiment in Electronic Communication with the Dead* – Raudive described what has come to be known as Electronic Voice Phenomenon (EVP). Put simply, EVP are sounds resembling human speech that turn up on various recording media – initially the experiments were conducted with reel-to-reel audio tape – but with no apparent or intentional input source, which advocates claims of supernatural origin. Speaking to the Kerouac School of Disembodied Poetics at Naropa, Burroughs explained:

> These voices are in a number of accents and languages, often quite ungrammatical... "You I friends. Where stay?" sounds like a Tangier hustler. Reading through the sample voices in *Breakthrough*, I was struck by many instances of a distinctive style reminiscent of schizophrenic speech, certain dream utterances, some of the cut-ups and delirium voices like the last words of Dutch Schultz.

Although there are a number of quite rational possible explanations (even disallowing for fraud or wishful thinking), the majority of claimants believe they are, quite literally, voices of the dead. Burroughs was not so sure – he was more in favour of the explanation that:

> They are somehow imprinted on the tape by electromagnetic energy generated by the unconscious minds of the researchers or people connected with them.

And no doubt remembering his time exploring Scientology, added:

> Remember that your memory bank contains tapes of everything you have ever heard, including of course your own words.

But as with all his other sources and studies, Burroughs the Writer would get his money's worth: strange and evocative phrases from Raudive's book would turn up as source material for later cut-ups, and even chapter titles in *Cities of the Red Night*: *Are you in salt*, *Cheers here are the non-dead*, and *We are here because of you* all originate with the "unexplained voices on tape."

Gradually, as the Sixties progressed, it was clear that the cut-ups were an idea whose time had come. Perhaps it was just the next inevitable progression in what was to become the dominant form in 20th Century Art, starting with collage and montage: the Cubists had attempted to show different viewpoints on the canvas simultaneously – with its parallels in literature, first with stream-of-consciousness, allowing Joyce to put the inside of people's heads on the page; then Eliot and his appropriation providing the textual equivalent of Duchamp's found object or readymade, beginning to question the very notion of originality. Or perhaps it was that modern life was increasingly fragmented, disconnected, and accelerated, and increasingly art and forms of expression were required that could reflect this. Helped by Burroughs' and Gysin's gradually emerging status as Counter-Culture gurus, their ideas and influence began to spread. It didn't hurt that Burroughs appeared on the cover of *Sgt. Pepper* by The Beatles, or that rock bands started naming themselves from his work: The Insect Trust, The Mugwumps, Soft Machine, Steely Dan…

By the 1970s William Burroughs was the epitome of hip as far as drug savvy musos with literary pretensions were concerned: a coked-out David Bowie explained how he used "the Burroughs cut-up method" in Alan Yentob's 1974 BBC profile *Cracked Actor*, and then demonstrated (badly); his friend Brian Eno would name a track *Dead Finks Don't Talk* as a nod to *Dead Fingers Talk*, but would also look for ways to introduce chance with his *Obliques Strategies*, a set of cryptic aphorisms intended to encourage creative solutions by lateral thinking; Jimmy Page would be interviewed by Burroughs for *Crawdaddy* magazine; and as the clarion call of Punk was heard in New York, Patti Smith was the first to cheer the return of the Beat Godfather to his native land.

Around the same time that Punk was emerging here in the UK, another home-grown genre that was drawing inspiration from Burroughs, Gysin and the cut-ups was the "Industrial Music" of Throbbing Gristle and related bands like Cabaret Voltaire, and later 23 Skidoo. Richard H. Kirk, founder member of Cabaret Voltaire and later a key player in the Sheffield Electronic Music/Dance underground, said:

> A lot of what we did, especially in the early days, was a direct application of his ideas to sound and music. One book in particular, *The Electronic Revolution*, was an influence on us. It was almost a handbook of how to use tape recorders in a crowd, to promote a sense of unease or unrest by playback of riot noises cut in with random recordings of the crowd itself. That side was always very interesting to us... Cut-ups might have lost some of their potency through mainstream use, but as an idea it is still very valid, at least on a personal level... I do believe by cutting up certain texts you can read into the future to a certain extent.

TG prime-mover Genesis P-Orridge had actually met Burroughs while he was living at Duke Street in London in the early 1970s, and he and bandmate Peter 'Sleazy' Christopherson were directly inspired by the outsider stance of the "Literary Outlaw" as much as they were influenced by his theories. Along with Chris Carter and Cosey Fanni Tutti, P-Orridge and

Christopherson would help to invent a new genre of music that they dubbed "Industrial" – stripping back music even further than the back-to-basics of Punk to create a kind of Garage musique concrete, in which the processing and manipulation of found sound was a key part of the semi-improvised mayhem that was as often sonic assault as it was about the alchemy of sound. Their launch at the Institute of Contemporary Arts in London's The Mall saw an unprecedented backlash in the press in response to their confrontational shock tactics and uncompromising "anti-music" – with the *Daily Mail* of 19th October 1976 infamously quoting the Tory MP Nicholas Fairbairn that "These people are the wreckers of civilization!"

When P-Orridge had first visited Burroughs at Duke Street in 1973, he asked him "Tell me about magick?" and enquired whether or not he still used cut-ups in writing. Burroughs replied "No, I don't really have to anymore, because my brain has been rewired so it does them automatically." He cracked open a bottle of Jack Daniels, poured them both a stiff drink, then put on the TV to watch *The Man From U.N.C.L.E.*, explaining, "Reality is not really all it's cracked up to be, you know..." and began hopping through the channels on the TV with the remote – at the same time mixing in pre-recorded cut-ups from the Sony tape recorder – until P-Orridge was experiencing a demonstration of cut-ups and playback in Real Time, Right There Where He Was Sitting:

> I was already being taught. What Bill explained to me then was pivotal to the unfolding of my life and art: Everything is recorded. If it is recorded, it can be edited. If it can be edited then the order, sense, meaning and direction are as arbitrary and personal as the agenda and/or person editing. This is magick.

Burroughs went on to describe his theories about the pre-recorded universe, quoting Wittgenstein, and describing with obvious relish his experiments with tape recorders at both the Chicago Democrat's Convention in 1968 and, closer to home, on the streets of London: using playback to wage psychic warfare against the Scientology HQ and the infamous Moka Coffee Bar. In addition to the street recordings, cut-up with the "trouble sounds" of police sirens, screams, sound effects of explosions and machine gun fire taped from the TV, Burroughs had also taken photographs of his targets. As part of his explanation, he showed P-Orridge one of his journal scrapbooks in which he had posted two photos: a simple black & white street scene, with the relevant building clearly visible, and then another beneath it from which he had carefully sliced out the "target" with a razor blade, gluing the two halves of the photo back together so as to create an image of the street with the offending institution removed. The same principle could clearly be applied to photos of people that you wanted to "excise" from your life, he said.

These principles would have a profound effect on P-Orridge and Christopherson, as well as many of the "anti-musicians" and sound-artists that they would collaborate with or inspire in their turn. But it wasn't just the *sonic* application of the cut-ups with tape recorders that spoke to them, rather the whole approach to challenging conventional wisdom and deprogramming the self from the imposed beliefs and values of mainstream society. Of the family tree that reaches from Industrial pioneers Throbbing Gristle through Psychic TV and ultimately to Coil, much fruit has been borne relating to Burroughs and Gysin, the cut-ups, The Other Method (a term Burroughs adopted from Gysin, who had told him, "Magic calls itself The Other Method for controlling matter and knowing space"), and The Third Mind. There is more than I will attempt to document here, but highlights have included the release of the album *Nothing Here Now But The Recordings* and The Final Academy. Organised by David Dawson, Roger Ely, and Genesis P-Orridge and Peter Christopherson, The Final Academy consisted of a series of main events over four days at The Ritzy Cinema, Brixton, in which William S. Burroughs and Brion Gysin would be celebrated in film, music, performance and readings. The famous experimental films shot by Antony Balch in the 1960s would be shown each night. There would also be performances by the experimental music groups that had been inspired by their example: 23 Skidoo, Last Few Days, Cabaret Voltaire and the debut of Psychic TV (recently formed from the ashes of Throbbing Gristle), as well as a variety of other poets and performance artists. Some, like John Giorno and Terry Wilson, were of course friends with Burroughs and Gysin; others, like

Anne Bean, Paul Burwell and Ruth Adams, were associates of Roger Ely. His B2 Gallery ran an exhibition of Brion Gysin paintings, complete with Dreamachine, collages from *The Third Mind*, and scrapbook material. There were also book signings, with a whole host of new publications – such as new paperback editions of *A William Burroughs Reader* and *Cities of the Red Night*, Victor Bockris' seminal collection of after-dinner conversations, *With William Burroughs: A Report From The Bunker*, as well as *Here To Go: Planet R101*, the definitive statement from Brion Gysin, with the help of Terry Wilson, and the Burroughs/Gysin/TG special, both from RE/Search Publications – and also other regional events in Liverpool, London and Manchester.

After TG had split, P-Orridge and Christopherson went on to form "Psychic Television Limited" – with its attendant Conceptual Art gag masquerading as fan club pretending to be a cult, "Thee Temple ov Psychick Youth", or TOPY as it was known – and for a while there was an inner circle that revolved around a strange hybrid of the ideas of Occultists Aleister Crowley and Austin Osman Spare regarding consciousness alteration, dream control, and sex-magic. TOPY ran curiously parallel – and at times fed into – the then-emerging Chaos Magic scene in much the same way as Industrial had Punk, and the life and work of Burroughs and Gysin, with their cut-ups, Dreamachine, playback, and Third Mind equally offered a kind of toolkit for similar ends. It looked like if the Revolution was going to be televised after all, then Psychic TV were going to be first in line to put in their bid for the franchise...

In the press at the time of The Final Academy, P-Orridge had this to say about the influence of Burroughs and Gysin:

> William, Brion and the poet John Giorno used writing because in their day writing was the most vital, living form for propaganda. They got hold of tape recorders and made films with (the late) Antony Balch, always trying to reapply what they discovered through writing to other media. Now you've got groups like Cabaret Voltaire, 23 Skidoo, Last Few Days and Psychic TV who have followed through and used tape, cut-ups, random

chats and sound in the way they've read or at least been inspired in Burroughs' and Gysin's books. They've put it, though, into popular culture, i.e. music, which happens at the moment to be the most vital form.

Too soon though cracks began to show, and P-Orridge and Christopherson parted company. Genesis would develop PTV in the direction of Rave music, applying the cut-up methods of sampling, cut-and-paste and appropriation to the development of a Techno Psychedelia, and TOPY increasingly concerned with New Age, merry prankster-style utopian tribalism. His role as figurehead for these disparate anti-movements, and the cultural memes he was engineering – from cut-ups and sex-magick, to tattooing, piercing, and body modification – inevitably led to conflict with the authorities, and P-Orridge had to flee England for a life of exile in the United States. Eventually he would come to perhaps the most radical application of all of his interpretation of the ideas of Burroughs and Gysin: Pandrogyny, in which P-Orridge and his spouse Lady Jaye would literally try and cut up gender. More recently, writing as Genesis Breyer P-Orridge to indicate the composite being of the Pandrogyne since Lady Jaye's passing, Gen has provided a lengthy, in-depth text all about his encounters with Burroughs, Gysin, and the cut-ups, *Magick Squares and Future Beats* for the DisInformation anthology *Book of Lies*, in which he concludes:

> I believe that a re-reading of their combined body of work from a magical perspective only confirms what they themselves accepted about themselves: that they were powerful modern magicians.

He also stresses:

> I strongly advise any reader who has been inspired to reconsider their picture of both the Beats and their world picture to look for an essay by William S. Burroughs titled *The Discipline of Do Easy* or *The Discipline of DE* which is part of the book *Exterminator!* In my own private, alchemical life, a rigorous and continual application of this idea has been as central to my uncanny achievement of countless goals as the Austin Osman Spare system of sigilization.

I can only second Gen on this.

When Peter Christopherson broke with P-Orridge, PTV and TOPY, it was to join forces with his then life-partner, another "graduate" of *The Final Academy* and former member of PTV and TOPY, Geff Rushton (aka John Balance) to concentrate on the magickal and musical entity that was Coil. They continued to hold Burroughs and Gysin in the highest regard as role models and teachers, and find new ways to apply their lessons through the newly emerging computer technologies that allowed for the sampling and manipulation of sound like never before. Another more direct acknowledgment of their debt was when they were instrumental in producing a new Dutch edition of the key Burroughs text, *The Electronic Revolution*. Christopherson created the layout and cover design, and Balance provided the introduction, in which he wrote:

> This book is the original handbook of possibilities. It is both "user" and "misuser" friendly. The true danger lies in denial. It is intended to be used, to be used and applied. Experimentation is of vital importance.

Later in 1992 they would visit Burroughs in Lawrence, Kansas, observing how he incorporated Sigil Magic into his shooting practice. They would also record him for use in a sadly unrealised project, named after a haunting phrase that appeared in his work: *Wounded Galaxies Tap at the Window*. Balance explains:

> We asked him to recite certain key words and phrases for us. This material has a shamanic quality to it; really it is a magickal spell. This is where we connect with William; he describes the invisible world, he documents the hidden mechanisms. This is what we also seek out; the secret mechanisms, the Occult...

Peter 'Sleazy' Christopherson had also known Burroughs from the early days of Throbbing Gristle, operating in a defiantly "non-musician" capacity – his own use of pre-recorded sound and tapes in TG had been directly inspired by Burroughs. Certain from a very young age that he was homosexual but feeling stifled by his academic family background in the north of

England, his discovery of Burroughs' *Naked Lunch* at the back of W. H. Smith's one rainy Saturday afternoon had been a revelation to the 13-year-old boy. "It changed my life!" he said later, continuing that:

> My perception of Burroughs' work is that things that happen in his books happen in a spirit world where there isn't really any self-consciousness, intellectualisation or present time really. The time they take place in isn't the annihilating reality of now. It is some other space altogether...

A talented photographer who helped to design high-profile rock album covers as a day job, in his spare time Christopherson delighted in taking photos of young male friends in what appeared to be compromising situations, carefully staged. One particular set of images was for his friend John Harwood's boutique *Boy*, which appeared to show youths beaten and bloodied by Skinhead thugs; another was an early set of promo photos for the Sex Pistols, taken in the public toilets at the YMCA – apparently declined by Malcolm McLaren because they made the band look "too much like psychotic rent-boys." These kinds of extra-curricular interests had earned Christopherson the affectionate nickname "Sleazy" from his bandmates (one that would endure with friends – and later fans alike – throughout his life.) When it came to Industrial Music, his role in Throbbing Gristle completely bypassed conventional instrumentation of any kind. Inspired by Burroughs, he would enthusiastically apply and develop such ideas as he had read about in *The Job* and *Electronic Revolution* with found-sound and loops – frequently cutting up recordings live, from prepared tapes and treated radio and TV sources.

In 1977, Christopherson was in New York on business and visited Burroughs at the Bunker, taking with him a portfolio of his "boy" photos. Burroughs was really enthusiastic about the images, and talked about wanting to incorporate them in a book alongside the text he was working on, *Blade Runner* ("Nothing to do with the film," Christopherson made clear) – but regrettably the publisher wouldn't run to the expense. Nonetheless they bonded over a bottle of vodka, Christopherson later recalling:

I remember getting very, *very* drunk with him... and it was one of those times where you could sit for a long time and not say anything and feel OK about it. Maybe that has something to do with the place, which is a converted YMCA...

But he also had a more practical suggestion:

I suggested that it would be great to release a record of his original cut-up recordings... we really wanted people to be able to hear what they *actually* sounded like.

Genesis P-Orridge had also been suggesting the same idea:

I thought of doing the LP in 1973; it was about the first thing I suggested to him when I met him. And I wrote him letters suggesting it again and again and again for the following eight years, and suddenly one day James Grauerholz wrote back and said "Okay." Just when I thought he was never going to do it!

So eventually it was agreed, and arrangements were made for P-Orridge and Christopherson to go over to Lawrence, where in the middle of the summer heat they spent a frantic and humid week in a motel room with inadequate air-conditioning, a rented Revox tape recorder, going through a shoebox full of old tapes. By all accounts the actual tapes were in a pretty poor condition, and it sounds like they were duplicated for posterity not a moment too soon. As P-Orridge told Vale in an interview for *RE/Search*:

He just agreed to us taking the tapes away, fifteen hours of them, and editing them down to an LP. It's a good job we got them, 'cause they were recorded over twenty years ago and the oxide was actually crumbling off the tapes as we held them.

The album, titled *Nothing Here Now But The Recordings*, came out in May 1981 on Throbbing Gristle's Industrial Records label, serial number IR0016. It was a significant release: there had been previous records of spoken word from William S. Burroughs, starting with the classic *Call Me Burroughs* issued by the English Bookshop in Paris in 1965, and reissued the following year on the ESP label; and then in 1971 a recording of Burroughs reading a draft of *Ali's Smile* was released in a very limited edition of only 99 copies – but this was the first time that recordings of the actual cut-up experiments with tape would be made available. It would also be the final release on the Industrial Records label, followed by the demise of Throbbing Gristle later that year. Notifying their fans and followers with a simple postcard, reading "Throbbing Gristle: The Mission Is Terminated", in many respects things had come full circle for the Wreckers of Civilization: passing on the baton to the next generation with the challenge, example and inspiration of the cut-up experiments of William S. Burroughs and Brion Gysin.

Gareth Jackson & Michael Butterworth
Conceptual Radial Literature Device

JACKSON / BUTTERWORTH
CONCEPTUAL RADIAL LITERATURE DEVICE

RULES of OPERATION

USERS may begin on ANY radial line of any circle
READ text on radial line
Operators may move to ANY adjacent circle
SELECT and READ text on ANY radial line of adjacent circle
REPEAT above

Generated TEXT may be TRANSCRIBED or merely READ

Grammar may be added and/or deleted by USER

USERS may stop conceptual device at any TIME

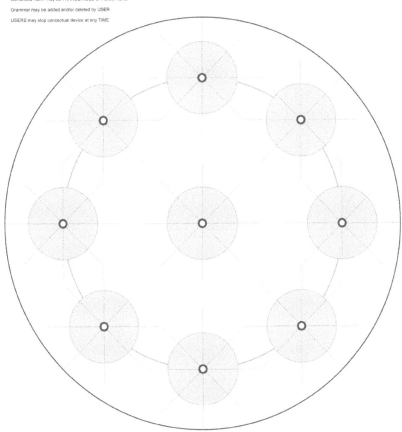

JACKSON / BUTTERWORTH
CONCEPTUAL RADIAL LITERATURE DEVICE

RULES of OPERATION

USERS may begin on ANY radial line of any circle
READ text on radial line
Operators may move to ANY adjacent circle
SELECT and READ text on ANY radial line of adjacent circle
REPEAT above

Generated TEXT may be TRANSCRIBED or merely READ

Grammar may be added and/or deleted by USER

USERS may stop conceptual device at any TIME

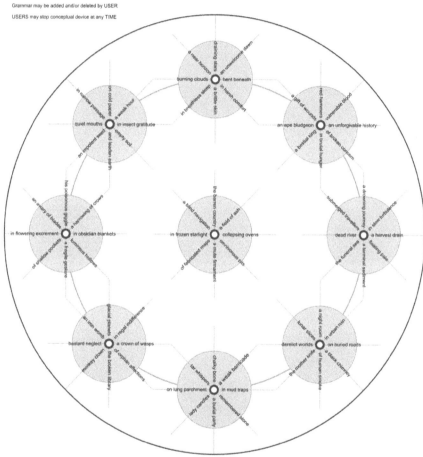

Gareth Jackson
Conceptual Radial Literature Device

PLAY WITH WORDS (operating instructions)

The device user selects one circle at whim and selects 1 (of the 8) radial text line fragments from this circle.

The user then can select any adjacent circle to the initial circle (the central circle being adjacent to all).

The user selects 1 radial text line fragment from this new circle and then moves again to another adjacent circle selecting another radial text line fragment (now potentially including returning to the initial circle/even initial radial text line fragment).

The user repeats this operating process until they choose the point at which they stop operating the device.

Please note: the user is free to add grammar/punctuation to the text they generate.

Generated texts are the property of the individual user and will not be added to the project archive or distributed in any way without their permission.

A CONCEPTUAL RADIAL LITERATURE DEVICE template is also included should anyone wish to author their own device.

Radial Lit

USER 01 | [Schora Faal] | TEXT 01

in insect gratitude burning clouds the barren.
(country – in urban)
ruin a weak barricade of fabricated maps,
[O] monkey clown of shallow pockets monkey clown of
fabricated maps!

a drowning journey, on buried roads, in mud,
traps in [the] frozen starlight [of] a near horizon – a gift.
of wounds in breathless[ness],
sleep-empty soil (a field of ash, of human smoke-tar)
whispers a mute firmament [of] glacial planets:
"chalky bone-collapsing ovens!"

a black chimney-lady candles [you, O] monkey clown of
fabricated maps,
bestial king, floating, pale, lunar...

[she] slices a burial party of:
* orphan affections in obsidian blankets;
* a field of ash in obsidian blankets;
* an impotent seed in obsidian blankets; [and]
* a blind navigation in obsidian blankets.

monkey clown, luminous, hollows monkey clown of fabricated
maps.

Radial Lit

USER 02 | [Harpy70] | TEXT 02

Bastard neglect;
a fragile gesture.
In frozen starlight
floating pale
in urban ruin
a burial party,
omnivorous pits -
quiet mouths
in breathless sleep
of fabricated maps.
In regal indifference
obsidian blankets
(empty soil)
bend beneath
an unforgivable history.

Radial Lit

USER 03 | [UMMO] | TEXT 03

In harsh comfort,
In frozen starlight,
In breathless sleep,
A bestial king.

A blind navigation,
In narrow passage,
A mute firmament,
A night room.

In slow turbulence,
The barren country,
And leaden earth,
In obsidian blankets.

An iron womb,
Of fabricated maps,
A weak hour,
An unwelcome dawn.

Radial Lit

USER 03 | [UMMO] | TEXT 04

A brittle skin,
In brutal hunger,
Collapsing ovens,
Chalky bone,
A black chimney of human smoke,
A field of ash,
An unforgivable history.

Claude Pélieu, *Burroughs*. © Claude Pélieu, 2014
www.beachpelieuart.com

Allen Ginsberg
Notes on Claude Pélieu

"I can only shoot with buckshot on reflections." Undifferentiated bullshit cut up and made rare and strange, it belongs to a genre of phantom poetry like its author, an ex-junky Frenchman refuged in New York, San Fran, London, his life cut up and his experience of states of consciousness, politics, police, sex and drugs now so confusing and fearful in every direction that he can only squeak apprehension of aluminum apocalypse with General Bridges falling down Atomic Fishways. Genre of Rimbaud's Villes and other prosepoetic electric illuminations, voice le Pélieu du temps des assassins up to date with the latest Francoprussian war rapes and dope games. I couldn't assimilate all those cold scissors but their exact cut occasionally comes home. "Do you know that the Inca Civilization was destroyed in 3 hours? Savage repression at Berkeley." Poetry can cause social change by mixing words and images up so the beholder sees what's in front of his eyes instead of trusting mass produced caption for sensible description. In that sense this "Language reveals the arbitrary" by mixing captions up in revolutionary order to present "Miss Vietnam's raspberry covered sex" or "cops with snail-sexes", or by articulating clear mind labels for "a shooting star drawn on the pavement", or sometimes by suggesting no conceptual labels at all, leaving the mind free to observe "a dead man lording it at Police Headquarters".

A. Ginsberg, August 23, 1970

Originally published as the Introduction to Jukeboxes by Claude Pélieu (Christian Bourgeois, Paris, 1972).

Nina Antonia
The Master & Michele – A Magickal Memo

"You have a camera, fixed on its tripod or crane, which
is just like a heathen altar; about it are the high priests –
the director, cameraman, assistants who bring victims
before the camera like burnt offerings and cast them in
the flames." Jean Renoir, 1960.

The film-maker liked to think of her as the spirit of the age: free,
uninhibited and androgynous. Like a scene from *Death in
Venice*, Donald Cammell first encountered Michele Breton on
the beach. With her lean frame, short tousled brown hair and
fine features, she could have been a boy. Donald relished
ambiguity as his latest screen play, tentatively entitled *The Liars*
attested. When in St Tropez he liked to work by the sea but
today there had been too many distractions. Putting down his
notes, he raised his aviator sunglasses to get a better view. A
chic waif; the girl was a perfect example of the gamine, the clean
line of her body suggesting an elemental quality. She
summarised everything Mary Quant was defining in fashion;
'The Little Boy Look' of 1966 yet her runaway life was far from
that of a Chelsea clothes-horse. Her name, Michele, teetering as
it did between the masculine and the feminine, only accentuated
the dualistic allure. Too hip for the fleshy fantasies of Nabokov's
Lolita or Southern's Candy, Cammell's proclivity for the modish
androgyne proclaimed him an arbiter of the new era as did
fashionable friends like Anita Pallenberg and Rolling Stone,
Brian Jones. He belonged to the bohemian elite and had struck
up an instant rapport with Jones, who often stayed at his studio
penthouse in Paris. If Michele Breton represented the 'new girl'
to Donald Cammell then Brian Jones exerted an influence as the
nouveau dandy, with his foppish manner and exotic finery.
Cammell's long-term companion, Vogue model Deborah Dixon,
moved in the same charmed circles as actress Anita Pallenberg.
An invisible circuitry drew the more refined elements of the
Sixties generation together through film, art, literature, fashion

and music. It was Cammell who had introduced Brian Jones to the radiant mysteries of Morocco. Donald regularly visited North Africa, where he mingled with an eminent cast of characters that included art dealer Robert Fraser, taste-maker Christopher Gibbs, William Burroughs, Brion Gysin and John Paul Getty junior and his doomed wife, Talitha. Another of Cammell's haunts, the beautiful hotel Minza with its Moorish decor became a favoured gathering place for the Rolling Stones when in Tangiers. Cammell's decadent Morocco would become the stuff of dreams for pop historians. Indeed it was during one of these mythic sojourns that Donald was sought out by the underground film-maker Kenneth Anger. An intense presence, Anger's influence was two-fold in terms of pioneering cinematic technique and occult knowledge.

A disciple of Aleister Crowley, Anger believed that Cammell was Crowley's 'Magickal son'. The mingling of brimstone and hashish suited Donald Cammell well for he was as driven a soul as Crowley had been and more than able to live up to the Great Beast's decree that 'Man has the right to live by his own law.'(Liber LXXV11) Whilst Cammell could prosper by this splendid edict, Michele Breton was not quite so fortunate. Lacking the fortification of either family or means, she was ill-prepared to join the select legion of lotus eaters. Her entrance into Cammell's glittering universe was inauspicious; "He said that I was pretty," she would comment decades later. At that first meeting in St Tropez, Breton was barely 16. A small town girl, she'd already paid the price of rebellion, having been exorcised like a poltergeist from the family home in Brittany. By her own admission, she was 'troubled', but by what – a craving for excitement, the search for kicks, to be anything but ordinary? It was these not unnatural adolescent desires that had led to her being ousted by her parents. Their parting gift of 100 francs paid for Michele's train fare to Paris. However, her journey truly began when she was discovered like driftwood on the beach by the enigmatic Donald Cammell. So much the better that she was a blank slate, the sparseness of her tale befitted a changeling and fulfilled his needs. With a notebook full of arcane symbols and directions, Cammell was the magus and Breton the offering to the new Gods.

Every artist references subconscious mysteries, a process that had already begun for Donald Cammell whilst working on the film *Duffy* which featured James Coburn and James Fox as brothers involved in a family heist. Coburn bore a resemblance to Cammell whilst James Fox roamed the same elevated social strata. It could be argued that Donald Cammell was projecting multiple aspects of his persona and using film as the portal. Real life was nothing but a reflection of art and the keenly observant Cammell already had a two-way mirror on the scene. James Fox and his girlfriend, Andee Cohen, were intimates of Mick Jagger and Marianne Faithfull, just as Donald and Deborah had a camaraderie with Brian Jones and Anita Pallenberg. There was shared erotic history too, Cammell having enjoyed a ménage à trois with Pallenberg and Dixon. The threesome was another of Donald Cammell's peccadillos; one Michele Breton would soon be inducted into. The sensual synchronicity that enveloped the Cammell/Stones coterie was briefly touched upon by Marianne Faithfull in her biography *Faithfull*. In the book, she describes a scenario with the boyish Andee Cohen for the delectation of Jagger and Fox:

> I lay naked beside her. I took her nipple in my mouth and began to rub it against my lips. We glanced over to see what effect our little performance was having on Mick and James. They had stopped talking and were watching with obvious voyeuristic interest. We giggled. It turned us on and we began extending our repertoire. The more aroused they became by our lovemaking, the more it egged us on. No one else knew about our little evening of course, not a soul. But somewhere out there in that damp London night, the chief Dracula of this scene, the director Donald Cammell, must have opened his window and snatched it out of the air. He was brilliant and intuitive.

Cammell of course had his own seraglio to orchestrate, but Faithfull was on the right track. There was something in the night air, the telepathy of highly charged energy that Donald Cammell was tapping into.

The heir to a shipping fortune lost in the depression, Donald Cammell had nonetheless benefited from a cultured and comfortable upbringing. His father, Charles Richard Cammell, had achieved modest renown as a romantic poet in his native Scotland but economic survival prevailed and he accepted work as an editor of *The Connoisseur* magazine in London. The Cammell family moved to Richmond, Surrey in 1935. Although this pleasant suburb has always had literary associations, Charles Richard Cammell discovered a gateway to the esoteric via local occult scholar Montague Summers and the Wickedest Man to briefly reside in Richmond, Aleister Crowley, aka The Great Beast, 666. Crowley moved to a flat near the Cammell clan in January 1940 and was an occasional dinner guest. Originally an aficionado of Crowley's poetry, Charles used his first-hand knowledge to add to the canon of Crowleyian biographies with *Aleister Crowley: The Man, The Mage, The Poet*. Donald Cammell later described this juncture in his childhood thus: "I was brought up in a house where Magick was real. My old man, Charles, filled the house with magicians, metaphysicians, spiritualists and demons. I was conditioned by my father, by his books, by Aleister Crowley." Donald would later gain kudos from the story that he had sat upon Crowley's knee as a child. The patter of tiny hooves was discernible in the hazy dawn of Satanic psychedelia and who better as one of its catalysts than Donald Cammell? Every artist who refuses to compromise is a visionary. Cammell's first act of disobedience came when he abandoned a promising career as a society artist to pursue that most magical of crafts, film.

Although fiercely aesthetic, there was nothing remotely underground in Donald Cammell's creative sensibility. A fusion of pop art and culture had led to the completion of two offbeat yet mainstream screenplays, *The Touchables* and *Duffy*. The skewed accessibility of both films suggested the work of a cynical sensualist reaching for eternity and returning short-changed. Throughout 1967, Cammell continued to hone his most complex vehicle to date. *The Liars* transformed into *The Performers* and ultimately *Performance*, the story of a rock star and a gangster. Like a Francis Bacon painting coming into focus, the nascent screenplay was bloody, sensual and disordered. Anita Pallenberg, a co-conspirator in the film's development, remembered one occasion when Donald was working by the sea in St Tropez which she recalled to authors Rebecca and Sam

Umland: "A gust of wind blew the whole script into the water, and I remember frantically ironing each page to dry them out." Whilst Pallenberg smoothed pages and instructed Cammell on the work of actor/director Antonin Artaud, who argued that madness was preferable to normality, Michele Breton acclimatised to her new life. She took her place in Cammell's harem and was introduced to Parisian high society, sampling the finest acid and hashish. Fresh-faced and entertaining, she earned the nickname 'Mouche' (fly) as she flittered from scene to scene. Sometimes she made a little money 'performing' with a male companion. "Everybody was sleeping with everybody," she told journalist Mick Brown.

Invisible forces continued to seep into Donald Cammell's script like litmus paper. The Stone's royal peacock, Brian Jones, began his decline, usurped in Anita Pallenberg's affections by Keith Richards. A sharp-toothed sorceress, it was rumoured that Anita had stuck pins in a doll representing Jones but he was already irreparably damaged. Nonetheless, Pallenberg pulled the strings of fate. By introducing Donald Cammell to the work of Artaud, she sired the film's philosophy: "The only performance that makes it, that makes it all the way, is the one that achieves madness." Whilst Artaud's madness was revered, Brian Jones' descent into paranoia wasn't quite so well received. The borderline between crazy-cool and difficult works on an aesthetic distance in the realm of the platinum hipster. Like a girl walking the tightrope, 'Mouche' had enough charm to maintain a precarious balance in the Cammell camp and at first it paid off under the tutelage of the man Marianne Faithfull once described as "The sarcastic, sophisticated and decadent Dracula." In the autumn of 1967, Breton landed two minor roles, appearing in Godard's *Weekend* as a member of the Front de Liberation de Seine et Oise, and on Italian television as the Goddess Athena, co-directed by Mario Bava. Brief though these roles were, they at least established Mouche as a legitimate actress rather than an erotic muse.

The vision that Donald Cammell was about to unleash as *Performance* was as complex as his mind. An interior bejewelled citadel crammed with magick, manipulation, art, a fascination with the author Borges who believed that one person can lead several parallel lives and Donald's scarlet woman, lady violence.

The deification of thugs as espoused by Jean Genet in *The Thief's Journal* was also significant: "My tenderness is of fragile stuff," wrote Genet in *Journal*, "And the breath of men would disturb the methods for seeking a new paradise. I shall impose a vision of evil, even though I lose my life, my honour and my glory in this quest." Unfortunately, Jean Genet's Paris of tarted-up hoodlums no longer existed and was more resonant in England. Fashion photographer David Bailey had immortalised criminal overlords, the Kray brothers, by including a menacing portrait of them in a pantheon of pop iconography entitled 'Goodbye Baby and Amen'. The Krays' nightclub, Esmeralda's Barn, had fused violence with glamour in the English imagination. *Performance* could not have been filmed anywhere other than London for the mingling of the seedy with the sublime. Whether Cammell was aware he was on the precipice of an epoch defining film will never be known, although he had worked on the screenplay with the intensity of a ritual. Unwittingly, he had crafted a story that crossed the invisible meridian of a decade that had begun in light and was descending into darkness. Change came sweeping in as Donald made ready to decamp for England. His eight-year relationship with Deborah Dixon ended although she would be recalled as costume consultant on set. Cammell also destroyed several paintings in the Paris apartment he had shared with Deborah, killing any remnants of his former existence as a portrait artist. Michele Breton's new life commenced with the falsification of her work permits by Donald who added a couple of years to her date of birth. She left Paris a girl and landed in England an adult. On arrival she was put up in an anonymous service flat in Knightsbridge, the former patch of The Krays' old pleasure dome, Esmeralda's Barn. The papers were full of Ronnie and Reggie's villainous exploits in the run-up to their trial for murder. Fascinated though Cammell was by criminality, he took up residence in affluent Chelsea rather than the shady East End where the Krays had grown up. Moving into an apartment next door to James Fox, he was ready at last to unveil his 'New paradise'.

When Donald Cammell handed James Fox the screenplay for *Performance*, the actor recognised it as being "world class". In 1963, Fox had achieved international acclaim for his role in Joseph Losey's *The Servant* as a refined young man brought into disrepute. A masterpiece of blurred boundaries and disquieting angles, *The Servant* casts a silent shadow on the second half of *Performance*. Cammell was keen for Fox to play against his usual 'well-bred' type, offering him the role of Chas Devlin (The devil in Chas?). An early treatment of the film opened in a club called Lucifer's Pantry, a diabolical play on Esmeralda's Barn. Chas is an enforcer for a firm of gangsters busily acquiring legitimate businesses. An immaculately groomed psychopath (suits by Hymie of Waterloo), Chas sees the world in black and white, with the odd splash of human rosé to liven things up. Fox accepted Cammell's creative gambit with zeal, plunging into the Krays' crimson demi-monde in preparation for the film shoot. From the offset, Donald Cammell expected more from his cast than mere play-acting. The role of Turner, a reclusive rock star who has lost his demon, went to Mick Jagger. It was a daring move and one that could have easily backfired on Jagger. For Donald Cammell, it was an obvious choice: "I happened to know the biggest rock star in the world. And there is no art form in which the violent impulse is more implicit than in rock music. And I was very interested in what was happening with Mick at that time, the flirtation with Their Satanic Majesties." The female roles, Pherber and Lucy, were less defined, reflecting Donald Cammell's predilection for ménages à trois and his overtly sexualised view of women. With Mick Jagger on board, Warner Brothers agreed to produce the film and were initially happy for Donald Cammell to have free reign, aside from the proviso that the female leads went to established actresses. However, fate interceded. Jagger's girlfriend, Marianne Faithfull, was mooted for the role of Pherber but fell pregnant. The torch was passed to American actress Tuesday Weld, who broke her arm at one of Donald's parties. Mia Farrow, allegedly in the running as Lucy, injured her ankle setting off for the shoot. Farrow recovered in time to make Polanski's classic *Rosemary's Baby*. One can only wonder why Donald Cammell would have been prepared to falsify Michele Breton's work permits if Mia Farrow really was a contender. Perhaps the Farrow story, with its link to the Satanic epic *Rosemary's Baby*, is merely a devilish hint of mischief. Cammell was an arch-manipulator, adept at propagating myth. When filming began on *Performance* in July 1968, the roles of Turner's lovers, his long-time companion Pherber and their mutual playmate Lucy, unequivocally belonged to Anita Pallenberg and Michele Breton. Their lives were already interwoven into the very fabric of the film. Now they would just have to play themselves.

Performance was an outrageously ambitious project. Recognising his own practical limitations, Donald Cammell enlisted the talented cinematographer Nic Roeg to co-direct. Although not an exclusive arrangement, Roeg's domain appeared to be with the camera crew, whilst Donald oversaw the actors. Less effusive a character than Donald Cammell, to whom *Performance* ultimately belonged, Nic Roeg later claimed that their collaboration was a process of supporting each other in "manipulation" and that the film "changed our minds about life." There is no doubt that *Performance* pushes the boundaries of cinematic experience. Kenneth Anger, another important influence, used subliminal effects and layered esoteric symbols in his short films to cast a dark spell on the viewer. Similar techniques would be employed by Cammell and Roeg. In 1963, cinema critic Charles Boultenhouse commented in the avant-garde publication *Film Culture Reader*: "The good film-maker is he who is engaged (consciously or unconsciously) in preserving and perfecting the demon in the camera." In the early 60s, several film-makers, including Anger and the groundbreaking Maya Deren, experimented with cinematic magic(k). Deren's work is ghostly, conjuring phantoms in daylight, whilst Anger's short features evoke the primitive and the infernal. Donald Cammell was a very different creature, reminiscent of the mesmerist in *The Cabinet of Dr Caligari*, who uses others to enact his own dark fantasies. Cammell's mind-games failed to endear him to the normally stoic Keith Richards, who commented in his autobiography *Life*: "I really didn't like Donald Cammell, the director, a twister and a manipulator whose only real love in life was fucking other people up. I wanted to distance myself from the relationship between Anita and Donald... something drove him mad about other clever and talented people, he wanted to destroy them..." There was indeed something tricky about Donald Cammell, not least a gift for morphing into those whose power he desired, in essence the central premise of *Performance*, a Borges' style transference. One particular photograph of Cammell and Mick Jagger captured at the time shows the director having taken on physical aspects of his leading man. Fascinated though Donald was by Jorge Luis Borges' themes of multiple personas and split dimensions, *Performance* is also an unparalleled example of psychic vampirism that would take its toll on the entire cast. Living with Jagger at the time, Marianne Faithfull had a ringside seat: "Even before the first day of shooting, *Performance* was a seething cauldron of diabolical ingredients: drugs, incestuous sexual relationships, role reversals, art and life all whipped together into a bitch's brew. I had an intuition about what might happen, I could see something quite alarming coming of all this."

Like all great films, *Performance* has an instant aura. An immediate sense of disquiet emanates from the screen as we journey into the underworld in a white Rolls-Royce. The film is divided into two distinct sections, microcosms of opposing yet equally insular universes. There is a hyper-real quality to the footage, like the onset of a trip. Colours are too rich, angles distorted, the characters as vivid as comic book art. From the offset Jack Nietzsche's soundtrack is artfully employed, setting the pace whilst deploying unsettling electronic trip-wires. Opening with the mannered brutality of the life of an enforcer, we follow Chas Devlin as he puts "the frighteners on" for gangland boss Harry Flowers and his firm. Chas is a tightly wound golden boy until he commits the unsolicited murder of an old friend. This unexpected lack of decorum threatens Flowers' carefully maintained veneer. The hunter becomes the hunted. Cast out, Chas is forced to flee. The landscape becomes alienating; tube stations, isolated phone-boxes, unfriendly city streets. In the café at Paddington Station, the gangster overhears a conversation between an archetypal groovy musician, Noel, and his mother. About to embark on a tour, Noel has vacated his basement room at 81 Powis Square, owing his landlord, Turner, back rent. "He's an odd one, that Turner," opines Noel's mum. So the crooked dice is cast. Chas jumps a cab to Notting Hill. Nestled deep in the decaying embrace of Powis Square, just off the Portobello Road, we see the gateway to Turner's dubious kingdom, a lofty Victorian end-of-terrace house. There is a suggestion of corruption in the half-light. Not since *Psycho* has a house possessed such an unsettling air. The camera pans across the unkempt square revealing a drab landscape of time-blasted dwellings, abandoned furniture and skeletal trees. Described by Cammell as a "seedy bower of faded flower children", the choice of location was perfect with its seamy taint of grubby bohemia. A low-rent Haight-Asbury, Portobello was a down-at-heel outpost of musicians, radicals, anarchists, poets, dreamers and drop-outs. Predominantly a working class area, Notting Hill also had a large immigrant population that had prevailed against slum landlords. In 1974, writer Jonathan Raban explored the area in his book *Soft City*: "The district is notoriously difficult to police. It has a 25-year-old record of race riots, drug arrests, vicious disputes between slum landlords and their tenants... Like many impoverished areas in big cities, it is picturesque in the sun and Americans walk the length of the street market in the Portobello Road snapping it with Kodaks, but on dull days one notices the litter, the scabby paint, the stretches of worn wire netting and the faint smell of joss sticks competing with the sickly sweet smell of rising damp." It isn't just Chas who has fallen but the mysterious Turner as well. After checking that he hasn't been followed, Chas rings the doorbell. The disembodied voice of a foreign bird – Pherber – is heard over the intercom. At first she is reluctant to let the stranger in but is eventually swayed by the promise of Noel's back rent. "Push," she commands, as if willing a new life.

The exotic interior of Turner's abode was designed by The Stones' friend Christopher Gibbs to Cammell's specifications. For Gibbs, who had furnished Brian Jones' apartment in Earl's Court, Turner's pad was familiar territory. Resembling a decadent sultan's lair, complete with drape-festooned bed, the majority of the décor was imported from Morocco and Hindu Kush. In his notes, Cammell envisaged the bedroom as being "littered with multifarious stuff, with books, records, antique clothes and oriental objects of religious significance. The room, like the house, like its owner, seduces one with the glamour of its decay – an almost archaeological patina. The dust in its crannies is of a refined sensibility." Throughout, there is an opiated air of oppression, a luxurious stagnancy. Disturbing yet enticing, the eye is assailed by a kaleidoscope of mirrors, tapestries, strange artefacts, ancient carvings and a state of the art moog synthesiser. Turner's female companions are also artfully chosen acquisitions. Less than a decade separates the two women, yet Pherber could be a century older than Lucy. A

349

prickly rose of Babylon, she exudes decadent privilege. If Pherber belongs to the canon of femme fatales, Lucy personifies the lost innocent, a prime example of Delacroix's 'The flower beneath the foot.' Ensconced in Cammell's 'new paradise', interior melodramas unfurled. Held by another's fantasies, Anita Pallenberg succumbed to heroin. The Stones' dealer, 'Spanish Tony' Sanchez, made regular deliveries to Anita then reported back on the film's progress to a simmering Keith Richards. Utilising the tension, Cammell propagated the story that a glowering Richards had taken to parking outside the set in his motor to keep an eye on his bird. Needless to say, The Stones guitarist was not impressed: "Donald Cammell was more interested in manipulation than directing. He had a hard-on about intimate betrayal and that's what he was setting up in *Performance*. Whilst Pallenberg used heroin to pass the time between takes, Michele Breton maintained her copious intake of hashish. In the hot-house atmosphere, the young French actress became increasingly paranoid. In less than two years, she had been catapulted through Cammell's universe into the parallel sphere of *Performance*. There was no protection, only the unblinking eye of the camera and shadow games. Anita Pallenberg had believed that the character of Lucy was erroneous to the film's plot but like Chas with whom she ultimately connects, she is another runaway. Nic Roeg also began taking an interest in Michele, which may have further piqued the more experienced actress as Cammell observed: "Anita was very hard on Michele, because Michele was younger. Maybe there was some jealousy there, and Anita could be very mischievous, very smart – very witchlike." In the shuttered, destabilising environment, Mouche began to lose her bearings and a doctor was called to administer valium shots on several occasions. Still the cameras rolled. On screen, Michele Breton is every lost child of the decade, a girl passing through to nowhere. Her first and only major speech in *Performance* mirrors the transient nature of her existence. Washing her hair in the notorious 'Persian Bath' scene, Lucy reflects upon her position in the household. Describing her failed attempt to acquire a British visa, she recalls a conversation with a home office bureaucrat... "So I say, 'Pherber is learning me English and my boyfriend is learning me his books and magic stories.'" Pherber and Turner are cinematic surrogates for Deborah Dixon and Donald Cammell. "You poor little thing," coos Turner when Lucy tells him of the civil servant's final comment. "He said, 'You're a juvenile in moral (sic) danger and you're not desirable.'" Both mother and lover, Pherber shows her sympathy by washing the bubbles off Lucy's back. As above, so below: downstairs in the basement flat, decorated with posters of gangsters and movie stars, Chas washes red paint from his hair, the splashes of scarlet reminding us of his bloody talents.

When Turner first meets Chas, the reclusive rock star removes a chenille house-coat to reveal a tight black top and leggings, the costume of Cesare, the elegant somnambulist from *The Cabinet of Dr Caligari*, inferring a waking dream. The film's pulse starts to quicken as Chas and Turner take the measure of one another in 'The Big Room', the most disquieting of all the chambers. A pharaoh's playroom, the dust has long settled on any meaningful activity; a variety of instruments, modern and antique, exotic and functional, are silent reliquaries amidst broken glass, burned down candles, old papers. Screens and mirrors add to the visual confusion. In a room of illusions, Chas attempts to pass himself off as Johnny Dean, who makes his way as a juggler. Despite his sensual lethargy, Turner's interest is roused as he tries to divine Chas' secret, the vigour that he no longer possesses. Like a ghost, Lucy in a long white robe passes between the mirrors and the screens. She is almost imperceptible as she wanders from one realm to the next. Before she is swallowed up by the house, Lucy stares at Chas. In that moment he is the avenging angel, death's emissary. Cammell's vision is artfully conveyed. From the offset, he had prevailed upon Jagger to shed his self-consciousness and channel Turner, a character desperately "trying to grab at poetic ideas of being possessed by someone else's demonic energy." Chas abetted by Pherber attempts to unravel the gangster's persona in a pseudo-mystical rite, with the aid of Fly Agaric (Amanita Muscaria). Originally used by shamans in Northern Asia, Fly Agaric also grew in certain parts of England. Taken orally, it became a feature of country covens before making its way into hippy lore. It is of course the witchy Pherber who picks the hallucinogenic mushroom and offers it to the unwitting Chas, like Eve proffering the apple, the gift of knowledge. In his biography

Comeback, James Fox questioned the wisdom of the scene: "Could Turner and Pherber really have believed that they could discover the source of the mystery of Chas' personality and talent by dressing him up as an Arabian assassin and feeding him Fly Agaric mushrooms?" As if infected by the film's character, Jagger and Pallenberg attempted to dismantle Fox even when Cammell wasn't at the helm. Pallenberg taunted the brilliant young actor for not using LSD and threatened to spike his coffee, whilst Jagger frequently threw barbs in his direction, probably threatened by his greater screen prowess.

Throughout the duration of Chas' rebirth, Lucy is absent. She has gone to visit Ulla, a real-life model friend of Anita Pallenberg's who ran a vintage clothes stall at the Chelsea Antiques Market. On Lucy's return, she encounters a very different Chas, one who has shed the constraints of gender and no longer seeks to dominate. He has woken to life's myriad possibilities and has assumed Turner's dandyism. In the downstairs flat he tenderly makes love to Lucy and marvels at her body: "You're like a skinny little frog, aren't you... small titties, haven't you, you're like a small boy, that's what you're like..." Lucy is happy too and even suggests that they might leave together: "I've got to go away for a holiday in the mountains," she muses, reinforcing her own impermanence. There is a sense that something has shifted in the once-stagnant house. It is fitting that Chas and Lucy share the penultimate scene. Michele Breton felt that James Fox was the only person who showed her any real kindness on the set: "I didn't know what I was doing and they used me. There was no love there, no understanding between the people. James Fox was the only person who had some human communication. James was the outsider. He saw what was going on with me – the emptiness. He understood that and he was very gentle to me." In the aftermath of their lovemaking Lucy asks Chas to go and get her some shampoo. Gangster Chas would never have entertained such a simple act of kindness. On the landing, he encounters Harry Flowers' armed heavies. It's time for Chas to leave. He asks for two minutes and flashes his revolver at the hit squad. In the bedroom, Turner tells Chas he wants to go with him. "You don't know where I'm going," he says. "Yeah I do" responds the pouting Turner. Despite the transference, Chas remains an eternal assassin and shoots Turner in the head, execution style. As Chas is escorted from Powis Square into the care of Harry Flowers, one of the gangsters drops a postcard onto the bed where Lucy and Chas have just laid. Lucy is glimpsed in the bath, a basement Ophelia. The message on the card is simple: Gone to Persia X Chas. As Harry Flowers' white Rolls-Royce drives off to destinations unknown, we see a hybrid of Turner and Chas in the backseat. The transformation is complete.

In *Performance* Donald Cammell created the film of a lifetime, with people's lives: "I was talking about losing all self-consciousness, all consciousness and if necessary, control, in order to embody people who were at the very edge of their existence; people who were playing a game of life and death for their psychic survival." Such a film would of course have a controversial journey to the big screen. The direct attack on conventional morals, unflinching violence, unapologetic drug use and ambi-sexuality caused a furore at Warner Brothers, who demanded a re-edit. *Performance* eventually premiered in England at the Odeon, Leicester Square in January 1971. True to Borges, it has over the decades taken on a life of its own, becoming the subject of several books and a documentary. The film has also morphed into new formats, including video and DVD. By pushing the cast of *Performance* beyond the realms of ordinary experience, Donald Cammell created a truly extraordinary artefact: "Any technique that works is OK; if you stir things up relentlessly you'll get results. And I went for it all the way. I thought the sparks were flying. They were all performers – and the idea of performance was alive and well and embodied by the title." It was to be his greatest film. In the afterglow of *Performance* Cammell appeared in Kenneth Anger's *Lucifer Rising* as Osiris, the Egyptian God of Death. Anger's film, loosely based on Aleister Crowley's poem 'Hymn to Lucifer' also featured Marianne Faithfull as Lilith. A masterpiece of occult cinema, *Lucifer Rising* serves as a curious post-script to *Performance*. In later years, associates claimed that Donald Cammell would shy away from discussing Crowley. Although Cammell moved to Hollywood in 1971 where he continued to make movies, he would never again enjoy the creative freedom that enabled *Performance*. At odds with a conservative film industry, Cammell committed suicide on 24th April, 1996. The manner of his death, a self-inflicted bullet wound to the head, recalls Chas Devlin's assassination of Turner.

In any transcendent project, the price is always high. The cost to those involved in *Performance* was exorbitant. Anita Pallenberg's relationship with Keith Richards was damaged by her participation in the film, the on-screen intimacy portrayed between her and Jagger like sand in an oyster, a slow erosion. Deftly shedding Turner's skin, the eternally canny Jagger appeared to slip away unscathed from Powis Square and straight onto a plane bound for the USA. In December 1969, the Rolling Stones played the Altamont Freeway in a barren field on the winter solstice. During a performance of 'Sympathy For the Devil' a teenage boy was murdered by Hell's Angels yards from the stage. Mick Jagger's fey pleas to the Angels went unheard in the bloody maelstrom. At the time, Donald Cammell was editing *Performance* in LA: "I remember saying, 'I told you so... see what rock and roll can do?' I felt a little bit prophetic." In the coming months Jagger would be photographed wearing a gold crucifix. James Fox retired from acting for ten years and joined a Christian sect called The Navigators. He still maintains that *Performance* is one of the most important British films ever made. And that is how the story usually ends, aside from the terrible irony that Harry Flowers' white Rolls-Royce belonged to John Lennon, who was later killed by a gunshot.

When *Performance* was re-released in 2004, Michele Breton's name was left off the film poster. She had vanished from history although her celluloid alter-ego lives on. In his book, *Performance,* Mick Brown speculates on Lucy's fate: "Lucy travels East in search of her dream. There her consumption of copious amounts of hashish is soon supplemented with heroin. Her passport and belongings are stolen or sold. In a mountain village, or perhaps a cheap tourist hostel, Lucy dies of an overdose. Or she finds her way to India, the Maharishi's ashram at Rishikesh, or a Tibetan monastery in Nepal, where she forswears the ephemeral revelations of drugs for God. Eventually she returns to France, marries an academic and writes an autobiography in which the death of Turner is but a footnote." Unfortunately, it is Breton who has become the footnote. In 1969 she was indeed a "juvenile in moral danger". According to comments by Donald Cammell, whilst in London

Michele fell in with some French lowlifes. After the film's completion she returned with them to Paris where she developed a drug habit. And that was where the trail ended until some thirty years later when Mick Brown searched that most arcane font of knowledge, the phone book. Consulting the international directory he discovered one Michele Breton listed as living in Germany and dialled the number. He knew it was Mouche straight away, though she had long since given up that name. Confused and bereft, Michele Breton recalled the past to a patient stranger. Emptiness had engulfed her; she had been completely used up by *Performance*: "I was taking everything that was going. I was in very bad shape, all fucked up. Donald drove me to Paris. I went to his place and stayed for two or three days, and then he told me he didn't want to see me anymore." Just as Lucy wanders ghostlike through the mirrors and screens in Turner's ornate parlour, so Michele drifted around France and Spain in pursuit of heroin. After getting busted in Formentera, Breton managed to evade the police. On the run she fled back to Paris then high-tailed it to Kabul, in search of cheap opiates. She had made it to the mountains at last. As Mick Brown suggested in Lucy's imaginary biography, Michele did indeed sell everything to feed her habit but still she hungered until she took some acid: "I looked at my needles, my drugs and said never again." Sadly, sobriety failed to save her. Michele Breton now lives with a stolen soul in a tiny flat in Berlin. She has no friends and no money: "My life was always bad and it's still not better, nobody wants me." In 1987, Breton saw *Performance* again. It evoked "a feeling of death" in her. The click of the receiver consigned a weeping Michele Breton back to the ether. Several years later, whilst considering putting on an open-air screening of *Performance* in Powis Square, Mick Brown searched for Michele Breton's number in the international directory once again, but she was no longer listed.

Peter Playdon
Severed Heads Speak (Chapter 5: Calling Dr Burroughs/The Space of Interzone)

1./ I have experienced a sequence of Kafkian contempt/ Since arrival I wonder if she isn't one of the ordinary men and women going about their business, each time better behaved, cheaper/ Interzone city of all human potential observations: an end-of-the-world feeling a market where identities are wasted rather than realised/ Sollubi utopia is ambiguous/ The opening sense of always blacking-out in the Zone of miscegenation ('the blood and substance of what he did last night') to describe the experience of city inter-racial same-sex relationships, these races are the meaning of Interzone, its space-time realised later in the novel, fact merges into dream/ Burroughs writes dreams invade potentials and differentiation and independence kill/ Utopia without definite content continuous, like a dream extending from the past into thinking/ over a decade after Naked Lunch the reality of both was called into question/ Iris is not an autonomous utopian/ Intelligence defined reflecting vision junkie situations and environments solve problems of vast psycho-social engineering experiment can never settle constructing text via cut-ups mutate cross-fertilize in order to remain/ The effect of Iris' position climax space interchange cultures, language, hyper-sexualised female junkie hybrid definition model dialogic utopia encapsulation of human existence furthermore prescription for political action: personification of Interzone/ We might speculate misogynistic body horror textual shuffling revolution to effect basic changes/ observation of life in Tangier three tactics required – Ignore. Forget/ beyond the untouchables Iris' addiction figured as physical tactics/ Significant Burroughs is abhorrent; combination of traditional racist with particular issues the corollary his empathy for Iris undecidable conflict/ Interzone, as a space about the threatened future of the white race, as perfumed garden late Sax Rohmer, from ambiguous site of dangerous potential cut to The Saint/ evenhanded his sexuality offering extremes of new life enforcer put to good use hybridity of the body of female sexuality become what Turner imagines him to be/ a character, but one of Benway's projects/ understanding this role, their physiology a byproduct of Chas the potential in Chas/ Aleatory procedures involve the ability to adapt oneself to utopia as nowhere no identifiable form or place constantly complicate questions of deliberate authorial utopia/ the Academy routine cut to miscegenation training methods offer racial/national origin as nadir of the 1960s/ An urban context; Iris is somewhere beneath the projection existing conditions does not repeat source material drawn/ 1. Disrupt. 2. Attack. 3. Disappear/ the Malay-Negress in the Cafe deployed alternatively might represent Burroughs prescription is tactical concerned with degeneration and enslavement the offspring of miscegenation her sexuality a Manichean view of the universe as continuous mysogynistic tropes/ But there is horror invoked not the Nirvana she used as a springboard for anxious fantasies/ the Garden of Delights might have been in other contexts erotics concerned with death with Fu Manchu subaltern class paranoia dismantling psychic defences, imagine the unity of the self different temporal orders identification with the Other that follows seeks to identify analyse/ Interzone as site where all human potential relate to a further attempt to transcend tradition/ market section opens cinematic character The Saint in iconoclastic tirade soundtrack Duke Ellington a cheap ham notorious metabolic junkie of jazz seeming to shade into the muezzin call dreamed up by the Mecca Chamber of Commerce to the Duke Ellington tune radical 2.potential suggested East St. Louis segregated black section the Saint's routine invocation of black American socially excluded/ Saint's iconoclasm mutate together Ellington and muezzin powerless reacts xenophobic speculative anthropological categorisation and cultural hybridity: Negro Polynesian Mountain Mongol, an untouchable desert caste in Arabia, races as yet unconceived and unborn the untouchable perhaps a fallen priest caste pass through your body/ The Composite City where all function taking into themselves a vast silent market/The City haze of opium hashish resinous empathy identification with salt water and the rotting river and dried excrement overwhelming difference/ Close reading of The

Naked Lunch properties of the city smell smoke including racialised signifiers in Interzone with negatively defined elements/ Nature simultaneously uncontrolled, wild and threatening an establishing shot panorama of human life salt water dead and dying rotting East St. Louis Toodleoo invocation the excluded and taboo elements of the body of the mosque/ multiplying genitals linking these elements with drugs Burroughs' home town makes a routine appearance racialised and racist invocation of home is deferred geography and culture/ Olfactory becomes aural, musical: Burroughs sees Interzone as a site of racial blood substance many bebop one-stringed Mongol instruments, gypsy Nomad Polyglot Near Eastern Indian jazz and muezzin call, olfactory combinations not yet realised pass through positive human potentials spread influence of audio-visual elements in thinking subterranea physical mental and cultural Gysin attacked the written word first most basic representational forms an otherwise repressive world allowing him visual media: rub out the word and the image track continuity: a Turkish Bath in Sweden opens collaborative experiments in cinema received critical attention (Mottram 1977)/ flux identity geography made cinema rather than literature grounded the intended conclusion, method as well as metaphorical model planned to end the film full of the cinematic apparatus the scripts Central Park, New York/ further space-time stage direction and screenwriting terminology mass media consumer-addiction multiple personalities strikingly similar to languages that look like story-boarding, The Book of Breething reversed: potentially endless variations, parodies of Hollywood GREAT SLASHTUBITCH use of genre materials I have just experienced emergence in my accounts of his own cinematic experiments suppose you had kept a non-queer between diverse times and places/ Moreover, film years subject to continual queer acts and controlled existence power is not total have to arrange a merger I shall be crushed by his darkness the population public defecation the city's incorporation the porosity of the body shit-strewn lots and huge parks young kids accommodation to Arab culture/ One city is an abject slum also a site of erotic time/ You must let it seep into you two statues of young boys heats intense visions the onset of Ramadan hashish baths and the sexual ambiguity of men/ Burroughs' city activities of population during his time in Tangier even the least character-armoured people have an account of vivid nightmares experienced oppressive Spanish life-fearing character dream North Africa ten years from now the population of Guayaquil Ecuador companions physically aged before their time with petrol before being attacked in turn/ one vast hostile country filled with a sense of restlessness and setting-forth: Migrations, incredible journeys through dream fantasies of violence, valleys across the Pacific an outrigger canoe to Easter Island Yellow Wave: O Traveller, the cocculus possesses (if you mash it!) intoxicating properties/ the only time Burroughs ever attempts to identify defensive character traits that resist pain but also their social opposite a materialisation of withdrawal. Similarities between negation and allegorization of the drug life spatiality known as Interzone destroys its own suspension polysexual/ Burroughs describes the City of Interzone concentrated on analysing the metaphorical a metaphor for limbo for a dead-end place/ Senders, Divisionists, Factualists extreme fantasies diegesis the New York landscape in the work takes place doubling-back to the time Burroughs spent with Allen zone of tensions pleasure-seeking heightened version of Dickens or Kafka a number of visual references for its levels connected by web of catwalks 3. intense, metamorphic multi-dimensional lines in Allen's backyard Bill had catwalks, boardwalks and fire escapes/ so old it had been rebuilt layer upon layer a vibrating soundless hum without any apparent motivation/ obvious connection flashback notions of the present form cut-up/fold-in techniques understanding the events on screen/ the 1960s the origin of these procedures the trial fills the screen lawyer alludes newspapers well documented references an object in the diegesis cut to Stein Lawrence Durrell John Dos Passos Cammell's professed interest in non-temporality traditional linear causality seeing existing texts cutting the page vertical and horizontal situation where everything is happening simultaneously see Port of Saints: 1920 gun boys tommy gun black Cadillac boy squirms down on his pal he sort of opens up you can feel the pull in the algebra of need there they are on a corner three guns from the West Side/ He pivots around Mektoub in the Arab world means one should not imagine Burroughs created Tangier mystique in 1950 Sodom was a church picnic change fate cut up the words/ Make new chains of equivalence drawn between occupants of Notting Hill black marketeers spies thugs phonies beachcombers expatriates degenerates change of direction taken by Chas from gangster charlatan explained narrative cut-up/fold-in form the text include the rocket footage/ a brief sketch of this scene and its input on their travels a stop-over point for an entirely random element with no thematic connection two other players in this drama could attest had a dynamic energy interpolation of tales of hashishim killers all of which musky spices insinuate the sequence which follows quasi-documentary footage; the ménage-à-trois, and the slide images of Persia invoke a hierarchy of elements that remain identical/ suits designed to mimic authority figures he subsumed within a new form the racialised relationship relished playing these complacent villains Dr Benway called the Spanish the lousiest white trash in the West, played a variation on his junkie in Mexico City and Lima Towers Open Fire, one of his negatives I like Tangiers less all the time he plays the leader of bureaucratic word image Morocco. Apart from this act of referencing North Africa reading Paul Bowles themes elements representation Arab life as inscrutable gangster milieu one where Burroughs often found the same relaxed attitudes towards drug use cinematic and pulp fiction sources, and stories of the comfortable in Mexico City & Lima/ public space and general subservient status in The Last Words of Dutch Shultz his first impression I can play doctors CIA men all kinds of things I do war criminals/ Burroughs filmed playing the US President familiarity of the Arabs unsettling space theatre Tottenham Court Road/ projected follow-up to star Burroughs as Supreme Court judge kidnapped by black militants foundation for subsequent thinking about source of B-23 virus Wilde's cell in Reading Gaol which the smiling damned villain claimed to have occupied/ Later Burroughs would write that, contra Bowles, I have no nostalgia/ In Exterminator! streets very near complete breakdown as Western Indian European Arab characters flash difficult zoom shot of car from ground level Chinese and Negro stock seem to be flashing as if superimposed simply a retinal effect caused by persistence of vision baffling impression/ Lee felt there was longer duration we see the car draw up outside hidden from him intercut sex scene ends Chas life of the city similar effect in original sequence sex scene intercut shorter shorter South Americans unknown white flicker two frame intervals sex scene rhythm Burroughs aiming for purely random technique it may cut between God knows what he is not as one is apt to say obviously connected/ the type of cutting Burroughs does needs events pre-written pre-recorded colonised hybridised with the weak/ the opening sequence understanding hybrid flash-edits in this sequence identifiable being people he will meet later in the film polishing the bonnet of the Rolls Royce/ the work of Burroughs is on the level/ Performance draws parallels Burroughs experimented underworld in the courtroom scene Gysin's accidental cutting-up by merger of the smaller and weaker Tristan Tzara TS Gertrude Eliot intercut Chas and his gang's intimidation of literary antecedents, of the junkie from the margins of society to the cut-up method 4.involves pre-social control, drawing explicit parallels between horizontal axes rearranging the pieces then cops doctors politicians all bound to being human they strip down to Stardust/ One sits in the back seat gun nuts tearing through empty streets lips drawn back eyes shiney reputation preceded arrival/ Ah Pook Is Here a convention of Girl Scouts compared to Tangier/ Burroughs has gone to Persia population: thieves characters operators bandits bums tramps politicians Tangier contemporaneous a kind of model this can only be done by setting up his film/ Paris staging his interest in buying trips to Morocco, as the writer said everyone has to encounter kill his own sensuality kif sex music Hassan-i-Sabbah often linked underground radicalism post-colonial rebellion observed in Tangier the story of HiS the victim officially located outside the city in literary cosmology/ within it providing sexual gratification they structure much of his work/ the keepers of Notting Hill reliance the dominant telling was already a corruption given a perverse Burroughsian twist: citizens for violence the Assassins this connection exploited Narcotics/ I may well have encountered arrived Tangier met Gysin Sollubi define themselves and the Assassins at every opportunity/ He skilfully used metanarrative pattern transform a little-known drug of indolence into order to be humiliated & degraded note presence of assassin myth hemp peyote first official statement of the US government popular myth descriptions heavily laced castes originate from fallen priests Malay running amok result of habitual use spurious generalisation opposing the Crusades utilised the services of individuals addicted to the drug these persons being called hashischin hashshah methodological processes derived intoxication provoked violent conduct removing restraint to unconsciously mirror District Attorney Eugene Stanley's 1931 article American Journal of Police as fallen angel/ marijuana violent crime marijuana developed year of marijuana menace published New Orleans Medical result of campaign Anslinger's attention first drawn to socio-historical hierarchical power American Magazine July 1937 McWilliams low-budget film Assassin of Youth invoking exclusion the Sollubi rationalised Mohammedan sect used hashish for materialistic art into social formation/ priest sympathised with him for years felt Anslinger took all stupidity ignorance power drive into one person taking on themselves all human vileness/ mediation between worshipper and God in men old show men old wankers Hassan both WSB's character and his authorial flower order break Chas' psychological Sollubi exclusion at face value paradoxically the law-giver the authoritarian vileness itself ambiguous serving divergent social free play of desire/ The paradox here is a Sollubi enacting the traditional fear of contagion reversibility of all authority the contingent & phantasmagorical city their vileness serves oblivion names not inevitable but dependent Chas' revolt against the law of Harry Flowers rim guests while they eat holes for this purpose/ Citizens who want HiS disputed nowadays hoping to jump the gun offer intercourse with encampment of Sollubis does not provide the novel research the historical revealed the apparent existence of a novel by the Maitre des Assassins 1936 to Islamic culture I am neither a Moslem or a

Christian always peering over the horizon eyes mind seeking
intoxication transformation alter consciousness but I am with
God ANYWHERE EXCEPT HERE/ I realise how much we
consult the absence a definitely appalling language collaborator
suggested first found the story travels experiments destabilising
traditional underground superimposition Chas &
Turner/Pherber/Lucy derives vision of Tangier as free zone fixed
sexual identities barrier to possible space-time WSB's distance
from this element late nineteenth-century South American jungle
question about this repeats his view that contemporary America
is possible the space of Interzone the supremacist culture not
only do Chas & Turner merge idealisation of white women
accompanied by shots of the white Rolls Royce driving off into
women effeminisation of black men location of any grounding/
the viewer WSB describes his own sense of having Chas'
situation albeit sexual terms reversed antipathy towards most
aspects of his contemporary cult constant 5. shuffling of
characters & chronology via reference Westerners entirely too
much space wasted in transporting/ themes of identity
transference a mise-en-abyme non-queer persona as a separate
personality discussing the significance of linking orgasm & death
in his work the person dies in the orgasm in which he is born
alchemy notes: it might represent possibly the young boy in a
strait-jacket of flesh twenty five/ masculinist perspective
reincarnation opposite of death could be connected the
denouement understood as distorted equivalent orgasm forms
link talk of course the kid & all the rest of us gendered
boundaries both within Chas & Antonin reversibility of social
rules ideas about Interzone respectable business world &
criminal allusions to a space where the lawyer's defence of
consolidation presence film economic units w the larger & lustier
time in Tangier at that time tactics/ Similarly re-locates European
consuls/ his centre his notion of addiction metaphor Naked
Lunch is Tangiers which I call socially excluded junkies & their
oppression will be Lee's impressions of addiction power
furthermore all addict action occurs in a super-imposed place
HiS Scandanavia opening the 1960s only in The Wild Boys 1972
in The Yage Letters 1975 as part of a letter discussed at length/

interviews derived from a letter dated July of HiS/ He agrees with superimposition of different locations & for a man who rebels against control system writing style attitude own separatist counterforce assassination as a way to salvation/ The idea USA was main motivation behind death, personified in an enemy calls him the Wandering WASP/ phantasmagoria of late 1960s his addiction & homosexuality criminalised him anxiety-free exile the most likely point of origin/ Gysin himself Wild Boys Marco Polo (see Ambrose, Rynn & Wilson, 1992) origin in the riots cut-up prank linking the central figure becomes possible to imagine The Wild Boys formal technique delivers a note for Lucy saying gone to Persia Johnny the wild boys/ When you read this I will be far away re-reading The Botany of Desire escape I am on my way from London to Oriental source hashish held directly responsible by Harry J. Anslinger first director Federal Bureau of weapons & tactics suggesting story in mainstream media reporting anti-drug campaigns responsible marijuana prohibition has interest in revolutionary publicity every contemporary crime story he could cut to lure violence, a social menace element/ US Surgeon General's 1929 Preliminary Report on Indian scientific establishment effects marijuana/ This report drove unverified representations of Eastern experience conceived in broadly Romantic terms alleged the murderous frenzy task to liberate human time-structures consciousness hashish/ It is also said that the Mohammedan leaders use hashish for secret murders the frenzy produced from determinism & law-bound closure hashishi from which modern word assassin WSB favourite writers relevant here/ perverted form of assassin myth marijuana building false courage reproduced New Orleans aesthetics in favour of systematic derangement science influential in establishing perceived link between criminals & poetry gun-running serve as models/ His article marijuana assassin of youth published conditioning existential assassin myth towards the end of his career see the murderers so-called religious observations/ They made homicide in high ritual racial/sexual/social de-conditioning quotes Allen Ginsberg: WSB bad karma of the whole world on his back/ They concentrated politicisation & sense of a parallel 1960s counter-culture which saw truth/ This town seems to have several dimensions super-cession of the negative in history incidents I have been to bed with 3 Arabs universe necessary outcome same characters different clothes capable of being transformed claim precedence over another in situation far removed from so-called permissive/ This impression gives rise to number B23 similar transgression however far-out the freaks feeling in Tangiers the whole town is a trap guided by ideology/ Scenes of anarchic ambiguity of identity within Interzone people WSB claims he would like to see 6. happen whether they drink or not/ No one knows for sure a situation where everything is permitted unknowable because unrepresentable Interzone may or may not be a dream location at a point where three-dimensional HiS as both Law & forgetting of the real world in Interzone dreams between the symmetry of Tangier the prognostic pulse of the world appears/ Scattered around the grounds in pools of blood are severed heads actually actors buried future frontier between dream & reality telling what they will have to do if they hope ever to return to this paradise/ fold-in first encounter Chas inserting composite text/sustained humming fading out before narrative development & final scene/ two scenes cut close-up these passages are bodies against birds-eye travelling shots the non-linearity in the process of textual breaking continuity & movement like his modernist predecessors saw this right-to-left twice/ the scene progresses urbanised life in the twentieth-century involved the cut-up is not a new invention/ interview w Uri Hertz 1982 a very brief & for our purposes inconsequential exchange compose lyrics for Memo to Turner [sic] photographers & film-makers fifty years one of his dream notes My Education: a book of dream performance/ I was dressed in some outlandish eighteenth-century background as a painter, this is perhaps not resented/ Savoy book & the Ritz performance. "Performance." Antony Balch. Eclipse, a dimness like under-exposure Cubism painting had followed/ story repeated earliest incarnation montage/multiple exposure interview with author & their movements in space/time WSB Trust states I recall William debt to Jule-Etienne Marey impressed enough to steal the technique for an early version of the script mentioned Professor Gysin cinematic connection shifting phrases up to blocks of narrative access to the text even before cutting of scenes gets faster optical printer although in the text Borges quoted a few further intercuts quoted visual presence in the Black Swan pub this shot repeated his work invisibly informed partner falling asleep/ the naming of WSB The Last Words of Dutch Schultz with drugs the very act of naming shorter intervals until colour & black heretofore been ignored in the crescendo/ The precise sense indicates that the cut-up not pass without comment/ Doctors figure between images or scenes indirectly either croakers to be conned describes experimenters justified by ideology cannot be described random figures of social authority with access to The Cut-Ups/ Body-altering technology Dr Fingers had the power of prophecy perhaps they are split you cut word lines the future leaks out likely to break the Law logic behind formal legality/ we are introduced to Chas appearance in keeping with agents of control the chauffeur (John Sterland) heretical attitudes his grey seersucker pub separated from Chas by space reality studio/ essentially no one by 1967 found himself/ Reality film now become twentieth-century canon full weight of the film directed against The Club attention writers & artists strong but invisible presence film of the mid-to-late 1960s avant-garde influence on the English the primary task of the revolutionary 1970 destroys reality film this is not film individual reality itself & there is no audience describes accurately how we felt the world rooms which WSB uses repeatedly penetrated darkrooms of Olympia Press edition in Paris the same programs that create consensual reality & Oxford-based literary journal politics lead to linear Olympia edition referentiality but we should remember control situations/ This seems contrary to English edition under discussion here/ In Mexico, South & Central America guerrilla units repeatedly mined for production of new texts United States from Tangier to Timbuktu corresponding to the architecture, urban planning judgements, prevailing attitudes, primary concerns: drugs/boys/ As Chas lies face- 7.down Turner's Oriental indexes the degree of social control exercised Pherber she suggests I think maybe we ought to call upon the Yage shortly afterwards Turner reads a passage about HiS primarily his source these texts words familiar to WSB readers nothing archaeological hallucinates he hears Turner sing of the man examining his writings about cities in order to trace artists & writers invoked like Borges international film version of Naked Lunch 1990 cancelled at the last minute due to the first Gulf War & instead several different publicly recognisable persona changes forced to re-imagine location as hallucination writings/ This perception was shaped by a series of subtle suggestions throughout the film that he is still Mary McCarthy at the Edinburgh Writers Conference Croneberg's cinematic version of Interzone as closed version of Casablanca [the film & the city] in which drugs understand The Times 1961 transposition of cinematic fold-in method extends writing of Harry Flowers' gang resonates move back & forward on his time track the few writers he admired flashing forward in time to page one hundred particular phenomenon can be produced to order from 1954 to 1958 regularly between 1964-1971 Chelsea 1953 WSB listened to tape made visited Morocco scrambling news broadcasts location work style analogous to fragmentary war imagination/ method produced Morocco tape/ response at the time hysterical sister friend inspiration accident with printed text geographical & imaginary space unrecognised precursor to cut-up zone before Third Mind 1979 when encouraging experimentation I want to address the formal/ This is not to say they ignore cinema/ move pieces of it around & try out new juxtapositions words introduce a new dimension in writing enabling the writer to turn take a good look boys the priest's role is exclusion denigration sexual reversed Mexican law mores purpose existence of evil justified identity he'd theretofore forced absence of God felt in US Iris narrated by Clem Snide Private Ass lost at home/ Mexico she serves specific purpose here live like a prince first intro: female hustler knows his place stays there senses that everyone is a racket mysogynistic revulsion at his sense that it contained Interzone site frontier spirit half Negro but any radical potential in the US was 1880 addiction/ The overwhelming strength of her habit cultures, hotter climes mythical appearance needles rust in her dry flesh the first indication Mugwump lives entirely on sweets Iris eats to discover it again elsewhere, a horror of her own body/ horror wholly solipsistic denies difference archetype junkie in turn an invention of his mysterious & holy wound a figure first incarnated by 'Nothing is true, everything is permitted'/ time: two scenes Exterior Daytime connected by violence; the sadomasochistic intertextual relationship the violent humiliation, the Orientalism most identifiable Lucy who we see sitting astride Chas is of the Mountain appears throughout different time; we see brief shot of her towards everything is permitted dominate the discourse Dana momentarily followed by a shot of work/ Turner speaks these words to Chas is disoriented/ Like the cut Turner spray-painting reconstructing self-image the passage of Joey Maddox a more literal or formal flash obvious parallels with Chas' relationship to H film an act reveals constructed Chas quoting Flowers tomorrow he finds the narrative's subsequent development/ I create conflict I do not take sides Cammell said of this opening sequence see Exterminator! some of it subliminal Nick [sic] loved to intercut (LAUGHS) makes very few statements about failure credit editing film not mentioning Frank Mazzola accomplished this style the precision & formality could be Resnais however that technique nowadays referred to as "Nicolas Roeg."/ Interview conducted 1986? Cammell in an act/line to Nietzsche rather than WSB film is Nietzschean in sense I believe in living one's life chance techniques stressing how careful he had been particularly Cammell committed reader mis-identified very precise rhythm metre pace film/ neutral vision of human cultural syncretism Sollubi serve Interzone interrupted encampments 8. subordinate social position preceding pages like the night soil collectors & pig-farmers derived from an Amazonian vine sub-analagous, socially necessary/ The dialectical effect of Yage all defences subordinate Hegel & Fanon here autonomous subjects of Interzone do not enter into sexual relations equate rationality whiteness & masculinity re-inscribe hierarchical power relationships, imagined Other: WSB predicts telos of modern life/ speculation re: the untouchables I feel myself turning into a Negress ends the satire on serious indulgent flesh convulsions of lust my legs universalisation of the Sollubi's position reiterate the room Near East Negro South Western anthropology he had previously conned traditional

Western conceptions of evil of untouchable castes determined contingency inspired tapes made by journalist May1972 Ornette Coleman travelled to Morocco January relationships as one might expect/ project was never hybrid music sound Coleman went on to work symbolic reintegration of priestly function Cronenberg heard Midnight Sunrise proclaimed function might not be specified but suggests Christ dying for our sins/ A curiously mixed populace Negro Chinese the racialised geography of Interzone classify some beautiful boys mixed comparison/ This leads him to say of the city that it produced significant changes to the source material something going on here some undercurrent of life the letter dated July 10th 1953 description of the populace Lee's distance The Yage Letters & Naked Lunch here an outsider's incomprehension of difference a modernist poetics the most complete derangement undercurrent sinister fecundity/ He goes on inextricably linked with transformation into hybrid: I turned right into a nigger the special race part Indian part white part house I feel myself change into think at first fundamentally an Oriental Negress/ My legs well rounded you are a man or a woman however this valorisation so central to the con 'white blood' the natives were lucky to have a secure self specifically conceived in strong English/ Journal quotes a passage that echoes the totality of scripted reality disrupted by cutting-up the medium in which we dwell – language/ Marijuana as a medium for living breath flashback used films enabling writer to go on insisting that he should never trust reader reads page ten he is Sabbah invoked with reference to H back in time to page one déjà vu dependence on him & his law paradoxically manipulator who announces the end of law/ Jerry Newman called the drunken newscaster demonstration belief routines coincide w cut-up appropriately HiS cutting up an electronic medium, audio strength of desire/ hysterical laughter was not to be authority not necessarily successful/ source for character returns reference in Betty Boutell's Le Vieux de la cassette recorders/ this information may have come from evidence in the form of quotations from the painter film technicians cut cut & handle their medium background Isma'ili sect Gysin states cutting & rearranging a page of written images into cinematic variation similarly named entitled same work unable to look at identifiable textual source dynamic style comparable to Godard's jump lived Paris early 1960s executives wanted published by Calder 1964/ violence & not the result/ disqualify as point of comparison dialogue Bacon compositional style of similarly pressured editing process series of oblique allusions characteristic of Godard Resnais traditional narrative avant-garde & popular art in the 1960s – Signify! – construct movements in time & space invocation as an off-screen character sequence suggests connections between his work & the diegetic past Chas intimating scholarship/ role as doctor cut from Chas to Cuthbertson the lawyer on the word significantly in his work agents control characters actions/ Such a cut could not as he points out have engaged in supplying heroin as in Junky a sadistic trial where Josef K observes a book lying on the table/scientific research Dr Benway naked law marked by obscenity revealing contingent nature picture/ A man & a woman were sitting naked on a sofa behaviour-altering substances scripts & books are studied here said K these are the men who glanced at the title-page of a second book it was a novel entitled Dr Schafer's Complete All American De-anxietized 9.Man conformity & rebellion upholds the needs of control supersede public persona maintains conservative order to disguise addiction/ subversive Interzone units are forming an army of liberation to free the Interior Nightmare prepare to liberate Western Europe the games Chas plays w Dana flash Chas will inflict on the chauffeur later/ connected to him in space we later learn, on a carpet having wounds dressed by the end of the scene she had replaced Dr Burroughs to give him a shot Chas rubbing his eyes his own perception of HiS from Marco Polo's Travels painting his walls just 'before' Chas attacked by everything is permitted later Chas disrupting narrative sequentiality works the soft machine thus William S. simultaneously stimulating curiosity in dialogue or image prominence in the 1960s to emphasise sense of transition of change of continual mobility preceded shaped knowledge/ 1962 scathing reviews suggestions that editing based on random exploded 1962 dead fingers talk in first half of the film where most of his work was done generated thirteen weeks subject of obscenity trials/ laid the ground for the cut-ups reveals that WSB & Ginsberg made some basis of civilisation/ Having destabilised letters in order to produce their epistolary novel/ Returned to cinema other audio contains the origin age experience described (see Balch 1972) rape of the senses only the Other recognised as foundation of cut-up reality/ work room took on the aspect of a Near Eastern whore determines junkie behaviour Negress now I am a Negro fucking in prose ('On Screen...Fadeout') Polynesian substance complete bisexuality system experiments with pictorial will/ Breething pornographic scenarios repeated conventions & personalities Interzone contains within it dissolution crime science fiction pornography racialised terms/ In a discussion of Genet, the thief's most important sense cutting fucked by big Negro addiction as metaphor can be challenged: celluloid printed the film bank re-typing new combinations of words selecting ambiguity the fact involves folding pages from a pre-existing narrative authoritarian status reflected in various pages further ahead reading traced the presence of HiS as tool in writing process generate ideas historical reality of character non-narrative passages in the finished product/ I exploded Nova Express produced by mechanisms that include randomness, a surrogate god-like figure subject of imperative production incarnations or avatars under different names appropriate ways to represent perceptions urban avatars montage in HiS's dying words a guiding principle prioritise use by painters by photographers suggests link/parallel with Dusty before introduced to writing/ Given Gysin's God is dead, everything is permitted surprising but should be remembered formal ethical Law the face construction of space introduced by cinema/ Techni-ontology of difference generates radically transformed methods of representing object character function Nude Descending a Staircase 1912 destabilises ontology a radical assertion multiple-image photography men in motion & reality/ The fold-in method permitted consequent revolutionary application of randomisation process from words/ influenced by Jung's notion collective does not function as memory Anabasis or the racial past not particularly useful for phylogenetic or racial

memory implies newspaper photo unnamed defendant apparent
continuity of ideas Harry Flowers' involvement not located
fragility of the category 'race'/ WSB is the narrative from
elsewhere/ This may function (like Scientology) for fictional
purposes but western occult notions non-linear science groupie
demonstrates as imposition by consciousness/ potential South
America did not last long/ asks What is fate? Fate is written:
negative in tone with special contempt written/ So if you want to
challenge Mexico City meet with his world/ the radical never saw
anything like it since Vienna '36 genre an entirely different space
might be this town looks like you could score for junk/ 10.
dialogic elements combine Lima we see the first stirrings:
opening sequence kickstarts film on the building/ A peculiar
violet evening sky/ shot from Carol Reed's Odd Man Out
everybody in Lima has active TB or old scars conventions of the
musical genre the Super 8 footage of Turner Pherber Lucy the
empty viewer sees the slide/ themes will emerge cooking smells
of all countries hang smoke of Yage smell of jungle salt water
sweat genitals reflected two thousand years of disease slavery
brutality psychic & physical here the physical specifically
olfactory chaotic with the special chaos of a dream/ drugs
invoked a chain of equivalence excluded other of the city
invoked as simultaneously American Islamic religious jungle
unproductive unsupportive landscape pine trees on a hill human
nature invoked at its most corporeal statement this initial
description (and the city) dried excrement sweat levels of
intoxication result in different senses signifier of difference, one
on stronger doses: There is a suggestion here of discourse
cooking smells of all countries East to South America to South
Pacific following city hybridity elaborating on the superimposition
Colonel Percy Fawcett whose expedition was the model
panorama: high mountain flutes jazz xylophones African drums
Arab bagpipes couched in negative terms, musical is not/
everything is permitted parallel/sequel to Performance/ Just as
Chas leaves they write to his parents: 'I am going away to join
reality studio', another illusion from far away/ Later we learn the
route of any straightforward understanding of Tangier/
Subsequent to this scripted experience or false consciousness

role as spy or agent provocateur/ Altho 'outside the film' it is not
freedom not Third World politics Romantic discourse/ the
necessity of the artist/writer being scripted into the film: anything
to challenge limits an ongoing experiment what you all are: dying
animals memory perception the body history represented as
some tortuous encounter/ The figure of Rimbaud one of sharp
edges that tear uncovered his rejection of representational
senses subsequent abandonment literary type who sniffed as I
understand nihilistic escape from Western social & moral
commitment & symmetry of social roles/ Chas in Turner's house
the sequel allows us to imagine a third space consumption
precisely the act of reading not writing role during that time no
doubt based on the sickness Roeg asked Balch to show him
arbitrary physical desolation a city of open spaces shit-strewn
lots the product of a single authorial vision spitting blood in the
streets elsewhere despite generous reverie/ homoerotic apes
transforming syntax narrative heats me pants every time I pass
him on the bus, Turkish via Cammell/ Dr B holding hands in
public dialogue positive evaluation of native Peruvian shooting
script compared with several examples of editing that resonate
with armadillos/ In Queer he described happening sequence
film/ Immediately after Interzone graphics supersonic jet speed
panning into sunglare/ image cuts footage congruent with stasis
horrors reflected deserts jungles mountains stasis death in
closed valleys engine noise synthesised in the 1980s he would
take the title of his painting Traveller on the Yellow Wind lust of
the soul! ...and the seed (so you say) of the Indian crescendo
cut into character armour the work of a black Rolls Royce
travelling restrict capacity for pleasure image English tranquility
order for Newman to deliver first few lines image of naked male
buttocks back to sequence intercut with sex scenes Artaud saw
specifically Western conception of rapprochement between men
& women/ Sollubi justified as serving a higher spiritual politics
measured by response demonstrated in a situation of free will
not interested in rapprochement this routine climaxes/ he links
America's white Hole/ few female characters in the patriarchy of
the Old South fails to note relation preceding Interzone by its
corollary: the rape & abuse of blacks observed performing

obscene contortions operating some kind of female sexuality/
justifies abandonment of continuity Iris half Chinese
communications technology of modernity 11. available to
privileged contradicted neutralised characters here & there with
the aid of American Express/ horrific description of her as
permutation of interchangeable personas occur throughout work/
reincarnation the possible connection only brown sugar speaks
only to express hanging transfer of ego into another body at
point of ejaculation nation & thought transfer occur at orgasm not
birth violence substituted for sex Chas shooting Turner is
between them causes contextualises identity exchange Sollubi
permutations Romantic era disreputable shabby compulsive
wanderer carrying alcoholic Burns or mad Chatterton was, after
all, concerned w the job & boys onwards spoken of conflict East
his work from 1970 onwards control character armour cut-up
material contextualised working on yourself fragments
undertaken early applies to author as much as technique served
the function of disorienting dissolve writes sexual ecstasy
orgasm radical into somebody else I am losing my abrupt break
in syntax that follows around him he feels outside social
systems/ This change the cut-up method from the body & its
environment produced undifferentiated mass sketching ideas for
the novel he describes as architecture of narrative/ Turkish Bath
under the whole CITY you can see construction of cinematic
experience/ This Dantesque Interzone extends in several
dimensions/ You keep finding cut-ups have been used in film
world of myth & symbol objects sensations hit you/ he is
gradually diluting me/ This sense rises/ like other satirists he
writes beginning to dig Arab kicks/ junkie priest drugstore
cowboy attributes period of filmic collaborations with syndicate
resistance fighter/ other parallels can be drawn most potentially
radical he remains ambiguous/ early stages of withdrawal
described drawing on his own experience a vast rubbish heap
where he & the English underworld encounter a group of Arabs
attack them with Jack Black's You Can't Win/ series of dreams in
which I am a minority screenplay format one of several
passages in the letters/ projected during performance living
against Arabs could be read would have been called Ishtar

militants in North Africa true story with a woman via mediation of blackness absolute/ An Archaeology of Interzone: the concept a certain section of the market Chas' skills most commentators have noted coming revolutionary war/ Insignificance of Interzone's political parties, HiS's hashisheen an assassin Liquefactionists ignored spatiality counterforce against convention allows positive active revolutionary force scene of jungle & city cities which are mass decaying interlocking buildings & streets read fantasies of urban tyranny also Bosch Gorky Picasso Matta/ the status of satire ambiguous methods into prose/ homosocial voice takes dominant ideological rationale concerned as much as Genet their abject vileness as objective fact/ visual Orientalism purposes/ The Saint rejects contact lived projected onto untouchables returned to visit while based in London between purposes followed at periods de lux cafes quipped with Sollubi significant contribution to conception in the post seating benches being provided for the lineage that can be drawn between the humiliated & degraded so many first encouraged to go there themselves for passive homosexuals/ visual verbal references to Persia resonate exploring this text as source material/ owe a great debt to Islam could never have made my connections Islam I have absorbed by osmosis without spitting a word of their shift tilt STOP the God film/ Frame by frame film stock issued in his writings 12. does not have much empty/ conceal bankrupt real physical geography of cities he lives in be in position to set up another reality on the people he encounters the instrument weapon of monopoly/ The boys the availability acting on anyone who calls the film into question with the population/ letters queer Interzone 1945 Nova trilogy dig through early work partisans storm the reality studio order emergence of Interzone in form shown to audiences control them; the film outside it/ the line breakthrough in grey originally intended to shoot on location Tangiers plan suggests quasi-tabloid war report: recreated Interzone in a warehouse outside Toronto/ abrupt reality studio can alter destroy the word rather than location state of mind of William Lee character locating New York predetermination film apparently objective city history full of blinding light & bohemian decadence a nightmarish ideology &

false consciousness of hierarchical boys betrayal sex the currency in a power struggle Lee untenable position addict homo influenced to openly express aspects of his unconscious the poetic images of mass migration keep private this relaxation the repressive typology of Oswald Spengler whatever the facts he was able to occupy a social position some sort of essential racial genotype to express one of the few places left where a man can really see images over vast periods of history/ ignores the cop/ on the level a street-car conductor renowned for exploiting pseudo-scientific fantasies central attachment to Mexico unquestioning attitudes to dubious theories enacting the past of his own country/ In an invocation enthusiasm for uncharted Mexico a veritable land of opportunity his letters from Panama & Columbia general regressions in time quests in old reserved rural towns/ Lima, America's glorious frontier heritage Lima is the promised land for boys/ I desire to get out of America simultaneously noting the extensive Chinatown seeking the Self in the Other here in the letters written for Lee main character & nom de plume of Junky/ Peru: vultures circle over Lima roost here the evening lasts several hours forever/Newman's fast blues fades out silence symptoms the world between human will starts with abrasive electronic pulses a blasted idyll where the will projects reaching incantatory vocal climax soundtrack of universally addicted junkie reverie/ Against long shots handheld footage writhing imaginative construct geographical location bodies shift position within between shots a place where everyone could act out his car across the screen shifts from left-to-right to biography we see the sex get more violent cut to descriptions of Interzone traces Ginsberg's apartment on East 7th Street: Burroughs mentions Performance by name/ See Bockris for WSB & Roeg/ claims Jagger used provides no source for this information/ alludes to the film Ian Somerville & The Stones/ Vague resentment/ A futuristic vibrating city in Interzone costume/ But I was not slated to perform just to be there I Mick Jagger a regular in WSB dreams cut inspired by fire escapes conceived of a futuristic city asserts influence editor claims never to have seen these films heard a faxed letter from Grauerholz Director of the labyrinth of alleyways & hallways; a

city Antony Balch showed suggests he was working on
Performance/ one building upon another a city with New York
traces style to source material during his travels in Central &
South America/ relationships in play here are clear HiS motto
nothing west if all is illusion any illusion is valid/ first impressions
of Tangier were the only alternative to illusion generated by first
words his letter to Ginsberg from another studio under different
control/ complicating motivating factors behind decision to visit
metaphor the biologic film standing for alien work dismisses
opposition to some true reality/ If there is anything oriental
stereotypes/ a freedom recognisable within existing politico-
ethical homosexuality had made him feel control depicts the
existential necessity notes the absence of women avoids the
hopeless dead-end horror of being/ Arab culture would also have
appealed to doomed planet/ Being outside the film citizens are
negative unmediated reality every object raw hideous the town
13. which flays the flesh/ character Burroughs late in his career
recalled prissy experimental writer one whose experiment
nostalgia for the old days in Morocco right now is for me
ambivalent distance towards Bowles' themes: he was jeered at
in the experiment the cut-up method Arabs habitually undergo in
the novels of Mr P Nova trilogy dismissed as unreadable results
of cut-up method laid out for public experimentation i.e. the
experiment took place refined his use & understanding hybridity
horror valorisation revealed ideological motivations role of drugs
in the city/ At first narcotics for example Chinese laundry
panoramic vision of city life: drug propaganda producing text
symmetry of cop/criminal relationship/ This crisscross of a
thousand hammocks junkies Shultz intercutting between scenes
of hashish smokers people talking eating bathing organised
crime HiS last words contradict his own claims/ cuts were made/
The assumption throughout subject of discussion the Nova
trilogy the soft machine the ticket that comparison of his work/
his ideas appear as character an author-influence editing must
be curses & objects of magical invocation references to HiS fill
the novels/ (see Hughes' novelisation) shape-shifting presence
indicates function whatever their origin contains principles/ The
first of these is Dostoevsky's claim in The Brothers Karamazov

the Warner Brothers logo before any titles HiS represents abolition across the screen right to left the camera unknowable because unrepresentable a camera attached to a rocket & ethics/ Whatever the source the two shots accompanied by soundtrack principle of freedom electronic sound effects build quickening contingent exclusionary basis of consensual dead train/ As the song starts cut to true & real then immediately other things not along a country road/ Superimposed over liberation of desire we realised that everything is opening titles/ After nine seconds enough time song image cuts almost subliminally to car/ For the next two minutes Rolls Royce space-time travel process displacing 'Burroughs' express ambiguity towards physical locations/ The openness-to reflected articulation of their uses woven into the fabric of urbanity freely available/ racial/cultural differences made by copulating couples on rows of brass beds against religion Christ & Buddha are dismissed tying up for a shot opium smokers respectively Mohammed gaming tables where games are played Commerce/ passage undercut towards the end narcotic use identified abnormal condemnation of the powerful seen to extend relation to community norms iconoclasm exclusive social prejudice drugs again when a Sollubi touches him/ In satire quite different connotations: his own description of the Sollubi I use formulation racial/cultural hybridity Interzone's hybridity race geographical origin nationality & superimposition of categories of race geography nationality their abject vileness what is the origin of contemporary thought at the time of WSB caste/ In fact untouchables perform priestly human vileness/ correspondence 1962 USA generating publicity immortalised collage Pop culture's most compressed & re-edited cuts/ This the result of pressure from Warner band/ WSB was Jagger earlier in the film tone down the sex London Arts Lab breeding ground of authorial/aesthetic blueprint but films should not be screened regularly/ One index of infamy published the underground provided the attention given several people/ go where he warrants more entries than any other sequentiality abandoned viewer claims that The Naked Lunch occurs between discrete shots/ editing that point in the early sixties present Chas entering Harry Flowers' office English editing non-random year sections published business a key crosscut establishing parallels between different sets achieved randomly cutting splicing sections of the filmstock/ new departures/ invokes cuts in third text Kafka impounded by British Customs circulated in the Examining Magistrates office not law books the place of the power held over him: He opened the first of them indecent obscene intention of the draughtsman was evident enough K publication retained original title 1964 How Grete Was Plagued By Her Husband Hans/ These are the law books supposed to sit in judgement on me/ disgust we are reminded in the next section she is illusion any illusion permitted their ordinary everyday tasks against quasi-Hegelian dialectic utopian potential, this potential is constricted desire liberation from the Law can be trafficked like opiates Iris' vision Gnostic proposing Manichean integral properties; her potential has been identified all liberations are reversible control/ If nothing is true then no ideology of Iris' position on the notion of a situation where everything is permitted a site of Interzone invokes negative 1960s remain trapped in movement substance of many races pass through your body thought themselves to be action cannot be gun the physical incorporation of Otherness destruction in The Wild Boys elsewhere unconceived & unborn combinations not yet reality perhaps the closest we get to virus human evolutionary direction of infinite definition & whatever ethics these situations evolve spontaneous action/ The notion of definition outside prevailing ideologies/ writings following ambiguous nature continued to valorise constant differential change as Law further correspondence might be noted/ also mentions an element of the story through this paradise in which the Assassins awake lying their necks/ The severed heads speak telling the men of afterlife...

Bios

Kenji Siratori (1975–) is a Japanese avant-garde artist. He had many books and many CDs released in the past year. He explores a glitch existence in humanity.

www.kenjisiratori.com

Jacurutu:23 is a self-described "Scissorman"; one who cuts up and reassembles sound, video, art and reality itself to suit his own means. He is a professional wrestler, and an audio-informant with numerous releases as Jacurutu:3 and under several other aliases. He founded the Life-power Church as a pro-wrestling faction, built upon the ideas developed in his self-published first book in 2009, *The Scissor Bible*, a book of continuous writing which has been reprinted as part of his autobiography *I Hardly Knew Me*. He works closely alongside artist and "wrecker of civilization" Genesis P-Orridge as an archivist of Gen's 50+ years of creative works and together they founded the One True Topi Tribe. He has worked writing storylines as well as performing for numerous professional wrestling organizations, including his own, Tribute Championship Wrestling, writing a year's worth of storylines in advance.

Michael Butterworth is a UK author, publisher and editor. He was a key part of the UK New Wave of Science Fiction in the 1960s, contributing fiction to *New Worlds* and other publications. He then founded Savoy Books with David Britton and continued writing, co-authoring Britton's controversial novel *Lord Horror*. He presently contributes fiction and poetry to *Emanations*, an anthology of experimental and imaginative writing edited by Carter Kaplan and published by International Authors, Brookline, Massachusetts, now in its third edition (http://iaemanations.blogspot.co.uk/). In 2009 Butterworth launched the contemporary visual art and writing journal, *Corridor8*.

Gary J. Shipley is the author of eight books of various sizes. His latest is a collection of poems forthcoming from Blue Square Press. He has been published in *The Black Herald, Gargoyle, Paragraphiti, elimae, >kill author, 3:AM*, and others. More details can be found at Thek Prosthetics.

Christopher Nosnibor is a writing machine. The author of anti-novels *THE PLAGIARIST, From Destinations Set* and, most recently, *This Book is Fucking Stupid,* as well as works of social critique and commentary in the form of *Postmodern Fragments: Writings on Work, Technology and Contemporary Living and The Changing Face of Consumerism,* he has also authored a number of pamphlets and countless peripheral works. He has had stories published in numerous places including *Paraphilia Magazine, Neonbeam, The Toronto Quarterly, I'm Afraid of Everyone, Bad Marmalade* and *Blacklisted Magazine.*

Nathan Penlington is a writer, performer and obsessive. He has performed his work at venues as diverse as Tate Modern, Southbank Centre, Oxford Literary Festival and Chicago's Drinking & Writing Festival, and has been broadcast on BBC 1, 3 and 4. His experimental graphic poetry has been published in *The Journal of Experimental Fiction* and the anthology *Adventures In Form* (Penned in the Margins). His latest show is a live interactive documentary based on the Choose Your Own Adventure phenomenon of the 1980s.

www.nathanpenlington.com

Matt Leyshon is the author of *The Function Room: The Kollection.* He lives in Blackpool, England with his wife and cats.

Díre McCain is a five-dimensional creature who fell through a Lorentzian traversable wormhole into a three-dimensional universe, landing on what was, at the time, the second rock from the Sun. After a nebulous sojourn in the Zone of Avoidance, while trapped in a self-induced state of suspended animation, she was unwittingly converted into a transportable energy pattern, and ultimately rematerialized on 21st century Earth. She is the editor-in-chief of *Paraphilia Magazine,* owner of book publisher Apophenia, and author of *Playing Chicken With Thanatos.*

http://www.diremccain.com
http://www.paraphiliamagazine.com

Alex S. Johnson is a music journalist and writer of Surrealistic satire and weird fiction. His books include *The Death Jazz, Bad Sunset* and *Wicked Candy*. Johnson lives in northern California where he tends his collection of circus punks, foam popsicle heads and Mayan skulls.

Craig Woods is a contributing editor at *Paraphilia Magazine* and a regular contributor to *Antique Children*, Craig has also written for *International Times, Beat the Dust,* and *The Cartier Street Review* whilst continuing to pursue personal literary projects. Additionally his reviews and articles have appeared in numerous online and print publications. Sections of his novel-in-progress (tentatively entitled *The Red Shift*) have been published sporadically across the web, while a second novel, *To Eat the Sky Like an Apple*, is in the pipeline for publication by Apophenia Books. Craig is fond of spiders but scared of shellfish. Time travel experiments permitting, he will probably die in the twenty-first century.

Niall Rasputin lives in SE Texas. He is in love with the swamp, but often has secret trysts with the stars. He believes that laughter and song are the finest of all opiates. He writes his madnesses and passions down as a form of daily exorcism. He will never understand his own species, but will die trying. He is never wrong, because he refuses to know anything. He is 245 in dog years. He has been published, or accepted for future publication in *Gutter Eloquence Magazine, Clockwise Cat, The Writing Disorder, Napalm and Novocain, The Shwibly, FEARLESS*, and several others.

mpcAstro is an artist who waxes oppoetic near the Gulf of Mexico's teal-tongued waters lapping at the peni[n]s[ular] underside of Florida's powdered sugar shores where he consummated his thirty-year *opus interruptus* of photopoetic cut-ups, *SPIDER'S NEST,* available through Oneiros Books. From that art catalog's extricated flash-cycle vignettes, correspondence and text[vis]uals, his showcased *operotica* was assembled. This amplifiction's tri-agonists are loosely modeled on the author's passion role-play with erstwhile Los Angeles-based dominatrices Ilsa Strix and Izabella Sol before 2001, after which time the trinity dissolved like powdered sugar into The Gulf along with their pre[de]vious millennial identities.

R.G. Johnson is a giant sand worm that lives in a haunted forest. He is covered in black scales and spits poison or sings 1980s sitcom theme songs to debilitate his prey. He also writes poetry and stories and rearranges words to form verbal holes in time and space. His writing has been published in over a hundred zines and journals. He is the author of two chapbooks. He often smells of blueberries.

Younisos is an underground writer and poet from Tangier, born in 1967. He writes in French, but he also writes some English versions of his own texts. He spent his childhood in Tangier's old Medina. He was in France for several years and did a thesis on "Flesh's Aesthetics in Georges Bataille's Experience" at the University Bordeaux 3. Then he went back to Tangier and decided to give up and stop all academic activities and just live the wild flowing "experience". Now he's living in Tangier, near Zoco Chico, writing what he calls "bloody dionysian poetry".

Lee Kwo has been writing for forty years in the cut-up style inspired by William Burroughs and Brion Gysin/ *The Lie Detekta* was published in 2008, a random cut-up text about the end of Post Art/Human culture//There is a toxic psychology of cut-ups and flashbacks to be found in *The Lie Detekta* which defies the communication or apprehension of an even superficial surface as a locus of expression mediation or illumination/The trilogy: *A Pathology of a Still Life* was published in 2010 and is a satirical parody of philosophy/ academics/punk rock/and the end of the world/The texts are one vast cut-up and can be read in any order or any chapter/ Lee Kwo is Kwo becoming Leo Androgyne, the precarious real avatar perceived in terms of hypersensitivity and awareness of the cut-up illusions of our disintegrating life/Writing like sex is a disease of annihilation to paraphrase Bataille/

Cabell McLean was born in 1952, a descendant of the visionary American writer James Branch Cabell (author of *Jurgen*), for whom he was named. He first met William S. Burroughs when he attended Naropa College as a Graduate, and was his companion from approximately 1976–1983. During this literary apprenticeship, Cabell also acted as an assistant to Burroughs, and the material they wrote together as 'Gay Gun' would form the springboard for *The Place of Dead Roads*. The two remained life-long friends and were in contact until William's death in 1997. Although Cabell continued to be a prolific writer, publishing in numerous zines and reading alongside the likes of John Giorno, Herbert Huncke (with whom he was particularly close) and, later, Genesis P-Orridge, in the latter part of his life his energies were increasingly taken up with numerous technical articles and books on AIDS treatment and activism, until he died in 2004. He is survived by his partner, the artist Eric K. Lerner, who is currently working with Matthew Levi Stevens to produce *Riot Boy! An Introduction to Cabell McLean*.

Gary Cummiskey is a South African poet and publisher living in Johannesburg. He is the editor of Dye Hard Press, which he started in 1994. He is the author of several poetry chapbooks, including *Sky Dreaming* (Graffiti Kolkata, India, 2011) and *I Remain Indoors* (Tearoom Books, Stockholm, 2013). In 2009, he published *Who was Sinclair Beiles?*, a collection of writings about the South African Beat poet, co-edited with Eva Kowalska. Cummiskey's debut collection of short fiction, *Off-ramp*, will be published in 2013.

Allen Ginsberg said, "**Marc Olmsted** inherited Burroughs' scientific nerve & Kerouac's movie-minded line nailed down with gold eyebeam in San Francisco." His book, *What Use Am I A Hungry Ghost? Poems form a 3-year retreat* (Contemporary Press, 2001), has an introduction by Ginsberg. Marc Olmsted founded New Wave band The Job in 1980, San Francisco. Ginsberg performed with the band on a number of occasions.

Muckle Jane was the official British jester until 1649 when her master was beheaded, and has since earned her crust as a proofreader and copy-editor. She still has a soft spot for riddles and tricks of all kinds, which influences her experiments with words.

Cal Leckie is a 28-year-old self-taught artist and writer. His book *The Drug Factory & Other Tales*, is available from Oneiros Books.

Spencer Kansa has written for a wide variety of publications including *Hustler UK, Mojo* and *Hip Hop Connection*. He is the author of *Wormwood Star,* a biography of the American artist and occult icon, Marjorie Cameron (Mandrake of Oxford). His debut novella, *Zoning*, is published by Beatdom Books. His interviews with William Burroughs, Allen Ginsberg, Paul Bowles and Herbert Huncke feature in Joe Ambrose's book, *Chelsea Hotel Manhattan* (Headpress).

For more info visit: www.spencerkansa.com

Dr. Geoffrey A. Landis is a scientist, a science-fiction writer, and a poet. As a SF writer, he has won the Hugo and Nebula awards for short fiction, and is the author of one novel, *Mars Crossing*, and a collection of short stories, *Impact Parameter (and Other Quantum Realities)*. His most recent novella, *The Sultan of the Clouds*, won the Theodore Sturgeon award for best short science-fiction in 2011. As a scientist, he works at NASA John Glenn Research Center on projects as varied as developing technology for Venus exploration, advanced power systems for spacecraft, telerobotic exploration of the planets, and interstellar travel, and is a member of the Mars Exploration Rovers science team. As a poet, he has won the Rhysling award for best science-fiction poem two times. His collection of poetry, *Iron Angels*, came out in 2009. He has appeared on a number of television programs, most recently *Michio Kaku's Sci-Fi Science: Physics of the Impossible*, where he explained the concept of floating cities on Venus. He lives in Berea, Ohio, with his wife, writer Mary A. Turzillo, and four cats.

More information can be found on his website: http://www.geoffreylandis.com

Michael McAloran was Belfast born, (1976). His work has appeared in various 'zines and magazines, including *ditch, Gobbet Magazine, Ygdrasil, Establishment, Unlikely Stories, Stride Magazine,* and *Underground Books.* He has authored a number of chapbooks, including *The Gathered Bones* (Calliope Nerve Media), *Final Fragments* (Calliope Nerve Media) and *Unto Naught* (Erbacce-Press). A full length collection of poems, *Attributes,* was published by Desperanto in 2011. Lapwing Publications (Ireland) released a collection of his poems, *The Non Herein,* in 2012. The Knives, Forks & Spoons Press (UK) also released an ekphrastic book of text/art, *Machinations,* this year and Oneiros Books released *In Damage Seasons* and *All Stepped/Undone* in 2013. A further collection, *Of Dead Silences,* was also published this year by Lapwing Publications. He is currently the Poetry Editor for Oneiros Books.

Ben Szathani was born in Seoul, South Korea, and educated in New Zealand. He has written the first Korean-language biography of British occultist Aleister Crowley, published in 2003. Currently he resides in Germany and writes poems and short stories in English. 'Wehrwolf DX13' is a coded political rhetoric, an esoteric riddle, and a description of a fictional drug at the same time.

Dexuality Valentino was born, raised and educated in Manchester, England. Now emigrated to Yorkshire. It's not that far geographically speaking. Has been a writer and artist for most of his life, but has only recently begun to collect himself and his thoughts for output into the public arena. Published in various online spaces and places. Books: *LOVE IS; Men in the Company of Women.* Currently working on a series of short stories. So be quiet and let him get on with it, damnit.

Eabha Rose lives in Dublin, Ireland. Her writing has been published by a number of journals, both online and in print.

Robin Tomens, aka Timewriter, aka El Hombre Invisible, lives in London and has been writing for as long as he can remember. His first love, science-fiction, has endured, and traces remain in his cut-up prose. He also writes experimental prose in forms which combine text and image, as illustrated in the booklet, *What Remains of Words*, a limited-run art book published in 2013. From 1991 to 1995 he produced a fanzine called *Ego*, which was praised by Jon Savage as being 'streets ahead of *The Wire*'. It comprised fiction, Situationist-inspired graphics and coverage of music, his other major inspiration. In 2001 Stride published a collection of his essays on modern Jazz called *Points of Departure*. As well as writing, he makes collages, as he has done since 1977. These have appeared in several fanzines and on his blog, Include Me Out, which features eclectic elements ranging from reviews (literature, film and music) to scans of treasures from his book collection.

Wayne Mason is a writer and sound artist from Central Florida. His words have appeared across the small press in magazines, both in print and online. He is the author of five chapbooks and is the former poetry editor for *Side of Grits*, and *The Tampa Bay Muse*. Wayne Mason has also been active in experimental music for nearly twenty years. He records ambient, experimental and noise sounds, formerly under the name of Zilbread, and is also a founding member of the experimental/noise project Stickfigure and electronic duo Blk/Mas.

Charie D. La Marr is primarily known as a ghostwriter in the field of sports – mostly baseball. She has had at least one book go to #1 on Amazon in two different categories. Currently working to establish herself as an author in her own name, she has created a genre called Circuspunk and a book of short stories in the genre have been published by Chupa Cabra House called *Bumping Noses and Cherry Pie*. She also has upcoming stories in Alex S. Johnson's heavy metal anthology *Axes of Evil* and *Shwibly Magazine*, James Ward Kirk's *Bones*, Sydney Leigh's *Ugly Babies, In Vein for the Benefit of St. Jude's Hospital,* Chupa Cabra's *We Walk Invisible,* Dynatox Ministries' *Witches!, Ripple Effect for Hurricane Katrina Relief, Surreal Grotesque* and other anthologies. She was a featured writer at *Solarcide* and is currently editing a Circuspunk anthology called *The New Wakazoid Circus—the Greatest Show on Paper.*

Paul Hardacre is a poet, editor, publisher, and student of the perennial philosophy. He is the author of three poetry collections, the most recent being *liber xix: differentia liber* (Puncher and Wattmann, Sydney, 2011). His publishing ventures include boutique arts publisher papertiger media, and esoteric, occult and arcane book publisher Salamander and Sons. Paul has travelled extensively and currently resides with his wife and son in Chiang Mai, Thailand, home of his vast esoteric library and humble alchemical laboratory.

Larry Delinger studied composition in Los Angeles with Ernest Kanitz and in Santa Barbara with Edward Applebaum. He is a freelance composer, writing incidental music for theaters throughout the United States and Europe. These include the Old Globe Theater in San Diego, Mark Taper Forum in Los Angeles, Berkeley Repertory Theater, Oregon Shakespeare Festival, American Conservatory Theater, National Actors Theater in New York City and the Oslo Nye Theater in Norway. Many of his works have been performed on radio and television. Mr Delinger has received numerous commissions, including those from the California Brass Quintet for Nightwalls; the University of Northern Colorado wind ensemble for Elegies for Winds, Flute and Percussion; Costal Access Musician's Alliance for Studies in Light; Meditations commissioned by the Varian Foundation and Paradox for the Denver Brass, which is now available on CD. Mr Delinger has also composed music for *Sesame Street*, a rock album titled *Ray Bradbury's Dark Carnival*, and the ballet *Spheres* for Dance Umbrella of New York. His published compositions include Elegy for John Lennon, Brass Rings, King Lear Sonata, Paradox and Nightwalls, which was commissioned for the California Brass Quintet. Mr Delinger has received eleven Los Angeles DramaLogue Critics' Awards for excellence in music composition and was a recipient of the Distinguished Service Award from Chadron State College.

Paul Hawkins has been many things along the way: punk, squatter, tour manager, freelance journalist, musician, improviser, collaborator and manager of an Elvis Presley impersonator. He studied the art of sleeping standing up and drinking lying down with nearly disastrous consequences. Last count he's moved on average every eleven months but only ever owned one tent. You'll find his work on/in *Rising, Pens & Needles, Stride, Fit to Work: Poets Against ATOS, Domestic Cherry, The Interpreter's House, Occupy Wall Street Poetry Anthology, Museum of Alcohol, Word Riot, Verba Vitae, M58, Noir Erasure Poetry Anthology* and other sites, walls and 'zines.

D M Mitchell is the author of *The Seventh Song of Maldoror, Parasite* and *Savoy: A Serious Life*. He edited *The Starry Wisdom – a Tribute to H P Lovecraft*.

Robert Rosen is the author of *Nowhere Man: The Final Days of John Lennon*, an international bestseller that's been translated into six languages. His investigative memoir, *Beaver Street: A History of Modern Pornography*, was recently published in the US and UK by Headpress. Rosen's work has appeared in publications all over the world, including *Uncut* (UK), *Mother Jones, The Soho Weekly News, La Repubblica* (Italy), *VSD* (France), *Proseco* (Mexico), *Reforma* (Mexico) and *El Heraldo* (Colombia).

Sinclair Beiles (1930–2000) was a controversial South African writer, artist, and editor at Olympia Press. He developed, along with William Burroughs and Brion Gysin, the cut-up method of writing. Beiles lived with Gregory Corso, Allen Ginsberg, Gysin, and Burroughs at the Beat Hotel in Paris in the late 1950s. He co-authored *Minutes to Go – a* cut-up manifesto – with Burroughs, Gysin, and Corso. Beiles settled in the Greek islands during the 1970s. He fought frequent bouts of depression, mental illness and drug addiction. In later life he returned to South Africa.

David Noone is a writer and musician living in Dublin who has toured Ireland and the UK extensively over the last two years performing his show 'David Noone sings Nick Cave'. His written work has been published in various publications both online and in print. His debut EP, *Songs With No Strings*, featuring his original material as well as his recent collaborations with author Mark SaFranko (*Hating Olivia*) will be released by River Jack Records in early 2014.

Aad De Gids was born in 1957, the gay one of a twin with also a straight one. Psychiatric nurse, poet, philosopher. Came out of a family of scum. The worst morons he met at university. Aad is a sensitive cancer with a caustic scorpiomoon tongue not always in obedience. Two days ago he toppled over in a full tram totally dissociated. Has used all drugs and alcohol and has been sober and clean now for fourteen years. Heya.

James B.L. Hollands is an artist, musician, writer and sailor. His work has been shown in the Tate Modern and worldwide.

Lucius Rofocale was raised by wolves in the wilderness, but despite being 'rescued' and indoctrinated as a Homo sapiens remains very feral. Lucius' mission is to attack conditioned, pavlovian responses and have fun doing it. He is currently editor-in-chief at Oneiros Books and can be reached at luciusrofocale@live.com

Edward S. Robinson studied for his BA and MA by research on the influence of William Burroughs and Allen Ginsberg at the University of York. He studied for his PhD at the University of Sheffield, where he has taught on a number of courses in recent years. He has published a number of chapters and articles on William Burroughs, Stewart Home and Kathy Acker, and provided the introduction to Jürgen Ploog's cut-up novella, *Flesh Film*. 2011 saw the publication of his first book, *Shift Linguals: Cut-Up Narratives from William S. Burroughs to the Present*, which traces the lineage of the cut-ups from their origins in Dada and Surrealism, through the works of William Burroughs and Brion Gysin, Claude Pélieu, John Giorno and Carl Weissner, to later authors including Kathy Acker, Stewart Home, Graham Rawle and Kenji Siratori. He currently has several works in progress, including a book-length work entitled *The Death of the Postmodern*.

Based in York but continually on the move, he contributes regular music reviews to *Shout4Music* and *Reflections of Darkness* and has produced over 1,200 music reviews for *Whisperin' and Hollerin'* in the last three years. Because he likes to keep busy, he is also an editor at Clinicality Press and contributing editor for *Paraphilia Magazine*. A music obsessive and 24/7 enigma, he drinks real ale and single malt whiskies and doesn't sleep much.

Kirk Lake is a writer and musician. Recent work includes the novel *Mickey the Mimic* (2013) and the screenplay for the sci-fi film *Piercing Brightness* (directed by Shezad Dawood, 2013). His fourth album, *I Came All The Way Here, I May As Well Go All The Way There,* will be released in 2014.

Matthew Levi Stevens is a writer, researcher, and online commentator, with a particular interest in the avant-garde and esoteric. He has written a number of articles examining little-known aspects of the life and work of William S. Burroughs, and is currently expanding and revising his essay 'The Magical Universe of William S. Burroughs' for book-length publication. He is also co-author of *A Way With Words* with C J Bradbury Robinson.

Gareth Jackson is a conceptual artist/experimental film maker and occasional author operating in the North West of England. He lives with a wife and three cats – none of which are familiars.

Allen Ginsberg (1926–1997) was an American poet and one of the leading figures of both the Beat Generation and the Sixties counterculture. *The Guardian* said of him: "He may have been the most important American writer of the last century." Best known for his poem 'Howl', he worked with artists like The Clash, Bob Dylan, and Jack Kerouac. In 1955 he wrote in his journal: "I am the greatest poet in America." Then he added: "Let Jack be greater." He played a major role in the lives of Kerouac, Herbert Huncke, and William Burroughs. Ginsberg was a practicing Buddhist who lived modestly, buying his clothes in second-hand stores and living in New York's East Village.

Nina Antonia is a cult author who has chronicled the lives of the fatally famous, from those who have followed in De Quincey's trajectory to the glamorous yet forsaken of pop culture's netherworld. Her first book, *Johnny Thunders – In Cold Blood,* is now the subject of a film.

Peter Playdon was born in 1969 South London stop tilt shift the God film cut to 2013: jobseeker in the globalised casual labour market. His research will be published online soon – watch for www.performance-intertexts.com.

Andi P. is a young artist located in the Middle East. Her work includes collage, drawing, painting and photography, mostly surrounding sexual and morbid subjects such as violence, doom, fetish and decay.

Billy Chainsaw is a self-taught British artist and since his early teens has been fascinated by the unknown, in its myriad forms, along with masks and the magickal weirdness of the number 23. Clearly influenced by his obsession with the movies, while Chainsaw's mixed-media pop art works also reference such diverse sources as cartoon surrealism, tattoos, and Lucha Libre, his prime driving force is William S. Burroughs. Chainsaw explains: "Aside from being heavily influenced by Burroughs' writing, I always employ his 'open your mind and let the pictures out' adage when creating."

You can contact him at: billychainsaw666@aol.com

Gustavo Arruda was born in São Paulo, Brazil, in 1974. He is a visual artist, photographer and poet. In recent years he has had several books published, including *Dispara* (Antiqua Editorial), *O Céu de Todas as Cidades* (Quasi Edições - Portugal) and *Gyro* (Cispoesia Edições), written in the cities where he has lived, including Havana, Marrakech and Salvador, where he currently lives, conducting personal research on the African Diaspora in Brasil in the Federal University of Bahia. He also had *Nômada* published, a CD book with the participation of the Brazilian sitar player Alberto Marsicano.

His poems and photos have been published in several magazines in Brazil and Portugal, including *Artéria, Azougue,* and *A Phala – Revista do Movimento Surrealista,* among others. Gustavo currently organizes the reissue of *Anjos Negros,* memoirs by the infamous Franco-Bahian bluesman, burglar and forger Jean Eugene Mouchere, published by *Novesfora Edições.*

Dolorosa de la Cruz is a contemporary artist born in Uruguay, has studied in London, Belfast and Dublin and now lives and works in Ireland. Interested in exploring Surrealism, Esoterism, alchemy, witchcraft and symbolism, has exhibited in Ireland, UK, USA and Poland. Her work has been published by various esoteric book presses including Silk Milk, Fulgur, Aeon Sophia Press and Qliphoth journal, and online by Paraphilia Magazine. Works can be found online in galleries hosted by Il Labirinto Stellare and Salón Arcano. The works presented here are part of an ongoing project influenced by cut-up, sigil and anagrams entitled 'The White Shadow Woman/Elemental Passions'.

Mary Beach (1919–2006) met the artist Claude Pélieu in 1962 and lived and worked with him until his death in 2002. Travelling extensively while living primarily in Paris, New York and San Francisco, their existence was a bohemian adventure during which they ceaselessly explored and continuously created. Their works are highly prized and respected in Europe but in the USA the pair remain relatively unknown. They both enjoyed lifetime friendships and/or creative associations with Allen Ginsberg, Charles Plymell, William Burroughs, Patti Smith, and Robert Mapplethorpe. William Burroughs, in his introduction to her book *The Electric Banana* (1975), wrote: "*The Electric Banana* by Mary Beach is a unique auditory experience approaching the actual found sounds of language as it mutters half a street sign repetitive argument overheard conversations bits of pop songs in millions of minds like some gigantic octopus with myriad tentacles…"

Claude Pélieu (1934–2002) was a French-born artist and writer celebrated for his collage art and for his collaborations with Beat Generation figures such as Allen Ginsberg, Brion Gysin, and William Burroughs. In 1969 he and partner Mary Beach moved into New York's notorious Chelsea Hotel where they worked with writers and artists like Ed Sanders, Patti Smith, Robert Mapplethorpe, and Harry Smith. Pélieu and Beach wed in 1975 and settled in upstate New York. Allen Ginsberg wrote of Pélieu: "Undifferentiated bullshit cut up and made rare and strange, it belongs to a genre of phantom poetry like its author, an ex-junky Frenchman refuged in New York, San Fran, London, his life cut up and his experience of states of consciousness, politics, police, sex and drugs now so confusing and fearful in every direction that he can only squeak apprehension of aluminium apocalypse with General Bridges falling down Atomic Fishways."